KEEPERS

Also by Brenda Cooper

Wilders

Edge of Dark
Spear of Light

The Creative Fire
The Diamond Deep

Project Earth | Book Two

KEEPERS

BRENDA COOPER

an imprint of Prometheus Books
Amherst, NY

Published 2018 by Pyr®, an imprint of Prometheus Books

Cover illustration © Christian Hecker
Cover design by Nicole Sommer-Lecht
Cover design © Prometheus Books

This is a work of fiction. Characters, organizations, products, locales, and events portrayed in this novel are either products of the author's imagination or used fictitiously.

Inquiries should be addressed to
Pyr
59 John Glenn Drive
Amherst, New York 14228
VOICE: 716–691–0133
FAX: 716–691–0137
WWW.PYRSF.COM

22 21 20 19 18   5 4 3 2 1

Library of Congress Cataloging-in-Publication Data

Names: Cooper, Brenda, 1960- author.
Title: Keepers / Brenda Cooper.
Description: Amherst, NY : Pyr, [2018] | Series: Project Earth ; 2
Identifiers: LCCN 2018007214 (print) | LCCN 2018011317 (ebook) |
    ISBN 9781633884229 (ebook) | ISBN 9781633884212 (softcover)
Subjects: | BISAC: FICTION / Science Fiction / Adventure. | GSAFD:
    Science fiction.
Classification: LCC PS3603.O5825 (ebook) |
    LCC PS3603.O5825 K44 2018 (print) | DDC 813/.6—dc23
LC record available at https://lccn.loc.gov/2018007214

Printed in the United States of America

*To Martín Espada. I was lucky to study with you,
and to sit at your feet and listen to your poetry.
Your character formed the seed for the rebel poet
Valeria in this book, and your love of
Walt Whitman inspired Jake's love of Whitman.
Thank you for being an inspiration*

PROLOGUE

I t is fifty years from now. In the wild lands between the megacities, there are almost a third as many robots as there are people. Many of them are large and imposing, able to use tank-like treads or multiple feet to traverse almost any terrain, and multiple arms to complete almost any job.

These are the ecobots.

They are bringers of death and cultivators of life. They destroy. They rip up rotten, weed-filled roads and collect the concrete detritus for recycling. They bring down wooden houses and separate out toxins and carry them away, burning the rest. They erase all of the things that were once human from places that were towns, that were farms, that were communes.

After, they restore.

To restore is to grade and to plant, to seed and to water and to tend. To restore is to protect from anything not natural, including humans, for humans are no longer natural to the wild lands.

A few humans are still tolerated here.

These are the Wilders.

They work for the NGOs, the nongovernmental organizations, which is a fancy way of saying nonprofits. Thus, they are legally allowed outside of the megacities. Sometimes they tell the robots what to do. Sometimes the robots tell the humans what to do.

The Wilders and the ecobots are on the same side.

This uneasy partnership exists throughout the United States. It bears the most fruit in the Northwest and the Northeast, for those regions are less ravaged than the Midwest, the South, and the rest of North America. A drone flying from west to east across the Northwest would see much beauty.

Imagine you are riding with that drone, that you feel it bob in the wind and see through its cameras.

On the westernmost coast, the Olympic Peninsula rises out of the sea. It is occupied entirely by people from the First Nations who have rewilded their own land with their own robots and their own hands. Mountains spike up from moss-laden forests, jagged dark scarps that kiss a bright blue sky. Ghosts of great glaciers hide in shaded ravines, their last life melting into streams and thin waterfalls.

Crossing the peninsula, one flies over water before crossing over the long, domed city of Seacouver, which fills the inner coastline of the Puget Sound. It rises high and sharp and colorful from the troubled waters, its weather-control fields sometimes faintly visible as a shimmer or a slight bending of light. Bridges link the taller buildings in its three great downtowns—Vancouver, Seattle, and Tacoma. In spite of its industry, its metal and glass, its new-material modernity, the city is decorated with green.

Emerald City indeed.

Hundred-story buildings fill entire blocks with indoor gardens, and almost all roofs are given to year-long farms. Red tomatoes and yellow and orange citrus and the slender wavy tops of carrots compete with deep green kale and lighter green and red heads of lettuce. Flowers, berries, and edibles line the roadways that people travel using all sorts of machines, mostly powered by the humans themselves, their companion robots, or the fire of the sun. Even inside the dome—maybe especially inside the dome—the air is so clear it is truly invisible, the sort of air that humans used to buy from oxygen bars.

For all its beauty and size, its spaceports and its fabulous architecture, from way up here Seacouver is a long rectangle teeming with movement.

On the far side of the city, land rises into the Cascades. Cedar and fir forests drape the rocky shoulders of the mountains with green shawls. Here and there, the scars of fires remain visible as slashes of desolation or pale new plantings.

Topping a drone over the Cascades makes the engine strain. They're big. The air grows thin and wind becomes a threat. From way up here, it's easy to see how thoroughly the mountains control the weather. On the west side, where you have just been, everything is bright green and blue, dense with trees and birds and deer and coyotes, wet with streams and bisected by rivers. As you fly east, the rivers are larger and far fewer, the land between rivers as much folded hill and low scrub as forest, far more of it scarred by fire.

Almost immediately, you spot the small town of Cle Elum, with perhaps fifty thousand humans or maybe a few more. Far to the south, on the north bank of the wide Columbia, orchards and fields of grain surround Yakima and Selah, and then there is nothing for a long time, or at least nothing human except a few roads left for convenience, and a few silent trucks traversing those roads, and the ribbons of hyperloop that carry people quickly between cities.

If you fly lower, you see a few humans, a few robots, and a few others who are not supposed to be there.

You are now over Promise, or what was once New Promise, an upstart state that still exists as a legal entity although there are no border markings for it on the grounds. It has no legislature and no police force and not much of anything else. Spokane, the largest city in Promise, can be seen minding the border between Promise and Idaho. Before that, the Columbia—which starts north of the drone—runs a lazy course through the land. A few miles west of the river, a fifty-three-mile-long lake starts inside of the lower part of the east Cascades, hugged by ravines and lined with trees. It looks like nothing so much as a great blue worm.

Even though you can see there are only a few humans, compared at least to the billions in the cities, you don't have enough sensors to count them. If you cannot count them, then you do not know that there are almost twice as many as there should be.

The ones who should be there are the people of the Wilders. Together, the Wilders and the ecobots are on the side of the spruce and the cedar, the prairie grass and the wild rhododendron. They support the coyote and the rabbit, the black bear and the wolf.

The other people? Some are merely lost. Some are wandering artists who have lost themselves in the wild on purpose. They are illegal but tolerated. Others are full of hatred for this new world. If they could be found, they would not be tolerated.

These are the Returners.

There are a lot of places for them to hide in land this empty.

CHAPTER ONE

Lou loved standing on the top of mountains, but standing on top of the Bridge of Stars made her twitchy. There were too many people, too much movement, and every patch of green was tightly controlled. The bridge spiraled nearly two thousand feet above Seacouver, taller than almost every building. Lou hated it.

In contrast, her younger sister looked buoyant. Coryn's face glowed with the buzz of the city. Strands of bright red hair escaped from her loose braid, and blew around her face like a moving halo. She sat cross-legged on a white bench in front of Lou, swinging one foot in the air, gazing over the water and the western horizon. There, the Olympic Mountains cut a jagged green line against a bright blue summer sky.

She'd missed Coryn when she left the city the first time, but she'd miss her more now. Soon. It would be time to go soon.

Below and around them, the city moved. Bicyclists whizzed past so fast the wind of their wheels fluffed Lou's hair. Walkers stopped and talked to each other, or their companion robots, about the view in voices that varied from hushed whispers to high, excited exclamations. A dog barked, and she searched until she found it tucked into a robot's backpack. Its probable owner, a teenaged girl with long dark hair and a red skirt, leaned against the railing.

The screech of a set of brakes made Lou jump, but Coryn didn't even seem to hear it. "Coryn?" Lou ventured.

Coryn turned, shading her eyes with one hand. "Yes?"

"Thank you."

Coryn cocked her head and smiled, looking inordinately pleased at the simple words.

"I should have said that earlier," Lou told her. "I'm glad you came out, glad you survived, glad you found me and joined me. I should have said that right away, that first day on the farm after I found you . . . after we found each other."

Coryn's smile broadened. "Well, I did make it most of the way. But if you hadn't rescued me, I'd be dead." She caught some of her flyaway hairs and tried to tuck them out of the wind. "I knew you were happy to see me even though you didn't say so."

When had her little sister learned to be graceful with words? "I was just too wrapped up in our plan to shake up the cities." Here on the top of the tallest bridge in Seacouver, looking down at the green and blue tops of skyscrapers and the gauzy skybridges that knitted them together, she again felt the sting of her own naive choices. "I shouldn't have believed Victor. I knew there were plans hidden inside plans, but I thought I knew the *real* one."

"You didn't. You wouldn't have gone into Portland if you'd known people would die."

Lou grimaced. She should never have been such a gullible ass that she got tricked into invading Portland, her well-intentioned peaceful protest hiding a far more evil attack on the city. Even thinking about it drove a sharp pang of anger into Lou's gut. "I intend to find the bastards who sent the second wave of ecobots in. Shortly, too."

Lou hadn't even noticed when the dark-haired girl left the landing. Now an older woman with two companion robots stood stiffly, looking out but not down. One of her robots crowded Coryn, who scooted closer to Lou. Her voice cracked as she reached up and took Lou's hand. "I know. Stay with me for a few more minutes."

"Of course." The whole time they had been growing up, it had been Lou and Coryn together and everyone else outside of that tiny circle. Everyone. Even their parents, who had eventually killed themselves. Because they were together, they weren't bothered by the lesser challenges of being teenaged orphans: children who teased them, professors who scorned them, the city itself when it ratted on them as they broke rules. It had been Lou and Coryn, and Coryn's old companion robot, Paula, against the world. Lou had thought she would always know Coryn inside and out. But these last few weeks had felt like getting to know a strange woman. Coryn had become more than Lou had expected her to, as if she should have always remained a child. As she squeezed Coryn's hand, a message buzzed through on her wristlet, and she twisted her hand to shift it out of the sun's glare.

Matchiko hurt. Come now. Yakima. Shuska.

Yakima was a place. Matchiko and Shuska were Lou's tribe now, her people. A stab of fear made her shiver in spite of the heat.

Coryn must have noticed. "What's wrong?"

"A message from Shuska." Her heart ran faster with worry and anticipation. She went around the back of the bench and sat beside her sister. "I'm sorry. I have to go to them."

The disappointment on Coryn's face shifted to worry. "Is everything okay?"

"Matchiko is hurt."

"What happened?"

Lou pulled her hand away and glanced down at her wristlet. No more information had come through. But then Shuska was unlikely to send anything she considered secret into the city. She wouldn't have sent a note at all if it wasn't serious. "I have to go to Yakima to find out."

"Now?"

Yes, now. But the look on Coryn's face made her say, "Soon. Julianna said I might be sent out today anyway." Julianna was Coryn's powerful protector. Lou looked east, toward the Cascade Mountains and her friends. "You wanted to race me down the hill. I guess we should go now?"

Coryn's eyes widened. "Not yet. Please. I don't know when I'll see you again."

It hurt, but Coryn was fine and well-cared for. Lou whispered, "If Matchiko is hurt, I have to go."

Coryn looked away. "They're your family now, aren't they?"

"Like Julianna is yours. You're my only sister."

"You are my only family!" Coryn said, a little too loudly. Then she sighed. "But I suppose you do have to go. Will you come back? Can you promise?"

Lou winced, remembering she had promised to come back for Coryn's graduation. She had screwed that up entirely. "Someday. I can't know when. You know how it is out there."

Coryn nodded and took a single deep breath. "I love you."

"I love you, too." There. They hadn't said that in years. It felt . . . good. Scary.

They stood, staring at each other for a moment, before Lou took a step forward and folded Coryn into her arms. She stank of the city, but she also smelled like home, like the past, and like family.

Lou pulled away before she could be weakened by any more emotion, and held her sister by the shoulders. "Let's go."

"Okay." Coryn walked her bike away from the wall, threw her leg over it, pulled down her AR glasses, and pushed off, all in what looked like one movement.

Lou shook her head, amused. She pulled her own glasses down before she mounted, and looked around carefully, waiting for a far bigger break in the traffic than Coryn had needed. The AR world folded around her, lines and colors and flashing symbols.

She focused, identifying the three things she needed: Her sister, her route off the bridge, and the traffic immediately around her. By the time she was moving well through the other bikes and people on the bridge, her sister was already a quarter of the way down.

✝ ✝ ✝

Lou stood on the busy platform outside of the hyperloop with Coryn, Julianna, and Jake beside her. City police and private security-bots surrounded them, thankfully keeping some distance. A growing crowd had stopped to gawk at Julianna and Jake, faces reflecting awe, curiosity, and, in a few cases, the extremes of adoration or anger.

At least she'd said goodbye to Coryn on the bridge and didn't need to say anything tender with an audience.

A news-bot dived at Lou, and she barely managed not to swat it. Julianna and Jake might not run the city anymore, but they both commanded attention. Whenever they went out, news-bots thronged them. Stupid, vapid, city-dwellers with their cults of personality.

Jake had bent with age, but Julianna had run her way through life, quite literally. If Lou hadn't known who they were, she might have thought them from different generations. Julianna stood straight and slender, even though her hair had gone to gray and her eyes were buried in wrinkles. She looked right at Lou as she said, "I can't thank you enough."

Lou glanced at Coryn, who had mysteriously gathered the patronage of this strong woman. "No. Thank you. I'm sorry I have to go."

Juliana's smile disappeared. "The city is about to kick you out anyway. Portland's court sent its list of incorrigibles from the protests up this morning."

Lou tensed. "I see."

"Eloise will meet you at Longview Station. Drop off there. It's the stop before Portland."

"Okay." Lou turned to Jake. In spite of his bowed frame and thin cheeks, he was still as handsome as a near-centenarian could be. He didn't do anything so physical as marathons, but Coryn claimed he rode a stationary bicycle and race-walked. He must do something to stay so alert. Another icon. The Canadian half of the Jake and Lake Show, the man who stood up to the United States government and survived. Together, Jake and Julianna had created Seacouver. True to his nature as the quiet power, Jake smiled and took her rough hand in his far smoother one. She squeezed softly, so as not to break any of his bones. "Perhaps I'll see you again," she told him.

"That's likely. Good luck."

"Thank you. I could use some luck." Then Lou was face to face with her sister again. Coryn had her small, white dog with her. Aspen. He licked Coryn's face, looking at home in the city. Coryn had collected him from murdered Listeners on her way to find Lou. Well, Coryn and Aspen were both safer now. Maybe.

Lou ruffled Aspen's fur. A sudden sharp pang of loss tore her breath, but she refused to show it. She hugged Coryn once, briefly, and turned away to climb up the steps. Even though she wanted to stop, she didn't let herself look back, afraid Coryn would notice the tears at the edges of her eyes.

Soon enough, the noisy station grabbed her attention. She'd never ridden the hyperloop. Orphans couldn't afford it.

Security-bots stood at the top of the steps behind a black line, watching with perfect and slightly creepy focus. They wore red-and-yellow Loop Authority uniforms. All of them had been designed to look female. They wore the same faces and bra sizes, had the same long legs and long arms and long-fingered hands, but different skin color and hair. Lou tried to avoid them, which might have been the point of making them so uncanny.

Flashing white signs pointed to where the security scanning area started. She stepped over the line, and an area of the floor right around her feet lit up, a sign for the guards that the building had recognized her chip and vetted her. The light under her feet went off, and she stepped forward.

Multicolored neon light rods arched right to left above her. Softer white light spilled up from the floor. Most people on the platforms looked well-dressed and walked fast. Companion-bots trailed teams of people sliding into pod gates. She shouldered her backpack and handed her ticket to a post with arms and a pleasing voice. It ran a palm over the ticket, reading her destination. "Go to pod sixty-seven."

"Thank you."

It was already looking at the next customer. She squinted at the signs and went right, walking past five doors before finding the one with a red flashing 67 on it. She stopped in front of the door and waited for it to open.

When nothing happened, she looked around, worry thrumming through her nerves.

Her wrist buzzed at her again. No pictures, just a place. *Hotel Shamiana.*

Well, good. She'd needed a more specific destination than Yakima. *Come soon.*

She whispered into her wristlet. *On my way.*

The door in front of her slid silently to the right. Inside, a square box sat in front of her. One gull-wing door opened up and she stepped into the pod. There was a single seat, a small table, and no windows whatsoever. She sat. The moment she clicked the seatbelt buckle, the door closed her in.

Whoever had been here last had left a whiff of musky perfume that almost made her gag. The car lurched forward, two hard jerks, and then the ride smoothed. Although she couldn't see outside, she knew her pod was joining with other pods to create a grouping of eight, some of which held cargo while others held people. She felt a whisper-soft bump as her pod joined others in front, behind, and to the right. She expected to hear clicks or whirrs or something, but it was silent in the car except for her own breathing.

The superpod started up, smoothly and with less fuss than she expected. A slight pressure pushed her back in her seat, and she wondered if they were in the main tube yet.

Entering main tube flashed on the wall in front of her.

Okay then. This would be fine. It would.

Travel time to Longview Station: 31 minutes and 15 seconds.

The pressure increased, but not badly. No worse than the farm trucks she occasionally rode Outside, and no worse, really, than being on a galloping horse. Smoother than a horse.

She hadn't brought anything to entertain herself with, so she imagined seeing Matchiko and Shuska again, sharing a three-way hug, talking over tea. She had refused to go with them when they broke free from Portland Metro after the failed attack. It had been an almost impossible thing to do, a thing so hard something inside her had ripped. But she *had* to be sure Coryn was okay. She hadn't known about Coryn's powerful protectors when she left Matchiko and Shuska—Lou had met them later, on the plane flight between cities. The same flight she was reversing now, if at lower altitude. She smiled at the thought. So much easy travel.

How badly was Matchiko hurt? What had happened?

Travel time to Longview Station: 16 minutes and 43 seconds.

The walls still felt too close. She shut her eyes, hoping they'd get there before the tiny space drove her crazy.

It felt good to be going home. Not that home remained. RiversEnd Ranch had gone bankrupt with the Lucken Foundation, in trouble for helping to fund the failed attack-within-an-attack on Portland Metro. But she didn't feel guilty about that anymore, not after the way she'd been grilled during her captivity in the loft where she and her friends had been held by the same foundation.

She'd been stupid. She wouldn't be that stupid ever again. She and Shuska and Matchiko would find the Returners behind the real plot, the one that had killed people and that had almost succeeded at bringing Seacouver to its knees. They were all trained Wilders, and they had a reputation as some of the best. A well-earned one. The three amigas. None of them were Hispanic, and she couldn't remember who first called them that, but she liked it. She opened her eyes, glancing at the trip timer.

Travel time to Longview Station: 9 minutes and 12 seconds.

The hyperloop might be twice as fast as an airplane, but she'd liked the plane ride. She hated being locked in a tiny box.

What could have happened to Matchiko? At least Shuska was whole and only Matchiko hurt. Shuska could carry either of them, but both of them together would be unable to carry Shuska. She'd met Shuska first, one cold fall morning when she was still new on the farm and she and Daryl were tracking a collared wolf that was broadcasting its mortality.

They'd rounded a sharp corner and entered a clearing where a big woman was holding off three burly male Returners. Shuska had wielded a machete and two of the men had rivers of blood running from their limbs—one an arm and one a thigh. Blood ran down the woman's face and spotted her clothes.

While she had the upper hand, it couldn't stay that way long.

A dead wolf lay beside the small game trail, a long gray beauty with blood matting her coat.

Somewhere nearby but out of sight, her mate howled.

Daryl pulled out his stunner and took down two of the men before the last one noticed. Lou pulled her weapon as well, but hesitated. Daryl had ordered her not to shoot any time he had the situation in control.

The remaining male combatant froze, disbelief flooding his face. Then he looked directly at Daryl and lunged toward Shuska, a metal knife-blade glinting in sharp sunlight.

Lou fired on him without thinking about it. He dropped, stunned, and Shuska spit on him, hissing, "Wolf killer!"

That one incident had started Lou's reputation for being ruthless, even though she hadn't killed her opponent. Killing had come later.

RiversEnd had just lost a seasoned ranger in a wicked snowstorm the week before. Daryl hired Shuska as a replacement on the spot. She'd been close to Lou ever since; this was their only separation since that day.

Perhaps Coryn had been the only force in the world strong enough to split Lou from Shuska and Matchiko.

Travel time to Longview Station: 0 minutes and 15 seconds.

The superpod drifted right and stopped. The light over the door turned green. She snapped the seatbelt free, gathered her things, and stepped out. Longview Station only had enough space for two super-pods at a time, although tunnels and bridges led away from the main room, which was much shabbier than Seacouver's had been. Two other people got off with her, so the rest of the pods must be full of cargo. Julianna had told her to look for Eloise, but she certainly wasn't waiting on the platform.

Well, maybe she was outside.

One of the people who had just disembarked drifted her way and whispered, "Follow me."

So Eloise had been in Seacouver with her? And Julianna had said nothing? Damn the whole city for its intrigue and secrets.

She kept a bit of distance since that appeared to be what Eloise wanted. Robotic cargo handlers passed them both, smart carts with flashing lights that made quick turns. Additional robots that looked like they were built into the pod bay doors began unloading boxes from the five cargo pods. The dance of the robots. It was always a part of the city, even a place as small as this northern end of the Portland Metroplex.

She followed Eloise up a moving walkway and along a straight tube only three times as wide as the hyperloop tube itself. Two of the cargo-bots ran ahead of them, whirring softly. Insipid music flowed down from ceiling speakers, utterly failing to calm her. A thin line of windows showed the late afternoon sun illuminating the Columbia River to their right and reflecting on the shiny metal of active train tracks to the left.

Eloise led her down another escalator. It left them off at a nearly-empty parking lot that looked old enough and outsized enough to have been built before cars with human drivers were outlawed. Weeds colonized the cracks and holes in the concrete, as if the lot were wilding itself.

Eloise led Lou across a wooden walkway above a weedy, damp wetland. The same boat they'd escaped Portland in on the day of the second attacks bobbed in the water, a low, sleek beauty with wide seats. The other woman gestured for Lou to climb aboard and took the taller pilot's seat. She pushed the on switch and the engine rumbled to life, the boat shaking faintly, as if it were a horse that wanted to run but was being held to a quivering stand by the will of the rider. After she glanced at all the gauges, Eloise pushed the scarf off of her head and said, "I can get you as far as Camas."

Lou leaned in. "Can you get me to Kennewick? That's the closest place to drop me for Yakima."

Eloise gave her a flat, unsympathetic look. "I haven't got that much time."

"One of my friends is hurt."

"The Asian girl or the big one?"

The tone in Eloise's voice pissed Lou off. "Matchiko. The 'big one' is Shuska." She forced herself to smile. "Please?"

Eloise glanced at her wrist and then at a slate she pulled out from a drawer near her right knee. She nodded and held her hand out.

Lou stripped her wristlet and handed it over. Eloise dropped it and her own devices into a bag and drew the top closed, then dropped that into another bag and then another one, and put the whole assembly down between her feet. This was the same way they'd hidden their identity from Portland Metro when Eloise took the three amigas out of the city before she left Matchiko and Shuska to fly to Seacouver with Coryn and Julianna.

Eloise smiled as broadly as Lou had ever seen her, as if now that she'd decided to go to Kennewick, she was going to make it memorable. "Hold on!"

Lou clutched the railing just in time. The engine gave a great high whine and then Eloise opened the throttle and the sound lowered to a deep thrum. They were off, the bow pushing waves away to each side and the wind of their passage blowing Lou's hair against her cheeks.

Eloise gave out a soft, happy yip at the speed, and Lou yipped as well, a statement of joy that she was Outside again, free again. Dark water flew by under the boat and the air smelled of cedars and firs, and of the great river itself.

CHAPTER TWO

Eloise was good with the boat, confident and sure. They hugged the starboard shore, moving upriver fast enough for a great wake of water to rise up behind them. The air smelled of trees and leaves and water. It had a bite to it, and the wind pulled at her hair and stung her cheeks.

Lou would see Matchiko and Shuska soon.

After an hour, the high bridges of Portland rose in front of them. Eloise slowed until the nose fell and the boat rode flat on the water.

The Portland-Vancouver Bridge spiraled up from the Washington side of the border and crossed the wide river in a high curve before turning gracefully downtown. She hadn't ever crossed the PV Bridge, but Coryn had, riding on the back of an ecobot with two more of Julianna's minions, Blessing and Day. That thought made Lou stiffen; Blessing and Day had worked for her once. Or so she had thought. "Have Blessing and Day always worked for Julianna?" she asked the back of Eloise's head.

Eloise turned with a half smile. "Always is a long time."

Lou clamped her mouth shut. Just one more way she had been naive.

The PV Bridge split the sky and threw a long, looping shadow on the river. Coryn's companion robot, Paula, had died somewhere on that bridge. Been shot. To hear Coryn tell the tale, Paula had gone out in a blaze of glory protecting Coryn from the city's police force.

Movement caught her eye as a figure flew above them. She blinked. A person?

Eloise laughed. "That's the zip line. The bridge's most famous feature."

She hadn't known that. Coryn could probably tell her everything about the bridge. But then, Coryn loved bridges and full, busy places.

Lou loved neither. She didn't mind the river though, or the boat, or even the silence of her companion.

As Eloise negotiated the tricky current where the Willamette joined with the Columbia, Lou glanced upriver toward the Pearl District. They were too far away for her to make out the loft where she'd been held captive for days before Coryn rescued her. But she knew it was there, and she shuddered at the memory of being locked away with the other protestors, fed water and paste, and questioned for hours.

Not that she had known anything useful. The questions had taught her a few things, though. It wasn't the city that held her, but the NGO she'd worked for. Her boss had tricked her into joining an attack on Portland, but her bosses' boss had known next to nothing. He was merely a lazy waste of energy covering himself in fancy clothes. Meeting him had explained why they were always short of resources on the ranch. At least she felt anger now, instead of the despair that had fallen over her those three dark days.

It had taken most of the plane ride to Seacouver after Coryn rescued her, but she had come to terms with herself; she would be smarter now. No one was going to take easy advantage of her again.

They passed the Camas Gate under a shielding line of drones. She pointed toward the gate itself, a large metal structure on the Washington side of the river. "Look at all of those police vehicles. There were hardly any when we came in a few nights ago." Now, two straight lines of cars and trucks blocked the road. Uniformed men and women paced along the shoreline, the airspace above them clotted with drones.

Eloise nodded, but she kept her face pointed forward into the wind, her expression grim, her lips thin, and her eyes narrow.

A light pop of air told Lou when they passed through Portland Metro's protective dome. As if leaving the dome had oiled her tongue, Eloise started talking. "The city is still on high alert. Drones out. Extra security. Twice the usual number of police-bots. Both cities. I suspect they'll stay that way for months." She leaned down and grabbed the nested bags, unearthing their electronics.

Lou sighed in relief. She was certainly persona non grata in Portland Metro, and now she'd gotten in and out of it with no notice. Some system somewhere would know that she had disembarked at Longview Station, but it would probably assume she'd walked away from it without ever entering the cityplex.

Good.

She liked confounding automated systems.

As soon as Eloise finished buckling her wristlet on, she gunned the engine again. The bow of the boat rose and they raced through the glittering waterfalls of the Columbia River Gorge. Water fell like ribbons from the tops of cliffs, sometimes like satin and other times like lace.

About half an hour out of Camas, they passed a team of robots carefully thinning a forested slope. The robots were five or six times as big as humans, hulking machines painted in camouflage greens and browns. Not full ecobots, but slave labor doing some of the more dangerous wilding. After Portland, she'd grown nervous of large robots, but these looked normal and uncompromised. Maybe because they had fewer brains and weapons than the far smarter versions that Lou usually worked with.

Long after they'd passed out of sight of Portland, but before they reached The Dalles, Eloise slowed the boat. The sun had gone down so far that the automatic lights on the bow and stern had come on. She turned to Lou, her face serious. "We need to talk."

A doe and two fawns stood like slender statues at the edge of the water, watching the boat. Luck. Deer were always luck for her. Maybe Eloise would answer more questions now that they were beyond the city's sensitive surveillance. "All right. What can I help you with?"

"You know there are layers to last week's attack?"

"Of course." The littlest fawn lowered its head to drink from the still water at the edge of the river. They moved slowly to avoid spooking the deer. "Sure. We were on the bottom, the clueless and pissed-off Wilders. The counters and burners and planters and cullers. The people naive enough to think the system actually cared." Anger choked her throat, and she took a deep breath and watched the deer, letting nature calm her. "We were too stupid to realize our bosses would trap us." She blinked back an angry tear and took another deep breath. "And of course, the rich people in the city."

"It's complicated, you know," Eloise mused. "You need the city."

"Not more than the city needs the wild," Lou snapped.

Eloise held up a hand, and her smile had a tiny bit of condescension in it. "Still."

Lou's hand tightened on the side of the boat. Did the world really need all those people? But she kept that thought to herself, and simply replied, "I know. When Julianna and I were doing research during the attack, we learned the NGO's board wasn't all evil either. Two or three at the top were, though—they were all about money and power. Liars who were already so rich they didn't need anything else, but still they stole from the land, from the future." She tensed, remembering the endless waiting and begging for supplies. "They shorted us over and over, killed some of us by doing that."

A spark of anger flashed in Eloise's eyes, and her jaw tightened. But otherwise she sat as still as the deer standing on the shore.

Lou took a few deep breaths, and when she spoke again, her voice was softer. "But beyond them, beyond the greed, there was something else. Julianna and I both felt it, even though we couldn't prove a thing. Just like my strings were pulled, someone else pulled the board's strings."

Eloise didn't even look surprised. "Any ideas?"

"You know how the Returners always seem crazy? Like they want the past back, but we all know it's not coming back, and they have to know it as well?"

Eloise shook her head. "I know more about the evils in the city than out here. I know a little. The Returners want to own the land again, and most of them came from it. They're the people the great taking displaced."

"Yes. They're angry people. They hate Wilders. They believe lies, and they hate science. Kind of like the people who didn't believe the sea would rise or that we were killing off the animals. They want to go back to a world that can't exist anymore, and they'll kill us to do it. But that's just stupid. After all that's happened, it's hard to imagine people being so simple that they think they can remake the world by wishing it back a hundred years. Julianna and I both felt there was more organization behind them, more resources. Someone molding their thoughts and aiming them at the city. It's not just crazy people, like I had to deal with on the farm. It's a crazy army." She shivered. "I hope we're wrong."

"Julianna doesn't think you are." Eloise moved them a few feet farther away from the bank. "Someone keeps the Returners alive, feeding them lines about a better world. We both hope you will help us look for this army."

That was a rather long speech for Eloise. "What should I look for?"

Eloise gave the boat enough power to leave the deer behind. "They're organized, and they have good communications. Maybe dedicated satellites or something. Remember all the dead Listeners?"

Lou nodded. "Coryn made friends with some, before the people I hired to help us hack the ecobots killed them." She wasn't proud of that. The admission made her shiver.

Eloise narrowed her eyes. "That's complex."

"Coryn's lucky she wasn't killed, too." She glanced upriver, eyes stinging. They'd all been lucky.

Eloise pushed her damp hair away from her face. "We're looking for a nest of Returners. We think they have a whole city hidden somewhere, someplace fully off the grid. The people who built that city killed the Listeners to be sure they didn't get caught."

"Because the Listeners know everything?" It was a common refrain on the farms. They'd always fed the Listeners well, and plied them for information.

"Yeah. And because—mostly—they weren't trained fighters. They were do-gooders."

There was that. The Listeners had wanted the grand dream as much as Lou had. A land with real wild places, a land with the interstate and the mansions and even the farms scraped off of it. Returners wanted the old world back, the one where they could do whatever they wanted, strip the land if they wanted, hunt whatever animal they wanted, throw down fences or even just signs, and own things that shouldn't be owned. "They're the assholes who kill the wolves and grizzlies and shoot at the ecobots. I've killed more than one Returner." She glanced at Eloise, who had probably also killed people. "In the line of duty. As part of my job."

"I know."

Lou refrained from asking how she knew. Coryn must have told Julianna, who must have told Eloise. "So you want me to help you find them. What will you do if you succeed?"

"That depends on what we find."

"Fair enough." Lou reached into her pack and took out her coat, pulling it on and zipping it against the cooling night air. "Try not to get this wet. Any idea where to look?"

"North. Somewhere near the border. But we don't know any more than that. They might try to take the city again before winter."

Lou glanced toward the bald hump of Mount Adams. "I don't think so. The vine maples are already starting to turn, even down here. There's no more than a few weeks of real summer left, and they won't want to chance the fall storm season."

"I hope you're right. We'll tell you if we learn different. Will you tell us anything you find?"

"Well, the first thing I need to come across is a job." And her friends. She could feel the full day that had passed since Shuska messaged her. It was going to be too dark to get to Yakima tonight. "Do you want anything else?"

Eloise shook her head. "Will you help, though?"

"I'll help. But I won't work for Julianna. I'm a Wilder, not a city girl."

Eloise flinched. "I predict you'll change your mind. We're creating a new foundation."

"Do you know what its goals are?"

"We will."

She hesitated. They would need to eat. "Maybe talk to me then. We need work now." She had some money saved, but it wouldn't last more than a few months.

"We can pay you," Eloise stated. "To look."

"I don't need money to hunt down Returners." She smiled. "I do that for fun."

Eloise laughed, and Lou thought she saw a flash of respect in the reticent woman's eyes. Good. Lou liked her, in spite of the fact that she worked for Julianna. Well, maybe Julianna was a little okay, too. But Lou wouldn't have thought that a month ago. A month ago she would have cursed anyone from the city except for Coryn.

To her relief, Eloise stroked the console again, and once more they sped closer to Matchiko and Shuska.

Yakima was eighty miles from Kennewick. After Eloise dropped her off, Lou made a sheltered spot to sleep in the woods. When she woke, she found a ride to town on the back of a truck carrying workers for the orchards. So she stood outside of Hotel Shamiana by just before noon.

The hotel looked like a place for itinerant workers as much as for tourists. It had been built before the taking. Its roof sagged on one side, and the glass in two of the big windows in the entrance had cracked. Still, as she walked in, Lou approved. A fireplace was filled with wood ready to light for the evening, and comfortable chairs made the lobby look like a great place for a conversation and a beer.

A real person stood behind the desk, a short man with a pleasant smile and an eight-inch-long graying beard that looked fluffy enough to hide small animals. As soon as he saw her, he asked, "Are you Lou?"

"Yes."

"Room 143." He threw something shiny at her. "Here's a key."

She caught it, shoving it in her pocket. A physical key, brass, hooked to a plastic fob.

He pointed down the hallway to her right. "Near the end."

She stopped long enough to pour half a cup of overcooked black coffee into a disposable cup. In spite of having the key, she knocked.

No answer.

She opened the door to find Matchiko sound asleep and bundled under blankets, her pale face as white as the bottom of summer clouds on a burning hot day. Sweat beaded her forehead. Lou stood in silence, her body flooding with happiness and worry.

Matchiko looked beautiful even in her sleep, even injured. Her round face had mostly Asian features, although her lips were fuller and her chin a little sharper than most of the Asians Lou knew. Her dark hair had been pulled into a ponytail. At rest like this, she looked younger than usual, but it would still be easy for anyone to guess she was at least ten years older than Lou. The real answer was almost twenty years older; Matchiko was forty-three.

Matchiko was their brains, Shuska their muscle, and Lou the planner and risk-taker. All of them together were heart.

A note rested on the round table. *I'm in town finding a doctor* had been scrawled in Shuska's precise print.

Too bad she hadn't bothered to note how long ago she'd left. Medical care was very different Outside than Inside, although here in a sanctioned city it shouldn't be as bad as they'd had it on RiversEnd Ranch.

"Matchiko?" Lou whispered.

Nothing.

She said it a little louder. "Matchiko!"

Matchiko lifted a finger and grunted, but didn't move her head or acknowledge for sure that she'd even heard her name or noticed Lou had returned.

Lou chose one of two chairs, an orange square that squeaked when she sat down. She finished her coffee quickly, watching Matchiko sleep. From time to time, Matchiko let out a small moan that echoed in Lou's chest.

What had happened?

After Lou finished the last sip of coffee, she went into the bathroom and took a hot shower, washing the scent of the city off of her. She pulled her last set of clean clothes out of her pack, and was just tucking in her shirt when Shuska trundled through the door, followed by a tall man with a neat brown mustache and brown eyes that almost matched his hair.

At the sight of Lou, Shuska's whole face lit with a broad smile. "Good to see you!"

"Good to be here."

Shuska nodded at the man. "This is David. He's a paramedic."

Good. "I'm Lou."

David smiled. He said, "Pleased to meet you." He bent over Matchiko. "Let me look at your friend."

Shuska said, "I gave her painkillers."

That explained the deep sleep. "What happened?"

"She broke an ankle. Maybe more. Badly. I couldn't splint it well enough for it to heal." Shuska looked a little guilty at that. "I had to carry her here from the river."

Lou could picture the tall, broad Shuska walking with slender Matchiko draped across her arms, legs dangling. It was kind of a sweet picture, other than the part about Matchiko being hurt. Or the part about how long the walk had to be. Days? "How did it happen?"

David drew back the blankets.

Matchiko stirred and flopped onto her back. Her eyes opened for just a moment but then closed again.

The paramedic murmured, "I see why you drugged her."

Matchiko's right ankle was three times its normal size, and the foot below it was black and blue. David bent down and gingerly touched her ankle.

Matchiko's eyes opened wide. "D . . . don't touch me!"

"It's okay," Shuska said. "He's trained."

"Doctor?"

"Paramedic. Lou's here."

Matchiko turned her head, and when she saw Lou she smiled widely and extended one arm.

By the time Lou got to her side, her eyes had closed again. "What did you drug her with?"

"Morphine."

Wow. Lou took Matchiko's hand, now flopped over the side of the bed, and sat stroking it while she watched the paramedic work.

David ran a portable device over Matchiko's ankle slowly, just a few inches above it. Some kind of imaging machine. It hummed softly and then clicked. He let out a low whistle. "Good news and bad news."

"All right," Lou said. "Give us both."

"It's not infected. Yet. There's a break that I might be able to straighten by hand, but it's not in her ankle. It's above it. It's going to hurt. A lot."

"And the bad news?"

He smiled tightly, as if knowing how unwelcome his news would be. "Her ankle is twisted and some of the small bones in the top of her feet are fractured. I can get her on the list in the hospital, but there's a five-month wait for surgery table space. You'll have to take her to Portland Metro."

If she went to Portland Metro she'd be arrested. Lou didn't say that out loud. Instead, she asked, "Will she be able to walk before it gets fixed?"

"If the bone heals well, a little. But with pain."

Good thing Matchiko liked to ride horses. This was grim indeed. It was never good to be seriously injured Outside.

Shuska almost growled at the poor paramedic, her underlying stress audible. "Go ahead and set the long bone."

"You're sure?"

"Yes."

"Good thing she's drugged." He glanced at Shuska. "Hold her."

Shuska placed her big hands on Matchiko's tiny, birdlike shoulders. "Go on."

Since Shuska was blocking her view, Lou couldn't see what the paramedic did, but she heard a bone crack.

Matchiko screamed.

Shuska put her lips close to Matchiko's small ear and whispered at her. "Shhhhhh . . . shhhh . . . it's done."

"Almost," David said. "Keep holding her."

Whatever he did this time didn't produce a crack. Nor did Matchiko scream, although her eyes and mouth stretched wide, every muscle in her face taut with pain.

"There."

"Are you done?" Shuska asked him.

He took the machine out again, scanning with quiet competence. "It'll be okay."

Lou let out a sigh of relief.

"I'll splint it. You can watch me. I can give her a shot to help her make new bone. But you'll have to stay put a week before you risk putting any weight on it."

"I can carry her," Shuska said.

David stared at her. After a few moments, he nodded. "After the week, you probably should. But for now, she needs to heal in a bed and have exactly zero movement of that leg. I've got plaster for some casting but we'll need to find materials to splint it."

Matchiko fell sound asleep again, her entire right leg wrapped in a splint that started above her knee and ended in thin air below her wrecked foot. The foot itself was encased in what amounted to a bubble of plastic and plaster wrapped around wood. "That's quite a splint," Lou said.

"It was cheap." Shuska raised a bushy eyebrow toward Matchiko's foot. "I expect it will also be quite effective."

Lou shook her head in something that wasn't quite laughter. There was nothing funny about having Matchiko badly hurt. If they'd been in a megacity, a new ankle might have taken hours. But they weren't. They were here, where a shot of cells to knit the bone would have to do. Worse, they were probably stuck in this room, with the one bed taken up almost entirely by the smallest of them and her enormous cast. But they were together. "How much did you pay him?"

"One bottle of recently expired morphine pills."

Now she did laugh. "Where did you get that?"

"Remember how the foundation stabled our horses just outside Camas? By the time we left, I figured our bosses owed us a few things. Between me and Matchiko, we managed to steal quite a few supplies from their dispensary, three horses, and a few good coats."

Lou's mood elevated instantly. "Mouse?"

Shuska shook her head. "We lost the horses. Didn't have Mouse anyway. Someone had already taken her."

"Dammit."

Shuska gave a long, slow smile. "I know. I looked for her."

"I know you did." Lou felt a sharp ache, just then realizing how much she missed her horse. She and Mouse made a good team. One more loss she could chalk up to being stupid. She got up and stood behind Shuska, opening her palms and rubbing Shuska's shoulders.

Shuska groaned with happiness. "I missed you."

"I missed you. What happened to the horses? And to Matchiko?"

"We got ambushed. Five men. I stunned one, and we left him. The others got away after one of them pushed Matchiko over a cliff. Rode the horses away, the bastards." She glanced at Matchiko. "At least she didn't go all the way into the water. Her foot got caught in a tree root on her way down. It slowed her fall, maybe kept her from rolling into the river and drowning. Luckily there was a beach down that cliff, and even a way down to where she fell. You can't see it, but her backside is pretty bruised, too."

Lou kneaded harder, taking her frustration at the story and the lost horses out on the knots in Shuska's upper back. "You couldn't take out five men all by yourself?" she teased.

"They had better guns."

If she'd been with them, this might not have happened. They might be riding north even now, no one hurt, everyone happy. "You'd think we lived in the Wild West."

"Don't we?"

"At least we have access to handheld x-ray machines."

Shuska drew a ball in the air with her hands. "It made a whole 3-D image. That's only the second time I've seen one. Pretty cool."

"You should see what they have in the city." Of all of them, Shuska was the one with no history in cities. "A robot would fix her in the city."

"She left the cities on purpose."

"I know." Lou dug deeper into Shuska's right shoulder, making her groan. "Your muscles are as tight as a steel rod. I have a little money, but it won't last until she's better. We'll need work."

"That knot's from carrying Matchiko. Tell me about your week. What did you leave us for?"

"How much do you know about Seacouver's history?"

"What does history have to do with anything?"

To be fair, Lou had never seen Shuska reading anything she didn't have to. Lou and Matchiko were the ones who carried tattered old books around in their saddlebags. "Humor me. Tell me what you know."

The big woman shrugged. "Seacouver used to be two cities in two countries. Now it's one city in two countries. And the city tells both countries what to do about that."

Lou laughed. "Do you know who Julianna Lake is?"

"Isn't she dead?"

"Nope." The knots were beginning to work out of Shuska's shoulders, so Lou started in on her neck and scalp. "Julianna and Jake and Coryn and I talked the city off a ledge while Blessing and Day drove the bad guys out."

"Tell me the truth."

"I never lie."

"Nope. Never. What did you really do?"

"I told you. We did a television show with Jake and Lake and told the city who was attacking them. When we get some network, I can show you."

Shuska shook her head. "That's all?"

"Oh. I got to ride the hyperloop."

"Really?"

"And fly in a plane."

"You should write a novel."

Lou sighed and left off on Shuska's head, coming around and planting a kiss on her forehead. "My gosh, but it's nice to be home."

"It's good to have you back."

"It's even better to be out of the city."

Shuska stood, stretching. "Are you going to run back to your little sister?"

"Not right now."

"Good. I'd hate to miss you all over again. Now sit down. It's my turn to work on you."

Lou let out a long breath. It was heaven to be here, to be all together in spite of Matchiko's injury, to be alive. There had been moments on this trip she'd thought they'd never make it out, but here they were, Outside again, in a tough situation they understood.

CHAPTER THREE

Coryn rolled over and groaned as the room's alarm clock turned up the lights and sound. It began with a rising wash of water lapping against a rocky shore, followed by calling seabirds, then the insistent bark of seals. She opened her eyes as gulls screeched right overhead. Yesterday, Coryn had been out of bed by the time the seabirds started. This morning the gulls forced her out of bed and over to the off switch. She stretched, her muscles tight and full of small complaints.

She'd woken twice. Once with worry about Aspen, who had licked her face until she fell back asleep. Later, dreaming of a man named Bartholomew who had almost had her killed. It hadn't been personal—he had hardly known her. But he had been a mystery, a man Lou knew and paid to work for her, a man who had threatened to kill Coryn. A hacker who was part of the attack on the city. In her dreams, he was big and silent, looming over her. She was as compliant and terrified as the women who lived in his little band, like she'd been when he first captured her. In the real event, she had been brave, but her dream-self was frightened and sweaty.

It took a few breaths to realize she was safe in the city, threatened only by being late for her training run. She'd been living in a spare room in Julianna's downtown Seattle penthouse for four days. Every morning had included a long run. Her limbs still felt heavy with exhaustion even after seven hours of sleep. Yesterday, when Julianna told her she'd get used to the pace, the only thing that kept her from screaming was that Julianna kept the same pace she demanded of Coryn, and she was at least fifty years older. If an old woman could do it, Coryn could do it.

Now she had thirty minutes to get dressed, take Aspen out, and be at the breakfast table.

She barely made it.

She had expected just Jake and Julianna, but for the first time since she'd moved in, a stranger sat with them at breakfast. A man. Slender. A streak of gold ran along the right side above his temple and glittered all the way through the dark hair in his ponytail. A pretty boy with a bicyclist's body. Or a runner's.

He smiled at her and stood, holding out his hand. "Coryn? I'm Adam."

Of course that was his name. He looked the part. She took his hand. "Pleased to meet you."

Julianna explained. "Adam will coach you today. I've got a meeting, and you're ready for someone better than me."

Coryn felt her sore muscles groan. Adam's legs must be almost twice as long as hers. But all she said was, "I'm looking forward to it." Her slouchy running clothes and loosely braided hair made her self-conscious, but there was nothing for it.

She sat and poured the fresh milk by her plate into the bowl of granola and garnished it with blueberries that had been counted out into a small white porcelain cup. Julianna's training table always had real food.

They ate in silence. As soon as a server removed their plates and poured them high-electrolyte water, Julianna's house manager joined them at the table. Ghana Loreto was a small, brown man of indeterminate origin with the energy of five or six bigger men.

Ghana pulled out a chair and started right in. "Good morning. The threat level for the day is normal, which means be careful."

Good. Maybe the police had finished ejecting most of the city-dwellers who had joined the uprising.

Ghana took a cup of espresso from a tray the server brandished by his side. "Both Portland Metro and Seacouver are dropping visible security measures one level but both are leaving general surveillance high." He nodded at Julianna and Jake. "You both have busy schedules all afternoon. Coryn will have three and half hours to train with Adam."

"Anything else?" Julianna asked.

Ghana looked a little more relaxed now that the formal part of this ritual was over. "There are rumors of another attack, but the city is not taking them seriously." He smiled. "I assess that it is merely nerves and will pass. The space station is launching tomorrow and that should rip people's attention from past threats to future ones."

Jake nodded in his usual sage and slow way. "I suspect you are right."

Julianna pursed her lips.

Coryn knew from previous conversations that while other cities had been building outposts in space in case the rewilding didn't work, she and Jake had spent Seacouver's wealth on defense and infrastructure. The current mayor was investing in space, though. A lot. Coryn liked the idea. After all, who wouldn't want to see the city from space some-time? The earth was supposed to be beautiful from up there.

Adam stood, extending a hand to her. "Shall we go?"

She hesitated. Adam was strange and beautiful, and he smelled like soap and freshly printed running clothes. Surely he wouldn't bite. She let him help her up and after they said goodbye to the others, she fol-lowed him out.

They exited the building onto a roof park and started walking at a steadily increasing pace. "Have you known Jake and Julianna long?" he asked her.

"Four years. You?"

"As long as I remember."

Just like Blessing and Day. Apparently Julianna gained loyal staff by harvesting the young.

Was Coryn being harvested? She pushed the thought to the side for now. "Where did Julianna find you?"

"In New York. She visited whenever she was on state visits for a while. She paid tuition for good schools."

They slid easily into a jog as they entered a runway that wound between buildings. It took them uphill, and Coryn gave herself a few moments to find her stride before she asked, "Did she want something from you?"

"I would give her anything she asked."

That wasn't Coryn's question, but she let it go. This man hardly knew her, and he certainly didn't owe her his secrets. As if he heard her thoughts, he changed the subject. "I hear you've been Outside."

"Yes. I just got back."

"How different is it? Can you describe the differences?"

Turnabout. She tugged her shirt down and thought for a moment. "Have you been Out?"

"Not yet."

"All right. I've only been Outside once, to find my sister. The weather is part of it." She gestured toward the dome. "There's no safe place, not really. Wind and rain and cold and heat—they're all extreme. A cold spring night Outside is colder than the dead of winter here. The wind almost picked me up, and I'm not light."

"You're not heavy."

She giggled. "There's almost no data out there." She touched her VR goggles. "These don't work, and you wouldn't want them on anyway. You have to pay attention Outside. There's no city to keep you safe, no AI, no nothing. And everybody wants a piece of you. You have to be tough."

He looked like he was assessing her. "How did you survive?"

"I had a companion-bot with me. But that was hard, too. People wanted to steal her. One guy almost did, and another threatened to kill me if Paula—that was her name—if Paula didn't come back for me."

"Did that frighten you?"

"Of course it did." She clearly hadn't convinced him how dangerous it was outside of the domes. But then she hadn't believed it either, not until she experienced it.

"But you're here now. You're okay. Do you still have your companion?"

Coryn added speed and led them through a small crowd on a roof patio. Once they were through, she let him catch up. "She died protecting me in the Portland Metro protests." A lance of pain threatened to make her fall.

Adam sounded surprised. "The riots last week? The ones at Camas?"

"They weren't riots."

"They were violent."

"Not at first." She didn't want to talk about that part. Seriously did not want to talk about it. "Everybody Outside wants something, and a lot of them think you have it. You have to be tough. The Wilding, that thing that's going to save us all?"

"Yes." He sounded cautious.

"It's pretty awesome, but it's not happening as fast as the news says it is. That's what my sister went out there to work on."

"You must be proud of her."

"I am." She blurted out a fresh question before he could ask more about Outside. "Do you race?"

That drew a smile from him, and in answer he sped up and she had to work hard to catch up. By the time she did, her breath was already sharp. "Your pace is a little fast for me."

In answer he pointed to his AR goggles, which still rode around his neck. He mouthed the number "seventy-six" and she nodded and directed her gear to that channel. They pulled their goggles on at the same time, and she found herself in a training simulation complete with audio. "Five minutes at this pace. Go. Go. Go." Jazzy music played in the background, and she focused on it, matching her pace to the beat. The first three minutes were almost fun, but the last one almost killed her. Her side stitched and her breath went from sharp to impossible.

When the voice of the simulation said, "Great job," she wanted to punch it. She also wanted to slow to a walk but it guided her to half the pace she'd just been on, and Adam stayed just far enough ahead that she felt pulled along in his wake.

Interval training continued for two hours, leaving her dripping. He was always ahead of her on the fast parts, and looking pleased with himself for it as well. At least he didn't say anything obnoxious like "good job" or "way to go."

When they stopped, sweat dripped from her forehead and stung her eyes. Adam waited for her in the doorway back into Julianna's building. "I'll meet you right here in twenty minutes."

So he was going to the library with her? A tiny flash of resentment gave way to curiosity. "All right. I'll see you here in a few."

‡ ‡ ‡

Adam had chosen far fancier clothes than she had, which made her feel shabby. He wore a flashy purple top and tight black jeans that looked more like evening wear than work clothes, while she wore jeans and a forest-green T-shirt she'd had made the night before using the basic shirt 101 design with a myriad of camouflage colors chosen to highlight the dark reds in her hair. Simple and dull compared to Adam.

Sure enough, women and a few men watched him closely as they took the elevator down to the rail station and caught that to the library stop. Since she'd lost Paula, Coryn's instinct had been to avoid standing out, but Adam clearly loved attention. She watched him notice women watching him and smile at the most interesting ones.

Jake met them at the outside door, wearing his signature black-and-gray outfit. He always looked clean and neat, and even powerful; a feat of understatement rather than overstatement. He greeted them warmly and led them up the brightly colored escalators to the top floor, and then down a hallway and into a private room. Eloise ghosted in just before the door shut, silent as usual.

Three people waited for them. She recognized the librarian from a meeting here two days before, but she'd never seen the middle-aged couple dressed in ragged cottons from Outside.

Jake sat opposite them, and, as she had come to expect, no introductions were made. The librarian logged into a computer and a detailed map came up. "These are last night's satellite shots. You can write on the screen with this." She handed the unnamed woman a pen-shaped device.

The woman pushed dirty-blonde hair behind her ears and used the light pen to circle an area that included the northeastern portion of Promise and bits of Canada and Idaho. Her circle enclosed a lot of mountains and rivers, and no approved towns or rewilding centers. Maybe it was one of those places that had never been anything but wild.

"We have rumors that the orders came from in here. We've searched sat shots for clues. We've seen some groups on paths and roads that are surely Returners, but none of the groups are big. We talked to a few people we met from there." She pointed at the map. "And they acted like everything they saw was normal." She hesitated, then spoke a little faster. "One guy told us a wild tale about seeing a cowboy army ride through a storm. He said they were all dressed in leathers and rode fine horses. He told us they were well armed and had full saddlebags *and* a few pack horses. They looked serious, he said, deadly serious. He called it a 'Cavalry from Hell.'" Her pale eyes flicked toward Julianna, as if afraid of not being believed.

Jake frowned over steepled fingers. "Any pictures? Anything to prove it's not an army of rumors?"

The woman stiffened. "If he got any, he didn't offer them to us."

Eloise looked up from her note taking, face sharp with intense curiosity. After a moment she put her head back down and became almost invisible again.

Adam leaned forward across the table, getting a little closer to the map. "Did he count?"

The man spoke for the first time, his voice deeper than Coryn expected. "He told us hundreds, but that can't be true. We only came from the edge of that circle—" He pointed at the screen. "But I don't see a place to hide many Returners. Not if they're all living together. There would be families." He gestured toward the map. "A satellite would show a town that held that many. They'd need food, too. So I bet they're in Spokane Metro, and that it's not a few hundred."

The librarian punched some numbers and logged them into

another system. She pulled up a list of names and numbers. "These are neighborhoods in Spokane. There's no evidence of a nest of Returners anywhere. If they're there, they've scattered throughout the city. I have compatriots from the Spokane library working on it, but they haven't found a pattern yet."

Adam held out a hand. "May I?" The librarian handed over the device, and he zoomed around on it, his fingers driving the map under them to move in steady flicks. "Are there any big cave systems around here? Any place you could hide a city?"

"What if the group is mobile?" Coryn suggested. "Bartholomew and his followers had a few small towns that they moved between, never staying long. They didn't settle them properly either. For example, they hardly used any lights at night."

Jake looked thoughtful. "Maybe. Maybe that makes as much sense as anything. Hide your people in plain sight by moving them around."

The man and woman glanced at one another with skeptical frowns. "You'd have to move around a lot of stuff, too. Weapons. And children. And I think, for these people, a lot of horses."

"True," Coryn conceded. "Bartholomew's band was on foot."

They zoomed in and poked at possible locations for half an hour, but nothing turned out to seem like a better idea than any other thing. This was the second meeting like this, only the players had been different. After a few hours of questions with no solid answers, the librarian led the two Outsiders from the room, closing the door behind her.

Jake turned slightly in his seat to face Coryn. "What did you learn?"

The first words that came to mind were "nobody knows anything." But that wasn't what he was looking for. She thought about it for a while. "It's more corroboration that a big group of Returners exists. But we didn't learn anything specific."

Jake leaned back in his seat. "Will your sister spy for us?"

Eloise spoke for the first time in a long while. "I asked her. I'd say maybe."

"I can't speak for her." Nor did she have any idea what Lou would say. Or if she was well. Or where she was. Lou had never been any good at sharing what she was doing Outside.

Jake watched Coryn. "If we send someone out to find her, what should they say?"

Coryn shivered, bracing for the idea of going into the wild again. "I can go."

Julianna cut off that idea. "No. You have a race in two weeks."

She blinked. Julianna had mentioned races in passing but not that there was one coming soon. The city loved physical prowess, and Julianna had been pushing Coryn, suggesting that racing was the best way for her to gain attention on her own. "Then who?"

"Blessing."

She struggled not to show how much she hated that answer. She'd always known that Blessing wouldn't stay. "All right. Have him tell her I asked her to help us, and to be careful." She realized she was staring at her feet and looked up. "Tell her everything we know, including the cavalry story. Let her know there might be hundreds of them."

Jake looked evenly at her. "Do you think there are?"

She swallowed. She couldn't really justify her conclusion. And yet, every instinct told her she was right. "I think there are more than that."

Jake finally looked away from her to glance at Adam, who nodded and told her, "I'm a data scientist. I pieced together every record of sightings I could find." He tugged at the gold streak in his hair, looking serious. "I think there are at least a few thousand. They may not all be in one place. If they can shield from satellite view, they could have a pretty good-sized city."

"And they could do that how?" Jake asked, clearly sure of the answer himself but wanting Adam to explain it to the rest of them.

Adam looked happy to try. "They could be underground. I'm not sure they'd need a cave. It's possible they could dig. Or they could use old infra-structure, like underground parking somewhere that's not occupied."

Coryn stared at the map. Based on what she knew from walking a sliver of that land, it was a big place to find a small town in. "So Blessing needs to tell her what to look for. And maybe you need to leave some people to help her."

"Will she accept help?"

"I don't know." She sat quietly for a few moments, suddenly worried about Lou. Lou hated Returners. What would happen to her if she ran into hundreds of them, all in one place? What would she do?

CHAPTER FOUR

Aspen snuggled into Coryn's chest, clearly aware she was leaving soon. "I'm sorry sweetie," she murmured into the soft fur between his drooping ears. "I'll walk you again after I see Blessing."

The little dog snuffled more loudly. She had been surprised at how much harder it was to have a pet here the city than it had been Outside, even though out there Aspen's life had been in danger every day. Hers, too, for that matter. Now, every minute felt full of demands, and there was no time for the dog. Every time she looked at him, she felt guilty. Right now, she only had five minutes until she had to leave. "You'd like to see Blessing wouldn't you? But I can't take you. Honest. He said I have to leave you home. But you can run with us part of the way tomorrow."

He licked her face and she shook her head, amused with him. As she put him down and closed the door on his hopeful face, she whispered, "I'm sorry. I'll be back."

He didn't look like he understood.

Twenty minutes later, Coryn and Blessing rode side by side on a bikeway through the center of Seattle. Other bicycles crowded them, but they were used to riding together and managed to stay close.

Blessing would leave tomorrow to meet Lou, Shuska, and Matchiko somewhere near Yakima. Julianna had asked her to be home by six. That was still four hours away. It felt like a vacation. She stood on the pedals, smiling, happy in the moment. She rode a new bike Julianna had bought for her, a sweet thing that responded to any request she gave it.

Blessing rode an oversized red bicycle that fit his tall frame. His dark shorts and jersey blended so closely with his skin color that he looked almost naked, except for a few neon yellow stripes.

She glanced over at him, catching his attention from the corner of his eye.

His face erupted in a smile as he teased her. "It's going to be strange to be Outside and not worry about you."

"Brat. Does Julianna work everyone this hard?"

"You're asking that after a week? Most people take a little longer to complain."

"I could barely get out of bed this morning. Everything hurt."

"Are you faster?"

"Yes."

"Are you smarter?"

"Not a fair question." She darted ahead of him and turned a corner under a big cedar, starting them up a hill. When he caught back up she said, "I know more, but I don't think that's the same as being smarter."

"True. Yes, she's always like that. And if you get lazy, she'll drop you. She selects and trains the best, and there are always more waiting."

"You're implying you're one of the best."

He grinned over at her. "I am." He powered up the hill ahead of her, stopping at the top. "Are you good enough to catch me on the downhill?"

His bigger wheels and weight gave him an advantage. She slapped her bike into high gear and pedaled past him, tires thrumming, gauges showing that she was hitting thirty-five miles per hour.

He glided past her. She swore and pedaled harder.

They coasted down onto a flat almost side by side, shedding speed. Joy filled her, joy at the free moment, at the speed they'd gotten to, and at being with Blessing. "Please be careful out there," she told him. "I don't have many friends. I don't want to lose any."

He shrugged, as if dismissing the idea of danger. "Let's go down to the waterfront."

"Okay. I can't be late getting back."

"We have time."

They dismounted outside of a small building with a long line around it. "This is a satay place. Very popular." He looked quite proud of himself. "All good on your training diet. Protein and a little seasoning, a fresh salad."

"I was kinda hoping to break my diet. A little forbidden dessert or something."

He shook his head as he locked up both bikes with his lock. "She's making you a champion."

Coryn frowned. "I know. I'm lucky. She's spending so much on me. Time. Her house. Adam. A full-time trainer costs a lot of money."

"It would be a fortune to an orphan from Kent. It's budget dust to her. She likes you. Accept that, but don't count on it. She loves to help, but she doesn't like people who get dependent."

They were close enough to the waterfront that she smelled the Puget Sound. A salty, working waterfront scent. They joined the line and slowly worked their way to the front. She chose chicken and he chose fish and chicken and ordered some mushroom as well. The food all came on sticks and smelled of soy and sesame and ginger. They took it outside and sat on a vast green lawn dotted with other patrons. The meat practically melted off of the sticks and the tofu was firm and quite fabulous. "That might be the best chicken I ever had," she said.

"I thought I should treat you to something good." He was laughing, teasing her. "After all, you might never see me again."

She stared at her last piece of chicken, her appetite suddenly waning. Blessing had a habit of thinking every day would be his last, which he'd taught her when they were both Outside, in danger, and used jokes to stay brave. "I forgot."

"Don't." He curled his tongue around a mushroom and pulled it free of the stick. When he finished chewing, he said, "The city is more dangerous than out there."

"Really?"

He cocked his head at her, uncharacteristically serious. "There're at least ten people who wish they had your position with Julianna."

She snorted. "I hadn't noticed."

"I know." He grinned. "You're still quite unaware of what's happened to you. So I shall enlighten you. Julianna will be loyal—that's her nature. But others may try to hurt you. The city is a dangerous place."

Julianna herself had said something to that effect. "You mean physically?"

"Politically. That hurts more."

They took their plates to the recycler. Instead of going back to the bikes, Blessing led her around the building and they walked for two blocks and came up onto the tail of the line for the Great Wheel. "Have you ever been?"

"No." It wasn't something her parents would have been able to afford. Certainly, it wasn't something orphans could do.

She stared up at the Ferris wheel. It stood well over two hundred feet tall, easily the tallest thing on the boardwalk that ran along the seawall. Long before the weather domes were perfected, a violent and unexpected storm tore the first wheel down and dropped it in the water. This one had been rebuilt almost fifty feet taller, which was a very Seacouver thing to do. The city liked grand gestures.

The gondolas were white with blue-and-green accents, and the wheel itself was a bright silvery metal with colored ropes and strings and circles of light built into it. She'd seen it from a distance at night, luminous even on cloudy nights, and brilliant with other colors on holidays. Last Valentine's Day, it had been bright red and pink. Today it was white, green, and blue. Seacouver's colors.

It looked smaller than she expected until they stood close to it, and then it loomed over them so that she felt small.

As they neared the front of the line, Coryn bounced on the balls of her feet. They still had two hours; there was time to get to the party even though the line inched along. No wonder Blessing had asked her to leave Aspen; the wheel was no place for a dog. What if he fell?

Their car rose slowly as other cars took on passengers. Every small bit of rotation made the view that much better. But nothing could have prepared her for her first unencumbered view from the very top of the wheel. While it wasn't nearly as high or vast as the view from the Bridge of Stars, it was intimate. She could make out the colors people wore, and almost their expressions. The lights of West Seattle glittered across the Sound, the top of the hill above the boardwalk that ran by Alki Beach roughly at eye level. Even better than the top of the bridge, there was only she and Blessing in the gondola. No crowd. No watchers.

Blessing slid an arm around her as the wheel began turning at a steady pace. The second time they reached the top, he leaned down and kissed her, his lips warm and sweet, undemanding in spite of the fact that the kiss sent shivers through her. The last time he kissed her, she hadn't returned it. It had been a total surprise, and she hadn't had time to think about it. This time she welcomed him, and returned his kiss with abandon.

He tasted like spicy satay and the wind of Outside, familiar and wild at once.

When they disembarked, he leaned over and whispered in her ear, "That's what you do when every day is your last."

They didn't kiss again, but she felt his lips on hers until she stepped into the shower to start getting ready for Julianna's mysterious party. Hot water poured over her head. She tried to assess her feelings as she washed her hair, and found she couldn't. She was just as confused about Blessing as she had always been. He was wonderful to be around, a little mysterious, and yet he always held something back. Well, except during the kiss, but she hadn't held herself back then either.

They both seemed to seek out the company of the other, but to then be awkward in it, like middle-school kids.

She turned her back to the water and set it on massage, letting it slam into her tight upper-back muscles. Blessing amused her and entertained her and made her laugh, but when she pushed at him for substance, his personality slid away from definition like jelly.

She reluctantly turned off the water and wandered into her room dressed in nothing more than a towel. An older woman in a white uniform waited for her. Three outfits hung from hooks on the walls. One was a purple pantsuit lined with sequins that she hated on sight, another was a small black dress that might do, but she went right to the third, a long flowing dress in deep blues with black accents. "This one."

"Julianna asked that you try them all."

Coryn smiled. "I'm Coryn."

"Ginger."

"I don't care what the purple looks like. I'm not going to wear it."

Ginger smiled as if in approval, although she said nothing.

Twenty minutes later, she was ready. The blue had fit beautifully, but it made her look like a high school girl on her way to a dance. The black dress hugged her waist and felt a little too short, but she had never looked so old or so . . . what? Poised, maybe. A pair of gold earrings glittered as brightly as Adam's streak of golden hair, and a gold necklace with a large fossil of a shell outlined in gold acted as a statement piece. Her shoes were nude, low-heeled, and comfortable. Ginger had dried her hair straight, which added to the years the dress gave her. She might be twenty-five instead of eighteen.

Julianna nodded in approval when Coryn entered the room. "I had thought that might be the best one."

Coryn touched the skirt self-consciously. "I hated the sequins."

"My designer recommended it for you."

"Purple would look terrible close to my red hair. At least that color purple."

Julianna looked amused. "I'll tell her you don't like sequins."

"Where are we going?"

"To the Ambassador's Ball."

"I've never heard of that."

Julianna raised an eyebrow. "I forget so much. I started the ball years ago. Thirty-seven years ago, I think. No, thirty-eight."

What must it be like to have so much personal history?

Julianna picked up a glass of water that sat on the hallway table, waiting for her, and took a sip. "The date and place of the ball changes. It's wherever and whenever the Association of Mayors meets. They invite me whenever it's in Seacouver."

"Do they meet at the ball?" She realized it was a silly question as soon as she said it and shook her head. "Of course not. That's where you've been the last few days."

Julianna leaned in and smoothed Coryn's hair. "You can be forgiven for not understanding the ways of the rich and stupid. I should have explained it to you. I've just been . . . rather busy. Jake doesn't go to the main conference anymore, but he'll be my date for the ball."

Coryn still hadn't figured out if they were or had ever been lovers. She suspected that the whole megacity movement had been started because these two loved each other when they were the mayors of Seattle and Vancouver respectively and didn't want a border between them. But that was a romantic way to look at things and she hadn't found the courage to ask Julianna.

Julianna stepped back, looking her over again with a pleased smile. "Are we too alike?" she asked, twisting so her skirt washed around her legs like a wave. She also wore black, although her dress was velvet and fell below her knees, swishing softly over boots that looked like they'd been printed in place around her calves. Some cleverness had hidden the zippers entirely.

"No. No," Coryn stammered. "I could never look that classy."

Julianna's high laugh bounced off the walls and the whole foyer seemed to brighten. "You have the infinite class of the young. Use it while you have it. It's time for you to meet people. Focus on the ones under fifty. They'll be staff, like you. They'll know more than their bosses in some cases, and you may need relationships with someone other than Jake and me someday. That's what you're here to develop. Political friends."

That sounded so cold. "So I'm just supposed to meet people?"

Julianna picked up a small, gold purse and handed it to her. "There are paper cards in there. I took the liberty of making them up." She smiled as she held the purse up close to Coryn's jewelry. "I threw a comb in, and a pen and paper. Write down the names of people you meet. Store nothing on your wristlet. No pictures." She hesitated a moment. "I wish we had a few more months. But this is too good an opportunity to ignore, and it will be years before this ball is here again." She frowned, looking concerned. "You need social graces."

Coryn stiffened. How to answer that comment? She paused, searched for words, and decided to simply exercise some social grace. "Thank you for the dress."

Julianna smiled and nodded. "You're welcome. After a few months of getting paychecks, I'll expect you to buy your own clothes. You'll develop a style." She picked up her own purse, a small clutch the color of midnight. "Follow me."

They took the skyway between buildings, threading their way through gardens bright with multihued lights designed to show off flowering plants. Some of the other people walking near them appeared to be going to the same place; they wore way too much finery for a simple summer night. Coryn had gotten much better at spotting the bodyguards who tended to surround Julianna. This time she identified three she was certain of and three more she thought were guards.

When they were halfway across the skyway, she asked, "Which mayors will be here?"

"Los Angeles, Portland, Mexico City, New York, Salt Lake City, Toronto, Austin."

"So all from this continent?"

"Yes." Julianna grinned, a slightly evil-looking grin for such an old woman. "We share the same federal governments to manage. Better to leave Europe to the cities there, and Africa to Abu Dhabi."

Coryn scraped up a smattering of her high-school geography as they merged with a growing crowd. "And China and Japan to the Chinese."

"Japan is still independent. Barely."

"Oh. I guess that's good."

"It is." Julianna took Coryn's arm and led her around a knot of young women who had stopped to fix something on one of their dresses. "There'll be hundreds of people at the party. When Jake and I ran the place, every staff member who thought they might be senior begged for tickets."

"So what do the mayors meet about?"

"Cities. There's so much. How do they think? How do we manage them? What rules will make them better? What do people need? How do you tell when people are happy? How do you know when they're not? There's a lot to running a city."

During the recent attack, waves of hacking had brought the transportation system to a standstill and almost compromised the city's water. "They must talk about security."

"Everything comes down to security. Even economics is about security. And yes, we've been discussing the attacks. There shouldn't be open discussion about that here. But if you hear anything . . ."

"I'll listen carefully."

"Don't worry too much." Julianna shot her a quick, sharp look. "Your job is to make contacts. If you look like you're spying, no one will tell you anything. Just be friendly."

The party took the entire top floor of the McBride Building, a newish building with cascades of edible gardens on the walls and purple and yellow flowers growing over the entrances. There were no robots anywhere near the huge outdoor patio where most things seemed to be happening. Just before they reached the doorway, Julianna stopped and took Coryn's hand briefly. "Adam will escort you."

That stung a little, but what had she expected? That *Julianna* would stay with her? Adam spotted them as soon as they walked in and strode over to greet them. He wore a black tux with an off-white shirt and matching shoes, all of that topped with an off-white fedora. Gold chains enclosed his wrists and hung around his neck, maybe thicker than they needed to be. He looked classier than she had expected. He took her hand and placed it on his arm, her fingers sliding along the silky material of his coat.

Julianna offered a small, gracious smile that didn't quite make up for being abandoned, but Coryn knew she should be grateful. She didn't belong here. She didn't belong in this dress, on this man's arm, or in the company of the powerful.

Julianna headed straight toward a roped-off area near a stage currently occupied by three rather small girls in matching white dresses playing fantastic piano. People watched her come, faces lighting up in greeting. Clearly she was still popular with the current governments of the great cities.

Jake stepped out from the press of the crowd and took her arm, and Julianna moved effortlessly to a position where they fit like two halves of a puzzle. They shared a brief glance before turning away, looking for just a moment like young lovers long parted.

Adam steered Coryn toward the outside of the room, which was occupied by well-dressed young people only a few years older than Coryn—exactly whom Julianna had suggested she find. Adam fit well with this crowd. He clearly knew a number of them, at least if smiles and handshakes and whispered conversations about the last year or so were any indication. He introduced her to so many people in the first twenty minutes of the party that the faces all started to blur together.

Everyone they met was as dressed up as she and Adam, the clothes so dramatic they caught her eye over and over.

She didn't quite know what to say, and so she tried to suck in the conversations to think about later. Names were hard to remember, and who worked for who was even more difficult to keep straight. She felt lost, as if she were taking a test but didn't know the answers and had to intuit them from the slightest clues.

Many people looked nongendered. There had been a trans boy in her orphanage, but she was still astonished at how easily Adam switched between "she," "he," and "they". She tried to note where he used "they" so she'd get it right. Jin was a tall person with female features and masculine clothes wearing way-too-high heels for their six-foot-two frame. Imke had slightly exaggerated tattooed makeup and many rings and baubles on their fingers and ears and nose and a ruby in their right eyebrow, and a high laugh full of good-natured energy. They leaned over her hand and pressed their fingers into her palm, a gesture somewhere between greeting and caress. Aro simply looked neither male or female, indistinct. Unlike the opulent Imke, they looked like they merely wanted to fit into any moment in as forgettable a manner as possible.

Waiters in red uniforms wandered the room with champagne and tiny appetizers. She took one of the glasses, expecting to be asked her age. Instead, the waiter handed it over without a second glance. She drank it quickly, a little guilty about it (surely not on her training diet!). It made her feel a little giggly and off-balance. She refused two more that were pressed on her. Adam took from all three platters, drinking the bubbly wine as fast as she drank water. He began to list to the left. She leaned into him to keep him on course between groups of people, hoping his unexpected weight wouldn't make her stumble.

They walked across a clear spot in the huge room, and she got a panoramic view of the glittering crowd. It looked even fancier than she had imagined when she was little and stared up at the tops of skyscrapers, trying to imagine living like the rich. Gold and silver and gems sparkled on almost everyone, makeup transformed faces to near-perfection, and low lights flattered even the old.

Her head spun and her feet hurt. Someone introduced a classical band and they started playing softly, adding a touch more magic to the moment.

Adam didn't seem as awe-struck as she felt. "What did you do in New York?" she asked him.

He smiled down at her and gave a small, off-balance flourish of a bow. It looked like an imitation of a gesture that would look natural from Blessing. "I worked for Julianna."

"As?"

"I was a . . . a person on her staff."

He had been about to say something else. Another waiter passed them, and Adam took a fourth drink and drained it so fast he was able to set the glass back on the same platter.

The waiter grimaced but kept moving gamely though the crowd.

She sensed that pushing Adam wouldn't help, although gaining his trust might. "So tell me who to meet next?"

He looked around, as if selecting a target. "How about Marisela Hu from Ontario?"

"All right. Why?"

His words came out slurred. "You're getting smarter."

For asking questions? He was the supposed data scientist. "What does Marisela do?"

"She manages immigration to and from Ontario. They have some great schools, especially in the bio . . . biological sciences. This will be good to know if Julianna starts the foundation she's talking about."

"I think she will." Julianna had talked about it quite a lot, and as if it existed. She had even had Coryn file some paperwork for it.

Another waiter stopped right in front of them, champagne bubbling brightly as if just poured. Coryn deflected Adam's arm. What was she going to do if he got too drunk to walk? What if Julianna blamed her?

Hadn't Blessing said there were people waiting to take her place? She didn't intend to just give it up.

Adam muttered something about her being a nursemaid.

"Where is Marisela?" she prompted him.

He stood as tall as he could, which let him look over the sea of sweating faces. "There." He leaned in close to her. "Take out one of your cards."

She had forgotten them! She opened the small golden purse and took out a card, tilting it into the light to read it.

Coryn Williams
Special Assistant to Julianna Lake
Cwilliams@jl.sc

She smiled. "I'm ready."

CHAPTER FIVE

Lou frowned as she added up Matchiko's word game points. "Thirty-five. That makes two hundred and seven. To my one hundred and twelve. You win."

Matchiko smiled at her from her position propped up among pillows on the bed. "That's because I'm not fretting as much as you are."

Lou shook her head as she picked up the pieces. "Most people make five points on their last move. Not thirty-five. And yes, you are fretting." Matchiko looked better. She'd started refusing narcotics the day after David set her leg, and a day after that she'd started eating regularly again.

A soft, familiar knock. Lou tucked the game away and hopped up to open the door. Shuska came through, balancing two bowls of sweet summer corn soup and a tray of bread, surely from the hotel kitchen. "I ate my soup. Couldn't carry three bowls. It's good." She handed Matchiko a bowl and set the rest of the food on the table. "I ran into David. He said maybe tomorrow."

Lou picked up her bowl and tasted the soup, then grabbed the peppershaker they'd borrowed from the kitchen on the first day and shook liberally. She waited while Shuska fussed over Matchiko, making sure she had everything in easy reach. They'd managed to build up a way for her to sit almost straight up in spite of the ungainly cast. Shuska had scrounged boards and nails and made a lap-table Matchiko could eat from or use for games or small puzzles. Anything to keep her distracted from the itch and awkwardness of the cast.

Shuska settled on the only other chair. She started on her story of the day by tossing a hundred and twenty dollars onto the table. About average for her work days. "Two more days and we can afford a horse."

Lou finished a spoonful of soup. "That's dubious."

"It only has to be able to walk."

"It would be nice if we could feed it."

Matchiko interrupted. "If my cast comes off tomorrow maybe I can do something to help."

"Yes, you can." Lou set her already-empty bowl down. "You can rest another day or two and be happy you can scratch your ankle."

Matchiko merely smiled.

Lou stood up. "Maybe I can find work tonight, as well as information."

"Try the Third Horseman." Shuska leaned back in her chair. "I noticed a help-wanted sign in the window this afternoon."

Lou sighed and started gathering her things into a bag she could throw over her shoulder. "I hate tending bar. But once more into the dark of night . . ." She spent every evening looking for both work and information. One of them was always with Matchiko, and most of the time the other was working or looking for work.

Shuska had better luck than the rest of them at getting hired. Muscle was useful for almost every farm or shop, and her native heritage played well in Yakima. She swore she belonged to sea and sky and land, and thus to no tribe, but the Latinos and Mormons who ran much of Yakima didn't know that, and it was always useful to keep the local tribes happy. The three groups balanced power partly by cooperating. Shuska made money every day, and Lou had found work once. Once.

The walk from the Hotel Shamiana to town took almost an hour. Mature orchards with gnarled trunks bordered the road. Pickers had started streaming out of the orchards to head home, laughing and talking, one pair of old men singing. Much fruit was still harvested by hand. Lou had heard that this was more to keep the orchard's owners from being mobbed by angry people who needed work than because it made economic sense. Nevertheless, in Yakima, everything that grew on trees was picked by humans.

Yakima was one of the few small cities that thrived legally on this side of the mountains. It survived to serve as a waypoint for delivery of fruit from the remaining orchards. Megacities grew most of their food in vertical farms, but apples needed orchards, and orchards didn't thrive in sterile environments. They did thrive all around Yakima, and food came in from a few nearby farms in Promise as well.

From time to time short convoys of trucks drove by carrying products, workers, or even farm animals. Almost every engine was silently electric. Both foot and farm traffic grew thicker as she neared the town, an odd mix of old buildings like the Shamiana and new, tall, glassy buildings that housed the hospital, the city workers, and a few of the bigger corporations, which ran much of the economy. Yakima had never seen a significant influx of tech or biotech or any other modern industry, and that showed in the aging infrastructure, the old-fashioned materials, and the way it looked the same every time Lou visited. She liked it far more than she liked Seacouver.

The Third Horseman did, indeed, have a help-wanted sign on it. It was a smallish building, with about twenty wooden tables and a long bar inside. The bar menu had five high-fat food choices on it and a varying special, and it smelled far more of beer and cider than of food.

Lou headed straight for the long wooden bar, which was almost empty this early. Still, she had to wait for almost five minutes before the barman got to her. He was a tall Latino man with kind eyes, and wrinkles dripping down his face. She had seen him before, when she'd been in here trolling for information. He'd seemed nice enough and somewhat no-nonsense. In spite of his apparent age, muscles showed in his shoulders and he moved easily, smiling as he came up to her. "What can I get you?"

"Can I help? I saw your sign."

His expression changed from welcoming to assessing. "Know how to tend bar?"

"For traditional drinks."

"Can you stay for the rest of the harvest?"

"I can stay a little while, but I can't promise that much. We have to be north before winter."

Regret showed in his eyes. "I need someone who can promise that."
He started to turn away.

"Wait."

He stopped, looking a little annoyed, and his face hardened.

"I'll tend tonight for tips," she blurted out. "You can keep trying
to fill your spot."

He hesitated. A group of three young men came in through the
door, and that seemed to decide him. "You can stay tonight. If it works
out, you can come back tomorrow. Tips only, cash only. You can have
one free drink and a bowl of soup."

It wasn't a very good deal, but it was unlikely she'd find a better
one. She smiled. "I'm Lou."

"Salvador."

He gestured toward the three men, who had selected a table near
the door. "There's pads for taking orders by the till."

"Thanks," she said again, and headed over to get a paper pad and
blue pencil and find a thirsty table.

Three hours later, the bar was so full that she barely had time to
think between orders. She overheard bits and pieces of conversations,
some in Spanish. The harvest was good. The worst storm had come
after the fruit had set and before it was hot enough to blow almost-ripe
apples off, so the year had been good, on balance. There were rumors of
attacks on the cities, but there were always rumors of that.

It turned out there was a lot of cash in this economy. Lou pocketed something over thirty dollars before the traffic started slowing down about eleven.

While she stood behind the bar pouring two home brews from a
keg for a pair of older women, Salvador came up. "Nice job. You can
come back tomorrow. If the sign's still on the door you can work again."

A dismissal. "Can I sit here and drink my drink?"

He smiled. "Better than drinking in the streets."

She chose a stool in the middle of the bar and close enough to the
main floor that she could overhear a few table conversations.

The most interesting thing she learned was that a pack of wolves had moved into the Cascades on old highway twelve, which was barely maintained. Although the table she was listening to talked about shooting the wolves, they didn't sound very serious, and one of the men kept suggesting ways they might live with them.

It was all Lou could do not to join the conversation.

Not a bad night, on balance. She had earned decent tips, sore feet, and no particularly interesting information.

David didn't come out the next day, and Shuska swore at the delay, while Matchiko picked up a book and ignored them all. Lou was happy enough to escape back to the Third Horseman and even happier when she saw the help wanted sign still hung in the window.

A group of ten motorcycles stood outside the bar. They were tall and light, with knobby tires, big electric engines that hung under comfy seats, and locked metal saddlebags. The current motored version of horses. They could do easy off-road riding and take most road damage. The battery cases were painted with glittering flames or sun-speared mountains or neon cityscapes.

Where had they come from?

As soon as she walked in, Salvador handed her a pad and gestured toward the far side of the room, where the bikers lounged across three tables. They held menus and downed water from tall, clear glasses. Five couples, all middle-aged and fit, faces burned dark and wrinkled by the sun, hair tied back in ponytails or braids, or in two cases, simply shaved.

She smiled and announced herself in her most perky voice. "Good evening! I'm Lou. What can I get for you?"

They mostly wanted beer, although two slender women who were younger than the others asked for mimosas but settled for ciders when Lou explained, "Yakima grows the best apples in the world, but no citrus. Not even the engineered stuff. Farmers who want a finicky crop choose grapes."

They smiled at that.

"But we make the best ciders in the known world."

The mimosa women and two men switched their orders to cider.

She delivered the drinks, managing to attract enough small talk to learn they had come down from Montana, cutting through Coeur d'Alene in Idaho and around Spokane Metro on side roads, then running down here via Highway 2 and the 97. "How were the roads?"

"Tough," said one of the smaller men, a pale thing with freckles, who looked too small to handle a big motorcycle. "It's summer. We had to take three detours, but they were okay on the bikes. Might have been hard for cars."

And by inference their bikes were far better. "Did you see very many people?"

A slender blonde held her hand out for one of the ciders. "A few groups of Wilders."

Her friend added, "A traveling preacher stayed with us one night. Tried to tell us we were going to hell for driving, even though we're all solar."

Lou had to hold back a laugh. They were undoubtedly illegals, people like her who'd fled the city. Since she didn't have a regular job or even a work contract, she was illegal as hell. Especially now that the city had kicked her out. Maybe the preacher would tell her to go to hell, too. "Anybody you didn't like?" she asked, taking her time handing out the last few beers.

"I didn't like the preacher," the biggest man said.

The youngest looking women said, "There was a town with no place to stop. We used the head in a park, and by the time we left there were twenty people staring at us. They lost a chance to feed us lunch and maybe have us a buy few things."

"Scared," another man added.

"I thought they were mean," the first cider-girl said.

Lou was out of drinks to hand out, but she stood there anyway. "Where was this?"

One of the men gave her a suspicious look, like she might be a spy or a policeman or, if they hadn't all been killed, a Listener. But the cider-girl didn't see his look. "Not far out of Coeur d'Alene," she said. "Maybe an hour. I wanted to stop in Coeur d'Alene but we didn't, and that was why we had to stop in that place full of creeps."

Lou decided they'd probably picked this girl up Outside instead of escaping the city with her; her language was too coarse. Maybe she was even an escaped Returner herself. Not that it mattered. Lou looked at the girl and smiled. Just as she was about to ask a follow-up question, a shrill woman two tables over gestured for her and she noticed Salvador watching her, so she swallowed her irritation, pasted on a fresh smile, and went.

The bikers left before she got a chance to ask them anything more, but she pondered what she'd heard all night. Coeur d'Alene was an outlaw city, a place no one had bothered to dismantle yet, but which didn't have any taxing authority or legal standing. It was as likely a place as any to look for Coryn's Returners. It wasn't a lot of information, but it was more than she'd had. Shuska had suggested they go east and north anyway.

The bar was busy enough that she stayed until they closed, until the cooks and the busboy had gone home. Salvador took her pad from her, looking as tired as she felt. "I would have had trouble getting through the night without you."

She managed a tired smile. "That was fun."

"I have someone coming for an interview tomorrow," he said. "Are you sure you don't want the job?"

Her feet hurt so much that she barely regretted telling him no. "I'm sure I can't stay that long. Maybe a week more, maybe less."

"I'm sorry."

She didn't want to walk back until she gave her feet a rest. "Do you have time to share a cider with me?"

He hesitated. "After the floor is done."

She helped him with the mopping, and then they sat together in air that smelled faintly of bleach. "This is a new cider," he told her. "My cousin makes it. He brought a keg over today."

She took a sip, savoring the dance of flavors on her tongue. Tart and crisp. "We should have served this today. It's good."

"I wanted to finish up the old first. Will you be back through here?"

She shrugged. "This is the first time I've stayed in Yakima for long. Our friend is hurt, and we've been working on making enough money to buy a horse for her to ride on. We're Wilders, looking for work up north."

"There's work near here."

She chanced a direct question. "We're heading north. Looking for work with any of the foundations up there. We also want to help find the people who almost brought the cities down a week or so ago. I have family in Seacouver and I want to keep them safe."

The look he gave her suggested he thought she might be a little small to take on any force that attacked cities. At least he didn't say so out loud.

She persisted. "So have you heard anything about who might have been behind the attack?"

Salvador sat back and sipped his cider. "A bartender hears a lot they don't talk about."

"Do they hear anything they share?"

"Just that the bears causing trouble have gone back to hibernate. But there are rumors of trouble next spring."

"Bears?"

"In human clothing. The best way to survive in my business is to listen to every story and tell none of them."

"Even to friends?"

He glanced at her, his eyes level and suddenly a little cold. "I think you should not come back tomorrow. Hopefully I will have new help."

She sat back, chilled. He had never been rude. "I'm sorry to have bothered you. I meant no harm. But I know I am taking my family into danger, and it's important to me to understand that danger so I can protect them."

"Go south."

"I can't do that."

He looked down at his drink. He stared it for quite a while before he looked directly at her. "I heard a story a week ago. Two days after the attacks. It's only a story an old bartender heard from no one, and it might not be a truth at all."

Since he was staring at the table instead of at her, she said, "I like to hear stories, and I know that's all they are."

He took a sip. A beat. Two. "A man and his wife came into the bar together. The man said he wanted a quiet table in the back near the door, and there is one." Salvador pointed at it. "And so I let him have it. When he got up to use the restroom, I took an order for a second glass of wine from the wife, who was a small thing with a black eye. I didn't like the black eye, and I didn't know if he gave it to her or if someone else did, and whether or not I should worry about trouble in my bar. So I asked her if I could help.

"She shook her head, but I think that was because she saw him coming up behind me, on his way back from the washroom. Twenty minutes later she came back to me and she told me her husband made them leave her brother. She said her brother might kill them both, since they lived in a secret place. I merely raised an eyebrow, being nothing but a bartender. She didn't say anything else then, but when I took them their food I over-head the word Chelan. He hushed her for saying it, but she was watching my eyes, like she wanted me to hear, and she wanted to know I had heard. Hard to explain that, but you pick up these little things in bars."

"I used to listen around campfires at night, wait to hear what people said and what they didn't say."

He glanced at her. "What kind of campfires?" he asked.

"Ranch. I worked RiversEnd Ranch." No need to tell him she'd been a crew boss.

"Wilding?"

"Yes."

He poured her another half glass of cider. "That's dangerous work. We appreciate it."

"Thanks. Is there anything more to the story? Did you see them again?"

He grimaced. "They disappeared without paying that night. The next night the brother came in. He was a Returner for sure, a right angry man who wore three guns in plain sight. He was sure they'd been here, even though I had no record of it, nor any memory of it. That would have been the end of the story, except that I heard him talking to a friend that was with him. They used the word Chelan, too. It's a place, you know. And a lake."

"I know."

He finished his cider and held his hand out for her glass. "Then may good luck follow you."

CHAPTER SIX

Lou walked in front, taking them up an overgrown path that paralleled the 97 without being visible from the road. Ecobots still maintained the 97, and once in a while they heard a vehicle rattle over a pothole. The sun shone from almost straight ahead, keeping their shadows short and drawing sweat onto Lou's brow.

The only horse they'd been able to afford was an older draft horse named Buster, so Matchiko rode well above them, acting as their best lookout. Shuska trailed. She always trailed, always shielded their backs.

They were far less likely to draw attention here on the trail than on the highway.

It bothered Lou to be on the move without data. When she was the ranch foreman at RiversEnd, they'd had adequate data. Their logins had still worked for the first few days they were in Yakima, but the foundation that provided them had apparently been wound down far enough that systems had been turned off.

They were on their own with no current information, no way to look for work, and no contact with Coryn.

Two coyotes trotted across the trail in front of them. Lou held her breath, but Buster didn't react at all.

Matchiko commented, "I guess he knows it would take more than two little canids to take him down."

"There could be more," Shuska muttered, barely loud enough for Lou to hear.

She ignored the comment. Coyotes wouldn't bother a group this big. Wolves wouldn't either, at least not now, in the flush of late summer, when rabbit and deer were plentiful.

She was going to have to get new boots soon. She could feel even small rocks under her right forward sole.

"Trouble!" Matchiko exclaimed, clutching the saddle horn hard.

Lou unclipped the lead so Matchiko could steer the big horse if necessary, looking around. Nothing. "Two men," Matchiko insisted, staring ahead. "Maybe more."

Lou tried to follow her line of sight, but the hill in front of them blocked her vision. "How far?"

"We're coming up on them."

Lou stopped to evaluate the terrain. There was an uphill scramble to their left, a small downhill slide to their right, and if they could negotiate that they'd be in a dry riverbed. Shuska spoke in a hurried whisper. "There's someone behind me."

Without giving any signal at all, Lou abruptly turned and started down. Matchiko and the big horse followed. Shuska stood her ground on the trail, just across it and slightly uphill, where she'd have some visual advantage. She looked imposing. She held up her hand with three fingers showing and shook her fist in a gesture that indicated uncertainty. There could be more.

Lou glanced up at Matchiko. She was probably the target. Not Matchiko herself, but the horse. They hadn't decided if Buster was fast or not, but she would be willing to bet he wasn't. She whispered, "Hold on. We'll follow you when we're done."

Matchiko nodded grimly and adjusted her seat into the loose body posture that would keep her on the horse even if he lunged away quickly. At least, probably. She only had one foot in a stirrup. The injured one dangled free in a cut-away boot they were using as a makeshift splint.

Lou picked up a stick and slapped Buster's wide, golden butt.

He stopped, lifted his leg a little, prepared to kick her if she did it again. He swished his tail at her as if she were a fly.

She swatted him again, stepping out the way of a half-hearted warning kick.

Again. The stick broke but he didn't move.

Matchiko made kissing sounds at him. He trotted off reluctantly, somewhat under Matchiko's control.

Lou drew her stunner from the inner pocket of her light coat and turned back to see Shuska had decided to simply sit and watch until there was something more interesting to do. She looked like she was laughing.

Clearly, she had assessed the situation and decided it was going to be okay. This was a good thing; Buster was at most two hundred feet away and slowing.

Lou watched Shuska for clues. She heard Buster breaking small sticks behind her as he walked, Matchiko encouraging him in an exasperated whisper.

Maybe they should have practiced moving him faster than a walk.

Two young men came at Shuska from her right, jogging, and looking in the direction Buster had gone. They moved like people familiar with work and travel, their gaits economical. One had a gun; the other didn't seem to have anything. No pack, no gun, nothing but a simple leather coat. Neither of them noticed her; all eyes were on the horse.

Shuska let them get almost right below her before she simply stood up and bellowed, "Stop," in a loud, demanding voice.

Surprised, they stopped and stared at the huge woman who had appeared out of nowhere just above them. With enough time to look, it was easy to tell they were a year or two short of eighteen. One was taller than the other, both ruddy and white-skinned with short haircuts.

They stared up at Shuska, faces set with a fierceness that looked like a slight wind could crumple it.

Lou moved to Shuska's left, below her, watching for the person she'd heard behind them. As soon as she turned, a young woman with unruly black hair badly in need of a brush crashed down the slope toward her. Lou moved in on her easily, catching her by the arm, turning her, and shoving her stunner in the girl's back. She spoke softly: "If you're still, I won't hurt you."

The girl only struggled once before realizing Lou had her tight. Perhaps she had been taught that the best thing to do when in trouble was to scream since she did so, immediately and rather loudly. Lou poked her in the shoulder. "Hush."

The girl clamped her mouth shut and glared at Lou.

All five of them held still for a long moment. Lou spoke mildly. "And your plan was?"

"We need a horse," the girl said.

"For?"

"We've got to move fast," the older of the boys said. "We really do." His face had gone white under hair almost the exact color as the girl's. Their noses were both on the long side, and they had the same color of brown eyes.

Probably a sister and brother. "Who are you running from?" Lou asked the girl.

"My father. This is my husband, Rick." She pointed to the younger boy, who might have been all of sixteen. He was also the one with the gun. "And my brother, Scott."

Such old-fashioned names.

"Your father doesn't approve of your marriage?" Shuska guessed.

"It's more complicated than that," the girl said.

"Well." Shuska drawled her words out slowly. "You can't have our horse. We happen to need him. If we didn't, we might *give* him to you. But he's more likely to slow you down than help you move fast." She paused and grinned, clearly having a little fun. "We are looking for information. If you'll tell us your tale, we'll trade for a meal." She held her hand out. "But I get the weapon. I'll give it back when you're done."

Rick didn't move. His hand shook and he looked uncertain and very, very young. "Maybe we won't eat with you."

Lou laughed softly. "Whether she's your wife or not, she's hungry."

He glanced toward the still-unnamed girl, who said, "They could have shot us."

"Good girl," Lou whispered. "That's a show of common sense."

He handed the gun over.

Lou and Shuska kept their own weapons out, but pointed at the ground. Lou led while Shuska, of course, trailed. As soon as she found a decent clearing, Lou left Shuska to regale them with her native silences and took off after Buster.

He hadn't gotten a quarter mile. Matchiko was usually good with horses, but they'd only had Buster two days and he hadn't shown any inclination to do what anyone said, except for Lou when she had a lead line on him. He stood with his head buried in the grass by the side of the path, completely ignoring Matchiko's weak tugs at his reins. Lou bit back a laugh. "You'd have better luck without a broken ankle, you know. You could stand in the stirrups."

Matchiko glared at her and then back at the horse's stubbornly bent neck. "What was that about, anyway?"

"We found some young people to tell us stories. But we need the contents of your saddlebags first. They're apparently in danger of imminent starvation."

"Do-gooder." Matchiko gave up on getting Buster to obey, letting the reins loose. Lou clipped the lead back into Buster and hauled his nose up. He gave her a resentful look and tossed his huge head once before he allowed her to lead him. "Maybe you need a sharper bit," she told him. "Or a week with Shuska riding you."

"That would do it," Matchiko said.

In five minutes they were back at the clearing, where the three teenagers had settled in on rocks and roots. They looked a little sideways at Buster. The girl said, "I didn't know he was so big."

Matchiko was already digging in their packs. They still had bread, cheese, and jam, as well as apples, and so they were able to make a decent lunch, which disappeared so quickly Matchiko relented and gave the boys each a second half-sandwich. After they fished, Lou said, "So . . . what are you running from and where are you going?"

The brother, Scott, talked first. "We're going south. To LA. I have a friend there and I think I can get work."

"Will the city let you in?" Matchiko asked, still perched on top of Buster.

The boy shrugged, not looking at her. "He says so."

Lou was willing to let the unlikelihood of Scott's assertion go. "What are you running from?"

"Who says we're running?" Rick asked.

"Your willingness to take on three armed adults and steal a horse was my first clue."

The girl blushed and looked away.

Lou had to work around rising anger in order to keep her tone soft. "You said it was because you're in a hurry. And something about her dad."

"Oh. Yeah." The boy straightened a little on the rock he'd chosen for a seat. "He'd promised her to one of his friends, but we found a preacher to marry us. Her dad doesn't think the preacher is legit, so he decided we're not married and he's going to make her marry his friend."

"That's the oldest story ever." Anger knotted her shoulders; she tried to force them to relax, failed. This time she didn't even manage to soften her voice. "It amazes me how much social devolution seems to go with small populations."

"Fancy words," Shuska said, smiling, her steadiness letting Lou release some of her tension.

The boy looked confused so she told him, "Never mind. It's not fair. That's all she means."

"What's the friend like?" Matchiko asked.

The girl shivered. "He's old. He wants me to have a bunch of kids. They want me to be a teacher, but I just want to get away. The world can't be as bad as they say it is."

Even Shuska's face softened a little. She almost smiled. "No. It's not. But it *is* dangerous. What if we'd just shot you?"

The girl paled, and her young lover put his arm around her. "You wouldn't have done that."

"No." Lou lifted her stunner from her lap. "We wouldn't have. But someone else might."

The girl flinched.

Good. "How long ago did you run away?" Lou asked.

"Yesterday," the girl replied, almost in a whisper.

So the father could be close. "You had better keep moving. But you'd also better be more careful. We could have been far more dangerous than we look, and in fact we are, to some people."

The girl glanced up furtively. "I bet you'd be dangerous to my dad."

"I bet I don't want to ever meet your dad. But maybe you should tell me about him."

"He's big. He's hates the way the world is. He keeps a whole collection of books and pictures about the way it used to be. It's the only physical thing we keep every time we move."

"Do you move a lot?" Matchiko asked from up high.

The girl toed a rock with her right foot. "We used to move every few weeks, but lately we've been in one place."

"Where?"

"In a town by a lake. In the hills."

That could be a lot of places in Promise. Including Chelan. "Do you know the name?"

She shook her head. "Every place is named home."

The boys had shouldered up to the edge of the conversation. The brother's face looked alarmed that his sister was saying so much. He took her arm. "Paulette. We should go."

There. A name. At least it would be easy to remember. It was like Coryn's old robotic protector. Lou had all of the information she really needed, and they didn't want to stand here until the father caught up. "Do you have any water?"

They showed her two bottles, both half-empty. She dug in her pocket for her container of water purification pills. She was a fanatic about them, so she had hundreds. She spilled about twenty into a napkin and folded it over. "Put one of these in every bit of water you drink. That'll keep you well until you get south."

"We boil it at home," the girl offered.

"Do you have a pot or stove with you?"

"No."

Lou did her best to look sternly parental. "You'd better start thinking. Going after our horse wasn't thinking and, frankly, neither was taking off without more provisions. We're a little short ourselves or we'd give you more. But look for orchards and pick apples. They'll help keep you going."

The girl quivered. "Can we go with you?"

And bring down the wrath of a Returner father on their heads? "We're not going anywhere near Los Angeles."

The girl swallowed. Her face had gone quite pale and she looked a little ill.

Oh, crap. "Are you pregnant?" Lou asked, and immediately wished she hadn't. There was nothing for it, except maybe getting into the city or the underground medical system, which was expensive and bad. Hopefully the girl wanted the baby, even though she wasn't old enough for it.

The girl looked down at the ground, but her husband looked Lou in the eye for the first time. "We are."

Good. He had some spunk. "Good luck," she said. "You'd best go."

They scrambled up. Shuska held the boy's gun out and he took it. His hand shook when he took it, just like it had earlier. She was willing to bet he'd never even fired it. He looked so resolute and so frightened that Lou felt sorry for him.

As they started walking away, Scott had the presence of mind to turn around. "Thank you."

"You're welcome." Matchiko spoke from Buster's broad back. "Be well."

"We will."

They watched until all three were gone. "What do you think their chances are?" Lou asked.

"Small," Matchiko said. "Pretty damned small. We should have done more."

"What more?" Shuska asked.

No one answered.

The encounter left Lou in a sour mood. Before her first job out here, she'd believed the great Outside would be fair and sweet and that everyone would be working together on the grand design of saving the earth. The city was intrinsically vapid and deeply striated by class, but Outside people starved to death and killed each other.

She hoped they would find somewhere safe.

The sun sank so low that the trees they walked between threw shadows longer than the trees were tall. Lou spotted two does, and a little later a one-prong buck. The deer made Lou smile, but they also served as a reminder that dark was coming.

No barn.

Matchiko pointed toward a copse of trees a little off the path and near a thin streambed, and led them there.

Lou nodded. They could put Buster on a lead between two of the trees and then camp a little above him so they didn't get stepped on in the night. "No fires," Shuska said.

"I know," Lou and Matchiko answered exactly together.

"It's good to be home," Lou said. "The city was too damned comfortable."

Shuska went and stood by Buster, looking up at Matchiko. "Slide down."

Lou held his head while Matchiko swung her left leg over the horse's butt and slid, giving a little gasp of pain as Shuska caught her. "You all right?" Shuska whispered.

"You try sitting on a draft horse all day sometime."

"I'll be happy to. As soon as you can walk." Shuska swooped Matchiko up in her arms, carrying her like a child even though it was an uphill climb to a rock big enough to set her down on easily.

Lou took Buster to drink in the stream. She led him to a spot where she could stand uphill of him and on a rock in order to loosen the cinch on the saddle and pull it off. "Good thing he's docile."

"Good thing we didn't need him to run today," Shuska replied.

"There is that." Lou handed Matchiko the lead and pulled the long line off of where it was tied to the back of Buster's saddle. She started stringing it between two sturdy trees. "So, does the kids' story tell us anything about whether to go to Spokane or Chelan?"

Shuska pulled a flask of wine out of the saddlebags. "Chelan makes sense to me because it's pretty private. But could you hide there? From satellites?"

"I don't know if the old buildings have been taken down," Matchiko said.

Lou poured some grain into her open palm for Buster. "Are there utilities?"

"We won't know until we get there," Shuska said.

"Think there's anything for three Wilders to do?" Buster's lips tickled Lou's open palm as he snuffled up the last of the grain. She took his lead from Matchiko and tied the end of it to a carabiner on a long line. As soon as she was done she sat by Matchiko. "How's it feel?"

"Like I'll be glad when I can walk instead of ride a board with a spine."

"Can I see?"

Matchiko lifted her right leg into Lou's lap and let her roll up the bottom of her pant leg. Shuska came and bent over to look, whistling. "It's twice as big as yesterday."

"It's been hanging over a horse belly all day. I'll keep it elevated."

None of them was a doctor, but Matchiko was a biologist, which counted for something. "All right. We'll look then." Lou touched the biggest part of the ankle, which was angry red and hot enough that her first instinct was to draw her fingers away from it. "We need a cold stream to stick it into."

"It's going to be cold in an hour or so."

Shuska started opening packs and pulling sandwiches back out. "So eat."

"I'm not hungry."

Shuska got her to eat half a sandwich, and Lou had a whole one, glad to be sitting down.

The light fled after the sun fell all the way down. There were too few clouds for much sunset, but darkness pulled the light of the stars and Milky Way into being above them.

Shuska passed the wine flask around and they were all three quiet together, the soft grinding of Buster's teeth as he cropped grass and the croaks of frogs someplace below them the only sounds. Eventually, a pack of coyotes started howling on a far hill, the howls interspersed with haunting yips and yowls.

"Hear the babies?" Matchiko asked.

Lou cocked her head. "Yes." This year's cubs would be half-grown by now. "It's still warm, but we'd better find housing before winter."

Shuska grunted in assent and put a finger to her lips. She liked quiet, especially when there was a summer night's worth of natural symphony.

A perfect night, Lou thought. A perfect moment. It didn't even matter that one of them was hurt and that the world was still deeply damaged. They were together and full and the stars were out and the coyotes calling. The only possible improvement would have been a wolf howl.

Shuska leaned forward, alert. She tapped Lou's shoulder.

Flashlights bobbed on the trail they'd been on a little bit ago. Two of them. Lou held her breath, watching. "Maybe it's our teenager's father," Matchiko whispered.

"Let's hope not." Lou rolled Matchiko's pants leg back down and started planning the fastest route to get Buster untied and saddled. It wouldn't be easy. "Maybe they'll just go on by."

Matchiko swung her leg down slowly, her face taut with pain. "If it's the father, we should delay him."

Buster whinnied.

One of the lights turned toward them. It didn't quite reach them, but it illuminated the rocky hill they'd climbed up, and showed whoever held the flashlight that there were fresh hoof prints.

"I'll go," Lou whispered. She took a light and her stunner, but she kept the light off and her stunner in her pocket. She scrambled down, placing each foot carefully to keep from knocking rocks loose. A small, flat rock gave way under her heel, and a large rock slid free and knocked into two others, and dirt and small rocks shushed even further down the trail.

The light slid toward her.

She snapped her own light on full, trying to blind them before they blinded her.

An arm waved. "Hello the hill."

She recognized the voice. Blessing. "Hello the trail!" She pointed her light toward the ground and let Blessing and Day come to her. "It's fabulous to see you."

Blessing hugged her, kissing the top of her head, smelling of clean sweat and laughter.

Day held back. She directed her light at his chest and looked at his face in the edges of it, and he was smiling as much as Day ever did. "It's so good to see you," she said. "How did you find us?"

"Three scared kids down the path told us about three old women who fed them."

"Ah. Being a good Samaritan does pay off."

Blessing had already started up the hill to find the others. She cocked her head at Day. "Wine and food?"

"Food."

He was always too serious to drink. But Blessing would share their wine, and now they were a bigger—and thus safer—group. Things might be better than she thought.

CHAPTER SEVEN

Coryn felt like her lungs were being pulled apart by glass. As she crossed the finish line, the announcer called out, "Second place, eighteen to twenty, Coryn Williams." The crowd clapped. News-bots dove around her feet, and she shied away from one, nearly falling.

Adam met her at the end of the exit chute, an open bottle of water in his hand. He managed to look handsome while dripping with sweat. She nodded thanks, took the bottle, and gulped from it between gasping breaths. She was never this starved for air after a training run; she must have really pushed herself.

Adam stuck with her, letting her release the heat of the run in a steady walk.

After she could talk, she asked, "How far behind was I?"

"Five minutes, fifteen seconds."

"That's a lot."

"Loraine is fast," he said. "I didn't expect you to beat her. I didn't expect you to take second."

She punched him lightly in the side. His clothes were a cool, sweaty damp. "How much did you beat me by?"

"Ten minutes, twelve seconds, and one one-hundredth."

"Your legs are too long."

"Your legs are perfect."

He was flirting. As usual, she both liked it and didn't. Sort of like Blessing. Shouldn't she feel enchanted with *someone*? "Can you see who came in third?"

"Not yet."

"Let's go look."

Before they could turn around, Eloise was there with bananas and juice and squeeze tubes of freshly ground almond butter. While Eloise didn't wear her usual scarf, she did have on outsized neon sunglasses, a black sweatband, and a black running outfit that showed off her heavily muscled calves under a multicolored short skirt. She leaned in to whisper in Coryn's ear, "Don't dawdle. There's a meeting in three hours. Salish Conference Room."

"Okay." She'd expected the day off. In fact, she was pretty sure she'd been promised the rest of the day off. Still, she nodded at Eloise. "Thanks."

Eloise faded into the crowd. Coryn turned to Adam. "Have you ever seen her train? She looks like a runner crossed with a bodybuilder."

He shook his head. "She must work out somewhere. I've seen her lift rocks as if they were paper."

"I usually think of her as Julianna's enforcer. I wonder why we have a surprise meeting?"

They stood in the clapping crowd, eating the bananas and cheering their competition coming in over the line. Coryn's second-place finish was solid. They'd missed seeing the third-place runner in her age-group, but she had finished two minutes and change behind Coryn.

Even though she'd been on multiple race podiums before, Coryn felt awed by this podium. This was her first time in the top three in an elite city-wide race, and hundreds of faces and almost as many hovering news-bots watched the medal fall around her neck and the race official lean over and hand her the pin.

After the announcements, she and the other winners, including Adam, attended a party designed to give the media easy access to the runners. Even though they could only stay half an hour, two news-bots and one human reporter interviewed her, the news-bots working together to crowd her away from people so they could get the shots they wanted. She managed not to give in to the temptation to stick her tongue out at the fist-sized bot that got right in her face. What did it want a picture of? Her pores? When she caught up with Adam near the end of the party, he reported four interviews.

The city was crazy about sports and entertainment, a side effect of almost everyone having time and no one being hungry. Football, hockey, and soccer drew huge crowds. Winning at endurance running wouldn't make her a household name, but elite runners attracted invitations to art openings and films and parties, which led to social contacts. They got sponsorships, and fame in some circles. And she could do it. All the days and weekends of running for the last years of high school after Lou abandoned her to become a Wilder were paying off. She hadn't started running to win anything. She'd run to stay sane.

She clutched her second-place pin and silver medal tightly as they left, resolving to train harder. Five minutes was a lot to make up, and she'd have to do better to survive the next age bracket anyway. Twenty to twenty-four had even fiercer competition.

"You can taste it now, can't you," Adam said.

"Taste what?"

"Fame. You don't have it yet, but this might be the beginning."

She didn't like the way he said "might." "I want to run harder tomorrow."

"The day after a race is always a day off."

She frowned. But that made sense. She'd just run her fastest time ever, and surely she would feel it tomorrow. But right now, she felt awesome. But as usual, there was no time to rest in Julianna's carefully planned day. "Our meeting is in an hour."

They'd partied too long. She started to jog home, but her muscles complained, so she settled for forcing them into a fast walk, and chose the tram and then the elevator instead of the spiraling uphill skyway.

Her hair was still damp from her short, scalding shower when she entered the conference room on the same floor where she and Adam and a number of other staff lived. It was an interior room with no views to distract participants or windows for news-bots to hover at. The cherry table was big enough for twelve to sit around, but the only two people in the room when she arrived were Blessing and Day. They'd clearly been back at least since this morning, since they were clean and dressed in city clothes that fit them perfectly. They were both odd sizes; Blessing tall and lanky and Day short and broad.

She could feel her smile in her bones. "Did you find her? Is she okay? Do you have news?" She drifted toward Blessing of her own accord.

He folded her in his arms and kissed her on the cheek. "Nice. I watched you finish this morning."

Something inside her demanded more than a kiss on the cheek, and her hands trembled. "I was on the news?"

He grinned, his voice teasing. "Only for a moment. But a glorious one."

It had been almost nine weeks since he left to get messages to Lou. That felt like forever in city time, but it wasn't long to be Outside, where travel times were slow and hard.

Someone cleared his throat, and she turned around to find Adam watching her closely, a slightly injured look in his eyes. She took one step back from Blessing but kept looking at him. It was so good to see him. He looked great. No new scars. He'd eaten well enough. He was alive.

Julianna and Jake came in, and Eloise as well, clutching one of the disconnected slates they used for secure note taking. As soon as Julianna and Jake sat, everyone else searched for seats.

Coryn ended up between Blessing and Day and opposite Adam. In spite of her rubbery limbs after the run, excitement and worry burned through her. It was hard to wait for Julianna to convene the meeting and ask Blessing and Day, "Can you tell us what you found? Did you see Lou?"

Blessing nodded. "They're fine. Matchiko almost destroyed her ankle, but she's healing. We settled the three of them in a small house on a hill, a place they can probably defend. There's no working sewer, but we helped them dig a latrine. They have a good fireplace and two cords of wood. It won't be a great place to winter though, and we promised we'd come back."

Julianna looked slightly amused at Blessing's firehose of disconnected information. "Day?"

"They're fine for now. We bought them a second horse and forced Lou to take it." He glanced at Coryn.

She asked, "Don't they need three?"

"One's a big as a house. Lou and Matchiko can share him." Day almost smiled. "Safety aside, they have been gathering information. There appear to be a lot more Returners than there were before they slaughtered the Listeners last year. They've only seen a few, but they've gotten a lot of reports of them."

Jake held a hand up. "Do you have proof the Returners were behind the killings?"

"It's common understanding Outside now." Day twisted his hands together, a sign of slight frustration in this man of few emotions. "But I have no idea how we'd prove it. We also heard rumors they're planning something big for next spring or early summer, but we can't tell what. There's rumors the feds are behind the Returners. They've got no taxing authority left, and they want some."

"That seems a little extreme," Adam said.

Day shrugged. "Frankly we spent as much time helping get the three amigas settled as we did spying."

Jake kept his focus on Day. "Can you tell if the Returners have specific plans? Or the feds?"

"Rumors go from attacking the cities again—only winning—to shooting found nukes."

"Surely that's ridiculous," Coryn blurted out. "Nukes?"

"A lot of Returners are ex-military."

Jake grunted. "I'm dubious about live nukes. There was a spasm of denuclearization before the taking."

Julianna paced. "Not everywhere. Maybe they came from another country."

Day raised an eyebrow. "Like Canada?" He waited until he had everyone's attention before he continued. "Or like Russia, via the arctic and down through Canada. That's one rumor."

But something else he had said intrigued her more. "Aren't the feds weak?"

Julianna laughed. "Weak bureaucracies can cause more havoc than good ones. Besides, the Outside is federal no matter what we say. That's why you had to apply to them for the wilding permits."

Coryn had spent the last few weeks helping to set up the Outside-N Foundation Jake was designing to gain more access to the Outside and information. And, not incidentally, to employ Lou. The project kept running into unexpected obstacles—waits for permits, forms that shifted from day to day. It felt as if the various bureaucracies were combining to stop them from succeeding. Coryn turned to Day. "We've been trying to figure out where the Returners are concentrated. Could you tell?"

Day hesitated, and Blessing stepped into the silence. "Lou thinks they're in Chelan."

Day added, "But we're not sure. They might be. But it sounds like they are on the move all the time. Moving would let them share information without using electronic networks. What have you seen on the satellite pictures?"

Adam raised his hand and waited for Jake to nod before he spoke. "I've been analyzing the patterns I can pick out of the daily satellite shots. I can't prove it, but based on the farms that are operating and a few boats that run all the way down from the top of the lake, someone is using provisions in Chelan. My current theory is that they keep women and children there. It's easy to defend; there's one road in and out." He pushed a few buttons. A map of Promise appeared. He zoomed in on a lake that looked so long and thin it resembled a blue earthworm.

He pointed at the south end. "This is Chelan. It should have been abandoned. The main utilities were shut off and the whole area is prone to wildfires." He was on a roll, enjoying the floor and the ability to hold a room's attention. "The topography makes it easy to defend, though."

He was a good speaker. She would almost describe the look on his face as blissful.

He zoomed in so they could see a big old hotel by the south end of town. Two big buildings stood by that, and opposite it, a new and fairly large warehouse with a green roof that looked tended. "That one," he said, pointing at the green roof, "could be a grow operation. You could do a lot of vegetables in there. It was built during the heyday of the marijuana industry, and a lot of grow operations turned into vegetable and food production after martial law."

Jake looked fascinated. "If you built tunnels to go between buildings you could hide a lot of people."

Julianna turned her attention to Coryn. "Do we have a permit request in to home the new foundation in Chelan?"

"Yes. There is a one-week wait time posted."

Julianna's lips thinned. "Be very quiet about it. I suspect that if the Returners find it, they'll lodge a complaint."

"On what grounds?" Adam asked.

"None whatsoever. But while the Returners are no citizens of ours, they long for the old world, and they could slow things down with the feds."

Jake leaned back, looking ready to settle into the meeting for some time. "Blessing, tell us the whole story."

"Don't we need lunch?"

Julianna smiled. "I'll call for some. But go ahead and start."

Coryn had to struggle not to go check the permit database right away. Julianna was right, but how was she going to wait a whole week without drawing attention to how much the permit suddenly mattered?

CHAPTER EIGHT

Lou and Matchiko walked slowly around the interior of the log cabin. They'd pushed all of the furniture to the center so the table butted up to the couch and the big comfy chair faced out as well. Matchiko's right hand rested on Lou's left arm, and she hobbled around the circuit, sweat beading her forehead. "That's five laps," she gasped out.

Lou chewed on her lower lip as she looked at her. "Do you need to rest?"

"One more."

Lou nodded and started the next lap. They'd been here almost a month, and were running out of staples. "Did you see the frost this morning?"

"It was beautiful," Matchiko said. "Like every leaf was it's only sparkling creation."

"Like we need to get north now."

"Blessing and Day are only a week overdue. They'll be here."

"I know." But still, Lou worried. They could depend on Buster to carry Matchiko. But horses were targets, and the chance of losing them was high. They also needed feed and water and vet care, none of which was cheap. They'd given up shoeing them, but Buster was developing what looked like a thin crack in his hoof. Not a problem yet . . .

The hidden house was roughly half the way up the state, and west of their old territory in the Palouse. It was far enough off any remaining roads that they hadn't seen anyone since Blessing and Day left. Since it was below the crest of the nearby hills, they had no horizon, no view. Living in a bowl made her scan the tops of the hills regularly for dangers. Matchiko did not seem to be as bothered, but Shuska actually climbed some of the hills near dusk on most days.

After they finished the last lap around the living room, Lou helped

Matchiko settle into the big chair and prop her foot up. There was no visual swelling now, but when Matchiko walked any distance, her face lost all of its color, her lips paled, and her eyes sometimes grew damp. She never actually cried, but then Lou had only seen Matchiko cry once, and that was over the death of a dog rather than anything that happened to a person.

Lou stared out the window at the cold morning while water heated up, then made coffee for all three of them. She handed Matchiko hers and took her own plus a cup for Shuska outside.

A simple bench occupied a third of the small, weathered porch. Shuska had put it together using nails she pulled from abandoned boards and rocks for a hammer, so it wasn't straight even though it was sturdy enough to take all three of them.

Shuska's eyes lit at the sight of the coffee. "I knew you were a goddess."

In truth, they'd been getting sick of each other, all of them. Lou marked it up to the strange stress of being unable to go anywhere. She handed Shuska the cup and sat down beside her on the bench. "We need to leave."

"Blessing and Day are coming here."

"I know. But what if something happened to them?" Lou sipped at her coffee, savoring it. "We can't winter here. There's not enough to eat."

"Give them a week." Shuska blew on her coffee to cool it. "If they haven't shown up by then, we'll go."

"It's going to snow before we get settled anywhere north."

"It's forty-five degrees," Shuska countered. "Nowhere near freezing. You just hate waiting for anything."

"Hey! You're the worrier. Why aren't you worrying more this time?"

"Matchiko needs the healing time." She scooted closer to Lou and put an arm over her shoulder. "It will be okay."

"Don't spill my coffee."

"Never that."

Lou laughed and leaned into Shuska's shoulder. Shuska amazed her. Sometimes she fussed about every choice, every moment they were in danger of any kind, every stranger. Other times she was so zen it was almost scary. Obviously this was a zen week.

Buster and his stable buddy, Pal, both lifted their heads and whinnied.

Lou spilled a few drops of coffee on the ground, and she and Shuska stood.

A row of six horses and riders crested the hill opposite them, just like in an old TV Western she'd seen part of once. The sun shone from behind them, making it impossible to tell if they were friend or foe.

Two dogs started down ahead of the riders.

Neither Blessing or Day had ever had a dog that she knew of.

Shuska lifted her rifle and Lou slid the door open, reaching in for her stunner, which was just inside the door. "Visitors," she hissed at Matchiko.

Should she expose herself on the porch or stay inside and watch through the window? Shuska backed in, convincing Lou to go the window.

"Can you tell who it is?"

"No. But the dogs are halfway here."

They waited.

The people on the horses waited as well, everyone still except the dogs.

The dogs were quite well trained. They stopped three-quarters of the way down, far away from each other, watching the house. Lou decided their heads would reach her waist with all four feet on the ground. They had not made a sound.

Two riders came down right between the dogs, slowly, their horses under perfect control. They held guns, but at their sides rather than at the ready. Once they descended out of the backlighting sun, she saw that they were a male and a female, both easily over fifty. They had weathered skin and graying hair, although the woman's had once been black and the man still had a few streaks of a light brown. The woman called out, "Hello the cabin."

Lou slipped out of the door, keeping her weapon at the same angle, pointed down. "Hello the hill!"

The man laughed. "We wish you no harm. This is a periodic stop of ours. We're surprised to see it occupied."

"Who are you?"

"Wilders."

"Who do you work for?"

"No Fences."

It sounded familiar. Lou called back through the door. "Anyone heard of No Fences?"

"Yes," Matchiko said. "It's okay."

Lou smiled and set her gun down on the bench. "Lou Williams."

"I've heard of you. You hate Returners." The woman turned and gestured for the other riders to come down. When she turned back around she was smiling. "I'm happy to meet you."

"I think this is a good moment to start some stew," Shuska commented from right behind her.

"I'll do it." Matchiko stood up. She was the usual cook, although they'd given her a pass since her injury. Lou considered, but then Matchiko could hardly go help put the strangers' horses up. "Don't fall."

Matchiko stuck her tongue out. "I won't."

On her way out to show the strangers where to put their horses, Lou whistled a tune Daryl had taught her in her first year at RiversEnd Ranch, something about frogs. The tune was easier to remember than the words. She danced a little, pleased at the reminder that they were not the only three people in the world.

Maybe No Fences needed help.

Lou admired the utter relaxation displayed by the two dogs curled into large balls in front of the fire, their tails sticking out. The furniture had been rearranged into a conversational group. The man and woman who had come down first sat near the dogs, which curled at their feet.

Lou, Shuska, and Matchiko filled out a half circle looking at the fire. The newcomers were Greta and Ray Silverstein. She had heard of them but never met them. They'd worked for the No Fences Foundation for twenty years. That was a long time to be Wilders. Their staff were outside singing and playing music beside a fire with bowls of stew, a little whiskey, and two tents between them.

Ray declared, "It's too bad the Lucken Foundation went under. RiversEnd was a good outfit."

"I liked it." She felt a deep pang of loss for the wide hills of the Palouse, the buffalo and coyote and golden eagles. The views. Some days, when she was in the highest hills looking east, she had thought she could see the curve of the world.

Greta sipped her wine. "RiversEnd used to have a great reputation."

"Greed," Lou said. "They were greedy and small."

"They forgot," Greta said. "It's easy for people in the cities to forget that they need us."

Lou took a deep breath, hoping that No Fences needed her. She glanced at Ray, getting ready to ask.

He was a step ahead of her. His lips thinned, and he said, "I wish we could hire. But we're out of money and we've got a waiting list."

"We could work for room and board for a bit," she said.

He shook his head. "No. We can only take legals."

And they needed an approved job for that. It was the right thing for Ray to say, and she respected him for it. She offered a toast. "To honest leaders everywhere!"

Glasses clinked, although Matchiko gave her a wry look.

Lou shrugged. She had meant it.

Greta brushed her hair out of her eyes. "So what are you staying here for? Are you hiding or waiting?"

So Greta had figured out they hadn't settled in for the winter. Of course, one look in the kitchen pantry was adequate proof of that. "Waiting. For some friends. They're due in a week or so. If they don't come soon, we're going to ride north and find a place to winter."

"Most people go south for the winter," Ray observed.

"We're interested in the Returners. There appear to be a few extra riding about. We're trying to figure out what they're doing." Lou sipped at her glass of wine. It was the last bottle they had, and she was on the last glass she'd have until they got somewhere with a stock of alcohol. "I guess in some ways we're acting like Listeners. Collecting data while we wait for work."

"That'll get you killed," Ray observed.

Lou decided she was warming to his subtle sense of humor.

Matchiko spoke softly. "No. We're not acting like Listeners."

"Sure you are. You're asking questions."

Shuska added a piece of wood to the insert in the fireplace and the room brightened, making it easier to see faces. "Aren't you curious? Any attack on the cities will hurt our efforts to save the world. Resources will go to defense instead of to bison."

Ray's laugh came out bitter. "Some days I don't think we can save anything, not anymore."

Greta shook her head at him. "You only say that when you've been drinking, old man. I'm going to cut you off."

He stood up, pacing a little. "We *have* seen more Returners. What bothers me is that they act more organized, and also more high-and-mighty. They seem to have new resources, or help of some kind. I have a paranoid theory. Do you want to hear it?"

Greta held up a hand as if she could forestall his words.

Ray was having none of her attempt to stop him and didn't seem to care that no one had yet asked to hear his theory. "I think it's the feds.

I think the Returners have infiltrated the feds and they want to change the rules, make land okay to own, maybe allow some farming. Hunting. Undo everything we've done."

Wilders were allowed to farm. But just to eat, and that was it. There was a black market, of course, but it wasn't huge. Lou leaned forward, intrigued. "I don't know much about the feds. There's an office in Seacouver of course. And one in Portland. But they're not big. They don't control the cities. Not anymore. Can they hurt us?"

Greta stood up and blocked Ray mid-pace. "The foundations wouldn't stand for it, and neither would the cities. They just wouldn't."

Ray didn't bother to try and get around Greta. She was his height, almost his size, and clearly stubborn. He put an arm across her shoulders and smiled at her.

She leaned into him, accepting it. That made it seem like a very old disagreement, the kind of words married couples carried on for years.

Greta kept talking, her voice less bitter than Ray's, maybe more resigned. "He's always seeing scary things in the night. The Returners do plenty of damage without a federal bogeyman. They kill the wolves and the bears and all the other interesting predators. They're idiots who don't recognize there will be more and healthier elk if there are wolves. Someone needs to teach them to read."

Lou felt like getting up to applaud. The Returners *were* idiots. Dangerous idiots. But she had her own theories. "I think it's more complex than that. So complex that some days I think the Returners shoot the predators because they *do* read, and they want the Wilding to fail."

"You're giving them too much credit," Greta replied.

Lou laughed. "Don't get me wrong. I'd rather be counting wolves and hunting Returners than hunting rumors. But it does seem like there is more . . . resource . . . around the empty places than there used to be. I used to think the old Returners would die off and we wouldn't need to worry about them anymore. But they seem to have become everybody's bogeyman during the last six months."

The conversation moved on to the various good points about the horses, one over the other, which led to the various bad points about Buster. They drank while Shuska watched, and Matchiko looked more relaxed than Lou had seen her since her injury.

After the fire wound down, Ray and Greta and their dogs went to sleep outside. Matchiko hobbled to bed, and Shuska followed her, undoubtedly to tuck her in.

That left Lou up to keep watch as the coals simmered down. Her mood felt black, roiling with ideas and worries about the Returners. She paced, and then opened the door to the crisply cold night and stood on the porch. The dark humps of their guests' tents were easy to see in the moonlight. The Milky Way spread above her like a promise. As the cold settled in, she listened to two owls calling back and forth to each other and the occasional stamp of a horse's foot. The company felt good, both the people and the owls. But the people would leave in the morning, and owls would not feed her and her partners. They had almost nothing left.

They needed work. They needed a ranch, an NGO. She paced, humming to herself.

Theoretically, Julianna was working on that. But Julianna was a city creature. She'd probably never been outside the weather domes after she helped set them up.

Lou didn't want to work for her. She didn't want to work for Coryn either.

But as far as she could tell, her best hope was to do both of those things. And what if Julianna and Coryn didn't come through? Then what could they do?

CHAPTER NINE

Lou looked up from the horse corral where she was working Buster on a long-lead. She had succeeded in getting him up to a full trot. The Silversteins had been gone for three days, but she couldn't stop thinking about the conversation they'd started. Was she sitting right here in the middle of a historical flashpoint when the things she'd spent her whole life dreaming of—working out here restoring wild places—was under threat? If so, did she have the strength to be a hero?

Pal let out a long whinny, and Buster slowed down and broke the circle of his lead, trotting toward her so she had to step aside to avoid being run over by a horse the size of a small mountain. "Hey boy, that's no good." But she turned to see what had gathered his attention.

Four horses showed up over the top of the hill, and for a moment she had to do a double-take. Then she realized there were three riders and a horse on a lead, and the man in front could only be Blessing.

A high-pitched whinny stopped her.

Mouse!

She unclipped Buster's lead, dashed past him, and ducked between the lower two metal rails on the corral. She ran toward her old horse, who was being led in full tack. She waved at Blessing and kept right on going, throwing her arms around the big buckskin's neck and drawing in a lungful of her sweat.

"Who knew you missed the horse that much?" Blessing asked.

"I did," she retorted.

"She's a bribe. We paid extra to free her from a string of pack horses."

Lou pulled back and stared into Mouse's eyes. "I can't believe anyone put you in a pack string." She kissed her horse on her soft nose. "What are you bribing me for? Whatever it is, you can have it."

Day rode up behind her. "Seriously, you'll need one horse each. You get us, too, for a while. And we brought you one other bribe."

She pushed herself away from Mouse and looked closely at the third rider. A slender man with a big hat and a long mustache. She squealed. "Daryl!"

He tipped his hat to her.

He had trained her, and then he had worked for her, swearing he was never going to manage a whole ranch. There were many things she loved him for, including that he could fix anything and was reliable as the sunrise. "Good to see you!" she called out. "Welcome."

She tightened Mouse's cinch, turned her sideways into the hill, and mounted right there, even if the ride was only a few hundred yards. It wasn't her old saddle, but it would do, and feeling Mouse's familiar gait under her felt fabulous.

They put the horses away, working as a team. She turned to Daryl. "Will you stay on watch?"

He leaned over and gave her a hug. "Of course I will. It's so good to see you."

"It is."

In the house, Matchiko and Shuska fussed as much as Lou had. Hugs were exchanged and stories babbled and everyone looked at Matchiko's ankle, even as she was trying to get them to leave her alone so she could cook.

After a fabulous dinner that Lou hardly tasted, Blessing and Day laid a series of maps out on the table and briefed them on Adam's theories of roving Returners, small towns full of Returners and maybe a secure one in Chelan.

"It makes sense," Shuska mused.

"We can't know," Matchiko said.

Lou touched her shoulder. "We can. We can spy."

Matchiko looked intrigued. "If it gets me out of this house, I'll do anything."

After Blessing picked the maps up and put them away, Day produced a brown paper envelope, tossing it onto the table.

Shuska reached for it, opened it, and took out the paper. She stared at it for a long time, and then handed it to Lou. It read:

> *Outside-N Foundation*
> *Executive Board: Jake Erlich, Julianna Lake, Coryn Williams,*
>   *Lou Williams, and Eloise Smith*
> *President of the Board of Directors: Jake Erlich*
> *Vice-President of the Board of Directors: Julianna Lake*
> *Secretary Treasurer of the Board of Directors: Eloise Smith*
> *Members-at-large of the Board of Directors: Coryn Williams,*
>   *Lou Williams.*
>
> *Purpose of Foundation:*
>
> *General rewilding with a special focus on predatory species,
> including the northern gray wolf, the black bear, the grizzly bear,
> the mountain lion, the cougar, the bald eagle, the golden eagle.
> Other animal-based rewilding. May join with other foundations
> working to rewild plants, including fungi.*

She stared at it, tears gathering in the corners of her eyes. Fungi? Coryn knew she loved mushrooms. But rewilding fungi?

She was on the board?

Blessing came over to her. "I have a copy that you need to sign. I'll carry the signed version back with me after we escort you to your territory."

A smile spread across her face. "You're coming with us?"

"We've got to stop in Wenatchee. Julianna's sending some supplies."

Lou wanted to comment on the strange grin on his face, but before she decided what to say Shuska handed her another piece of paper.

Nonexclusive Operating Permit: Two Years
Territory: Area previously known as Chelan County, including the
area around Lake Chelan and the taken territory for seventy-
five miles.

Below that, it repeated much of the information that was on the previous piece of paper, explaining how they could help with any mammals, and particularly with predators.

The last piece of paper appointed her as the foreman of the operation and gave her permission to hire up to ten people and any robots she could afford. It listed a budget that might just do.

She swallowed and sat still. Mouse. Working with her sister. Taking on the bad guys. Really being in charge. Everyone's safety up to her. Being on the board of an NGO. The safety of at least two packs of wolves up to her. The safety of an unknown number of grizzlies. The ability to provide for Matchiko and Shuska, hell, the ability to hire them so they could all provide for each other. She walked over by the fire and stared at the crackling flames.

Could she do this? Run everything out here? The unexpected weight of so much responsibility made her knees weak. The change. As she stared at the fire, she realized that there had always been some shadowy and competent boss when she thought about this possibility. Someone who wasn't her.

If she accepted this, she had to see it out, no matter how hard it became. She wouldn't be able to leave for a better chance with any of the other foundations, or quit until the two years had passed. That would be selling her sister up the road, and she couldn't do that. It was a pair of handcuffs, but they came with food and shelter for the people she loved and work for land she loved.

She left the fire and went to Blessing's side. "I'm ready to sign it."

He went to his saddlebag and drew out another envelope, a shiny, white-linen paper, and a blue pen. He smiled as he handed them to her, and she had the sense he knew how much it meant to her.

Everyone gathered around. Matchiko held the document at arm's length and stared at it for a moment, and then nodded.

Lou sat at the table and signed.

Blessing produced four extra copies. "Why so many?" she asked him.

"I'll take two, you'll keep two, and we'll have one extra just in case anyone wants it."

She frowned. "Feds?"

He merely smiled. "Anyone."

She shrugged and kept signing.

When she finished, everyone clapped, and Blessing smiled as if he'd just won a race. Luckily, Day had thought to bring a bottle of merlot with him. Lou had a rather large glass.

A few minutes after that, she went out to the paddock to brush Mouse and think.

The horse refused to answer any of her questions about how to succeed at this impossible job, but Mouse smelled of old successes and long rides and comfort, and she whickered softly when Lou scratched behind her ears.

CHAPTER TEN

Aspen looked content, his belly flat on the table and his head up while Jake stroked him behind the ears with one hand. Jake used his other hand to show Coryn how to search an old land records database for Chelan to find property boundaries and to cross-reference that data to records that showed old reports on wells. Information scrolled on two walls, some of the data so old she had to read handwriting.

She scribbled notes. "Then I use the satellite shots?"

"Yes. Look for people, or for green gardens, or, of course, water." He sat back in his chair and pulled Aspen into his lap. "People know we're looking, so they try to screen gardens. They'll put up lean-tos, for example. But growing things need sun, and they can only be a little hidden. You should be able to spot them."

"How many people live there?"

"The last estimates we have from Listeners in that area is under a thousand. That's not many. It wouldn't have been enough to spend resources dislodging."

She nodded. Her high school education had insisted it was all empty Outside, that the great taking had returned every scrap of land between cities to the wild, but she'd seen that lie when she'd gone out to find Lou. There had been people everywhere. Some good, some mean, all a little desperate in one way or another.

It was a crime to occupy a house without a permit in the rewilded zones, but some crimes were ignored as long as they weren't crimes against nature. People could shoot each other Outside, but they couldn't shoot a bear. They could occupy an old building before it was torn down, but they couldn't build a new structure. Not without drawing ecobots to destroy it.

Chelan was so remote that no one casually rode through on the way to anywhere else. Roads weren't maintained. Wildland fires weren't put out. She drummed her anxiety out on the table, tapping her fingers. Lou and the fledgling NGO needed a place to land. She had to find one this morning if she wanted to be sure there was time to file a permit for approved occupancy. "What if I pick the wrong house?"

"You may never know." Jake stood up. "Some choices aren't ever clear."

He was lecturing her. She stared at the screen so he wouldn't see she was frustrated with him. He was brilliant and driven, but it bugged her when he treated her like a child.

"Pick a good one. That's enough. If I were you, I wouldn't pick the best house in Chelan. Lou might have to fight for that, if it's occupied. Pick a good one," he repeated. "Look for a water signature. That's the most important thing. Water. And access to the wilds."

She stared at the zoomed-out version of the sat shot she'd left loaded on a tablet for reference. Everything in Chelan oriented around the lake, and thus around water. But it was fed from the mountains, and the town nestled in hills where water flowed when it rained and summers were fire-dry. Water to drink, water for food. Things she never needed to even think about in the city.

She couldn't fail Lou.

As Jake walked past her, he put a hand on her shoulder, as if he understood the stress she felt. She looked down at it, noticing again that the end of his little finger pointed the wrong way and the knuckle above it was huge and swollen. It must hurt to be so old. She smiled up at him. "I'll find something."

"Okay. I've got a meeting to go to, but I'll try to come back before you need to file the permit."

"Thanks."

"If I don't get back, you will have to choose."

He walked slowly out of the room, bent and a little shaky. As he opened the door, a companion-bot stepped in and held out an arm, and

Jake leaned on it. After it closed, she stared at the door for a moment. He seemed far more fragile than when she first met him.

Even with Aspen warm in her lap, the room felt empty. Jake could make her smile so easily. He spent time helping her almost every day, and she sensed he valued this time as much as she did.

She spent the next hour flipping through screens, trying to narrow her choices down. One house was too small. Another had no roof. A third went in the *maybe* pile. A fourth only had one entrance and exit, and they'd talked about the need to be able to defend and to flee. Yet another table contained a hand-scrawled list of parameters. Water, right at the top. Barns and outbuildings. Multiple entrances. Access to the wild.

Another task where it would have been easier to have Paula.

She was pretty sure someone, maybe Adam, was running the same analysis with the help of machines and that they'd check her answer that way. She loved working on the foundation and learning the tools, but every day felt like a long, protracted test. Did she run fast enough? Did she learn fast enough? Did she answer questions right?

She sighed and stood up, stretching. This was so important and she just wasn't sure she was good enough at it. How did you pick the most useful river rock out of a whole pond full of the damned things?

All the richest people in the city were tech people. How did they stand staring at data all day?

She flipped over to a real-time satellite shot of Chelan, and then stood and studied the three properties she liked the most. There was no way to tell which would be better.

Aspen whined at the door, breaking her attention free.

As she took Aspen out, she reviewed the three houses she liked the best. All of them had problems. All three appeared livable. She couldn't tell if they were occupied or not, not with the data she had. The shots hadn't shown people, but they did all seem—not abandoned?

Time wasn't slowing down for her. So when she got back, she chose and filled out the permit paperwork, ready to pull the trigger. She watched the door and the clock, willing Jake to come back.

With just a few minutes left to spare to get a filing that day, Jake sent her a brief message. *I can't get back. Remember, there's no perfect choice.*

Her stomach flipped at the responsibility, at the utter lack of backup or confirmation for her choice. But she pushed the button, called Aspen to her, and closed up for the day.

CHAPTER ELEVEN

ou sat at the kitchen table. Early morning light poured in on her through the shattered window in the house the six of them had "borrowed." The horses shuffled outside, penned in a backyard rather than a barn.

It had only taken two days to ride here, to Wenatchee, from their hideaway. Two more days had passed since then, waiting for something Julianna had promised to Blessing. And he, in his turn, was being all secretive about it, promising her she'd be thrilled.

Julianna was her new boss, her benefactor, her funder. But what did she know about what to send here for Lou to use?

Lou went to the window and stood in the cool morning air, which smelled of autumn. She wanted to get to Chelan and find the wolf packs. They would already be out teaching pups to hunt, and every day made it a little less likely they'd find the animals before spring.

Waiting almost hurt.

She could still smell yesterday's rain, and the air felt damp enough to glue dust to the ground.

The town took its name from a river. Right now Day and Daryl were off getting water from the Wenatchee. Most would go to the horses, but they would purify some for themselves. Wenatchee was still decent to live in, after a fashion. The ecobots had started destroying it, but they'd stopped after Leavenworth burned to foundations and chimneys. Wenatchee was never made into an approved town, but it was allowed to exist as a half-broken ghost. Some houses had been repaired, and a few people hauled water for gardens in plastic-lined wheelbarrows or old orange buckets. Hollyhocks lined the fence of the house next to them. That was part of why she'd chosen this street. The tall peach and pink flowers made the damaged street cheerful.

Behind Lou, Shuska and Matchiko banged around in the small kitchen, bossing Daryl around from time to time. The air had started to warm, and she felt a restless need to *move*. Not only did they need to get to Chelan, but they needed to get away from here.

The responsibility for all of these people and animals weighed her down. On top of that, she was responsible for a rather large and specific scrap of wilderness she hadn't even seen yet. And a limited budget. Maybe there was more money where that came from. Maybe not. She hardly knew Julianna.

So much obligation made her mind run through scenario after scenario, possibility after possibility. What if they never even got to Chelan?

She drew in a deep breath of the fresh, damp air, and fretted.

Blessing's voice, loud with jubilation: "Lou!"

She blinked. She couldn't see them, not yet, but they'd be coming from the river. She grabbed her stunner from the pile of weapons by the door and headed out into the empty, crumbling street.

One of the many feral cats almost tripped her, but as soon as she had a good view, she spotted them. They weren't carrying any water. They were walking upright and grinning, coming fast. Right behind them, two of the most common ecobots—the same kind she had ridden into captivity in Portland Metro—carried the water. The jugs looked like small bubbles balanced on the big robots' flat backs.

A flock of drones followed the robots.

The procession looked quite military, here on this side street with the hollyhocks. Utterly wrong.

Anger pounded at her temples. They wouldn't be safe here. Not with these. Could they get them into Chelan? Did they have time to manage them?

Shuska and Matchiko spilled out of the house and joined her on the road. "Oh no," Shuska said.

Matchiko's lips thinned and her jaw tightened to steel. She took a deep breath. "I'm going to finish breakfast. Better that than shoot Blessing."

Lou stalked across the street and stood in front of Blessing. "Is *that* what we were waiting for?"

He looked like a cat who'd caught a hummingbird. The bots stopped behind him, looming, as wide as the road.

She loved Blessing, but there were times he made her want to tear her hair out. "Were these used in the attack on Portland? Were they hacked?"

"They've been upgraded."

"Great. Hopefully they were also tested."

He grinned and shrugged, his look suggesting she was worrying about nothing. As if having big machines solved problems.

"Well," she said dryly, "I had been wondering how we would defend ourselves if the current residents of Chelan didn't want us around."

The ecobots stopped in the road, waiting.

"Breakfast is ready!" Matchiko called, her voice twice as exuberant as usual.

"I suppose I can't send them back where they came from," she observed.

Blessing's smile was still on his face, but he managed to look crestfallen in spite of it. How could a grown man be so good at emotional drama?

Well, Julianna had sent the damned bots. They must have been expensive. "I suspect they're coming with us."

Blessing's smile widened. "I think we should name them."

She sighed. "Whatever. Let's eat, water the horses, and head out."

Daryl had come up beside her and taken his hat off, staring up at the metal beasts. He grinned. "That gives us a lot of muscle."

Men. "I had hoped to ride in without being noticed." She turned toward the door and headed for the kitchen, following the scent of toast and eggs.

Lou sat beside Matchiko on the lead ecobot. They nestled between three sets of folding arms right behind the large rounded head where it rested, retracted, near the front of the robot. The bot's multiple drones all occupied their parking slots, making the wide top feel crowded. Daryl, Shuska, and Blessing all rode horses. Day rode the other bot, and the other three mounts walked on a long lead attached to one of the bot's arms.

Lou practiced giving the ecobots commands. Now that they were out of town and in an empty place on a wide stretch of decent road, stopping and turning the bots seemed like a good idea. Matchiko held on tight, and wore a sour little smile, so Lou asked, "Is anything other than the ride bothering you?"

Matchiko reached for Lou's hand. "I have a hunch that Chelan is going to be rough. And I don't know if the ecobots help or hurt. I'm guessing hurt."

"They don't exactly let us ride in quietly."

"Especially not if you keep driving them like drunken cars."

"Hey! We need to practice giving them orders."

"They might just be humoring you."

"They're machines."

"Smart machines. Can we just go straight for a while? I'm trying to count hawks."

To be fair, Matchiko did have her notebook resting near her. Lou stopped asking the machine to do anything. She'd already tested voice commands and using swipes on her wristlet.

It did matter whether or not she could command the bots, but in her experience, ecobots sometimes had their own agendas, and those would have priority. They would obey her if they had no higher calling associated with saving the world. Or, as proven in Portland Metro, they'd give her no warning at all if they were hacked. They might even turn on her and her people.

Ecobots made fickle staff.

Chelan was roughly fifty miles from Wenatchee. Two days, if they pushed the horses. Three days if they didn't.

"I wonder if they've blocked the roads?" Lou mused.

Matchiko shifted to a new position, stretching her injured leg out and reaching toward the ankle in a pose that looked like yoga, the move oddly graceful on the metal back of the robot. Like a single flower in the middle of a rocky cliff. "We'll find out in the morning."

"If they're organized, they'll know we're coming."

Matchiko nodded.

"What if there's no good place to stay? No usable water?"

Matchiko sighed. "It's a big lake. You have your stash of water pills."

"There's only one big road on either side."

Matchiko reached a hand out and touched her cheek, her fingers warm. "Stop worrying so much."

"I'm not worried. I'm looking forward to finding a nest of Returners."

"You know," Matchiko smiled, "we're used to dealing with one or two Returners at a time. Once, we had six. Remember? This might be a hundred. Or five hundred."

Lou laughed, a little high and nervous. "Are you telling me to be careful what I wish for? We'll find a way."

"Don't brag. You'll tempt the universe."

Lou shut up, balancing on top of the big bot, which rocked less than a horse and differently. It made her ever-so-slightly queasy. She watched the riverbanks for animals. The recent rain has driven some dark green up through the brown grasses of early fall, all of that mixing with the softer greens of low sage bushes. A doe and a fawn drank from a low bank on the river and farther on, a yearling buck struggled uphill on the far side, watching the bots with suspicion. A few minutes later something bigger than her head splashed in the water. It was too far away for her to tell if it was a fish or a river otter. Maybe a salmon. They should be between the summer and fall runs, but the exact timing of the fall run varied. Since the biggest dams had come down, the quantity of fish had more than doubled. So maybe a salmon.

She wanted to look at maps, but they had nothing for Internet way out here. She expected premium access from Julianna, but it hadn't shown up yet. So when her wristlet buzzed, it had to be one of her party; they had no better connectivity way out here. She glanced down.

Day. Economical, as always. A single word: "Stop."

She raised an eyebrow and swiped to tell the ecobot to stop. It obeyed so abruptly that she had to steady herself against its metal arm. She and Matchiko both stood.

A party of five men had appeared in the road. She'd just looked that way and seen nothing. The youngest looked like he was in his thirties, the oldest probably twice that. Each of them held a gun and more than one had another weapon as well. She spotted a hunting crossbow and some kind of sword. They wore leather vests in spite of the heat and old-style sewn jeans and leather boots. Hats covered every face. They were so over-the-top her first instinct was to laugh, and she barely managed to stop herself from at least smiling.

Returners. They had to be. Well-dressed, if stylized. She smiled. Game on. A jolt of adrenaline added speed to her racing thoughts. The ecobots wouldn't help in a fight unless the humans were hurting the natural world or attacking the bots directly; they allowed people to kill each other with no interference. These people probably knew that. But being able to stand on top of mobile machines gave her party far better angles to shoot from, and the men on the road had no cover whatsoever to speak of.

For just a moment everyone stood still, as if they'd all paused for a photo. Then Blessing urged his gray horse forward a few steps. He smiled his signature wide smile, looking so relaxed Lou was sure he wasn't. He gave them a moment to speak, and when they didn't, he said, "Good afternoon. Can we help you?"

"Don't go up there," the man said. "You can turn around and go across the river and go up the other side, but don't go to Chelan."

Blessing cocked his head, looking curious. "Why not?"

"There are sick people up there. The city is quarantined."

Blessing kept his smile.

Matchiko's hand curled around Lou's forearm, her nails digging slender moons into Lou's flesh.

Blessing answered the man. "We have business in Chelan." He paused, as if thinking carefully. "What kind of illness?"

"The kind that kills people."

"That's not very helpful."

"Trust us. You don't want to pass us. It's like a flu and contagious."

He was lying. It didn't sound like he had even thought much about his story. Maybe he'd made it up on the spot. Lou moved two steps closer to the edge of the ecobot. She was at least twelve feet above the Returners, so they looked foreshortened. She cleared her throat. "We're Wilders. We won't do you any harm. We don't care what's happening in town. But we have a job to do, and Chelan is our newly assigned territory. We'll take our risks."

Matchiko let go of her arm, and Lou rubbed it.

The man kept watching Blessing. "We don't care what the city told you to do. The city has no rights out here, and we're telling you not to go." He sounded disturbingly sanctimonious as he added, "It's for your own good."

"I'm not a city girl." Lou moved her hand closer to her stunner. "We have a federal permit."

Beside her, Matchiko sank to a sitting position.

Blessing stared at the man, as if contemplating his next answer.

Daryl cajoled his horse into a light prance and came up beside Blessing. The two of them looked imposing.

Matchiko twisted so she lay on her stomach, braced on her elbows, peering over the edge of the ecobot. She held a small, capable gun in her hand.

None of the men had raised a rifle yet, but the air screamed with tension, thick and brittle.

Matchiko whispered, "I've got the leader in my sights."

"Hold," Lou whispered back. Shooting their way into town did not seem like a terribly good idea. But maybe the threat would help. She glanced around for Shuska, who had been riding in the last position, acting as rearguard.

Not visible.

Wherever she was, chances were good it would be the right place. Lou spoke again. "We're not asking for permission. We have it, and we're going up there. We may be able to help with your sick."

Matchiko gave her a soft kick in the shin.

"We've got the bots and we've got our orders. We won't bother you, but we're not turning around."

Only one of the five men looked up at her. The other four all watched the two men on the horses in front of them.

By now, Lou was used to being underestimated. It amused her.

Shuska's voice. "Please move out of our way." She appeared from around the side of the second ecobot, mounted on Buster. Not the mount Lou would have chosen. But Shuska and the horse were of a size, and they looked good together. Shuska's hair had been caught back to stay out of her eyes, and her left hand held the reins, leaving her right free. She repeated her command. "Please move." When Shuska said it, *please* was a command.

The man who had been doing the talking stared at the huge native woman for a long moment. One of the men behind him poked him and said something Lou couldn't hear.

Lou chose to risk Matchiko's ability to get a clear shot by urging the ecobot very slowly forward, reminding the men that they had machine power.

Just in case they didn't have enough advantage, Blessing and Daryl had both managed to get their weapons pointed at the men while they were distracted by Shuska.

The men guarding the road were thugs, but they weren't strategic thugs. So far. Once more, Lou almost wanted to laugh. She knew it for nerves. She knew better than to underestimate opponents.

The men stepped slowly to the side of the road.

Shuska glanced at Lou. Although she said nothing, she might as well be lecturing Lou on the inadvisability of leaving armed men behind them. But there were too many to capture, or to watch well if they did. She wasn't going to fire the first shot. She gave a slight shake of her head, signaling to Shuska that she understood her, and had chosen differently.

Lou nodded at the men. "Thank you for the warning. I meant what I said. We may be able to help. We'll see you in town sometime tomorrow."

She watched. No one raised a rifle.

Lou told her bot to lead them off.

The men stepped aside, watchful. Lou tried to memorize their faces, but they were hard to see at this angle and under hats.

Shuska stayed behind until the party was a little bit ahead, and then, by some miracle, she managed to convince Buster to trot fast enough to catch up.

Lou glanced soon at her. "Sorry," she mouthed.

Shuska glared at the machines. She was good with them, better than Lou, but she didn't trust them. "I can manage. It'll be a long night."

A quiet entry into Chelan would have been too much to hope for. At least with the damned ecobots. She turned to Matchiko. "I'm going to have figure out how to manage Julianna so she doesn't send any more inappropriate gifts."

Matchiko had clearly been thinking along the same lines. "I hope Julianna has to ride one of these things someday."

Lou stared at the river. "She's trying to run an NGO from inside the city. She knows nothing."

"Our last bosses didn't either." Matchiko reached up and took Lou's hand. "At least we know Julianna means well."

"I suppose."

"If you want me to have time to cook anything decent for dinner, we should stop soon."

"I won't mind a cold dinner."

Matchiko smiled her patient smile.

Lou woke at dawn, mildly surprised that they had survived the night with no interruptions. She rolled out of her sleeping bag into the cold morning. Pristine light graced the great river, illuminating every blade of grass with its own glowing frost halo. She sat up and looked around in all directions. No bad guys in sight. Just Daryl, on watch, his slender figure throwing a long stick-thin shadow over the horses.

Good. But she didn't trust the silence.

Her wristlet buzzed and hummed. She glanced down to read. *Accept connection from Coryn?*

She tapped *Yes*. Finally. Connectivity.

Audio?

Yes. Yes! She glanced down. Video, too. A tiny image of Coryn stared at Lou. She'd cut her hair.

Video took excellent connectivity. A weight of relief slid from her, followed by concern. Why was Coryn calling before six o'clock in the morning?

Her little sister sounded worried. "Lou?"

"Good morning."

"There's going to more trouble."

"You know about the trouble we had yesterday?"

"We've had you on satellite since you left Yakima. But we weren't able to finish negotiating and placing the bandwidth we needed to talk to you."

Coryn spoke fast, as if she were as relieved as Lou to be back in touch. "There's a barricade on the road. It wasn't there yesterday. It's showing up on satellite shots but we haven't been able to get a picture with enough resolution to analyze whether or not the ecobots can break through it."

"I hope not."

"What?" Coryn sounded surprised.

Lou took a deep breath and tried to stay calm. "I'm going to have to live there. In Chelan. I can't afford to enter in a fight. What was Julianna thinking?"

"She's not here right now."

Lou forced another deep breath. Coryn was her only support?

"Did Julianna send the ecobots?"

"Yes."

"Did she suggest that we try to go through a barrier?"

"No. That was me. That *is* me. I'm in charge of getting you into Chelan."

Across the ashes of last night's campfire, Shuska sat up, staring at Lou. Lou swiped her wristlet to make Coryn's side of the conversation audible. "So let's think a little more about this. If it's a barricade, it's not coming after us, right?"

"Uh . . ."

Lou smiled. She had known something would happen. This was better than being shot at from behind a boulder. She glanced at Shuska, who had stood and headed toward her. Matchiko's eyes were open, but she hadn't moved. "Look, we've just woken up. Can you hold on for five minutes and we'll have a regular meeting with all of us? I want Daryl, too, since he's actually been to Chelan. Give us a second."

She muted the call and filled the other two in, then said, "Shuska, can you get Daryl? Maybe put Day on watch?"

Matchiko climbed out of her bag. Shuska had already started toward Daryl. Lou hastened through a minimal set of morning ablutions and lit the clever little solar-battery stove under the coffee water, then stood waiting with the other three gathered. Moving around helped her shed some of her anger with Coryn. It probably wasn't Coryn's fault she was the only one available. At least she was there.

Shuska clutched a tablet in her hand, not looking at it. Daryl stood quietly beside her, half her girth, a few inches shorter, and all wiry muscle. His hair had already grayed and the lines in his face were marked with dust from traveling on horseback most of the previous day.

Lou swiped the connection back open and started with a question. "Tell us what you know about this barrier?"

"It just went up last night. It's on the 97. Jake and I reviewed the sat shots from the last week, and the material was staged three days ago. It looks like a metal. There's a small solar cell installation to run the gate. So we don't know that the barrier is all about you, but we do think they put it up quickly last night to keep you out. It's about three miles in front of you, after the road starts winding up into Chelan. It's a narrow spot—"

Lou cut her off. "We'll go around it."

"What? It might be soft enough to get through—you know, unfinished or something."

Matchiko looked up from where she was spooning instant coffee into cups and held her finger up to speak.

Lou nodded, noticing the deference. It wasn't like Matchiko to defer to her. But then Matchiko worked for her now. It made her uneasy. How could she be the boss and one of the three amigas?

Matchiko started with a simple question. "Why would we break through the barrier?"

"To get to Chelan." A beat of silence. "Oh. But then you have to live with these people."

Apparently Coryn had finally heard the obvious. Lou asked her, "So maybe you can find a way we can go around?"

"I'm looking."

Shuska spoke up. "Do we have access to maps now?"

Coryn answered. "I have five connection IDs."

Not enough. "Please give Shuska and Matchiko each one now.

You can send me the others." Lou turned to take a cup of coffee from Matchiko while Shuska and Coryn negotiated the ID. The wind blew the smell of the river toward them from the east. The tops of the ecobots already glowed with direct light. Here and there, lanky jackrabbits grazed cautiously some distance from them, periodically looking up as if to check and be sure no hawks circled overhead. When Shuska had clearly established her connection and become lost in data on her tablet, Lou spoke again. "We'll need more IDs. I'll need one for everyone I have permission to hire, even though we haven't got them all yet."

"Did you add anyone in Wenatchee?"

"No. I wanted to get set up in Chelan as fast as possible. Now that I have network I can get the word out, but I thought I should know where we'll be before I add to the team."

Blessing appeared, looking quite put together and ready of the day. Matchiko immediately handed him cup of coffee, probably the one she had intended for herself.

"We found you a headquarters. I'll send you the address."

Daryl raised an eyebrow. Shuska grimaced. "You didn't sign anything long-term, did you?" Lou asked. Matchiko laid a hand on her arm, reacting to the tone in her voice and patting her as if she were a child who needed to stay calm.

What was it about little sisters? Lou loved Coryn, she even trusted her, mostly, but so many of her ideas were so naive. But Coryn had brought connectivity, and funding, and those were no small things at all. "All right. We'll check it out and let you know if it's any good. In the meantime, can you look for alternate ways in? Shuska will do the same. What else have you learned about Chelan?"

"There are at least a thousand people there. There aren't supposed to be any, but there are a lot more than zero. Adam thinks there could be up to fifteen hundred."

Something in Coryn's tone made Lou ask, "Who's Adam?"

Surprisingly, Blessing answered the question. "Her running coach."

Her *what*? She could ask later. "That's a lot of people."

"And there are more up at the top of the lake. There's a town up there called Stehekin. It's fifty miles from Chelan, on the lake. The only easy way to get there is on the water, on a big boat called *Lady of the Lake*. It goes up and down once a week."

Lou took a sip of her coffee, and then asked, "Are you telling me there's a boat that goes up and down the lake once a week even though there's not supposed to be anyone in Chelan?"

Daryl had moved over beside Shuska and was pointing at things on the tablet. "I've been to Stehekin. It's pretty. Might be where we'll find some wolves as well."

Coryn apparently agreed. "There is a pack north of there, and the other one is closer to where you're going. I'll send you a summary after you get there. It's not important now."

Lou was still a little stuck on the boat with no town. "Why does Stehekin exist?"

"Stehekin kept the right to exist, way back on the way to the great taking. It's a single line in the agreement with the feds. Jake has a cabin there, and he argued that since it's so rustic already and rewilding efforts could go forward from there, it should stay. It's not a city and it can't tax, but it never was a city. People who lived there during the taking, and their children, get to live there as long as they want. They don't get any services except that Seacouver sends them enough engineering support to run the boat and maintain their power arrays."

Matchiko finally got her own cup of coffee. "How come no one told us that before? Does Jake still have a cabin there?"

"Yes, and you can use it. But it's not big enough to be a headquarters and Jake would prefer you to be near Chelan so you can figure out what's going on there."

"Me too. But we still have to get there."

"Okay." Lou glanced over at Shuska. "Can you take this call? Work on a route with Coryn? One the robots can manage?"

Shuska nodded as if it were a great favor indeed, her distaste for Coryn evident on her face. Well, that went both ways. Lou was going to have to work on that someday. In the meantime, she pitched in to help Matchiko heat up bread and eggs in the skillet.

They separated from the 97 shortly after the place they had camped and climbed laboriously up a steep ravine that added at least two hours of travel time. It forced Lou to close her eyes twice for fear of falling. After that, they connected with a strip of dirt that had been a road in some far past life. The sun shone so brightly on the ecobots it was hard to look at them, and equally hard to touch them. The bots themselves seemed noisier than usual, clanking and rumbling. While they couldn't talk, Shuska knew how to read their diagnostics, and once she stopped and cleaned out a leg joint.

"What would they do if you weren't there?" Matchiko asked her.

"Clean each other. You know how you almost never see just one?"

Matchiko smiled. "Oh."

"But humans are better," Shuska explained. "Our fingers are smaller."

Lou burst out laughing, the laugh turning to a dust-clogged cough. "I wish it would rain again."

Daryl stood nearby. "Be careful what you wish for. There's a wicked thunderstorm due in day after tomorrow."

They reached the top of the hill and looked down. Lake Chelan lay there, bright blue, thicker than she had expected given its shape in pictures, but then she could only see one end. The other end of the lake wound all the way back into the hills, which rose up and up, and above the hills she could see the tops of the Cascades, brown and gray and sharp at the tips and then folding down into forested ridges that must—somewhere—enclose the other end of the lake. No wonder people wanted to live here. It was truly beautiful.

She signaled for a stop. After everyone dismounted from horse and robot, she and Matchiko broke out sandwiches they had made before breaking camp. It was the last of their fresh bread from Wenatchee.

Matchiko handed out the sandwiches.

As they ate, Lou gave simple directions. "Don't look threatening. We'll ride in front of the ecobots so no one thinks the robots are attacking."

This made Blessing smile. She smiled back at him. "Shuska will stay in the rear, and Daryl with her. Blessing will be with me. Matchiko stays on a bot. As soon as we see anybody we'll go slow. We want to make friends."

Matchiko shook her head in amusement. "You sound like you're telling us how to go meet the savages."

Lou laughed. "Maybe we should have brought some trade goods."

Shuska glared at her so hard that her cheeks reddened. "Sorry," Lou said. "We'll be nice to everyone."

"Until they're not nice to us," Shuska finished. It was a thing they used to say when they approached people who weren't supposed to be on the RiversEnd Ranch property. Appropriate. This was half of that crew, and the best half as far as she was concerned.

CHAPTER TWELVE

Aspen wriggled in Coryn's arms as she passed Jake's personal bot and pushed open the door to the conference room Jake had dubbed the Outside-N Foundation Support Office. She noticed someone had put up a sign that said just that, in formal lettering. It made her smile. Inside, Jake waited for her at the big conference table. He held his hand out, and she released Aspen on the top of the table. The dog bounded over multiple devices and piles of papers and into Jake's embrace. His tail brushed a vase of red and yellow flowers, and Coryn leaned across the table just in time to catch it. "Good afternoon!" she said, laughing.

Jake pushed Aspen's face away from his for a moment and said, "Your sister is on her way into Chelan."

She glanced at the wall screen, which showed tiny people on horses dwarfed by the two robots that followed them. She identified Lou and Blessing out in front. In back, the big Indian woman sat on a horse so big the two of them looked normal sized together. Shuska, who refused to trust her. For just a moment, she wished she was there with them, and with Blessing. Then Adam came in and greeted her with a slightly sultry smile, and she had to look away from him so he wouldn't see her blush.

Both men attracted and confused her. When she tried, she could still feel Blessing's kiss like a ghost against her lips.

Adam sat down and stared at the screen. "How old is that picture?"

"Twenty minutes." Jake pulled Aspen into his lap and scratched him behind the ears.

The image refreshed every thirty minutes. She sighed and sat down. "Any news from any other source?"

"No. Not about Chelan anyway. Or the nukes that woman told us about. I doubt they exist. But we did find a strange link." Jake looked up again, smiling softly when he saw Adam looked interested. "Money trails going into Chelan. Supply purchases ordered into Wenatchee or even Stehekin."

Ever since she had stopped being poor, everything came down to money. But why did it matter here? "We knew there were people in Chelan. They'd need to buy things, don't you think? Lou will."

Adam leaned in. "How much money?"

"More than a thousand people could possibly need. We haven't been able to trace it to its sources yet." Jake set Aspen down and drew a few papers closer to him. "We can see the smoke, but the fire is still hiding, waiting for us to find it."

Adam asked, "Do you know the source?"

"We're seeing loose linkages through a particular policy pod."

"Can you link it to bank accounts?" Coryn asked.

"Of course not." Jake focused on Coryn. "Money doesn't work that way anymore. The ultrarich seldom directly tie money to bank accounts. The great taking went with the great taxation, and that drove a lot of assets underground."

Adam drummed his fingers on the table, looking like a coiled spring.

Jake referred to the papers in front of him. "Even without direct account ownership or other easy threads to pull, the correlations are strong when you run analytics on the data. The probable fiscal link to the policy pod is only 33 percent. It's called the Modern Training Institute of all things—a name so benign I have trouble remembering it." He shook the papers to make the point.

Coryn had learned to stay interested in Jake's conversations even when she didn't quite follow them. So she asked, "What do they do?"

"Teach Outsiders how to get into cities. Mostly what the culture is like and how the technology works. It's of interest primarily because that's also a way to get dissidents in. But no one has been able to prove they're doing anything dark, and no one they tutored has broken any laws. Not even in the last uprisings." He frowned. "Yet." He glanced at Coryn. "Do you know what policy pods are?"

"They replaced the old think tanks after they were banned. They're designed to influence laws, so it's money that goes into politics. They have to be small, and they have to say where they get their money, though, right?"

"We kept even these illegal for a long time." Jake's jaw looked unusually tight, and his eyes seemed to be gazing into his past. "But there are always ways for the greedy few to act, and there's a lot of money out there."

She stared at the screen, willing the image to change. "So what does it mean that there's more money in Chelan?"

Adam glanced toward Jake for permission before he answered. "The money trail might lead us to whoever is financing the Returners." He frowned, hesitated. "I keep thinking that almost-perfect data analytics can trace anything, but that keeps insisting on being an illusion."

Jake laughed. "You can't analyze the real world."

Adam merely frowned.

"If this is about money, does that mean it's really a war against hackers again?" Coryn stretched, still watching the wall screen.

"We know there's enough money to run Seacouver for a year out there," Jake said. "It's underground."

"Like in caves?"

Jake and Adam both smiled, and Adam said, "Electronic caves."

The screen finally refreshed, drawing all three of them to stare at the wall screen. Lou's group had made good time for twenty minutes. The flat image made it hard to tell elevations, but it looked like they had almost reached the road that ran around the lake.

Adam walked near the image and stood in front of it.

She went over, careful not to block Jake's view.

"What do you see?" Adam asked.

He was close enough that she smelled his shampoo. Mint. "They're in the same formation. Everyone looks good."

"What else?"

She scanned the picture. "There are people over there. On the right." She gestured at the wall, zooming in. "Ten. And dogs. Three dogs. They're walking toward Lou and the others."

"Do you see guns?"

"I do. But Returners always have guns." She hesitated. "Don't they?"

Jake cleared his throat and she and Adam both turned to him. "First, no. Of course not. *Always* is a sloppy word. But they are often armed. Of note, your sister is rather well armed herself, and everyone in her group is a good shot. But a battle would be devastating."

Coryn squinted. "It looks like the same people who met them on the road."

Adam added, "Which means operation sneak-into-Chelan isn't working."

She bridled at his tone. He'd never been Outside! "Did you really think they could sneak in with ecobots?"

Adam stiffened. "I don't know."

"I bet there's no other ecobots in Chelan." She glanced back at her sister's image, now a minute old, at her likely pursuers, coming toward her unseen on the road. "What do you think will happen?"

Jake answered her. "Anything."

She pursed her lips. "Sometimes you're as exasperating as Blessing."

That made him laugh out loud. It always pleased her when she could draw a laugh from him. She really liked the dour old man, and he looked a little younger when he smiled or laughed.

Jake kept smiling. "Blessing spent a lot of time with me. Maybe I chose to be more like him."

More likely the other way around. What would Lou do? "I want to call and warn her."

Jake stared at the screen for a long time. Every breath drove Coryn a little crazy. They should be calling. Finally, he nodded. "They'll know. They should, anyway. A call could be a distraction, and it could be traced. You don't create leaders by babysitting them."

Coryn whispered, "But what if we don't warn her, and she gets shot?"

"That's a risk," Jake said. "But I think she'll do okay."

Coryn leaned back in her chair, staring at the screen. She wanted to smell the hills, to feel the unfiltered sun on her face. She wanted the danger.

Blessing often said he expected to die every day. That, he had told her, was why he was still alive.

CHAPTER THIRTEEN

Lou sat easily on Mouse, Blessing riding on one side of her and Daryl on the other. They led the group, the robots behind them in a line, with Matchiko on the first one and Day on the second, the two spare horses tied to that bot with a long line and tended by Shuska.

The road was marred by potholes so deep that the horses had to weave to avoid them, and the sides of the road cracked and crumbled away so that it was no more than a lane wide in a few places. It felt more dangerous than the rocky trail they'd just come down. Above them, the sky was blue and clear, the edges of the mountains and hills sharp against the sky and almost as sharp in their reflections on the lake.

It was the kind of morning when even though Lou was surrounded by the damage that made the world break, it felt as if they might be able to fix it.

She could barely wait to set up house, to have a base to work from and daily rosters of work to do. She hadn't let herself look forward to that until now, but the logistics of creating a new headquarters were starting to run in the background of her brain. She had never created a home before, and when she was a child, she'd never had one. RiversEnd Ranch had felt like home, like they were all working together. That was where she had first met Matchiko and Shuska and Daryl, and where they had all been happy. Once. She yearned to create something close to that.

They rode past what had been estates with vineyards and wine-tasting rooms. These had surely once been well-tended parts of sophisticated gardens. Years before the great taking, even the rich had stopped trying for grass lawns.

They passed a car rusted into the earth, partly obscured by tall ornamental grasses and butterfly weed in full yellow bloom. Her stomach twisted in a brief flash of anger. So much toxic junk just left behind. Greed had made the world into a place that needed Wilders instead of a wild place. Blessing must feel the same, since he said, "Such wasted opulence," just loud enough for Lou to hear.

"That's an unusually big word."

His only response was to look serious.

"There's someone close by," Daryl said, for no reason that she could see.

Blessing stood a little in his stirrups, alert.

Lou shook her right wrist to loosen it up in case she needed her weapon. She glanced up at Matchiko, who rode above and behind them, seated in a lotus position on top and near the front of the ecobot. She had dressed in blue this morning, just slightly brighter than the sky, and she reminded Lou of a picture she'd seen of a woman riding an elephant.

Lou gave a fist shake to indicate possible danger, and waited for Matchiko's nod before she turned around again just in time to see Daryl raise his rifle.

A woman strode out into the road in front of them, stopping with her legs a little apart and her hands at her side. Confident. She wore old jeans and a flowing top that had once been white, and which was still white enough to contrast with her dark hair and flint-colored eyes. Latina. A beautiful Latina, tall. Her hair had been braided away from her face, but fell down her back freely, blowing behind her in a soft, warm wind.

Daryl watched the place she had come from. Blessing glanced toward the other side of the road, a strip of long bank leading to the lake, the water level ten feet below the footings of a dock that had almost crumbled to dust. He pulled his gray back a little.

That left her to ride Mouse toward the woman, stopping about ten feet away. "Hello, I'm Lou."

She answered in a raspy and deep voice that carried well, a performer's voice that had been overused. "I might be able to save you. Perhaps."

Lou blinked at her. "From?"

"Yourself, and your foolish courage. You are coming into a dangerous town, and since you came over the hills, I suspect you know that. Will you accept advice, woman to woman?"

Lou considered this while assessing the stranger. She had the muscle and wiry strength to hold her own in a fight. She appeared to carry nothing on her, no purse, no weapons, not even a coat with pockets. As far as Lou could tell, she was alone.

What desperation or courage had caused her to step into the street in front of them? They could kill her easily. The woman waited patiently.

The silence had gone on long enough. Lou asked, "Do you want to talk now?"

"No. After I save you."

Daryl narrowed his eyes at her. "Save us from what?"

Blessing asked a different question. "You found us. Were you looking for us? Did you know we were here?"

The woman smiled and chose to answer Blessing. "You were the talk of the town last night. There were bets about whether or not you would try the new wall. Many thought you would give up. But I did not think so. It takes power to command two ecobots, and capability to keep and care for horses." She looked grave. "There is little time. I want to get you through town before there are more people arrayed against you."

Lou had developed a good ear for lies. Whoever this woman was, she believed her own story. Perhaps she could help them find the place that Coryn had chosen for them, and maybe even help them tell if it was a good choice. "Do you want to come with us?"

The woman nodded.

"Do you have a name?"

"I'm Valeria."

Lou held out a hand. "Lou."

"Lou Williams, the protector of wolves and the scourge of Returners."

It shook her a little that someone out here knew of her. "People have called me that."

"After the foolish men came back to speed up building their foolish little wall, they talked of who they met. I thought it was you. You're rumored to travel with an Indian and Chinawoman."

Lou winced at her word choices. "I travel with friends."

Valeria's smile lit her whole face. "I'm happy to hear that."

Lou glanced from Daryl to Blessing, giving them light nods to communicate her intent. When Blessing smiled and Daryl said his usual nothing but offered no contradiction, she turned back to Valeria and pointed at the ecobot behind her. "Would you like to ride?"

"I would." She didn't approach the bot though, but came up beside Mouse and extended a hand. Up close, Lou noted that she was older than she looked, with nests of thin wrinkles around her eyes and lips. Not Julianna's age; maybe sixty or so. But like Julianna, she moved like someone younger. She looked utterly confident, not pleading for a ride, not demanding one. The hand she extended bore the scars and calluses of someone who had worked on a farm.

Lou hesitated. She would be vulnerable with Valeria behind her. What if she had a knife?

"I won't hurt you," Valeria said.

Lou pulled her foot free of the stirrup and extended her hand, and Valeria nearly flowed up, settling behind the saddle. She sat calmly on Mouse's broad back, as if she were quite familiar with horses.

As they started off, she moved easily against Lou, rocking appropriately with Mouse's gait.

In spite of Daryl's usual sixth sense for problems and Matchiko's high perch, Mouse was the first to spot trouble. Her ears swiveled forward and she pranced and tossed her head ever so slightly. A slight sheen of sweat appeared on her arched golden neck.

"Hold on," Lou whispered to Valeria.

"No." Valeria slid off Mouse's rump, a movement as soft and silent as possible. She stepped aside immediately even though Mouse showed no inclination to kick her.

Lou slowed Mouse and let Valeria move around them to the front.

Matchiko called down, "Strangers!" loud enough that the strangers undoubtedly heard her.

Lou considered this wise. It had never worked out well when armed intruders startled them on RiversEnd Ranch.

Lou assessed the terrain. Just ahead of them, the road bent to the left. She couldn't see or hear whatever had spooked Mouse, but horses were prey animals, and good at sensing danger. She stopped, signaling the others to stop.

Shuska rode up from the back, so that everyone on horseback was in front. She glanced at Valeria, and then at Lou.

Lou merely shrugged.

Shuska raised an eyebrow, but offered a grim smile to signal grudging acquiescence to the stranger in their midst.

Two men on foot rounded a bend in the road, heading toward them, rifles already raised. Another two followed, flanked by beautiful dogs that walked stiffly right beside them, obviously under their control.

The first men noticed Valeria and stopped.

She kept going, walking up close to them. It was quite a contrast. The men were big. The dogs were big. Valeria was slight.

They looked like they wanted to back up, maybe turn around. They didn't, but as others came around the corner they also stopped. The moment was a quiet one, a small and still one, pregnant with the possibility of argument or even of gunfire.

Valeria stopped in front of one of the men, and Lou kept Mouse moving forward very slowly, hoping to overhear the conversation. Now that they were this close, she could tell that this was one of the men who had tried to stop them on the way up, the one who had claimed the town was sick and that they should stay away.

Once again, Valeria's voice carried. "John Smith! I know you must have been doing like I was, coming out to greet these people and lead them into town. They can surely help us, since there is so much restoration work we might want done."

John Smith—surely a made-up name—John Smith stood there with an insincere smile, his face white.

They were afraid of this woman. It didn't make any sense, but it was true.

Valeria's voice sounded like steel wrapped in cheerfulness. "They're here because we need them. They're here to help. I will work with them, and if you want the things I provide, you will let us through."

His reply was harder for Lou to hear, but she bent forward over Mouse's neck and that helped a little. His voice was low, resentful. "You never worked for anyone else in your life."

"I said with," she replied. "Not for. They're going to be good for us, make some balance. Besides, I'm doing this for you."

He stiffened. He and Valeria were of an age, the primary obvious differences being race and gender. Otherwise, both looked entirely sure of themselves and sounded accustomed to giving orders.

His expression, slightly belligerent and clearly doubtful, challenged Valeria.

Valeria let a few moments of silence slide between them before she said, "It's for the best. They have power. You can see that by the bots and the horses. We can use that. It will be better to let them in. If you stop them, there might be more power sent, and more, until it's more weight than Chelan can bear."

These weren't words to inspire Lou to trust Valeria. But they served an immediate goal, so Lou fumed quietly. When she glanced back at Shuska, she noticed her jaw was clenched and her eyes narrow.

John didn't respond directly to Valeria but stalked right past her as if he were as furious with her as Shuska was. He went right up to Daryl and addressed him. "You may come through here. You may be here. But know that you will be expected to follow the rules."

Lou was tempted to ask what the rules were. Her fist tightened on her reins and she held her silence.

Daryl had never been a man of many words. "Thanks for the warm welcome," he replied in a completely deadpan voice, as if all of the subtext had gone right past him. He urged his horse forward, and she followed, then Blessing. She didn't look back, but she heard the low rumble of the ecobots.

Given that they were on horses and robots, they passed right through the standing men so fast that Lou wondered if the word that they were being allowed in would reach the back of the line of men and dogs before they did.

The people they passed stood eerily still, watching them. Lou watched back, trying to memorize every face.

She had expected them all to be men, but near the end of the line she spotted a tall woman with broad shoulders, short blond hair, and a black dog. Her eyes were as hard as the men's. Lou wondered about her story. Men who only recognized white men as worthy to talk to were not the type she expected to include a woman in a party planning a battle.

Well, Matchiko was certainly taking pictures. She would study them all if they got settled and had time. These would be faces to know.

About a hundred yards past the sullen Returners, Lou started shaking. These people would have attacked despite the ecobots. She and the others would probably have won—but surely not without cost. She had lost friends out here before; she couldn't imagine losing anyone with her now.

Valeria caught up with them and jogged beside Mouse, looking up at Lou expectantly.

Lou let her jog alongside for a few minutes, and just as her breath was starting to rattle, Lou asked, "Do you know what we came here to do?"

"The first thing you came to do was get through town. I just made that possible."

"We might have found another way."

"Not without fighting, maybe killing."

"That could be true."

"There's no easy way to get in here unless you're called in." Valeria paused, caught her breath. "And we still need to have that talk."

If she didn't let her up soon, the woman was going to fall behind. Lou relented and extended her hand, again.

Valeria needed more help this time, but she was soon mounted and they neared town.

"I didn't offer you a job, you know," Lou said without looking over her shoulder.

"You might find you need me."

Lou forced herself not to answer. Patience.

Valeria began to hum, and then to sing softly in Spanish. She sounded fabulous, her singing voice high and clear, utterly devoid of the roughness that edged her speaking voice. Her singing added to Lou's frustration. Singing was something she had always wanted to do, but she had never been good at it. Sometimes she sang around campfires, drunk.

Shuska trailed behind again, Daryl with her, but Blessing rode beside them and smiled broadly at Lou as if he knew how conflicted she was about Valeria. Well, she could talk to him later. "Do you know where we turn?" she asked him.

"Bradley. And then on Union Valley. But we have to get around the bottom end of the lake first."

Valeria leaned in toward her. "Good choice. I think I know where you're going."

Blessing smiled at Valeria. "Why is it good?"

"There's water there."

"A well?" Lou asked.

"Yes."

"Is the house any good?"

"It hasn't fallen down. You'll have to repair the barns."

"It has more than one barn?"

Valeria's laugh was bright. "Three."

What had her little sister done? "How big is this place?"

"You'll see." Valeria fell quiet.

Near the eastern end of the long lake, they passed two women and a young girl wearing patched coats. They turned away from the ecobots, rushing down a side street, the girl twisting her head behind her to see while she was rushed away. A group of three young men in boots and hats stopped in a doorway and watched them go by, looking like they were trying not to be curious or afraid but also looking like they were both. An emaciated dog crossed the street in front of them, intent on some clear goal.

The streets were emptier that Lou expected. She spoke softly to Valeria. "Are people hiding from us?"

"Yes."

Old hotels hunched along the side of the lake, mostly intact but with an abandoned look to them. An overgrown park threaded through the hotels on one side and buffered a small neighborhood of houses from the lake on the other, complete with broken children's swing sets and layers of graffiti on every metal surface. Further along, they passed a rather large parking garage, which Coryn had told her might house people who didn't want to be seen by airplanes or drones. Inside, she spotted dimmed lights and hanging sheets, and the silhouettes of people moving slowly and quietly.

Lou squinted at the garage, and Valeria leaned in. "Don't look too close. You'd do better to look ahead of you."

Lou obeyed, and whether it was from anything real or merely Valeria's warning, her skin crawled with the regard of unknown watchers.

They passed through without any hindrance.

Ahead of them, a row of small shops appeared to be in pretty good shape, and a few awnings even looked fairly new, bright red with no appreciable damage from sun or storms. Lou wanted to look closer, but they didn't go that way, turning left to follow the lake. Shortly after, they turned right on Bradley Street.

They wound up and up, getting as high above the lake as they had been when they first saw it, the roads passable even though they had to skirt a few large potholes and one whole section that had washed out. A trail had already formed around it, a good detour that put them back on the road in a few hundred feet.

"There," Valeria said, pointing at a nondescript driveway.

They turned in and Lou stopped in the drive, assessing.

A line of half-dead trees lined a long driveway. On the far side of the trees, a vineyard had withered to a series of dead sticks clinging to metal lines.

The fences looked like they were in decent condition, although they would all have to be checked.

She nearly jumped when Valeria whispered in her ear. "It was beautiful once."

"How do you know?"

"There are pictures in the library."

Lou twisted far enough around to get a glimpse of Valeria's face. "Chelan still has a library?"

"No. But we saved some of the books."

How had Coryn picked *this* place?

Matchiko interrupted the conversation with a good-natured call down to them. "You're blocking the road!"

Lou laughed and pressed her legs tight against Mouse's sides, asking her to move forward. She broke into a short trot and Daryl and Blessing let their horses have some head as well. Then Mouse sped up; the three of them cantered up the dry driveway, driving clouds of dust up toward the ecobots.

The main house looked big enough for the headquarters Lou imagined in her head. They could fit staff in with room to spare. Three barns spread across the property. Part of the roof had fallen into the biggest barn. Another barn that was almost as big had slumped on one side. The third looked like it was still maintained. It was small, but it might do for the horses they had so far. She urged Mouse toward the barn, waiting to see if Valeria would complain. She didn't.

Between them and the barn, a tall wooden fence looked big enough to hold a few of the horses. She rode toward it and found that, mounted, she was just tall enough to peer over the edge. Inside, spent pea vines and nearly spent beans with yellowing leaves filled raised beds. Pumpkins poked out from underneath wide leaves in another bed, some pulled up from the dirt and set, still attached to vine, on the flat wooden benches that ringed the beds, as if they had been set to finish ripening. The bright reds of at least three different kinds of tomatoes gleamed in the late afternoon sun.

Lou stiffened. She whispered through clenched teeth. "You live here, don't you?"

Valeria didn't answer, but Lou felt her nod.

Valeria wasn't making any sense. "So then why didn't you want them to stop us on the road? Why would you want us to take over your house?"

"We need protection."

Lou shivered. "We?"

CHAPTER FOURTEEN

Lou struggled not to show her dismay at the fact that her new headquarters was already occupied. Anger wouldn't help anything. She stayed silent on Mouse until they got to the barn, the problematical Valeria right behind her, and gestured for the others to come close. As soon as she knew they could all see her, she extended her arms overhead and opened her hands and stretched her fingers wide and then closed them before bringing them down in the signal for *possible danger*.

Matchiko stood up on the ecobot, which would give her a better view, and Day gestured for her to get down as he peered around, trying to find the danger.

Matchiko flattened herself.

Maybe she was overreacting.

If only there had been time to learn more about their claim in this place. Chelan wasn't sanctioned. Property could not be owned, not by Valeria or by the foundation. Rights to use *could* be vested in an NGO, and they had a permit. But having a right and exercising it might not be the same thing.

Valeria hadn't stabbed her on the way in, but Lou wasn't ready to trust her.

She turned. "Please get down."

Valeria slid down the side of Mouse this time, a less showy move than when she had slid off his rump. She turned and looked at the entire circle of people, gazing up at each one for a moment, gathering attention, turning the rocky soil under into a stage. "Perhaps," she said, "I should introduce myself."

Instinct warned Lou not to let Valeria dominate the conversation. She dismounted, but gestured for her team to stay where they were. "How did you know we were coming? Tell me again."

Valeria's smile was confident and even a little elfin. "I am a poet and a singer. I often provide entertainment in bars. And I'm *very* good."

What did that have to do with anything? "How did you know we were coming here? Not to Chelan, but to this place?"

Valeria turned and spread her hands wide, as if taking in the land around them. "You live where you can out here. Only a few places still have working well pumps. We can't get parts any more, not easily. So our home was a likely choice. Besides, when—." She hesitated "When the black man gave you directions I knew you were coming here. Everything else on this road is too small or has no water."

"His name is Blessing."

"Okay. Blessing."

Valeria didn't look at all contrite, but then why would she? Lou was taking over her home, not the other way around.

Lou felt a need to stay in front of the conversation, to be the interrogator. "You and who lives here?"

Valeria tipped her chin up, smiled. "I have sons. Foundations have paying jobs. We will work for you."

Lou stiffened at the presumption in her statement. "How many sons?"

"Five."

Five! They already had five of the people they could hire. At least if Blessing and Day stayed. She was under no illusion about what they'd do if Julianna called them back. The new foundation would need specialties that it didn't have, and that Valeria almost surely didn't have either.

Valeria wasn't done yet. "And daughters. Two. And three grandchildren."

Clearly this place had a *lot* of water and a small army to defend it. Her thoughts raced. What were the chances there was someplace else that was this well-suited to them? Or would that offend Valeria, who clearly had enough power to influence the Returners. They'd need that.

Could she forge a deal here? "I can only hire a few people. How big is the house?"

"Big enough. I will show you." Valeria bowed ever so slightly, the bow of one leader to another.

Lou gritted her teeth. She glanced at her team, trying to sense their mood. No one except Blessing gave away any emotion at all, and he appeared to be amused. Damn him.

She turned back to Valeria, trying to keep her inner doubts from her face. "Gather your family and bring them all to the front of the house, outside. We'll be along in a moment and we'll meet them."

It was an order, and at first she though Valeria wouldn't take it. But then she said, "We'd be happy to meet you. You'll find my family quite fabulous." With that, Valeria walked away—head up, in full control. Whatever else she might be, she was impressive.

Was she friend or foe?

Lou gestured for her people to gather around.

Shuska dismounted, walking far more quietly than anyone would expect such a big woman could move. Daryl was already off his horse. He and Shuska approached the old barn together, neither of them saying a word. Daryl held his handgun ready at his side.

Shuska opened the barn door with a jerk, stepped back with the door, and stayed out of the opening. Daryl hugged the other side of the door.

It was too dark to see inside.

Shuska pulled a light out of her pocket and shone it through the dark opening. Nothing. She called out, "Hello?"

A donkey brayed.

Shuska smiled and went in. The light disappeared, and then a few moments later Shuska's head poked out of an upstairs window. "Clear. One old donkey, two pigs, and two goats."

"Thanks," Lou called up to her.

Shuska came back out and closed the barn door. "I think the pigs are for food, but the others look like pets. The goats are wethers."

They had enough resources to keep pets? Lou clapped her hands for attention. "I'm going to want to hear what you all think. But I'll say a little first."

Shuska crossed her arms, Daryl stepped closer in to them all, Blessing fidgeted, and Day nodded. Matchiko had gone to total stillness, her features giving away nothing. "Go on."

"We expected one thing and got another. I'm guessing this won't be the last time that happens. We don't want to come in fighting the locals. That woman doesn't like the Returners and neither do we. We'll start from there." She glanced at their faces. No arguments appeared there; they were waiting.

She wasn't used to being in charge yet, but she was, and she would keep going. "I can't tell if there are enough resources for all these people and for us. Maybe there are." She looked toward the big house. "We may need to assert our right to be here."

She shifted her gaze to Blessing, her closest tie out here to Julianna and Jake, and thus to funding and authority.

His grin surfaced. "We might have to fight for it."

All the more reason to negotiate. "So let's hear from all of you," Lou asked. "You first, Blessing. What do you think?"

While he looked more thoughtful than usual, his answer wasn't very helpful. "We can do anything."

Shuska shook her head. "We're outnumbered. I don't think that's good."

"We need to know more." Daryl. Taciturn—and correct—as usual.

Matchiko said, "Kindness is better than unkindness."

Such a Matchiko answer. It forced a smile to Lou's lips.

Day nodded as if he agreed with all of their conflicting views, but then he answered practically. "Daryl's right. We need to go up there and learn more. But we shouldn't leave the horses alone."

"I supposed we can post a guard," Lou replied. "Let's leave the ecobots and two of you here to watch the horses. Daryl and Blessing?"

Blessing looked disappointed. But if she could only take one of the two, she wanted Day. If they needed to fight, he was better than all of them, better even than Shuska. She told Blessing, "I need two good hands to watch the horses. Surely they're valuable out here."

His voice had a slightly bitter edge, very unlike him. "For those who can afford to feed them."

"Anyone can eat them," she snapped.

Blessing dismounted and started clipping leads onto bridles so the horses could be tied to posts, the sharp jerky motions of his hands suggesting anger.

Matchiko said, "The animals will need water."

"There's a small trough in the barn," Shuska told Blessing. "And I saw a hose leading outside, so look around back."

Daryl looked relieved to be left behind. He started whistling low under his breath, a thing he often did to soothe animals. Perhaps he was trying to soothe Blessing, too.

Lou gathered the others and they started off on foot toward the big house. A wide front porch had tables and chairs on it, and even little umbrellas. They'd be invisible from the sky since the top floor had wide empty decks or awnings most of the way around it.

She approved.

The windows were either glass or boarded, the yellow paint fresh. The steeply sloped roof and the grounds looked pristine. All natural, with some of the plants already dried for fall and others wearing yellowing leaves or tinged with red. Someone who loved gardens tended them, keeping plants cut back and cared for, deadheading flowers, and sweeping the walks.

Three men, a woman, and a child waited for Lou's party on the driveway. A woman carrying a small child was just coming out of the door.

Lou stopped them at the edge of the lawn and they watched the house disgorge people. It took a long time. Lou counted to herself. Fifteen. Valeria came out last.

She should have asked how many of the children were married.

They all looked healthy and like they were accustomed to work. Most of the people shared Valeria's Spanish features and coloring. One of the women was almost as dark as Blessing, and almost as beautiful as Blessing as well. One white man stood out both for his pale skin and for being taller than most of the others. He was also quite thin. One little girl looked frightened, the other was old enough to feign boredom. Two of the men looked defiant, but most of the others just looked confused or slightly worried. They spoke in hushed tones. One little boy, who might have been all of five, perched on his father's shoulders and pointed toward the small barn and proclaimed, "Robot!"

The father's quick hushed reply reached Lou's ears. "They're dangerous. Don't go near them."

Valeria introduced them all, carefully stating their skills.

Lou tried to remember all of the names, but some of them ran together, the Hispanic names full of vowels.

Lou introduced the people who were with her. She even named the horses, which delighted the children.

Everything felt polite and only a little strained, as if everyone— literally all of them—waited for some answer. Surely, they wanted to keep their home. She sensed pride in them, and trepidation.

Valeria, Lou decided, had raised her children to be a lot like her.

She realized they had been standing for almost half an hour and that the sun was already throwing long shadows. It had to be close to dinnertime. She asked Valeria, "Is there a room big enough for everyone to sit in?"

Valeria laughed. "No. Well, uncomfortably. Perhaps you and I can talk?"

Lou shook her head. "I have advisors to include in this conversation."

Valeria spoke with no hesitation. "I would like my daughter and granddaughter along."

Valeria's oldest son, Felipe, took Day onto the front porch, sitting where they could be seen while they looked outward like guard dogs.

Valeria led Lou, Matchiko, and Shuska to the main living room. Valeria included a daughter named Astrid with dark hair that flowed past her waist in a thick braid, and Astrid's daughter, Alondra. The girl was somewhere between ten and twelve, just prepubescent, with big dark eyes, a wide mouth, and a noticeably serious demeanor.

The room looked comfortable, with couches and chairs in front of an outsized fireplace. Shuska stood. Lou and Valeria took two dark blue stuffed chairs, and the other three occupied one of two couches. Large windows overlooked the driveway and gardens outside. The light had taken on the soft gold of pre-dusk, which made Lou itch to start talking. She was tired. Her crew was tired. They needed to know where they were going to sleep soon. She opened with a compliment. "The gardens are beautiful."

"Astrid keeps them. She studied gardening in Spokane Metro, and earned a Master Gardener's certificate." Valeria's voice was full of glowing parentage. "She also oversees the vegetables and makes sure that we all have enough to eat."

"I'd like to see the gardens." She herself was thinking that someone who knew plants might be useful. So, of course, would food.

Valeria didn't react, but Astrid's eyes widened. The vegetables mattered to them.

As Lou chose to move into the business of the meeting, she understood why Valeria had included Alondra. She found herself speaking very carefully, trying not to upset the girl. "We have a permit from the federal government."

"A permit for what?" Alondra asked from her perch on Astrid's knee.

"To help the wild plants and animals in the area, to help them survive in spite of us. It's good work."

Alondra smiled, and said, "I would like to be a Wilder someday."

Maybe that was another reason Valeria had included her. If this was what her grandchildren thought of Wilders, the family must be supporters.

Astrid looked piqued, but said nothing more.

Lou turned her attention to Valeria. "We can bring some work to you and your family. Maybe two positions, or at the most three."

Valeria nodded. "I believe that there might be other things you are interested in as well. Such as knowing about some of the people in town who may not agree with the Wilder policy position."

A strange phrase to come from Valeria's mouth. *Policy position.* She did intend to spy on the Returners, but that was a secret she wasn't ready to share with this woman. Not yet. "We really are only interested in doing our job."

Astrid spoke quietly. "Do you need killer robots to help the environment?"

Julianna and her damned ecobots. "They are also builders and planters. Here, we may use them to destroy." She smiled, realizing that destroy wasn't the right word after it escaped her mouth. "It looks like it's past time for the old vineyards to be taken down."

Surprisingly, Astrid laughed. It made her look younger. "I might like to see that. We've been planning to get that done, but there is little time."

Matchiko spoke from behind Lou. "What occupies your time—so many of you? Do you mind sharing?"

Valeria smiled. "We run a store in town, and on Friday and Saturday night we run a bar, and both of those are much work."

Astrid's chin lifted. She sounded defensive. "We grow many vegetables, and hay for winter feed."

"We weed," Alondra added, "and chase off the bunnies."

Lou smiled at the girl's earnestness.

Matchiko changed the subject. "Are there many stores in town? We didn't get to see."

Valeria shifted in her seat. "Four or five. Ours is the only one with fresh local foods, and we do some traveling back and forth to other places to acquires staples."

Lou silently thanked Matchiko for the excellent questions. She once again felt the pressure of the failing light. Hopefully Blessing and Daryl were feeding the horses. "We'd love to talk more about all of this in the morning, but, for now, you know why we are here and now we know some of what you are doing here. Is it possible to have a tour before the sun sets?"

Valeria looked at Astrid. "Will you take them?"

"Yes," Astrid said, her voice flat.

Alondra stood and looked beseechingly at Valeria, who smiled and nodded. "You may go."

Lou stood and extended her right hand to Valeria. "Thank you."

Valeria took the offered hand, her handshake strong and warm. "You're welcome."

No return *thank you*. This was, perhaps, going to be interesting.

She was no closer to deciding how to set up a headquarters in an already-occupied stronghold than she had been before. But she would figure something out.

CHAPTER FIFTEEN

Outside, Valeria stepped gracefully close to Lou and gave her a quick, formal hug, leaving a faint scent of lavender hovering in the air where she had been. "I'm leaving you in good hands." She nodded toward Astrid and Alondra, who stood silently and very formally as well.

The sun had almost touched the high mountain peaks to the east. The lake and the sky had become the identical shade of blue, as if you could trade the two of them and stand on the sky and look up at the lake.

Valeria walked off with the confident sashay of a far younger woman. Lou pursed her lips, feeling outdone.

Astrid offered a small guarded smile and started along the side of the house at a quick walk. Lou and the others followed. They strung out into a line, with Alondra in the back position, behind Shuska, watching them all so intently that when Lou looked back she felt as if the child scorched her with her gaze.

She seemed full of the same fey focus and charisma as her grandmother.

The main house was large enough that it took some time to walk around it. About halfway along, they went through a gate and into a large garden enclosed in tall deer-fence and covered with netting to keep birds out. They found row on row of raised beds, most of them full of ripe fall vegetables. Lou leaned over to Shuska, "Isn't this at least an acre?"

"A little more."

The tall black woman, Tembi, and her husband, Valeria's youngest son, Angel, bent over the beds. Tembi snipped cucumbers free of bushes, and Angel shook dirt from fist-sized potatoes. They piled the vegetables into faded red and yellow crates.

The garden smelled of damp dirt and mint, of lavender and thyme.

Were they working this late in protest or to impress her?

Lou leaned over to Matchiko and whispered, "I think this is why the town allows them to remain here. The Returners need someone to grow their food."

Matchiko elbowed her gently, and she turned around to see Alondra watching her, perhaps close enough to hear. Lou turned back to Astrid and listened carefully as she described the work of the farm. "We use soaker hoses and raised beds to save water, and the nasturtiums planted in the beds are a natural pesticide. They're edible, too."

Valeria's other daughter, Sofia, came out and began harvesting lettuce and bright orange nasturtium flowers, cucumbers, and garlic. She placed these in a single basket, and Lou assumed this would be for the evening meal. She was the smallest of the grown women, thin and short and long-armed, with tattoos and short hair. Astrid, and even Alondra, looked like they might have been on this farm a hundred years ago, but Sofia looked like a recent refugee from a city.

Shuska moved deliberately, passing all the beds, looking carefully. A few times she bent down and felt the soil or fingered a leaf. The look on her face was somber, perhaps even sad.

Sofia watched Shuska's inspection, eyes wide. Did a hint of anger flicker in that stare? When she noticed Lou watching, she looked down.

A woman sang from inside the house, and chickens clucked and called from somewhere nearby. *Chickens? Eggs?*

Astrid stopped at the end of the vegetable bins. "We grow almost everything: peas and snap peas, pole beans and runner beans and bush beans, green and red leaf lettuce, early girl tomatoes—"

Lou began to lose track of the details, drowning instead in the possibilities, the variety, and the challenge of all this. The permit allowed the foundation to grow food for themselves, but not to sell it. That was akin to farming and needed a permit that would only be granted inside of a sanctioned boundary. Those bins of cucumbers and potatoes weren't all destined for the dinner table here.

She couldn't just kick them off. She had known it from the moment Valeria uttered the word "we," but she had been slow to make herself accept that reality.

She would have all of these people to help protect.

Valeria had promised they would help protect her as well, and her people. Perhaps some would become her people. But that complicated things. Didn't it?

She couldn't allow Valeria to tell her what to do.

Astrid finished her list. Alondra stuck close to Lou, watching her face closely. She picked a single ripe cherry tomato and held it out, her palm open as if she were feeding a horse.

Lou plucked the fruit from the girl's hand and bit into it, smiling as the warm juices trickled through her teeth and filled her mouth.

"Do you like it?" the girl asked.

"Very much."

Alondra whispered, "You won't destroy the garden, will you?"

Lou smiled at her. "It will be all right. Somehow."

Alondra nodded as if she understood all of the complexities.

On the other side of the fence lay another enclosure, this one full of chickens. Hundreds of chickens. Red ones, white ones, chickens with barred patterns on their broad chests, and smaller chickens with bare necks and funny rings of feathers right under their heads.

Piles of chicken feed lay behind fine screens inside a covered patio, and piles of green and white chicken manure sat near the door ready to remove with a small army of scratched green and gray wheelbarrows.

Coops lined two of the interior fence lines, although at the moment the chickens were mostly in the yard between the coops.

Lou wandered close enough to hear Astrid explaining that the chickens would put themselves to bed at dark, and that this whole area was guarded enough with tight fencing that none had been taken from here except three that a neighbor stole once. Astrid explained, "We slaughter about two thirds of them every fall and start over with new chicks in the spring."

It all looked quite neat—unexpectedly neat—and just like the kind of operation that the Returners always claimed they should be able to create when they argued that open-land farming should be legal again. This little scrap of land could be a picture postcard for the way the American West was before the damage, before climate change, before the great taking.

How could she leave it intact without being a hypocrite? Her chest tightened with worry and a bit of dismay.

The tour didn't go near the barns, but they did pass another out-building with bunks in it. Two men and a woman cleaned walls with brushes they dipped over and over in soapy water. Ignacio, Ana, and she'd forgotten the other's name. Something else that ended in that *o* sound. Three of Valeria's boys had names like that; something-o. She was surprised she'd remembered Ignacio.

How could she ever remember all of their names?

She'd had a simple vision of riding into a damaged but empty place with working water, maybe fixing a few walls or something, or even getting the ecobots to do the hard work while they set about the business of locating the local wolves. She turned to Alondra. "Do you ever hear wolves?"

Alondra's eyes widened and she hesitated, then spoke softly while not looking at Lou. "We hear coyotes almost every night. They hunt in town and even out here. One night they were right under my window and something screamed."

"Was that scary?"

Alondra shrugged. "Animals need to eat. They are not as scary as people."

"Do I scare you?" Lou asked her.

Alondra was quiet for a long time before she mumbled, "No," in a manner that Lou interpreted to mean quite the opposite. Was it the ecobots, the power Lou had to take their house, the weapons they all carried, or the fact that they might draw in enemies from town, like John Smith or whoever else was here? What did this girl understand? She was the oldest child here, her body about to bloom into a woman's but still long-legged and coltish. Lou had a nagging feeling that she was underestimating her.

Had the tomato been a peace offering?

The pale red glow in the western sky had faded to gray by the time they returned to the house. Light-blocking shades made it look empty from the outside, but inside light spilled through every room. Alondra left her side to help her two younger cousins set a large table in a formal dining room on the opposite side of the house from the room they'd held the meeting in. The children were at best half of Alondra's age, a boy and a little girl. The girl might be even younger. She could barely reach the table to tip spoons onto it.

Lou glimpsed a door that led into a kitchen, a big one that might have originally been designed for parties.

She stopped Astrid as the other woman strode by on her way to the kitchen. "We'd like to see the rest of the house."

Astrid's lips thinned, but she nodded as if compelled to politeness. "Of course."

Lou had the sense that Astrid couldn't wait to get away from her. She wanted to reach out to her like she had to Alondra and tell her that everything would be okay, but she probably shouldn't have even said that to the girl. It might very well be a lie.

Astrid pointed down the hall. "Should we start with the library?"

Lou was about to say no when she noticed the look in Matchiko's eyes. "Sure."

The library could hold more people than the sitting room, except that shelves covered every wall and some even stuck out into the middle of the room. Based on a quick estimation, there must be thousands of physical books here. What a strange thing to find anywhere, much less way out here. In the center of the room, tables and chairs and armchairs provided places to work or to sit.

Matchiko, who loved books, started reading spines. Lou plucked at her shoulder. They wouldn't be sleeping in here. "Later. We'll come back later."

Matchiko kept walking, staring at all of the bookcases, although she did speed up. As she finished her circuit of the room, she asked, "This was the city library?"

Astrid nodded.

Matchiko narrowed her eyes. "Can people from town come use it?"

"If they want to."

Lou heard the unlikeliness of *that* in Astrid's voice. "All right. What else is down here?"

"There's an office that's been turned into a bedroom, a really big pantry, and some storage. Do you want to see them?"

Lou nodded, and they followed Astrid on a tour of a messy ex-office with two beds and shelves full of supplies from ragged green army blankets to cases of dish soap. The pantry was the most impressive food storage she'd ever seen, although over half the shelves were empty. The top shelves were lined with wine bottles.

Astrid took her up a wide staircase. It wasn't a decorative stair, merely wide in a functional way, as if there was a need to drag couches up it or walk up and down two abreast. At the top of the stair, they had to turn right or left. Astrid took them down the left hallway and stopped in front of two doors, one on the right and one on the left. "There are two bedroom suites on either side of the house—each has a bedroom, a bathroom, some storage, and a small office."

She hesitated, but before Lou asked she swung one doorway open. "Mathew, Alondra, and I share this room. You might remember Mathew is my husband."

"He's the tall white man?"

"Yes."

That explained Alondra's long legs. The room was neat, the furniture homemade and sturdy, and flowered curtains hung in front of the two windows. Lou only went in far enough to count beds. Two. One was a twin, presumably Alondra's. A small stuffed horse rested on the pillow, brown with a black mane and tail.

Astrid continued, "Angel, Tembi, and Mary are in the one across the hall from us." She pointed. "Mary is the littlest. On the other side, Sofia has one room and Ignacio and Ana another. We keep all of the children up here on the second floor where it's safer."

Lou sensed a touch of the defensive in Astrid's posture and voice. She decided to ignore it. "Isn't Valeria's oldest son Felipe? Isn't he married?"

"Yes. He and his family have one of the master suites, and the other one is Valeria's."

"May I see one of the suites?"

Astrid gave her a look that bordered on resentment. "I'll show you Valeria's."

Tall windows would spill morning light into a high-ceilinged sitting room with a fireplace. The walls were hung with pictures of brightly colored vegetables and beautiful Hispanic women. Astrid showed them a separate bedroom with enough space to add three beds to it if you had to, although now it held a single king bed with a canopy and three chests. There was a large bathroom and a tiny bar with a sink and a hotplate. A huge closet. The suite was as big as a small house, warm, inviting, and just cluttered enough to look lived-in.

Lou thought about the bunk room they were cleaning out, and about who she would put where if it were up to her.

It *was* up to her.

But playing dictator could be the wrong move. And so could giving up her right to be one. The more she thought about the complexities of moving children away from reported safety and assessed the deep undercurrents in Astrid's manners, the hollower her stomach became.

If she turned these people into enemies, that's all she'd have here. That and two ecobots.

Shuska, Matchiko, and Day still trailed behind her. As the group went back down the stairs, Lou told Astrid, "We need to go check on the horses, and on our people. We'll be right back."

"I'll stay," Matchiko said. "It looks like the kids can use some final help with the place settings."

She didn't like the idea of Matchiko being left alone, but she wanted Day's opinion. She glanced at Shuska and gave her the sign to stay. Shuska nodded, the look in her eyes telling Lou she hadn't wanted Matchiko alone either. But it felt like a smart choice in spite of the obvious dangers—they'd have privacy and Valeria wouldn't, at least until after dinner.

Lou walked beside Day down the drive in the near-black of early evening, shivering slightly from a cool breeze. The thick band of the Milky Way glowed velvet in the sky. The moon had risen a waxing half, and threw enough light to see bumps in the rough road.

"What do you think?" Lou asked Day.

"It's up to you."

She pressed him. "You really don't have an opinion?"

"You need to choose," he said. "You're in charge, and we won't be here forever."

"Not helpful."

He answered with two words. "But true."

Before they got to the barn, Lou whistled for Daryl and Blessing, making sure they knew who was coming.

"Everything okay?" she asked, as soon as she heard their familiar footsteps.

"Boring," Blessing said.

"Good," Lou said. "Sorry. It's complex up there. There's fifteen people in the big house."

"Small for twenty-one," Daryl observed.

"Yeah, I can do math, too."

Day laughed, soft and low. It startled her a little; he seldom laughed.

"We're sleeping out here tonight. It's already dark, and I'm not moving children around in the middle of the night in a situation I don't understand yet. And we're mounting a guard."

Before Blessing or Daryl could complain that there wasn't enough daylight, Day said, "I'll set up camp. I can explain the situation to Daryl. You," he said, nodding at Blessing, "should go up and charm some folks for the evening."

Blessing smiled.

Lou decided to accept it even if she hadn't given the order. "Let's go."

Blessing ambled fast, the way he always did. Half cowboy, half fighter, always appearing relaxed even when he wasn't. She felt pretty sure he wasn't relaxed tonight—it wasn't like him to border on insubordinate or to pout, and tonight he'd done both.

She took a few little hop-skips to keep up with him. "What are you thinking?"

"It's our job to get these people to leave Chelan."

She walked backward so she could see his face in the faint starlight. "It's our job to save the wolf packs up here."

"Our permit for this place is for us," he countered.

"But we're not police." Lou had been thinking similar thoughts, and feeling uncomfortable with them. "I wish they weren't here. But they are."

She tripped on a rock, and Blessing grabbed her hand and kept her from falling. "I like them. That woman—Valeria—she's strong. They're not going to want to go."

Her reaction came out a little bitter. "Maybe *they* can help us save the wolves."

He laughed for the first time that night, and she decided there was reason for hope. Blessing always left her feeling a little hopeful.

As soon as they got back to the house, Alondra led Lou into the dining room and sat her at the foot of the huge rectangular table. It was lined with wildflowers and leaves that had started to turn red for fall, and the placemats were real fabric, although if she looked closely she could spot stains. She noticed that hers had none. Extra chairs had been brought in, and the placemats overlapped.

She found Alondra seated on her left and Astrid on her right. Someone—probably Alondra—had put name plates by each setting, small squares of real paper with block letters handwritten in colored ink. She called Alondra over and introduced her to Blessing, and the child made a new nameplate for him.

Dinner was surprisingly formal. The children served water and wine and the youngest two of Valeria's grown children, Angel and Sofia, served food.

The delicate formality of the meal covered awkward phrases and strained looks. After they finished the salad course, Lou stood up and waited for the room to grow quiet.

Valeria looked curious, Alondra afraid, and the others mostly, again, confused. Or maybe startled. She felt like she was violating some unwritten rule of the household, but she started anyway. "I am pleased to meet all of you and grateful for your hospitality."

Valeria glanced around the table as if catching everyone's eye, or sending them all a silent message. Her family smiled, or at least relaxed a bit.

Lou took a deep breath. "We do have rights to this place which is your home, permitted and granted to us by the government. We will be using those rights to help with the wilding. Accommodating us will require changes. In the meantime, we see no reason to move families around at night, and we are used to camping. Our robot companions will keep us safe enough. So please rest in the beds you are used to tonight. Changes will start tomorrow."

Valeria stood at the other end of the table. She spoke formally. "Thank you for your gracious understanding. Shall we talk at lunch?"

"Yes."

Valeria raised her glass. "To finding options that are of mutual benefit."

Everyone raised whatever glasses they held. Lou's had water in it.

"In the meantime, please feel free to stay after dinner for music and perhaps some poetry."

Poetry?

The mood during the rest of dinner seemed lighter, as if now that she and Valeria had traded polite public statements everyone could relax a little.

The last course was a bowl of wild blackberries that stained her fingers dark purple. As soon as they finished, the children and Matchiko quickly cleared the table. Matchiko went to help with the dishes, and Blessing and Shuska went with Lou, Valeria, Astrid, and all of the men to the sitting room.

Valeria opened a closet to reveal a motley collection of instruments in various stages of repair. She pulled out a flute case that she slung over her back, and a drum, then smiled at Lou. "Your turn."

This was a game she should be able to match Valeria at—there had been many nights of singing and dancing in the old RiversEnd Ranch great room, particularly in front of the great stone fireplace in the winter. She didn't have Valeria's voice, but she could play.

She selected a guitar, purposefully choosing the best one even though she felt a little guilty for it. She was not at all surprised when Blessing ended up with a fine hand-drum made from a tree trunk and stretched leather and Shuska chose a rattle more suited for a child. It looked tiny in her huge hands.

After everyone had a seat, some on the floor for lack of adequate seating, Valeria stood by the window and sang single note, a G.

The children came running in, babbling in excitement. They quickly settled into various places on the floor, however, faces turned eagerly toward Valeria.

She sang a solo song, a sort of lullaby. Her voice was truly beautiful, low and strong and with a reasonably wide range. Her pitch was perfect. The two youngest children were taken off by their moms then, which explained the lullaby. More evidence of discipline.

After, others started songs, and it became a general free-for-all jam session. Matchiko led three songs, and Blessing two, and Valeria and Astrid and few others all led songs, too. After two hours Lou signaled an end and rose to make her people's excuses.

On the way back down the long drive toward the barn, Lou said, "I think we survived that. They liked our music."

Matchiko spoke softly. "They liked your heart."

"I liked them," Shuska said.

Lou was glad it was so dark that Shuska couldn't see her startled expression. "Since when do you like someone the first day you meet them?"

"I never do."

As she snuggled into her sleeping bag, Lou heard the high yips and calls of a pack of coyotes a few hills over. She listened until they finished hunting.

CHAPTER SIXTEEN

The next morning, the lake glittered in bright sunshine although thunderclouds hung over the mountains. The storm Daryl had promised appeared to be getting itself ready to slide over the mountains and bear down. Lou took Mouse and rode to the edge of the property where no one could hear her. She could see much of this end of the lake and some of the town below, the streets ribbons of dark and the houses and buildings bright squares. It looked far different than Yakima, which virtually hummed with activity every morning.

She called Coryn on her wristlet. After establishing that they were both healthy, she blurted out, "You didn't know this house is occupied?"

"Every place in Chelan appears to be occupied. Every place with water."

"It's a working farm. Surely there was something emptier?" How could Coryn have even allowed this? How did Lou end up relying on Coryn, who had barely managed to survive out here?

A new voice entered the call. Julianna. "Tell me everything that's happened."

Lou felt a flash of guilt for berating Coryn, followed by a brief resentment of Julianna for interrupting. But Julianna was financing this, and she had a right to know what was happening. So Lou slid down off Mouse and clipped a lead to the halter she wore under her bridle, letting her crop grass. She told Julianna everything that had happened since they arrived in Wenatchee, including her assessment that the ecobots had been a very bad idea.

Julianna replied, "You got there, right?"

"Yes."

"And you haven't been attacked?"

"Right."

"I'm no lover of robots."

True. Coryn blamed Julianna for Paula's death. "Okay. Coryn told me."

"So I had a good reason to send you with some or I wouldn't have done it. You may need to show their power."

"They aren't war machines." Lou moved a few steps, following Mouse to better grass.

"They can be defense."

"Not reliably. I've been working with them for years." Lou heard the edge in her voice and took a long breath. "Sorry. I'm just not sure it wouldn't have been easier to sneak in here as a small group."

"Would Valeria have led you home without the ecobots?" Julianna asked.

Point Julianna. Lou kept trying. "Ecobots aren't the best defense, you know. They don't engage in minor crimes like killing humans."

"They will defend you. Now that you run a rewilding operation, they will obey you in almost all things, as well. I made sure of it."

Irritation crawled up Lou's spine. "How do I find out handy things like this?"

Julianna laughed, which only made Lou more irritated. But she knew herself well enough to know she shouldn't be. Her ego was getting bruised. She picked up a rock and threw it.

Mouse tossed her head, startled by the missile flashing past her.

Lou stepped into her, whispering, "It's okay."

"What?"

"I was talking to my horse."

Julianna laughed. "Tell us more about the people?"

Lou tried to name them all, got through over half and then just described genders and ages. She spent time on Valeria, though, since she was the key to everything.

"I know who she is," Julianna said. "Not directly. I'd like to meet her. She was a resistance fighter for Promise when she was a kid."

"That was a long time ago!"

"She hasn't always been on the same side as I am, but in this case I think she will be."

"Why?" Lou led Mouse a few more steps forward.

"She believes in the wilding, but she also thinks there should be more people, more settlements, than came out of the agreements. My sources say that she hates factory farming, and I think she understands that the land needs the cities. She won't like Returners much. She's famously stubborn."

"I noticed that."

Julianna ignored her. "I've heard she's also a raving pacifist."

"That's good."

"Does that fit? You've spent time with her."

Lou liked being asked. A little of her anger drained away, although under that was only a need to get moving, to go resolve the housing issue and start her real work. "I think so. And she got us in here. It wasn't the ecobots that did that. It was her. She told people to let us though and they did. And she's a damned fine singer."

Julianna ignored that last observation. "Is she honest?"

The question was so direct it surprised Lou. But Julianna was like that sometimes. "I don't know yet. I think so."

"Very well. I'm sorry we didn't have better intelligence."

Lou thought of those rows of raised garden beds. "The Lucken Foundation would have made me kick these people off. Or at least most of them. Can you give me permission to hire more of them? Will that protect them?"

A pause on Julianna's end. Evidently, she hadn't expected the question. "We're not permitted for more than the papers indicate. I doubt we'd get a better number without establishing some success."

"Is there money? Extra money? Can I be given enough to build another house?"

Julianna actually laughed. "You want to use rewilding money to build a house when you have a perfectly good permit for a perfectly good house?"

Lou threw another rock, watched it smack against a boulder.

"You'll have to be more creative than that. I do have resources, but the permitting is difficult. You could lose our permit if you do anything illegal."

"These people have young children."

"So do the Returners. So far, you made the—" A slight hesitation. "You made good choices. I'm pleased with you. You will have to be more creative than you have ever been. Blessing and Day can help you."

Julianna's pets. "But I am running the foundation." She hesitated at how bold the words sounded. "Or at least our operation out here."

"Yes, you are."

Lou swallowed, pushing away the stray thought that Julianna was housetraining her. She needed the old woman, and she did appreciate her. Without her, there might be no wilding, or no land to rewild, anyway. "I have things to do. But we should stay in touch. I'll call if I have any questions. Can we set up a call once a week?"

A brief moment of silence. Then, "Yes, of course you can. We'll send you a schedule for when Coryn will be available."

"Will you be there, too?" she asked Julianna.

"Coryn will be your main support."

"Okay." That meant she would largely be on her own. "Is there anything else?"

"Yes. We didn't put this in writing, but Blessing should have delivered the message. Wolves matter. The rewilding matters. We want you to work on that. But you must find out what the Returners are up to. There are rumors of another attack soon—on the city. We think the leaders are *there*."

Lou wanted to see all of the Returners scraped from the land. But just starting up was going to be so much work! "Can Blessing and Day work on that while I start hiring?"

Julianna's response came swiftly. "Finding out what the Returners are up to is one of *your* highest priorities."

Lou took three deep breaths, biting her tongue. She did care about that, but right now she had more immediate troubles. "There's a storm coming in. I have to make sure the horses get put away."

"Watch for messages. We'll be looking at satellite shots as they come in, and we may see threats before you do. Find the Returners' plans."

She sighed. It was bound to take all afternoon just to figure out who was sleeping where. "Okay. Thanks." She hung up, and then realized she hadn't said goodbye to Coryn. Dammit. She took a few deep breaths, forcing herself to notice the trees and birds around her, to be here in the moment and not worried about some future she couldn't control.

She rubbed Mouse behind the ears and mounted, starting back toward the house and barns.

The sky looked like it was about to unload on her, and a wicked wind had started twisting the tops of the trees.

She flirted with the idea of talking with the others before she found Valeria, but this was her moment to lead. Back to the amigas question; they couldn't talk about everything. There wasn't time. "Dammit, Mouse," she addressed the horse's ears, which swiveled back at the sound of her name. "Why is this so hard? All I really want to do is save wolves."

The horse didn't answer.

The family would need to stop selling food in town. That was a legality thing. Anyone who worked for her would have to stop that entirely.

Alondra waited for her at the end of the lane. Lou stopped Mouse and leaned down with a smile. "Do you know where Valeria is?"

"She wants you to go for a walk with her. She said I could take the horse."

"Really? Well, wasn't that nice of her?" Lou kept her smile friendly and relaxed. "You can follow me to the barn and help Daryl if you like."

"Daryl is helping clean out chicken coops. But Shuska is in the barn, and she said I could."

She didn't believe that Shuska had allowed any such thing.

Lou slid off of Mouse, clipped the lead on, and handed the girl up onto Mouse. Alondra clutched the reins awkwardly, but Lou kept the lead, and thus control of the horse. There. That was a creative solution.

Valeria waited by the barn. She wore a small backpack and carried a sturdy walking stick. She smiled. "We'll be going uphill."

Lou nodded. "Give me a minute."

"We have about three hours before the storm hits," Valeria said.

Lou nodded again and held her hand out toward Alondra. She stayed seated. "I want to ride more," she insisted.

Lou shook her head firmly. "We'll take the saddle off with you in it." The girl leaned over and half fell into Lou's arms. The move was less graceful than it looked like it was going to be, and Lou moved with her, swinging her in an arc and then landing her with her feet on the ground, giggling. Lou tousled Alondra's unruly dark hair. "You can help Shuska brush Mouse and put her away."

She packed paper and a notebook, her wristlet, her stunner, water, and some of the last of their dried fruits from Wenatchee into a pack of her own, and met Valeria out front.

Apparently jeans, boots, and a ruffly off-white shirt were Valeria's signature outfit. Her boots looked better than Lou's.

They walked side by side down the long drive, to the end of the road they'd come in on and then up a thin set of long switchbacks. The sun was still largely in the east, warming them while the clouds drifted toward them from the mountains in the west. The air smelled of dust. She was fully winded by the time Valeria stopped at the top of the hill and turned toward the lake and city, which now looked smaller.

Though Lou had ridden through the partly ruined streets and the runaway gardens, and seen that a quarter of the roofs were falling in or even had fallen fully into the houses or blown away, Chelan looked picaresque and whole from their high perch. Hills folded down to the town, a few living trees sticking up here and there amid many dead ones, burned to outsized black toothpicks in past fires but never taken down. She could see the black onion of fire-ravenged earth, each fire bringing new wildflowers and a fresh bloom of grass except for the last two, which must have been superheated and fast since the earth itself was still black in some places.

Valeria broke her silence. "This was a thriving tourist town. Vineyards everywhere. Half the houses—including the main house on the property—were bed and breakfast inns. That's why the kitchen is so large and so fine. It's the best room in the house."

"That also explains the way every bedroom has a bathroom," Lou commented.

Valeria added, "And the locks on most of the closet doors. The bunkhouse was built for hands and harvesters." Valeria looked down at the house, a slight wind plucking at the dark hairs that had escaped her braids. She looked proud of it, and quite proprietary. "They used to have wine-tasting events. There's a downstairs cellar you get to through the mud room."

"We missed that in the tour yesterday."

Valeria pointed at the clouds. "Maybe we have a little less time. I asked Diego and Santino to move to the bunkhouse. There's three other places in there as well. I thought you could move your three men in there."

So that was her opening. "We prefer to stay close. I had thought we three women would take one suite, and Blessing and Day one of the small suites, and Daryl the other for now. One of us will sleep outside with the bots and horses each night for a while anyway."

"I want my grandchildren upstairs. Surely you understand."

Lou took a long sip of water. The thunderclouds were breathtaking folds of grays with brilliant white tops. "Has anyone ever attacked you?"

"Three times."

She wanted to ask when and over what. "There are four small bedroom suites. If you take three—one for each child—we will use the downstairs bedrooms where Diego and Santino were staying."

"Sofia must stay in the house. She is only twenty-one. And she is very beautiful. None of her brothers would harm her, but it wouldn't be seemly for her to stay with them in the bunkhouse."

"Can she stay with you?"

Valeria stood up, the rising wind drawing her hair all of the way back now. "You will understand the value of having your own suite. I could not operate without it. I will allow Sofia to take the downstairs room. Felipe and his family will take the room she is leaving. Ignacio and Ana can join Sofia downstairs. That leaves you one bedroom and one of the two master suites upstairs. If you choose to have your women with you and put your men in that room, that's on your head. But if I were you, I would put them with my boys in the bunkhouse. People will need to get to know each other anyway, and we will be working for you."

She let that go for the moment, thinking through the housing. "I need to keep Blessing and Day near me. Daryl can bunk outside. Matchiko and Shuska will stay with me."

Valeria shrugged, as if to say that there was little she could do about it if Lou refused to accept her advice. But she also made sure Lou saw the shrug.

"I cannot hire all of you," Lou reiterated. "I don't have enough permits or enough money. There are some specific skills I will need to bring in from outside." She paused. "That will mean housing more people."

Valeria faced the rising wind, looking for all the world as if she were calling it rather than merely reveling in it. "In spring. We can build then."

Lou hoped to add people before that, but she could argue that point later. "I cannot pay you to farm. Anyone who is on my payroll will work for me. The foundation and our mission will be the top priority."

"Which is?"

"It means finding the two wolf packs that are up here and supporting them. It means surveying the deer population and tagging as many animals as possible and tracking their movements. Knowing what kills them. It means inventorying plants. It means using the ecobots to destroy man-made things when that is necessary to save animals."

"I know you came for the Returners as well."

Lou ignored her. "I can hire three."

"Felipe, Diego, and Angel."

Lou stiffened. "I will interview anyone who is interested."

"That's fine." Valeria glanced at the sky. "We should start down."

The air had begun to smell of rain and to draw the fine hairs on the backs of her arms up. "Okay." She was pretty sure that those three were the only people who would show up for any interview, and that any one of her team might have done a better job negotiating.

Going down was harder than it looked. Valeria took it almost at a jog, and Lou was soon focused on managing not to fall, and getting down before the rain came. Wind plucked at her, and then, on the flats, it threatened to knock her down.

As if by magic, Valeria timed it so that they closed the door of the house just as the first driving blast of rain slammed into the windows.

CHAPTER SEVENTEEN

The morning after the disturbing call with Lou, worry plucked Coryn awake even before the water of her alarm started lapping the shore. Had she picked the wrong house for Lou? But it was the biggest, and it was available. It had looked neat and in good repair. That had been something Coryn wanted so Lou could work on the things that mattered.

Getting up early put her in the breakfast room on time, and to her surprise Julianna waited for her instead of Adam. For just a second she had mixed feelings—but Julianna was actually better. Adam sometimes knew things Julianna didn't, but Julianna was really good at seeing how the city and the Outside worked together.

The older woman has chosen blue and green running shorts that hugged her legs tightly to just below the knee and a long bright-orange shirt. Coryn had chosen her black shirt because the lower cut emphasized her breasts, which felt foolish around Julianna.

Her boss appeared to be all-business this morning anyway. "Fifteen minutes," she said as soon as Coryn entered. "I've added five kilometers to the run so we can go a little slower. Endurance."

Pancakes with blueberries and a light syrup graced the training table. Well, at least she'd have plenty of fuel to burn.

They left via one of the many bridges that connected the most expensive buildings, eventually hooking up the Bridge of Stars and doing the long run up at a slow pace. Even so, they passed far more people than passed them, even the slowest bicycles. Clouds streamed around the weather dome this morning, their rain withheld by a sophisticated combination of temperature, wind, and the electrical charge of the air. The difference between the Inside and Outside was clearer than usual this morning, a sharp demarcation of color.

In response to the weather outside of the dome, the in-city temperature had dropped a few degrees from normal, and the cooler air helped Coryn keep her pace consistent up the long slope of the bridge.

Coryn left her AR rig around her neck and dug into the climb, practicing form. The steady hill eventually taxed her breath anyway. Last weekend she'd come in fifth in a race, a disappointing fall of three places.

The little things mattered. How she flexed her feet, the rhythm of her breath. She focused hard, hoping Julianna noticed.

At the top of the bridge they passed a dark woman wearing a golden veil over her head, sitting in a yoga pose and staring at the storm streaming around the weather dome. She occupied the same observation spot that Lou and Coryn had used the day Lou left. They went on to another one, leaning on the rail and panting. The clouds and mist outside made it hard to see the line of the horizon and completely hid the Olympic Mountains.

As she got enough breath back to talk in a normal voice, Coryn said, "It's a pleasure to see you."

A small smile touched Julianna's face. She looked off toward the horizon, as if it were visible, and said, "You need to up your game with the Foundation."

Coryn swallowed. Just like Julianna to pull no punches. "You mean I chose the wrong house?"

"No. I think that turned out even better than we thought. But we need algorithms built to analyze the sat shots. I sense danger."

"Adam is doing those." Coryn took a long, slow drink of water. "He's better at the math anyway."

That comment earned her a disgusted stare from Julianna. "I need him for something else for a few days," she snapped. "I want a list of what you're looking for by the end of the day. Adam will be around to help this afternoon, and then you'll have to do without him for a few days."

"Okay." He kept trying to talk her into drinking, and no matter how pretty he was or how good he smelled, she felt wary. "What do you need him for?"

Julianna stayed silent for so long that Coryn began to think she wasn't going to answer. "We have some faint traces on the weapons people have been hinting at. He's got the skill to help the analytics team pluck threads. There is also a rumored timeline for the next attack."

That startled Coryn. "Soon?"

"In the spring. I think Lou was right when she suggested our enemies will use the winter to regroup."

"What about this Valeria? Is she an enemy?"

Julianna stretched. "What did I say last night?"

"That she's not a full Returner, but she doesn't really support the wilding."

"That's right. That means she might be either. Maybe both. But I bet her enemies are ours."

The idea of Valeria being both friend and enemy reminded her of Bartholomew, who had in truth been enemy. That encounter had taught her to mistrust gray people. "What if Lou has to get Valeria in trouble?"

A frown crossed Julianna's face. "That will probably happen."

"Oh."

"That's one of the things you need to learn." Julianna spoke without looking at Coryn, her diction low and precise. And cold. "Leadership. Leadership means taking the hard things on and following through, fighting uphill like we just ran that bridge. Harder if you have to." She finally looked at Coryn, her gaze level. "I've got another job for you."

Coryn was again startled. But that was Julianna's mode of operation, at least lately. "Okay. What?"

"Not here. Let's use the West Seattle touchdown and go to Jake's Park."

One of their quiet places—a spot the city didn't have sensors in. Coryn swallowed. "Let's move before I cool down."

That made Julianna smile at last. "Remember not to push it down the hill."

A fair warning. Coryn loved the wind in her hair, and she loved this bridge. The slow run down was glorious. Nothing automated was allowed here except for companion robots. Lines of bicycles passed them on their left in the wheeled lane. A stream of at least twenty runners in the bright purple and silver uniforms of the University of Washington passed them, most of them tall, with longer legs than Coryn had. That was who she had to beat. People built like that.

She and Julianna raced down and down until Seacouver's bright green roofs and silver buildings, twisting and arching bridges, and tall in-city gardens enfolded them again as they ran above the waterfront. Then the bridge spiraled up again, less brutally and not as far, before it dumped them on the running surface along Alki Beach. Fancy buildings rose high on their left. To the right, only the seawall and the Sound. They joined cars and busses again, robotic and real dogs, companions shepherding children or the old, or even acting as trainers for the middle-aged.

As always, Julianna's guard robots ran a few hundred feet ahead and a few hundred feet back, invisible in the crowd unless you knew what models to look for, and how to expect them to behave.

They ran up to the lighthouse and made a left and kept going along the coast, the Sound washing angrily against the seawall just outside the weather dome here. Twice, salty spray surged over the wall, spattering them with briny water.

"Are we going to have to build the seawall higher again?" Coryn asked.

"Work has already started. It's supposed to be done before the winter storms."

"How bad is the storm going to be over Chelan today?"

"Don't you know?"

She swallowed. There was no point in saying she'd just gotten up and come down to breakfast and hadn't checked anything.

Silence would result in fewer demerits.

Julianna led her into a privacy-screened gazebo in a waterfront park that faced Bainbridge and Vashon Islands. It didn't look any different from the other picnic shelters, but the posts and roof had jamming equipment in them, and they could talk without being overhead by the city. It might know they'd been here, but not what they said. The silencing mechanisms worked when Julianna was present. She had places like this scattered throughout the city, places designed to fool it and let her have privacy.

Coryn reminded herself not to think of the city as a single entity. She had learned better working with Adam. It was a collection of data and analytics that served many masters in addition to its job of keeping the people in the city safe. Sensors listened everywhere, but they didn't save every single conversation. They could be fooled by simply making sure you did nothing far enough out of the utter ordinary to draw attention. It seemed like a single entity, acted like one. People talked about it as if it had a personality. But Adam swore it was just many systems with many interfaces.

She drank water and pulled salted nuts and some boiled small potatoes out of her pouch. "What did you want me to do?" she asked.

Julianna paced, at least to the extent that the small space allowed. She stopped long enough to look directly at Coryn, her expression stern. "I need for you to start stretching your thinking. In addition to the list of analytic targets I want from you today, I want your own assessment of the three biggest risks to Lou while she's in Chelan and the three biggest risks to Seacouver."

"I can tell you what I think they are."

"You can write them down for me."

She nodded, dismayed that Julianna seemed so unhappy with her. But this wasn't what she needed privacy for; Coryn had been the subject of even more cutting lectures in more public places.

Julianna kept pacing.

It felt like being locked up in a room with a very anxious animal. Coryn waited, eating slowly, letting her body recover. By her reckoning, they were halfway through the run. A strange time for such a long stop.

Julianna stopped again, and again focused her stare on Coryn. "I'm testing you for a purpose."

Coryn smiled. "You've been testing me since I met you."

"And teaching you." Julianna paused. "But I've only been testing you for a narrow band of skills—helping your sister. You've not been doing anything complicated."

Coryn stayed silent, stung again. Getting and keeping all the permits up had been complicated. Negotiating for and testing connectivity Outside from Inside had been almost impossible. The politics of supporting an NGO in the field was crazy-making. Other NGOs wanted to fight you, regulators wanted to slow you down, logistics and supply were hard. She'd learned so much!

Julianna continued. "Jake has always understood the interior politics of the city the best. He is a dancer; I am a klutz."

Coryn blinked at Julianna's strange statement. Julianna was brilliant at politics. She ran like a dream, graceful for any age and certainly for her age. Her words made no sense.

"I need to know if you are a dancer or a klutz. I need you to learn how to move in the world outside of my household. I thought there was more time to train you. Maybe years. But maybe there isn't." She stared out over the seawall just as a muscular wave sent up a spectacular spray pattern that reached high over their heads. "I'm sorry, Coryn. But I am about to be very hard on you. You will succeed, or you will fail." She turned her attention more directly to her. "You will work with Jake— apprentice under him, if you will—every afternoon in the foundation offices. That's in addition to your existing work for the foundation and your athletic training."

Coryn felt as if she'd been slapped. "I don't know how to do one more thing. I barely sleep enough now. You keep telling me to be mindful, and then you want me to work harder." She realized she sounded like she was whining, and Julianna hated whining. "I'm sorry. I'm just . . . I don't know how to do more."

Julianna didn't look at all moved. "We're at war. When we're at war, we stretch. You'll have to find a way." She looked out at the Sound. "There's more. You will move out of my house tomorrow. We're putting you into an apartment in a building where a lot of the young politicians and support staff live. I'm covering the cost of moving you, and giving you a furniture allowance and raising your salary to cover it. You will still work for me. After the move is completed, I will not pay your bills directly. You will need to do that, and you'll have enough money if you're careful."

She didn't even know how to think about that. It reduced her to a monosyllabic response. "Okay."

"You need to learn from more than me."

"Okay." She still didn't see why they'd had to run all the way out here. "Maybe it will be good for me to be on my own."

Julianna smiled for the first time since they left the breakfast nook. "That's the idea."

Coryn nodded, feeling abandoned in spite of herself. It made her feel weak.

"It won't be as fancy."

"I spent three years in an orphanage," Coryn reminded her.

"You probably only have three months with Jake." Julianna stared at an invisible point on the horizon. "Maybe less."

Coryn stopped. "Why?"

"He has an inoperable brain cancer. More accurately, there have been attempts to operate. He decided to stop them, to die with dignity instead of in a hospital." Julianna looked away and spoke so softly that Coryn had to struggle to hear her. "Cancer still kills the very old. After all, we have to die of something."

Coryn swallowed, suddenly immensely sad and even more adrift. When she first met Jake, he had helped her and Lou talk to the city about the attack, or perhaps they had helped each other. Since then, he had become part of her. Family. Her voice came out thick, trailing to a whisper. "I was starting to think of him like a . . . like a father. I'm so sorry."

"Not as sorry as I am."

Of course not. Coryn stood up beside Julianna, slid an arm around her waist, leaned in to hug her.

Julianna smiled at her, but pushed her away. "We can block sound here, but not visuals. No one must know this, not right now. I can't break down, not here."

"It's a secret?"

"Jake has significant economic resources. He has no heir except me, and I am old and already a target. If the news that he is dying comes out, it will affect the markets. Jake matters to the spirit of this city. We both do. I don't talk about that much, but our deaths will matter, and how we die will matter."

She straightened, as if gaining strength from her own words. "More importantly, there is much good he can still do if he is not discounted. He hates this. We cannot afford it." She had gone back to staring at the islands and beyond them at the mountains. Her jaw looked like an iron bar, and she blinked from time to time. "People in power can't show weakness. Not this much weakness. He agreed that I could tell you, but *you can tell no one.* No one."

"I understand." A fierce spark of love for the old woman replaced all of the frustration she had felt. It explained why Julianna was being so hard on her.

Maybe this was why Julianna ran. To show strength. "Are you ready?" Coryn whispered.

"Almost." Julianna stared out at the Olympic Mountains, then back at the city, still blinking. "Let's go."

Coryn followed her out. At first, her steps were slow and leaden, as if her sadness had filtered into her joints. But Julianna ran strong ahead of her, and Coryn had no choice but to find a way to catch up.

CHAPTER EIGHTEEN

Coryn was not at all surprised to find Jake sitting alone in the conference room when she returned. She stopped in the doorway, looking closely at him. Did he look more tired lately? Thinner?

"Come in."

His small smile offered very little reassurance. She sat down, fiddling with a pen. He liked real paper, told her over and over it was more secure. As a result, colored pens always cluttered the table.

"I see from your face that Julianna told you what's . . ." he paused, swallowed. "What's happening to me."

She managed a soft nod and a long pause. Then something broke free in her, and she rushed to his side, put her arm around his shoulder, and squeezed. A tear gathered in her eye and she willed it away, wanting to be strong for him.

His bony hand crept to cover hers for a moment, and then he said, "Sit."

She did.

He gazed at her for a few minutes, as calm as usual, and then when he asked her, "What do you want?" his words were laden with seriousness.

So he knew the content of her grim conversation with Julianna. She looked over his head at a blemish in the nearly perfect wall, her eyes stinging. She took a few long breaths before she said, "A place to belong. I love working to support Lou. I love running. I love my dog." She was babbling, so she shut up.

"What would a place where you belong be like?"

Lou had always known she belonged Outside. But Coryn had no idea what a home was. Her favorite place was on a bridge staring down at the city, but that was no answer. "We had thirteen homes growing up. All over the city. Then we landed in an orphanage. You know we lost our parents."

"Julianna also lost her parents at a young age."

She glanced past him at the current satellite shot. Clouds. Not even a scrap of lake, much less ground. Everything light gray on slate gray on ash gray, light and dark shades caught swirling over each other and frozen in time. She had looked up the storm while she showered. There were warnings for local flooding and rain, but the city only carried some news of Outside, even with her current access levels as staff here.

"She grew up in an orphanage, too," Jake added. "She never remembered her parents at all. They died of drugs, and she never learned whether they killed themselves or died of stupidity or if it was just an accident."

"I suppose I knew some of that." She reached for a piece of paper and started doodling. "It was in my high school history book."

"She believes that she accomplished so much because she had nothing to lose."

"I can see that." The doodle was turning into a purple horse, with the head and tail both too big. "You grew up richer, though, right?"

"Middle class. My parents were small-time politicians for cities that are now dead. They taught me to care deeply about politics."

And now he and Julianna were two of the richest people in Seacouver. Not *the* richest anymore. They had once been the most powerful, and while they weren't that anymore either, they were still icons.

The satellite view refreshed. A bolt of lightning arced between two clouds. She pointed at it. "See that?"

He smiled. "Yes. I've seen lightning storms from airplanes many times. They're strange from above, and beautiful. That bolt is pure power."

It looked small and bright on the film, caught in a twist of air like a striking snake. "Is it dangerous?"

"To Lou? Sure. But she should be okay." He leaned back, thoughtful for a moment. "What do you think Lou wants?"

Coryn laughed. Wasn't it obvious? "She wants to save the world. That's what she's always wanted. The wild world. She doesn't care if all the cities just blow away. She blames all the people for the death of the world."

A half-smile played around his lips. "It's not dead yet."

"Lou loves to look at pictures of what it was like from before."

The screen refreshed to all grays, the lightning bolt gone from the room as well as from the storm. "I see." He circled back to the first question he had asked her. "What do you want?"

"For Lou to save the world." She hesitated. "To win a race."

He stared at her for a while. "Really? Just to win a race? Haven't you already done that?"

"Second place." She sensed danger in these questions. He liked her, but he and Julianna always put power over friendship, and they had goals for her. She was being kicked out of Julianna's house. Maybe. Maybe it was a reassignment. Who knew? It unsettled her, though. And now Jake was asking her questions when maybe she should be asking him questions. "I want the big dream to succeed. I want the city to be safe so people don't kill themselves like Mom and Dad did. I want the wild places to get wild again, I want to see the earth repaired. I maybe even want to help with that. I want to matter. Doesn't everyone?" She was rambling. She'd given up on the horse doodle so she started over, talking while she drew. "I want to know the things you know. How to be effective at politics. How to hide from the city's systems, and how to work with them. How to negotiate." She stopped for a moment, focusing on the curve of the animal's neck. "Julianna says she's no good, but I've seen her work a crowd. She's incredible." She glanced up to see Jake watching her carefully. She was used to him being the one distracted by paper notes, and now they had changed places.

He stood and circled the long table slowly, talking as he went. "Julianna broke her heart over and over on the world. It sprawled then, you know. People everywhere. *Everywhere.* There were almost no roadless places, almost no truly wild places. We were destroying *everything* and most people didn't care. They played games and they danced and they ate richly fed cows and pigs fattened in pens and they traveled. They beat each other up for religious and racial difference, and for differences smaller than that. We were still on oil then, a lot of us. The feds had power." Jake paused, turned, started walking the other way. "Julianna saw the way to keep humanity safe was to scrape most of them off the land. I agreed. It seemed harsh. Hell, it was harsh. We failed, and failed, and failed. But then we didn't. What do you care about enough to fail at over and over?"

She stared at him, blinking. "Lou. Saving Lou. But I'm not going to fail."

He kept coming at her verbally, leaning on her with words. "What will you do if you can't save her? You might not be able to, you know. You might make a mistake, or it might be out of your hands. What will you do if she dies? What will you do if she's hurt? Is taking care of someone you can't protect your biggest goal?"

She loved him for his honesty but it made her squirm. "I want a world where no one needs to commit suicide, and where Lou is safe, and where . . ."

He let her trail off, and then he spoke what she was already thinking. "The next few weeks will feel like a test. We *are* testing you, and Lou. We're testing Lou by making her solve her own problems. So far, she's doing fine." He paused as if thinking hard. "She could be a stronger negotiator. She's softer than her reputation."

"That's good," Coryn immediately responded.

"Maybe."

"She always cared about other people and how they feel."

"She may need to care less about that."

Coryn frowned.

"You want her to survive, right?"

"Of course."

"We want you both to survive. We're going to test you. I know the questions Julianna gave you. I'm going to add three. What makes you so happy you want to sing? What makes you want to cry? What would you die for?"

The last question drew a surprised smile from her. "You're reminding me of Blessing again."

"Is that bad?"

"Of course not."

"Blessing might be the strongest one of all of us. We're getting old, and we need to choose who and what will be supported after we die."

A sudden fear made her shiver. "Is Julianna okay?"

"So far."

She scribbled Jake's three questions down. *Happy? Cry? Die?* She added the word *Belong?* before she folded the paper and then shoved the questions, and her poorly drawn purple horse, into her pocket.

"You should go now," Jake said.

"I was going to meet Adam to work on the analytics."

"He's not coming today."

"Julianna said she needed him tomorrow."

"Not today. You need to go pack. We'll send staff to move you in the morning. Train as usual. Then come back here, on time, to work. I'll manage the morning shift for you. You'll need this afternoon to pack out."

Why was he being so gruff with her?

"Go."

She glanced back at the image from Chelan. No lightning this time. Just clouds. Gray clouds, as indeterminate and roiling as her own feelings. It almost made her ill to look at them.

She barely managed to close the door behind her with some sort of civility before hot tears raced down her cheeks. She kept her head down, pushed the elevator button, and tapped her toe as she waited for it.

It opened to reveal Julianna stepping out. Coryn tried mumbling hello and pushing into the elevator.

"Stay strong," Julianna whispered as she swept past her to go to Jake's side.

Her room door opened as she approached. Aspen careened through it and jumped, landing in her arms. She clutched him so tightly that he yelped. "Sorry . . ."

He licked her face, forgiving her.

At least someone loved her no matter what she did.

A small stack of boxes had been set just inside the door. Maybe five boxes. She stared at them for a long time, so surprised to see them that it took a moment to register what she should be doing. These little boxes would hold everything she owned.

She sat down on the middle of her bed, cold and shivering unexpectedly. Aspen leaned into her, too light to knock her over even though he dug his back feet in and pushed with his shoulder. "I'm okay," she murmured, entirely unsure if it was true.

Was she being kicked out of the inner circle? Blessing had told her that might happen, but she hadn't really believed him.

Jake had told her to report for work.

Had she done something clueless and lost the game of politics?

If so, what would she do?

Her limbs felt so heavy with remorse and guilt that she couldn't move. Not only could her dog not move her, but she couldn't move. It was the strangest feeling, like being trapped inside her own fears.

What if she just walked out? She couldn't imagine it, but what if she did? She knew how to live on basic, how to live in the myriad itinerant housing pods.

A full half an hour passed before she slowly slid off the bed and stood. She looked in the mirror and saw her mother looking back at her, the same hopeless look, the same deep sadness.

That wasn't okay.

She would never kill herself.

She had sworn that to Paula.

Who wasn't here anymore.

She missed Paula. When bad things happened, she still felt the loss of her lifelong companion. She was intellectually past it, would never get attached to a robot again. She knew better. A child's addiction. But times like this, when she would have teased Paula or been held by her, been comforted, at times like this, her emotions ignored her brain.

And Jake.

If she was supposed to be okay without Paula, then she needed her people. *Jake.*

Now she was going to have to be okay without Jake.

She took three deep breaths, feeling a cleaner emotion creeping up. Anger. It made her strong enough to start filling the boxes. Three pairs of running shoes and two clean running outfits.

Would Julianna still send her new outfits? Or have them sent, more accurately?

Aspen watched, quiet, his little ears back.

Would Adam meet her in the morning to run?

Three dresses and two pairs of shorts and a pair of jeans, a pair of sandals and a pair of boots. Some make-up.

She eyed her covers and pillows. They were soft and she was used to them.

But they weren't actually hers. They stayed.

She opened drawers and found small things. A hairbrush. Her electronic journal.

She filled four boxes. She stared at them and then she stared at the bed and then she took three deep breaths.

She still had a job. She still had a place to live. She didn't know where it was, but she had one. So she wasn't at the mercy of shared housing. Yet. Her chin quivered. She wasn't in the orphanage. She would see Jake tomorrow.

Jake, who was dying. After he died, she had Adam the drinker, and Julianna the elusive, and, somewhere out in Chelan, her sister and Blessing.

What was she going to do without Jake?

She had Aspen. She called him and he came, curling in her lap. She scratched him behind the ears, an almost mindless movement, as soothing to her as it seemed to be to the dog.

He had clearly picked up on her emotions. His ears drooped and he gave off tiny little moans.

She hated the sound of her own mind in this state. She hated herself for feeling sorry for herself. Pathetic.

She tried some yoga poses Julianna had taught her. A full sun salutation, complete with high stretches and a long downward dog that teased some of the stiffness out of her thigh muscles.

Aspen went to the corner of the room and sat, still solemn, still watchful.

She dug the crumpled piece of paper with the few words and the purple horse on it out of her pocket. She dug her journal out of the box.

She threw the covers and blankets into the empty box and sat on her bare mattress and started working on the answers to the questions.

CHAPTER NINETEEN

Coryn woke long before the alarm. The covers that she had unboxed to sleep in had wrapped around her like a straightjacket, and she had to strain to free herself. Aspen jumped on her chest and she pushed him away. "You're hot."

He jumped down and stood by the door, looking slightly desperate. She pulled on one of the two outfits she'd packed the night before, changed, and repacked her bedding and everything dirty.

Just as she reached for Aspen's leash, Adam came in, followed by two house-bots. "Good morning! Julianna asked me help you get things settled in the new place." He sounded gratingly cheerful.

"Good morning." She bent down for a box.

"Robocart. Right outside."

It took two minutes to load up. As they followed the cart down the hallway to the elevator, Adam said, "She wanted me to remind you that you needed a place you will be able to afford." He wasn't looking at her. "It's not as nice as this. But the people are great and there are shared amenities. You'll like it."

How did he know? She stifled a frustrated reply and glanced at her dog. "Aspen needs to go out."

"We'll stop by the park."

She'd realized how little she knew about his life when he wasn't around her. "Where do you live?"

"I'm moving into your old room. We're switching, you and I. It's easiest. Julianna needs me inside of her security perimeter."

That jolted her a little out of herself. "Are you in danger? What have you found out?"

"Not here."

She should have asked him before they left the security of Julianna's household. "Where's your room?"

"Your room now?" He smiled down at her with an insincere politeness that she found annoying.

"Wait, I don't deserve any security?"

"What? The city's not enough for you?"

He was teasing her. He probably *could* tell her whatever he knew, but he liked to treat her half like someone to flirt with, half like someone just a little below him. She had fallen for it on her first few training runs with him, but no more. Aspen wriggled in her arms, and she turned her attention to the dog. "We need a park."

They pulled off of the bridge. The robocart waited while they took an escalator up to the top of the building. The city was going to allow rain—the air smelled of it, and clouds gusted around the dome. Fall, coming in with a threat of winter. She'd read it might be early this year, and hard. Seacouver hadn't been snowed on in twenty years, but there were rumors about snow this winter.

It was so early they almost had the park to themselves. A few companion-bots and one human walked dogs. They didn't stay any longer than necessary.

Five minutes later, they entered the Scholes Building, with its wide, comfortable corridors, the robot's wheels bumping along the slate tile behind them. They went through Scholes, and out on the north side into one of the newer buildings. Well, not brand new; a decade or so old. It had been built for tech workers, converted to regular housing, converted back to tech, and was now out of favor since there were even newer buildings for the tech elite.

They turned off the corridor, and went through a door to interior elevators. The sign by the elevator said Salish Building: Floor seventy-one. She could remember that—it made her think of orcas.

She peered down a hallway, noting moving art on the walls and three older people walking together, hand in hand, talking.

"Hurry up!"

Her training schedule. She jogged a little to catch up. Behind her, the bot sped up. She was too distracted to note which floor he pushed, but as soon as the door closed she realized the elevator was going down to a part of the city below the bridges and the best views, below the roof gardens and the most powerful people. Well, Julianna and Jake owned whole top floors. If she was leaving their real-estate bubble, then she had to go down to pay for it.

Adam had survived. She would, too.

The elevator stayed empty. It was big enough for ten people, maybe more, but Adam stood so close they were a hair from touching. She stepped a little back from him, enduring a slightly hurt glance with as much stoicism as she could manage.

They went all the way down to twelve.

Twelve? It was going to be faster to go down to street level to get anywhere. Except then you had the doors to contend with. The security chipset Julianna had dropped in her hand let her travel the bridges, or at least most of them. Did it let her in and out of street doors?

Adam leaned back close to her, in position to kiss her. As if she'd let him.

She pushed him away, knocking him a little off balance so he had to take an extra step. His eyes widened, and he mumbled, "Sorry."

"It's okay." She stepped through the doors. "Which direction?"

He just stood there, making no choice. "I'm sorry I'm leaving. I picked this place, and Julianna approved it because this whole building is infested with diplomats and midlevel techies and government types. It's a good listening post. But that's why she likes it. I like it because it's the best apartment of its size on the lower floors."

He was babbling. He sounded like he felt guilty and also like he was praying she'd like it.

They turned twice more and he opened the door, standing aside and letting her walk in. Across from her, wide windows looked out on the city. The view was a corridor between two buildings that made it look like the apartment was in a canyon. She could see a narrow rectangle of the Sound, green walls on one side and old brick walls on the other, and above her, the grungy bottom of a bridge. She walked to the windows. The room she had just left only had virtual windows. This one had a real window, and a myriad of things to see through it. She reached toward a spider web that hung in the corner of the window before realizing it was on the outside.

Aspen wriggled, and she glanced back to be sure the door was closed before letting him down.

The water view mesmerized her. The steel gray sea looked angry, darker than the sky. She smiled; in that moment, nothing else mattered about her new home. The view. The view would save her.

This—even this—was better than any place they'd ever lived while she was growing up. Nothing like being in one of Julianna's own rooms on the top floor, but the view was not a plain and somewhat grimy street in Kent.

Outside the window and off to the right, she spotted rails and an open balcony. No entrance from this room, but there were two doors out to the balcony, so there had to be more rooms.

Adam spoke, bringing her back to the moment. "I left you two chairs. Julianna ordered a bed. The rest is up to you. There's an allowance."

"Okay." She turned around to look at the room she'd just walked through. Sure enough, two chairs. Big, rounded, overstuffed, and cringe green. The deep, narrow room felt oriented toward the view. Maybe she'd put a yoga mat down in front of the window. She could do sun salutations to the sea.

"The bedroom's this way."

She followed him. Sure enough, there was a bed in the small room. Also, a door to the balcony. No window. A strange woman sat on the bed.

She stopped, staring. A robot.

Companion grade, taller and thinner than Paula, with wide dark eyes and long dark hair tied back in a long ponytail. She had skin two or three shades darker than Paula's, in that shading that could be any of a number of races. The fine dust of robotic makeup turned her eyelids into seascapes when she blinked. She would be beautiful dressed up, but at the moment she wore a basic working uniform and looked a little like a fancy maid.

A shiver of anger ran through her.

Aspen came up beside her and growled slightly.

Coryn glanced at Adam. He didn't even look guilty. But then, he had never met Paula.

"She's a top-flight security-bot. She's going to be your trainer when I can't participate. Julianna said you neither own her nor have to pay for her, but she hoped you'd see her as useful."

The robot stayed seated and extended a hand. "Hello. I'm Namina."

Who named these things? Coryn inclined her head but didn't take the offered hand. Could she send the robot back with Adam? "Pleased to meet you."

Adam interrupted. "You two can talk in a minute. I've got to leave pretty quick. Namina can unload the robocart and send it back up here. To stay on schedule, you should start your sprints in half an hour, and I think you still need to eat. Namina can set out breakfast. I'll show you the kitchen."

The kitchen turned out to be on the other side of the balcony, so the whole apartment was the big central room dominated by the glorious window, the one bedroom and bathroom on one side, and everything utilitarian on the other: kitchen, pantry, laundry room, printer, and a tiny storage closet. The whole thing might be five hundred square feet. Maybe.

Adam watched her carefully. "Do you like it?"

"Did you have to pick green chairs?"

"Do you like it?" he asked again.

"Sure." She didn't really know, except for the window. She loved the window.

"I left you food printer stock in the pantry, and the grocery drones are willing to land on the balcony. There are public spaces. Namina will show them to you after you finish your run. I liked living here." The look on his face didn't quite agree with his voice.

He looked desperate for some form of approval, so she said, "I'll be okay. Just go."

She felt grateful when he closed the door behind him. Damn him for being beautiful, for being an asshole, and for trading up to her room. Damn him for everything he was.

Coryn left for work with Aspen wriggling in her arms.

Namina slid out of the door after her.

"Stay home," Coryn told her.

Namina cocked her head disarmingly to the side. "My orders are to be your bodyguard."

Coryn sighed. "I don't want to be followed."

"Then I'll walk beside you."

She was going to be late. "Behind is fine."

Namina obeyed, the whisper of her footsteps a sound-shadow that grated on Coryn's nerves.

The wall image in her office showed scudding clouds and soaked land, a few swollen streams. She called Lou, relieved when she heard her voice. She began to write down the things Lou wanted, but Namina whispered, "I can record."

Coryn frowned but let the robot record.

A piece of the biggest barn wall had fallen in and some of the beds had been damaged, and so the list was rather long. When they stopped talking, they'd said nothing of substance, only spoken of tactics and immediate needs. Coryn felt a bit put out after the connection closed, but nonetheless she watched Lou appear to skip from spot to spot on the farm as the sat shots refreshed.

"Shall I place orders?" Namina asked.

"I thought you were a bodyguard."

"I am."

And undoubtedly part of whatever test Julianna was putting her through. "I'll do it," Coryn told her.

It took most of the afternoon to sift through websites and place orders for twenty-five hoes and two spools of three-inch rope and ten boxes of three-inch nails and twenty or so other particular things that Lou needed. Some, like lumber, couldn't be had. She added a few things Lou hadn't ordered that came up as available in Wenatchee. A box of apples. Another box of old tools. A good winter coat. It took another hour to schedule a truck delivery to Wenatchee, secure a spot on a delivery caravan going to Chelan a day later, and find a guard to watch the goods in Wenatchee overnight. It would be easier to send diamonds to Chicago.

Namina sat, silent and unmoving, a robot at rest until it was needed. She looked dead.

Jake came in just as she was closing up screens for the day. He looked smaller and thinner, and maybe even more bent. It had to be her imagination—no one fell in on themselves so much in one day. Still.

She straightened her shoulders, reacting to his slumped posture. "How are you?"

He sat down with a long sigh. "The doctor says my brain will keep working for a few more weeks." The smile that he tried to add to his words looked light and insubstantial. "How are you? Do you like your new place?"

"It has a nice window." Then she decided to be a little more charitable. "Sure. It'll be fine."

"I'm glad you brought Namina."

"Julianna hates robots. So why did she assign me one?"

"Julianna bought Namina for you. She's the same base code

model that she uses for her own protection-bots. Namina will do more than that—she can care for Aspen, and she can shop or cook for you. We . . . thought you might not have time to do all of that for yourself."

"Do I take her on runs—even ones with Adam?"

"If Adam is along, you can decide."

Nice of them to leave her some free will. She squelched the small surge of anger in her throat and reached across the table to take Jake's hand. He was dying, and they were still thinking of her. "Adam said something. He said there were weapons. Tell me."

Jake's fingers tightened in hers. He gazed at her for a long moment.

"How do I keep Lou safe if I don't know what's going on? Besides, she needs to know, and I'm the one who talks to her."

His eyes narrowed, almost disappearing into the wrinkles around them.

"Please."

"We've been telling her everything she needs to know. We're looking for supply caravans and we're looking for leadership. Who is running the group in Chelan? Do they report to someone else?"

"Why shouldn't she know about the weapons?"

"It might be dangerous if she asked the wrong questions."

"What do you know?"

He sighed. "The great taking was a chaos. States did it. We made it happen, but we didn't carry it out."

"I know."

"Well, you weren't even born yet. Because the states did it, it was uneven. And some, like Washington, led. All of the battered coastal states, all of the burning and drowning southern states, every state on the East Coast except Maine, we were all leaders. But some states, like Idaho and Wyoming and North Dakota and Colorado . . ." He paused, either thinking or recovering his strength. "Some states worked with the feds, at least at first. Weapons disappeared. Some were real weapons. Rocket launchers and small nukes and some early experiments in nanoweapons before they were banned. There might even be weapons factories in a few places in those states or in Canada. If there are, they're hidden, but we hear rumors."

That was a long speech for him. "What about Promise? What side was it on?"

"It's complicated. They started out hating us, you know. They hated the idea of the cities, they hated getting out-voted by Seattle. That's how they became a state in the first place. I think that might have been my fault, and Julianna's."

"Surely not!"

He looked amused.

"Well. Didn't that start before you even combined the cities?"

"It ended after. That doesn't matter. We made mistakes. Promise hated us at first, but then Promise's government—such as it was—fell, and the people aligned with us. That part of Washington always valued the wild and the land, and when we helped them with a large contingent of Returners, they decided, formally, to let us lead them. There really isn't a Promise any more. Not really."

She nodded. "You still haven't told me about the weapons."

"Some rumors say there are enough of them to take Seacouver."

"Even with the dome?"

"The dome was built for weather, and as a simplistic sort of security. Our real security is the constant check-ins between your chips and the city's systems. The city knows where everyone is, all the time."

That had always been true. She thought of it as convenience. "I suppose it is our security." She let go of his hand and sat back in her chair.

"What about my questions?" he asked.

She had journaled about them and thought of clever things to say, but only a few things felt authentic. He wasn't going to settle for clever. "I want to sing when I'm running, and when I'm high above the world and can see forever." She glanced at him, shaking a little—was this what he wanted?

He nodded, his face unreadable.

"I want to cry—but I don't—when . . . when I'm alone, but Aspen makes it better. I also want to cry when I see the disaffected. The ones with drones." She realized she had seen no such thing for a long time. Living in the tops of buildings, you didn't see the ones living at the bottom of society.

"And you would die for?"

"You. Or Julianna. Or Lou."

He stood up. "We will all die, even you. What bigger thing would you die for? Lou would die for the land."

"Like you and Julianna built the city?"

"I'm not going to answer my own question."

She still had Julianna's questions to answer. She got up and gave him a long hug. When he returned her hug, she felt a tiny bit better.

When she left, it was nearly evening. Namina trailed behind her, helping once when Lou got lost. By the time she sat in front of her window, the sea had turned dark with a single road of light on it linking the setting sun and the city.

Namina sat in one of the awful green chairs so Coryn took the other one, staring out the window. She felt more tired than she had in weeks, and she had a long set of intervals in her training the next day.

"Is there food here?" she asked.

"I have your training diet. I can order out."

At least Namina wasn't going to be a fussy mother type who did things Coryn hadn't asked her to do. "Sure."

Someone knocked on the door.

Namina started to get up, but Coryn forced her tired body out of the chair. "No. I'll get it."

CHAPTER TWENTY

Coryn opened the door, and gaped.

Pablo. The old preacher looked better than she'd last seen him. That had been at the height of the hacking runs against the city, right before she and Lou and Jake had been calm voices talking the city down from fear. She hadn't thought of him since. She should have.

While she stood in the doorway, hesitating, Aspen knew what to do immediately. He barked happily and leapt into Pablo's arms, twenty-plus pounds of dog thumping into the compact man's chest. Pablo laughed and grabbed the dog, grinning and making a half-hearted attempt to keep Aspen from licking the skin off of his face.

Coryn opened the door all of the way and stepped back. "Come in."

He did, pulling the door shut. "Julianna said I could find you here. She said I should. She wanted you to tell me what you know and me to tell you what I know." He glanced at the Namina, who sat quietly in the bright green chair, watching.

Coryn turned to Namina. "Can you go get us some food?"

The robot glanced at Pablo. "Is a salad all right? And a glass of wine?"

He nodded. "White."

Namina's expression remained completely neutral. "How long should I be gone?"

"Are you hungry now?" she asked Pablo.

"Only a little."

She glanced at the robot. "Half an hour? We can always post you outside the door."

"Fine. A salad and white wine."

Pablo sat in the chair the robot had vacated, and Aspen leaned into his leg, looking for all the world like he wanted to become a single dog/man being with his old friend. "Nice view."

"I just moved here."

"I heard. It appears you are doing well."

Given that the last place she'd found him was leading a ragtag band of the poor from a campsite in Issaquah, she had to admit it probably did look like she was doing pretty darned well. She chose not to mention that she'd just left rooms on the top floor of an even fancier building. "Did you get your people settled?"

"Mostly. Three of them decided the city was too much and left again. Everyone else is either studying for the tests or has already passed them and started working."

It seemed too easy. "Did Julianna help?"

"Yes." He looked down, his gaze stuck on the dog. "That was what I bartered for . . . for helping you all."

She wondered why he sounded ashamed. "You traded for things your people needed. That was selfless."

"I would have done it for nothing. Bartholomew needed to be stopped."

"He almost killed me once."

Pablo's eyes widened. "I'm not surprised. Will you tell me the story sometime?"

She shrugged, more interested in the future than the past. "What did Julianna want you to tell me?"

Pablo smiled. "You know her well."

"How well do you know her?"

His smile softened. "I worked for her once. The last two years when she was mayor. As chaplain. I tried to help her make sure there was some kind of spirit in the city."

How did you tell if a city had spirit? What was that anyway? "I had no idea there was such a job."

He picked Aspen up and put him in his lap. "It was good work. I suppose it helped. It's harder to see in a place where everyone is safe than in one where you can see the ways to die. But it's safer here, and I guess that lets the spirit grow. I brought people here, after all."

She nodded.

"I'm going back Outside tomorrow. To Chelan. Julianna wants another set of eyes there."

So this was work, following her home in the guise of an old friend. A slight twist of envy made her straighten her shoulders and stretch, sending it away. She was needed here. "Have you been there?"

"Twenty years ago. It was almost empty, then. Just a few families caught behind the taking."

He sounded wistful, like the past had been a better time for him. But maybe he could help her. "Did you know a woman named Valeria?"

He nodded.

"What can you tell me?"

He looked like someone remembering good things, a small smile appearing and disappearing. "So she's still there."

"Yes. Did you like her?"

"I did. I respected her, too. Anyone does. She's a wicked singer. Writes poetry good enough to take your breath way. Fights for her own." He shook his head, still apparently lost in memory. "I'm a priest. Sometimes she came to me for advice. I wouldn't want her as an enemy. It's been years, but I suspect she's still the same."

"Lou seems to think she's formidable."

"She must be old," he mused. "She's Julianna's age."

"I hear she's tough like Julianna."

"No one is that tough." His smile broadened his cheeks as he changed the subject. "Julianna said to include me in the same data net."

"Okay."

It was good to see him. She wanted to tell him all of her troubles. Maybe that was the preacher in him. Maybe everyone around him wanted to talk to him. But she didn't say anything. If she started, how would she ever stop?

He hesitated, looking like he didn't want to ask the next thing. "Can I take Aspen with me? I'd like the company. I'll keep him safe, and I'll bring him back."

The idea hurt. She chewed on her lip. Aspen hadn't left his side since he came in. Aspen wasn't his dog—but he wasn't really Coryn's, either. She, Pablo, and the dog had all met on a Listener's caravan, and after the Listeners were murdered, she'd adopted Aspen. So she'd rescued him from a dead master, but the dog had known Pablo before he met her. He was used to being Outside. It couldn't be good for him to live in a conference room.

"He'd like that," she said past the tightening of her throat "I'm pretty boring for him."

"He's alive because of you."

She called Aspen, and he came to her, but turned and watched Pablo while she petted him. Nevertheless, she kept him with her while she told him everything she knew. Except that Jake was dying.

Namina came back with food, and Coryn put Aspen down carefully to eat at the small table in the kitchen.

She wasn't hungry.

Tears backed up behind her eyes. Maybe because Aspen was about to leave, or because Pablo was, or maybe because she couldn't go Outside, or even because Jake was dying. Maybe it was everything.

Pablo reached out and touched her cheek. "What's so hard?"

She swallowed. "Just being alone."

"Maybe I shouldn't take Aspen."

He was misinterpreting. "No—that's not it. And then you would be alone." She heaved a little, coughing. "Maybe that's it—a little bit. But I went all the way out there to find Lou, and we never stopped and had a quiet meal together. I talk to her every day, but that's still not living in a family." Jake was dying and Julianna was breaking because of it, but she couldn't talk about that. Her cheeks flushed with embarrassment as tears started in earnest. "I'll be okay."

He nodded. "You are strong. And we are doing God's will whenever we help anyone else."

She shook her head. Talk of God had never excited her. He was born and died before robotics and cities that knew everything. It didn't seem likely his advice was any good for the modern, broken world. She stood up and washed her face, embarrassed and somehow relived. When she came back she felt more composed. "I'm sorry. It's been a rough week. But we are alive, and the Listeners are not."

"And now I'm going to do their job."

Of course he was. She hadn't thought if it that way. "Don't get hurt."

"I'll be back in a few weeks," he said.

"Bring my dog back safely." She stared at him.

"I won't come back without him."

She closed the door behind him, tears still hot behind her lids. It was possible she wouldn't see either of them again.

She would have cried in front of Paula, maybe leaned in for a long hug from her. But Namina wasn't Paula, Aspen was gone, she hadn't seen Julianna for days, and she couldn't bear to be vulnerable. She went to the bedroom, rummaged in her clothes box for a decent dark blue shirt with glittery gold thread at the arms and neckline, and a dragon embroidered in the same thread on the back. It slipped over her head like water. "I'm going out," she said.

Namina looked up from picking up the table. "You should be ready to sleep in an hour. You have sprint training tomorrow."

She would have obeyed Paula. But as she went out the door, she expected that she wouldn't be back for a while. The thought made her smile even though Namina followed her.

Coryn allowed Namina to follow and didn't bother to engage in a conversation. The robot knew her ID, so she might as well try to lose her own shadow.

She stalked over to the closest common area. One older woman sat there, knitting, and a young child played blocks with her mother, while a robot companion sat in resting position with her hands folded in her lap and her eyes closed. Three programmer types sat in the far corner, heads bent close to each other, talking so fast she couldn't understand them. They didn't even look up.

Nothing here.

She sighed and walked right through.

Perhaps she could make use of her robot shadow. "Namina?"

"Yes."

"Where is the nearest good bar that I can get into?"

"Alcohol is not on your training diet."

"No shit. I'm not old enough to get served anyway. Where is the closest good bar?"

"May I walk in front of you?"

"Yes."

The bar turned out to be a full building away and at street level. A red awning identified it as "Roco's Rest." Flowers spilled out of pots by the door, and light pulsed and flashed through the darkened windows. The door opened to spill out three young people, the scent of designer fruit-drinks and the beat of decent dance music coming into the street with them.

Namina held the door open for Lou. "Will this do?"

"I suspect." The burly robot bouncer glanced at her long enough to ID her, and slapped a red bracelet on her wrist and locked it down.

Without being asked, Namina went and stood in a line of robots along one wall. Although there were emergency exits, this was the only formal way in and out. Every robot would be able to pick up their charges as they left, even though they really couldn't see them easily from the waiting alcove. They looked strange, all of them in rest poses, lined up like extremely large dolls.

Good.

She headed for the dance floor, stress burning a hole in her stomach and driving her to move. The band was live, with a young red-haired lead singer of indeterminate sex and very determined energy, an older drummer with a long gray beard, and a small handful of less-noticeable people on various instruments.

The lead singer looked familiar, but Coryn couldn't place her. Them. Not a her.

Even though she didn't recognize the music, she stepped right into the crowd and began to stomp her feet and sway, her shirt flipping and swishing around her hips with the music.

She hadn't danced since she graduated from high school.

It felt good. No, it felt great.

She lost herself in song after song, sweat beading on her forehead and running down the middle of her back and the backs of her knees. Most of the songs were fast, which suited her perfectly. She could lose herself and her worries and her anger in the precision of movement, the attention to others around her, the shifting beat of the drum, the high wails of the singer.

The band called a break, and the lead singer hopped off the stage and scampered to the bar. They were shorter off-stage than they had looked on-stage, but just as bright as they turned around with a beer and a cup of water. The singer headed right for Coryn and handed her the water. "You must need this. You danced that whole set."

"Thanks." Coryn sipped at the water, and then upended the whole thing and filled her mouth. It was the best thing she had tasted all day. "I guess I did. Need the water. And dance the whole set." She sounded tongue tied, awkward. "Thanks," she said again.

The singer took her arm and tugged her back toward an empty table. "Good to see you again."

"You look familiar."

"I saw you at the Mayor's Ball."

Oh. There had been so many faces there. "That was an overwhelming evening."

They smiled. "I only have a few minutes' break, but I wanted to tell you I love your dancing."

It made for such a horrible pick-up line that maybe it wasn't one. "I've had good music to dance for."

That earned her a smile and an outstretched hand. "I'm Imke."

Coryn remembered. A pretty name, indeterminate. "Coryn."

"I've never seen you here."

Coryn laughed, feeling bit drunk in spite of the fact that water couldn't possibly have that effect. Maybe she was drunk with newness, with change, with making a choice of her own. "I usually don't have time to dance."

"That's almost criminal."

Coryn shook her head. Lou needed her. Jake was dying. "No. There's just a lot to do."

"You're far more earnest than you looked on the dance floor."

"Dancing felt good."

Imke's gentle laugh made the jewels in their hair and ears sparkle as they moved in the light. "Music is always good for the soul. Will you stay after and talk to me?"

Coryn swallowed, suddenly feeling light and a little nervous. They were beautiful, with creamy brown skin the color of good tea, long lashes over wide dark eyes, and lips so russet they must be enhanced. Imke's ears dripped with metal and stones and they had a few small tattoo marks on their face, although Coryn couldn't tell if they were real or merely paint. "How long?" she asked. "I mean, until you are done? I have to run in the morning."

An eyebrow went up. Not in an exaggerated way. Merely—interest. The singer glanced up at the stage. "At least a few hours."

"Do you play every night? Perhaps I could come back."

"I play Thursday through Sunday."

Coryn tilted her empty water cup into the light and stared into it. "This is Monday."

"Yes. I have a meeting tomorrow. But I'm free Wednesday night."

Coryn watched them carefully, uncertain and interested. They obviously drank, and she despised the way Adam drank too much, or at least avoided him for it. But they were far more interesting than Adam, even though Coryn could put no finger on why. They were quick and creative and moved like a dream.

They noticed her hesitation. "Dinner? At a reasonable hour?"

She didn't know what to think. Blessing? But he was far away. Besides, what would he say? *You might die every day. Get your work done and be brave.* Coryn stammered. "6:00 p.m.? Meet here?"

"Not here. Meet at the waterfront?"

"By the big wheel?"

"That's too crowded. There's a park just south of it. Near where the middle spiral of the Bridge of Stars touches down in the city center. Do you know where that is?"

"Yes. I'll see you there." Maybe best not to meet where Blessing had kissed her anyway.

They climbed back up onto the stage.

Coryn stayed through two more songs, watching them as much as the area around her, and she even stumbled once, looking up to see if they had noticed.

They had. They smiled and touched two fingers to their brow.

Coryn smiled back and turned to the doorway, and her keeper. She was already looking forward to Wednesday.

Damn.

CHAPTER TWENTY-ONE

The world smelled of old fire, dry fall grass, dust, and horse sweat, which was just fine with Lou. She was finally searching for wolves.

She and Mouse topped a ridge, and the view made her feel small and in tune with the world. The deep blue of Lake Chelan peeked here and there through brown hills. To the east, sharper ridges and then soft hills spread for miles, damping into high plains that would eventually hit mountains again. Sharper features rose to the east and north, blending into the Sawtooth Mountains.

Felipe came up beside her on Blessing's horse, and she asked him, "Where's the water from here? How far?"

"An hour that way." He pointed almost straight north. "Two if those two don't go faster," he suggested, with a lazy grin that softened the square features of his face. He nodded toward Valeria and Matchiko, who were still a bit behind, Valeria on Daryl's steady mount, and Matchiko on the slightly more fractious Pal.

"It would be worse if we brought Buster." She licked her lips, lifted her canteen, and sipped. "Is it always so dry in the fall?" They'd passed two small lakes, only one of which had been accessible for the horses to drink.

"Almost." He fell quiet, watching the skies. Even though Felipe was a few years older than Lou, he'd taken well enough to her leadership, and proven as useful and steady as Daryl. But Daryl would thrive anywhere. Felipe's life revolved around his mother. Lou suspected that all of Valeria's children would turn to dust if anything happened to her.

Felipe had sworn he'd seen wolves out here three times, and that he saw tracks almost every trip he took up into these hills, so she had asked him to show her.

They'd seen nothing.

As soon as the other riders caught up, Matchiko slid from her horse, grunting when her feet hit the ground.

Everyone dismounted except Felipe, who shook his head when Lou reached toward his horse's reins. "Someone has to watch."

Matchiko took her notebook out and started writing.

"What did you see?"

"Coyote tracks. Two green snakes." She held up a slender feather. "I think I found a peregrine falcon wingtip feather."

Felipe held his hand out for the feather, looking closely at it. "I haven't seen a peregrine in years. Been too hot."

Matchiko nodded. "Still too hot, I think. And dry. It's probably migratory. Still . . ." She tucked the feather neatly into one of her sample bags and tucked that into her saddlebag. She grinned up at Lou. "Do I get a shower tonight?"

If they turned around now, they would have to push hard to get back to the farm. "No."

"Good."

"I love you," she whispered.

Matchiko merely laughed and climbed back on her horse.

It took more than an hour to reach Felipe's promised water. Lou selected a flat spot with some nearby rocks for seats, and glanced at Felipe. "Why don't you and Matchiko go look for tracks? You can make it all the way around the water and back here around before dinner."

"Hey!" Matchiko said. "That means we have to eat your cooking."

"You're the best tracker."

"Felipe might have me beat."

"You can test your skills. Take paper. We'll manage the horses and setup camp."

"I'll bet on Felipe," Valeria declared, apparently willing to support Lou's plan.

"And I'll bet on Matchiko."

As soon as Matchiko and Felipe set their saddles on the ground, pommels down, damp blankets spread on tops, they were gone. Lou turned to Valeria. "They look like a panther and a bear."

Valeria smiled.

"Two wild things, anyway." Lou wished she were going with them. She wanted to spot the first wolf track out here. But she also needed time with Valeria.

Valeria turned to her. "Tents?"

"Sure." As they were stringing up the top pole on the smaller tent for Felipe, Lou asked, "Where did Felipe learn so much about tracking?"

"His father was a guide. His name was Immanuel. When the taking started, he kept his job, since he was in Stehekin and it was sanctioned. It was one of the few jobs that survived. It didn't pay much, but it fed us."

"What happened to him?"

Valeria shook her head. "He disappeared one day. Felipe looked for his bones in the hills for years but never found him. I think he still goes out to look sometimes."

Lou imagined that, Felipe riding the hills and looking down. How sad. "How old was Felipe then?"

"Twelve. He used to accompany his dad sometimes, even that young, but that trip I didn't let him go. He had school. They all went to school in Stehekin, every one of my kids. I made them learn."

"Of course you did." It was probably twenty years ago, maybe more. She could picture it, too. A younger Valeria with seven kids stuck to her, dancing to her demands, all of them a pack that no one in their right mind would challenge. "You had to raise them all, didn't you?"

Valeria smiled at that, as if raising seven kids was like having a glass of wine or making a single complex meal. "Sofia was only one year old when he died."

"I'm impressed." Julianna had described Valeria as a revolutionary. "You had to be quite the matriarch. How did you survive?"

Valeria didn't answer until they finished the first tent, pounding in stakes on each corner to hold it in case of wind. "I went to work for Henrietta at first, saved money, then started farming."

"Who's Henrietta?" Lou dragged the bigger tent out of its folds in her saddlebag.

Valeria took one corner and pulled, then grabbed a second corner and walked toward the spot they'd chosen for the women's tent. "If you think I'm a matriarch, you should see her."

"Tell me about her?"

Valeria laughed. "There are no words for Henrietta. She's John Smith's mother."

"Surely that's not his real name."

"It is. Henrietta named all of her children as white-bread American as she could. But more later. She depresses me. I will sing you a song about her tonight, while we're watching stars." She flashed a wide smile. "If I remember."

"Okay." As they settled on a space for the tent, Lou realized how grateful she was for Valeria's help. She had expected to fight the older woman, but Valeria took Lou's orders, and if she disagreed she did it in private, to Lou's face. A little too often, that, but Lou had made peace with it. Felipe, Astrid, and Angel all worked for the Foundation now. The parents. They were perfect.

Felipe knew how to track, Astrid's knowledge of plants rivaled Matchiko's, and Angel had started following Daryl and Blessing around like a puppy.

She shook the door open and held up the front of the tent for Valeria to attach a rope to. "Will Felipe or Matchiko see more animals?"

"Felipe will win."

"You are very stubborn. There's something else I wanted to ask. That road we passed way down by town?"

Valeria bent down to pick up a pole. "What about it?"

"There were a lot of tracks on it." It had been a forest road once, a maintained gravel way to get up here into the Sawtooths. "Horse tracks. They weren't more than a week old."

"Caravans."

"Caravans?"

"Traders. People who take things from place to place and let people trade other things for them. They've gotten busy ever since all the Listeners were killed or sent back to the city."

Maybe they'd driven the Listener purge. She tugged on the back wall of the tent to get it square while Valeria went for the hammer and stakes to finish it off. "What do they trade?"

"Food. Sometimes they buy it from us. They trade horses. Donkeys. Information. They take our fall chickens sometimes, use them for a few meals, give us a tool or two. It's a way to make a living, out here." She shrugged and arched an eyebrow at Lou. "You have a golden life."

A common perception: Wilders as spoiled because they drew salaries for living Outside. "I've lost a few friends in this business. We're targets."

"Everybody dies Outside."

Lou stiffened. Valeria was nowhere near that casual about her family. "How often do they come through? The traders?"

"Here? More often than most places. We need the supplies. They just rode through a week ago."

That jived with Coryn's statement, or close. Good. "Any juicy information?"

Valeria shook her head. "Not for a while. Everything's gone quiet since the last attacks."

"There will be more."

"We Keepers will always hate it when the city tells us what to do." She'd never heard that term. "Keepers?"

"Yeah. Keepers. We don't want to go to the city, we don't want to go backward. Returners think the past will save us. Stupid. The past is a dead god." She brushed a stand of hair from her face. "The way to look is forward. There's room for sustainable living out here. Small farms." She glanced at Lou, smiled. "Like you and I share."

Lou's stomach tightened as she watched Valeria kneel and tap the last tent peg into the ground.

"No factories, no big farms. No cattle. We get that. But farms like ours, and the ability to live out here?" She swept her arm toward the lake. "Don't you want that?"

Lou stiffened. "We haven't stopped the warming yet, or put back enough wild places."

"There are many."

Lou was saved from having to respond as Felipe and Matchiko walked into camp. "Dinner ready?"

"What did you do? Run around the lake? How do you find tracks that way?"

"We saw a black bear with two of this year's cubs. So we turned around."

A bear with cubs! Lou smiled.

Valeria cocked an eyebrow at her. "See, there's wild for you."

Lou's smile soured. She'd seen more dead bears than living ones, and not many of either. They were nowhere near ready for more humans out here. Nevertheless, She forced a little humor into her voice for Matchiko's sake. "Who won?"

Felipe smiled. "We have to count."

Matchiko tilted her head, looking briefly younger. "I counted five different things. Rabbit. Deer. Snake. Coyote." She smiled. "And bear."

"No wolf?" Lou asked.

Felipe held up his notebook. "No. But I saw three distinct coyote. Different animals."

Valeria glanced at Lou, smiling. "We'll call it a tie. I presume the bear isn't coming this way?"

Felipe answered. "It ran off to the north, so I think we're safe."

Matchiko was already reaching for supplies and pulling out cooking implements.

Lou teased her, "So you really don't like my cooking?"

"Mine's better."

"No argument." If only they'd seen a wolf. Maybe tomorrow. Damned things were elusive as hell.

That night, from her tent, she heard the calls of at least one coyote pack, maybe two. The howls and yips bounced off of the hills and there was no way to tell where they came from. Not close, anyway.

She hoped she wouldn't have to shoot coyotes. It happened. Wilding meant managing populations while you drove them into balance. She'd shot buffalo and coyote. The coyotes were hard. She admired them. They were small, cooperative with each other, and fierce, but also beautiful.

As she drifted off, she remembered that Valeria hadn't sung to her about Henrietta. She hadn't sung at all.

The next day warmed up slowly from a near freeze. They heated their hands with cups of coffee before getting the horses saddled and ate lunch three hours northeast of where they had camped. Most of what they'd ridden through had been marked by fire. The trees were no higher than the horse's bellies, mostly spruce and subalpine fir here, now that they were higher. The recent storms had driven spears of green grass up through the summer's sun-dried tans.

They'd seen no wolves, no deer, nothing but three coyotes at a distance and plenty of rabbits. Lou sighed, disappointed. "We need to start home."

Matchiko nodded. Her foot was mostly healed and they'd been on horses, but she still looked a little drawn.

Valeria and Felipe exchanged glances. "Let's go for one more hour," Felipe urged. "I know a faster way back."

She hated going back with nothing. "Do you have a particular place in mind?"

Valeria merely smiled, but Lou interpreted that as a yes.

They rode up a series of steeply cornered switchbacks, the sun blazing down on them. Sweat covered the horses' necks, Lou's neck, and stuck her hair to her scalp.

Surely it shouldn't be this hot here?

They topped the hills, finally, and Valeria immediately dismounted. In front of them and below, a stream ran through a narrow valley. "This is Grade Creek," she said. "Felipe has offered to watch the horses so we can go sit by the water."

Lou glanced at Matchiko, who smiled and said, "Maybe I can put my ankle in cold water."

"You can." Valeria led them down a long, rocky trail bordered by small trees.

"Why did we leave the horses?" Lou asked.

"So they don't spook the wildlife."

Lou swallowed, uncertain what to think. She walked just a little behind Matchiko, prepared to steady her if she twisted her ankle or fell.

Valeria led them along a faint trail near the creek, which was thin this time of year but still fell in small, singing waterfalls. She settled them by one of those, where the water itself sounded like music. She pulled a flute from her shirt, surprising Lou.

When Valeria began to play, it surprised her more. Each note rose by itself on the air, crisp and resonant.

Matchiko settled on a rock, took off her shoe and sock, and dipped her foot in the creek. A sigh of happiness escaped from her.

The music lifted Lou's mood. So did the creek and the fresh air. All of it. The wolves would come in time.

Matchiko pointed upstream.

A doe and a spike had stopped to drink. They looked curiously toward the women but continued to the water, the doe watching while the spike drank. They traded places. After both finished, they backed up carefully and turned, twitching white tails, then walked away as if nothing about the strange sounds or the three visitors disturbed them.

Valeria stopped playing and folded her hands over her knees. "That was beautiful."

"Did you call them?" Matchiko asked.

Valeria smiled. "Do you believe that a flute could call a deer?"

"Not really."

"Then I did not."

CHAPTER TWENTY-TWO

Lou stood outside on the lawn. She tapped her foot, standing with her arms crossed while she waited for Valeria. A dry, cold week had passed, with no time to go into the hills looking for wolves again. The bright green had died back, the hills again russet and tan. A few hard frosts had pushed the deciduous trees to declare fall in unison, and to become simultaneously busy dropping fat brown and yellow leaves.

Valeria came through the front door, followed by Astrid and Alondra. Together like this, they looked like versions of the same woman at different ages. With no apology at all for being fifteen minutes late, they started the long walk to town. Each carried a bag of produce.

Valeria began to sing, and her daughter and granddaughter joined her, and after a bit Lou sang as well, her voice soft since she neither knew the songs nor sang as boldly as the other three. They sang in English and then in Spanish, and the Spanish was sweeter. Lilting. Maybe it just sounded better because she only knew about a third of the words, so it seemed mysterious.

They wound down and down, passing among wrecks of houses and, here and there, houses that had been painted or newly fenced. Once, a dog ran out to greet them. Valeria called it by name, JoeJoe. It jumped up and put its big paws on her shoulders and she let it lick her face. It followed them for a quarter mile before turning back.

The singing and the dog and the carefree walk lifted Lou's spirits.

As they came into the outskirts of town, Valeria made a sudden left turn and led them into a large warehouse with white paint peeling from the walls. A pair of young white women guarded the door, although they merely nodded at Valeria and watched Lou with naked curiosity.

Inside, light filtered through high windows to illuminate tables full of goods, each with one or more tenders nearby. Here and there, would-be barterers wandered between tables. Boxes lay stacked against the short walls. Small locked rooms that appeared to have been built from scavenged doors and garage walls lined the longest wall.

While the other three headed to tables to sell their cucumbers and squash and late-season carrots, Lou walked slowly down the two wide aisles, looking at the merchandise. Scavenge, mostly. Old clothes. A pile of leashes and dented dog bowls. Shoes, tied together in pairs by the laces or thin scraps of material. Glassware and dishes, some chipped. All of it useful in some way, none of it new, and very little printed. Two tables of homemade crafts for Thanksgiving, all clearly made by children. She bought a rock painted like a turkey.

She had been in the city a few months ago. The contrast looked stark. In the city, almost everything was made and recycled in days, always fresh, never old, never stained. The things Outside were mostly old, except the children's crafts, and those had been crafted from recycled junk. Outside enjoyed more freedom, but the poverty depressed her.

A few of the proprietors looked hopeful as she approached.

She stopped in front of a table that held knives and machetes. The visibly pregnant girl behind it was cleaning the rust from a long blade with a soft stone, her stringy black hair hanging over her eyes. Lou's heart raced, and she cleared her throat.

The girl looked up, and her eyes widened.

Sadness softened Lou, almost made her dizzy. "Paulette."

The girl set the machete down and swallowed. "Yes."

For a moment Lou felt tongue-tied, but she tried a few sentences in her head before she spoke. "I'm sorry you didn't make it to California."

Her eyes darted around the warehouse, and when she was satisfied that no one was near she spoke softly, her voice filled with a deep emptiness. "They killed my husband. Rick. Henrietta made Scott help them beat him. My brother? You remember."

"I do."

"She made me watch."

Anger drove Lou to look around. She wanted to stare, but that would draw attention. Who had done this? She remembered how earnest the boy had been, and how desperate. How young. She shivered and made herself look briefly down the aisle. She wasn't going to be cowed by the evil in this town. The room was mostly women and children. The children played quietly, the women talked quietly, and a few glanced at her from time, or toward Valeria. She glanced back down, forcing her body to look relaxed. Paulette didn't need the attention. She turned back to her and whispered. "I'm so sorry."

"Your big horse, is it still alive?"

"Yes. We live here now."

The girl's eyes widened again, and she flinched. All of the fight that Lou had admired had been stripped from her. Did she think Lou had given her away? That she would put up with such evil. It was still sinking in, the evil. *They made me watch.* "Not with your people," Lou replied. "Never that. We are not them. Not like them. We live in an old vineyard up in the hills."

"I thought you were Wilders?"

"We are. Even Wilders need a place to sleep at night. We're sharing a house with Valeria." Surely the girl knew who Valeria was?

Apparently. Her eyes grew even wider and her lips thinned into a slight smile. "Valeria is good," she pronounced as she looked around. "Please move on before anybody notices you talking to me."

"Is your family here?" Lou asked.

Paulette ran a finger along the dull edge of a blade. "Some."

"Are you related to John Smith?"

She hesitated a moment. "He's my uncle."

Lou picked up a machete, feeling the heft and balance of it. Not too bad. She made her hand into a knife-edge and balanced the weapon just below the hilt. A finger identified the blade as sharp. "Did you have to marry the man you don't like?"

She shook her head. "He doesn't want me now. Maybe after I have the baby."

Lou stiffened. She hissed, "I hope he never wants you."

"I don't get to choose."

Lou handed the machete across the table, her arm still and her muscles tense. "Can I buy this?"

Paulette nodded briefly. "For what?"

Lou held her hand out, full of old jewelry and coins.

Paulette's fingers moved birdlike across her palm picking up five items, looking up at Lou furtively, and adding a small cross.

"I hope you're okay," Lou whispered. "I'd like to talk to you more. Can you ever get away?"

Her right hand curled around her belly. "No."

But she had gotten away once. "If you can, if you need to talk, or you need help, we're up there. You can even get me a message."

Paulette put the money into a metal box and nodded. "Go, now," she said. "Please."

Lou wanted to know why, but Valeria and her offspring were two tables away and headed toward her, so she gave Paulette a last look that she hoped the girl would interpret as caring.

Paulette was looking toward the door, her gaze slightly vacant. Her eyes looked damp.

Lou headed for Valeria, machete swinging at her side. It was all she could do not to grip it tightly and swing it at something. Who could do such a thing to their own child?

As soon as she came near, Valeria pulled her aside and whispered, "Are you okay?"

"No." She glanced at Alondra. What if she ended up with these people? "No. But I will be. I can't talk about it right now."

Valeria nodded. "Okay."

Alondra said, "Come see our bar?"

The storefront was one of ten or twelve that lined the road north out of town. It looked abandoned. Old show posters covered the windows, making it impossible to see inside. There were also handbills and signs that might have come from protests. Bits of history.

STOP illegal Taking!
LAND RIGHTS are HUMAN RIGHTS
Keep your cities off our land!

The graphics were rather beautiful, if faded. Two notes had been pinned to a board by the door, and Valeria grabbed them and then held her palm up to the lock.

The door clicked.

Valeria motioned them through, and only as the door shut behind them did lights bloom on, letting Lou see the interior. Tables and chairs were strewn artfully in front of a big wooden bar, the colors a mash of dark greens and browns and blacks that somehow went together. The floor was polished concrete. When Lou turned back toward the door, she spotted a plywood wall, acting to block the light more effectively than the posters outside would by themselves. It had been hand-painted with a mural of mountains and animals. Alondra watched her admire it, curious.

Lou nodded. "I like it." She pointed. "There's a wolf."

Sure enough, a stylized wolf howled from the top of a mountain on the far side of the mural. "Felipe drew that," Alondra said.

Lou nodded, stepping closer to the image to look up a little at it. Not realistic, but good. Even though it was only three colors—a white, a brown, and a gray—the wolf looked alive. Her estimation of Felipe rose another notch.

If she wasn't careful, this entire usurping illegal family were going to be her new heroes.

"It's from memory," Alondra said. "From when Akita was young."

"Akita?" She knew that name. A legendary name, from an old story. *The Jungle Book*. "It's a real wolf?"

Alondra nodded. "Felipe knows how to find him."

Wolves usually traveled in pairs or packs. "Is he a lone wolf?"

"He has an alpha female."

"Does she have a name?"

Alondra hesitated, and then whispered, "Ghost."

Had Felipe really been trying to find the wolves when he led them into the hills? "Do you know how to find wolves?"

Alondra nodded. "Sometimes Felipe takes me with him."

The girl looked hesitant, and Lou decided this wasn't the time to press.

Lou turned to look at the rest of the room. A full kitchen took up the back, and shelves held books and papers and a few goods that might be for sale. She had expected vegetables and the like, but if so, they weren't here now. Fresh air coming in through the door diluted the slightly sour smell of old alcohol and rotting wood that permeated the place. Valeria must have noticed it as well; she threw open two other windows, letting natural light in with the air. "At night," she told Lou, "we have discipline about the light. We have to. So anytime we're here during the day, we air it out."

"It's so quiet," Lou said.

Astrid laughed. "Not on Saturday. You should come down. They let us serve from Saturday before dusk and stay open until dawn on Sunday. Some other days we open for poetry and singing, but mostly when the weather is bad. Those days they only allow us to serve a single glass of beer or wine to each person."

"Who is *they*? John Smith?"

Astrid nodded. "He leads the enforcers, Outside. His sister runs the town. I suspect that's why there's only one night of alcohol. If the men were in charge it would be more."

"Why do they get to tell you what to do?"

The slightest cloud passed across Valeria's dark eyes. "We negotiated. Everything out here is barter. They leave us alone outside of town, we follow their rules inside of town, and negotiate the rules in here. They *will* let us keep Saturday night. You'll see what it's like if you come. They'd have to fight their own people as well as us." Valeria slid into a seat, gesturing for Lou to do the same. "I just wanted you to see this, to know where it was. You should come down some Saturday."

Lou sat across the table from her. "I'd like that. But you don't sell the produce from here?"

"You told us we couldn't."

Lou filed that away. She had told them that, but she'd only half-expected to be obeyed. A sign of how much Valeria thought she might need Lou? Or at least the ecobots? She had finally calmed down enough to talk. "The girl I got the machete from? Do you know her?"

Alondra nodded. "Paulette. She ran away."

Lou wondered what Alondra knew. "Why?"

Valeria stepped in before the girl could answer. "She didn't do what she was asked in a family where the women behave."

"Isn't that disturbing?"

"Young girls get little say in things. It wasn't always like this, and these people weren't always like this." Valeria steepled her hands and looked lost in thought for a bit. When she looked back up she glanced at each of them, gathering attention. "I once fought side by side with some of them." She gestured toward the door, a reference to the posters outside. "But now I mostly avoid them."

Lou nodded. "It feels like a patriarchy."

Valeria smiled. "There are powerful women."

"Henrietta?" Lou asked.

"And her daughter, and her daughter's daughter."

Lou swallowed, thinking of the line of women right in front of her. "Like you?"

"I do not have such a tight hold on my family as they do."

"Then they must be formidable."

Astrid giggled.

Alondra brought a pitcher of water around and filled their glasses.

Lou savored the cool water, noting they had the wherewithal to make ice. "But still, it seems like the men run things."

"They like to think they do. Maybe that is how patriarchy has always worked."

Lou sat back, thoughtful. "I have a friend named Bartholomew who makes all the decisions for his band."

"The hacker?"

Lou wasn't quite able to hide her surprise that Valeria knew him.

"It's a small world," the old woman said. "I know most people who ride through here from time to time."

Surely Bartholomew was locked up in Seacouver somewhere after his attack there. It had only been what—a few months? He wouldn't be at trial yet, would he? "Bartholomew is trouble."

Valeria nodded, her eyes a little wary.

"Why would people like Bartholomew come here?"

"Because there are powerful people hiding here. Why do you think the feds allow Chelan to exist?"

She had heard this idea before, that the feds might be behind the attacks on the cities. "Why not Wenatchee? There are fewer ways in and out of Chelan, and strangers would be noticed more here, wouldn't they?"

"Wenatchee used to be overrun with Listeners. And there was a Wilders recruiting station, as well. Too many people go through Wenatchee, and an increase in population would be impossible to hide."

Maybe she should have spent a few extra days there. "I might go to Wenatchee to recruit in a few weeks. I need a few more biologists."

"I can go with you," Valeria offered. "Make it a trade trip."

"That might be helpful. How fast has the population grown here?"

Astrid shook her head. "We aren't sure. Strings of people walk or ride down from Canada from time to time. Some have federal insignia. Most don't stay. Some do. No one tells us these things, and to stay safe we don't come to town except to trade and to do our business here on the weekends. We try to be necessary and not to be targets."

Lou blew out a long breath and stood up, wishing this would all go away and that she could just go into the hills and count birds and deer and wolf. Who would have thought Valeria would submit to being bossed around by people who would kill a young girl's young husband? She shivered. Maybe even their own daughter's husband?

For just a moment, she contemplated ordering her ecobots to strip all of the houses downtown to their foundations. But that would make her as bad as these people, wouldn't it? That realization turned some of her anger to contemplation, but enough remained to drive her fingers to tap on the table and make her body to feel a need to move.

Alondra came by and collected the glasses, taking them to the sink to wash by hand.

Valeria rose. "We should start back."

"Where does Henrietta live?"

"Wherever she wants to." Astrid stepped aside to let Alondra out of the door first.

CHAPTER TWENTY-THREE

Coryn stared over the seawall railing at the dark shifting Sound. The great wheel's reflection glittered with fall colors. The baskets were lined in orange and the circle shone a deep red-orange that reminded her of Imke's lips.

Blessing had been beside her the last time she was here, and they'd kissed at the top of the wheel. But Blessing hadn't kissed her properly since, and he wasn't here. He'd asked her for nothing.

She had no idea if this qualified as a date or if she wanted it to, but it was certainly the first time she had met someone outside of Julianna's circle for a meal. Nerves goaded her into walking while a desire to look calm kept her pace slow.

The waterfront seemed overcrowded, filled with people showing off new coats and boots. People who weren't Imke. She stopped by the railing where she'd asked Namina to wait for her, and asked her if she'd seen Imke. The robot shook her head, and Coryn went back to walking.

She spotted Imke before they saw her. They looked older off stage. Their black pants and pale blue T-shirt seemed printed to an exact fit. Their face was an amazing palette of blues and browns, even their hair was blue tonight, pulled up in a braid, with long strands of jeweled string or chain glittering along their neck and shoulders and swinging with every stride. Their lips were the same enchanting russet, and immediately, Coryn wanted a kiss.

She felt plain by comparison, in spite of the hours she'd spent poring over designs for her outfit. She'd ordered black pants with geometric cut-outs that loosely mimicked stars and planets, and a flowing sage-green shirt that highlighted her green eyes and contrasted with her red hair. She had felt fabulous, and now she felt understated.

Imke seemed to appreciate Coryn's look just fine. Coryn's chest felt light as Imke's smile spread all the way across their face, lifting their cheekbones and looking so genuine and unforced it made Coryn smile. She sped up as she went to meet them.

They led her back to the railing, leaning out and looking over the wide seawall. "I like the wild places," Imke said. "We have water like this, huge lakes that are security holes in our wall, but beautiful. They are the only places we really have with horizons."

"Where?"

"Oh." Imke smiled. "I feel like I know you so well, but I don't, I suppose." Their words drawled off as they stared out over the water. "I'm from Chicago. Assigned to our embassy here."

Up close, Coryn could see that the jewels hung on small nanoribbons so thin she could barely see them. Metallic. Tiny knots held the jewels and faceted beads apart from each other, the whole long assemblages light enough to blow in the wind and tinkle against each other. There were maybe twenty or twenty-five strands curling down from Imke's hair and lying all along the left side of their neck. Fascinated, Coryn stayed quiet, her gaze skipping between the water and Imke.

What a stunningly beautiful human.

Imke pointed. "Is that a fish?"

Coryn squinted. The city's lights only illuminated a few hundred feet of water, maybe inches deep. The surface shifted and moved around, and rings of water moved through it. Then a gray form rose and fell, slick and finned. Coryn watched while it breached and breathed, noting its slightly flattened face. "It's a harbor porpoise."

"Is that a dolphin?"

Coryn smiled. "Close enough."

"Do you know a lot about dolphins?"

The porpoise disappeared, and Coryn watched the places it seemed likely to surface. "I'm fascinated with cetaceans. Particularly orcas, but really everything that lives out here."

"I'm impressed."

Heat flushed Coryn's cheeks. "I was glad you wanted to meet down here."

"Do you want to go on the Ferris wheel?"

"No."

Imke smiled. "Good. I've been on it three times already. What's your favorite place in the city?"

"The top of the Bridge of Stars."

"Really, a bridge?"

"I love the view. I'll show it to you. But not tonight. It's work to get there. We're not dressed for all that."

"Can we take a car?"

"No." Coryn gave up watching for the porpoise. "That's why I like it. You have to work for it. Walk up, run up, or bike up."

"So where else can we go?"

All Coryn could really think of was bridges and running places and parks and places Julianna owned. None of them seemed right for Imke. So she countered. "Where would you like to go?"

"Were you born here?"

"I'm really boring," Coryn countered. "Mostly I was poor. I can show you the places poor people go, but once more, we're not dressed right."

Imke raised a bright blue eyebrow. "Are you really? Boring? I don't think Julianna suffers the boring."

Coryn swallowed. Maybe she was boring. Maybe that was why she'd been cast out of the higher levels and of her room. But this wasn't the moment for that either. She had already decided this was important, and that whether or not Imke liked her mattered. Just being near them made Coryn's palm sweaty and her words tickle in her throat. "You said you liked my dancing. Do you know a good place to dance?"

Imke stood up. They and Coryn were almost equal in height, or would be if Imke weren't wearing platforms that made them a few inches taller. "I know just the place."

"I'm not twenty-one."

"I saw your red bracelet in the bar. Where I'm taking you, age doesn't matter."

"Oh."

Imke glanced at Namina. "Can you ditch your companion?"

Can you, rather than *will you*. Imke didn't appear to have a robot keeper, but they were giving Coryn room.

"I can't."

A sigh slid though Imke's lips. "I didn't think so. Well, she'll have to stay outside. There will be a few more like her."

Coryn shrugged.

Fifteen minutes later, Imke led Coryn into a large round hotel building and took an escalator to the top. After traversing a long hallway and taking a tiny set of stairs to the roof, they stepped onto a big square patio. The lighting was all ambient—light from other buildings, light from stars. A cool wind plucked at Imke's jewels.

Three or four other companions sat at tables, all of them young models with chiseled features and spare clothes. Coryn nodded, and Namina went over to an empty table and sat, staring out over the city. She was beautiful, maybe as beautiful as the others left out here, but she also looked a little plainer in ways Coryn couldn't figure out until Imke leaned down and whispered in her ear. "See that girl-bot over there?"

"Yes."

"She's almost half a million dollars."

"Oh." After moment she leaned up and whispered, "Why?"

"She's . . . precise. Clearly a sex-bot and a companion. But see how fine her features are? Don't get too near—I'm sure you wouldn't be allowed to touch her, but doesn't she almost glow?"

The robot turned toward them, her eyes picking up enough light for the soft green-blue of them to show. They looked deep and wise and a little thoughtful, dripping with empathy.

Coryn leaned into Imke. "She looks more than human."

"She does." Imke brushed their lips across Coryn's cheek, a touch so hot it almost burned. They tugged on Coryn's arm. "Let's go."

Imke opened the wide door at the far end of the patio while all of the companions watched them. Just inside, a male robotic guard stopped them for a moment. He stared at Imke and then at Coryn, and then nodded sagely.

They passed through yet another door, the setup reminding her of the security vestibule for Julianna's private offices. On the far side of the doors, a patio swept across the top of the building, the crowded dance floor pulsing with pastel colors. Mist rose from the edges, swirling across the dancer's feet, up as high as their knees in a few places. A beautiful wrought metal and wood fence with glass panes and fantastic dragons and birds enclosed the patio, which was lined with tables for two and potted trees covered with pale yellow lights. Robotic gargoyles bigger than humans occupied the corners, turned in toward the dance floor. The lead singer of the band played on a raised pedestal. He nodded familiarly at Imke.

Imke pulled Coryn into the crowd. Her feet moved awkwardly for the first song, and then Imke moved into her, putting a hand on the small of her back, and Coryn let out a long breath and started *dancing*.

Imke directed her, and then let themselves be directed, moving easily to cues.

Dancers began to give them room, and a few patrons clapped after Imke swirled Coryn under their arm, picked her up, and twirled her away.

Five songs later, sweat covered Coryn's skin and soaked her shirt. Imke called a brief halt and led Coryn over to a single open table that appeared, as if just for them. A pair of stylized eagles decorated the fence nearby. Imke nodded at the outsized birds. "I'll let them keep you company for a moment. I'll be right back."

Coryn had barely recovered her breath when Imke showed up with two glasses of water and two glasses of a pale white substance that didn't quite look like wine.

"What is that?" Coryn asked.

"Dessert wine. It's sweet, but you can use the sugar after all of that dancing."

Coryn reached for it and took a sip. "Sugar's not on my training diet." She took another sip, letting the wine rest on her tongue and trickle down her throat. "But this is good."

"Training?"

"I'm a runner."

Imke raised their eyebrows. "That explains your finely tuned energy."

Coryn didn't know how to react to that, so she didn't. "If you've only been here a month, how did you know this place existed?" Coryn asked. "I never heard of it." She didn't bother to ask how Imke managed to get wine for her. This place stank of the privilege of the super-rich. Not the quiet rich like Julianna. The show-offs. The chair she sat on probably cost a month's rent for her apartment.

Imke sipped their wine, their jewels clinking against each other as they moved. "I work for the mayor of Chicago, and he sent me here a few years ago. I split time between the two cities now."

"So you're more than a singer?"

"Aren't you more than a dancer?"

"Sure. I'm a runner. And I work for a foundation."

"You're not a Wilder."

"My sister is."

"So what are you?"

Why did everyone want to know that? Coryn finished her wine in a long swallow. "That's a good question."

Imke cocked their head at Coryn. "You have a job a lot of people would love."

"Working for Julianna and Jake?"

"Yes."

She blushed. It still amazed her as well. "I mostly support my sister. I'm helping her get things done. She's in Chelan."

"What is she working on?"

"Wolves."

"Is she safe there?"

Coryn shrugged. "Is anyone safe anywhere?"

"No." Imke grinned. "But every time I feel safe I also feel bored." They leaned in a little. "I'm here to spy. My boss thinks the recent attacks were designed to test Seacouver, figure out the strength of your defenses. And that there's worse to come. We have walls, but they can be breached. So we're worried for ourselves, too."

"Is that why you're making friends with me?"

Imke reached a hand across the table.

Coryn lifted her hand up, let it slide into Imke's while keeping her eyes locked with theirs. Their eyes were huge and beautiful, as exotic as everything else. Imke's fingers were long and slender, as gender indeterminate as everything else about them, as beautiful. Warm.

"I like your dancing," Imke said. "It's that simple."

Coryn's chest lightened, and the bottom of her throat grew a small lump. "Let's go." She stood, pulling Imke toward the floor again, feeling a little naughty for insisting, a little frightened at her own bravery.

Imke danced more aggressively this round, bumping up against Coryn, swirling hips, smiling with abandon, lifting their arms up and clapping.

Coryn matched Imke's movements, exaggerated them.

Imke smelled like roses and sweat.

Other dancers surrounded them, clapping.

Coryn danced harder.

Imke added sensuality, slowing down and staring at Coryn, looking utterly and only at her, and yet as if they didn't care what anyone, even Coryn, thought about them.

Coryn lost herself in the response, gazing back, her body moving of its own accord, reacting to rhythms she hadn't known existed. She had learned to dance with Paula, but Paula had never taught her to move this way.

Heat slammed through her center, becoming a spike that she danced upon. Light pounded her half-closed eyes, and her hair dripped with sweat. She felt wet and ragged and starved.

Imke slowed, backed off, smiled.

Coryn slowed in response, her breath sharp.

Imke offered a small curtsey accompanied by a wide smile.

Coryn laughed, almost stumbling.

A small crowd clapped.

"Let's go. I have somewhere else to take you."

Coryn followed Imke through a different door, leaving Namina behind with the fancy companions.

CHAPTER TWENTY-FOUR

Imke led her along three tall skybridges between buildings, all of them crowded with late-night partiers and their companions, their railings and roofs blinking with bright white and blue lighting. Glass candy canes hung from one roof, clinking together just above her head. She went from hot inside the building to cool on the skybridge, stumbling once.

Imke took her hand, and a brief look of concern crossed their face. "Time to feed you."

Coryn nodded, realizing she'd had wine and air and water and excitement since lunch. And nothing else. She felt lightheaded and dizzy.

She could stay out and eat. Namina was nowhere to be seen. Maybe no one except the city knew where she was. Well, also except Imke. She didn't need to get back to Aspen any more. He was gone. With Pablo.

A small chill of danger eddied through her, a sense of being alive. Here she was, out with a stranger, and no keeper in sight. She smiled as she followed Imke toward a tall, rounded building with orange pansies and dark lavender violas lining the doorways, and a harvestable winter cabbage garden right outside. She stopped and reached for the tiny blue and purple flowers. They were edible, and she was starved. Before Julianna hired her away from the basic income system, she'd paid for her keep by weeding gardens. Not this fancy; down by the streets. But she knew her flowers.

Imke tugged at her. "Let's eat."

"Okay."

The bright hallway shocked Coryn a little awake, and her feet slowed as they encountered plush carpeted walkway. A fancy building. They took an elevator up five floors to the top, and emerged on a patio restaurant. A handsome dark-skinned robotic greeter wearing a powder-blue suit led them to a table close to a waterfall. Imke waved a hand at him. "Water and something to eat please? Even just house bread?"

He glanced at Coryn and grinned, making her wonder what she looked like.

When the water came she drained her glass and then another. The bread tasted like delicate and savory air, melting in her mouth.

Menus appeared.

"There are no prices."

Imke laughed. "Dinner is on the Chicago Embassy."

"Oh." Coryn frowned again. "But what for? I don't work for Chicago. And Julianna isn't the mayor of anything right now."

Imke's response came out soft and sure. "Because I get to decide what happens here. Don't worry. I have a budget, and we get a discount anyway. I come here once a week or so."

Coryn shrugged and stared at the menu. It was the kind of food Julianna had served her, but in spite of the fact that Julianna owned restaurants, she seldom ate out. Coryn didn't recognize all of the words on the piece of paper in front of her, but she found something that looked like Julianna might not shoot her for eating a few days before a race.

It turned out to be a little rich. Spiced eggs and vegetables, with a thick sauce, which she mostly scraped off.

"You might have danced enough to earn that sauce," Imke said.

Coryn felt herself blush. "Maybe. That was fun. I feel like you're showing me my own city."

"I love Seacouver." Imke leaned forward. "Tell me your story. One of the aides at the embassy told me you showed up out of nowhere, from an orphanage, and now you're working closely with Julianna. Poverty to power and all that. I didn't believe them, but now I do. How did you end up here?"

Coryn shrugged. "I like to run."

"To run? You got here by *running*?"

"That's how I met Julianna. She ran by me and I kept up."

Imke looked bemused. They shook their head and sipped some water and leaned back with a small smile. "It takes people years of school and scraping to get to where you are. Lifetimes. Or connections."

Coryn took a few bites, buying time to evaluate the slight distrust the questions brought up in her. "I think Julianna tries to meet people when they're young and train them herself."

Imke nodded. "Makes sense."

"So how did you meet the mayor of Chicago?"

"Mayor Rufus Broadbridge? Hard not to know him."

Coryn let out a sigh of relief. Imke wasn't going to press her for info on Julianna. "Really? How can everyone know the mayor? I hardly know ours."

"Everyone has a different story. I went to school with his daughter. We were in DC together, studying city government and international relations between cities. She brought me home one Thanksgiving. I guess he liked me."

"So how is that story different than mine? School with a daughter, or running together?"

"It didn't sound to me like you were in the same circles at all."

"I guess not." Coryn dipped a fork in the sauce and let herself taste the peppery fats. "Was your family rich?"

Imke's eyes narrowed for a moment. "A little. Dad owned a company that built skyways and consulted on some of the skyscrapers that went up in Chicago. But it was all money he earned. He didn't inherit any of it. My parents still live there. I'll go back and see them for the holidays."

Coryn took the last bite of carrot and realized she was still hungry. She picked the menu back up. "International relations between cities? What does that mean?"

"Well, there are countries that are still strong. Russia. Australia. But not the US and not Europe, not really. Cities broker trade deals, and sometime even mutual defense."

She had heard of such deals. "I just didn't know people studied that stuff. I knew it happened. We have a mutual aid deal with Portland, for example."

"You have one with Chicago, too. And we're cooperating on building space stations. We have two up with our brand, but you built the propulsion systems. The Seacouver station is going up with our life support systems."

"I didn't know that."

"Are you interested in space?"

Coryn shrugged. "I don't know. What can you tell me?"

Imke smiled. "Later. I can see it's time to tuck you in."

She glanced at her wristlet. Midnight. "I'm not five."

"But you *are* busy. And important."

"I don't think so." But she did have to take care of Lou, and there was a storm coming. So she put the menu down and stood as Imke did. She let Imke take her hand and they walked out together.

Namina waited for them in the doorway.

Coryn had expected it, but she still stiffened. She nodded at Namina and managed to get out a polite greeting.

Imke went with her all the way to her apartment, Namina trailing behind like a guard dog.

When they got to the door, Coryn looked meaningfully at Namina, who smiled and went inside.

Imke waited outside the door, looking down at Coryn contemplatively. "Are you going to tuck me in?" Coryn asked, not sure what answer she hoped for.

"No. Not on the first date. But I'd like to see you again."

Coryn nodded.

Imke leaned into her, backing her against the corridor wall gently, and kissed Coryn so hard and so furiously that her lips felt both bruised and fantastic.

She closed the door behind her, plopped down in the ugly green chair, and stared at the water, wishing Imke had stayed. She was used to living alone, but at this moment, her whole chest hurt with loneliness. She blinked back tears.

Namina came up beside her. "You should not leave me."

Coryn kept watching the moon on the water and the varied lighting in the buildings that lined her view. "You didn't have any trouble finding me."

"Julianna would not like you so exposed. I can be discreet. I'll show you how to set my privacy levels if you like."

Coryn laughed, too tired to engage with the robot. "Later."

Namina shook her head, but her programming was apparently fine enough that she didn't push it. She merely held her hand out to Coryn, and Coryn took it.

Namina led her to the bedroom, where she had turned down one corner of the bedding. After Coryn climbed out of her clothes and got in, Namina tucked her in exactly the way Paula used to, almost down to the minutia of how she moved.

After Namina left the room, Coryn stared at the ceiling for some time, feeling the emptiness of a place with no one in it except for a robot. No dog. No sister. No Julianna a few rooms over. Not even any other stray orphans.

But she was important now.

Maybe.

Coryn felt more refreshed than she had expected to when she woke, and she hummed through breakfast and getting ready for her run. Namina served her and otherwise said nothing, and Coryn left it just like that, content with quiet.

Outside, the morning air felt crisp against her cheeks as she limbered up with a mile-long walk, keeping Namina behind her. In spite of how devastating it had felt to be alone after Imke left last night, she felt good this morning, happy to be out in the city. She picked up speed as she slid along the waterfront, heading north. Today was a long run day, and as soon as she had been running half an hour, she started to feel the steadiness in her body and to drift into her own thoughts while she managed the route almost on autopilot.

She left her AR gear hanging loose around her neck and exposed her senses to the city, experiencing the burned-coffee taste of a latte stand, the rich damp saltiness of the Sound, and the slight wind.

Clouds scudded over the sky, largely kept up and over the city by the weather dome. The forecast was dry, and the long beds of flowers and vegetables beside the path were damp from overnight watering. Here and there, Basics had weeded and deadheaded and harvested food, either to take home for free or to sell at the farmers' markets that would open soon.

She had been one of those, but she wasn't now.

Imke thought she was important.

Julianna thought she mattered enough to provide her with Namina. To be fair, also to demand that she answer questions.

Jake always smiled when he saw her.

Her sister needed her.

She had come close to winning races, and she was now listed on the boards as someone to watch going into every race.

She rounded a corner and took a hill, digging into it, focusing for a moment just on her running, her breathing, her form. She made small adjustments.

She had a race soon. Next week.

Her body worked great. She hadn't done too much damage being Outside.

Imke. Imke thought she was lucky and important, and Imke had asked her what she wanted.

Blessing had suggested she was lucky but she might not stay that way. He had warned her to be careful.

Could she trust Imke? She wanted to.

She crested the hill and started down, Lake Washington glittering deep blue in the sun in front of her.

Julianna's questions demanded answers. She had been trying to avoid them, but she was running out of time. Coryn pulled her AR gear up and set it so she could talk to it. She dictated, and ran, and dictated some more.

What flaws was she missing? Julianna would want Coryn to state the obvious, but she'd be pleased with an accurate surprise.

At the bottom of the long trail she joined up with the historic Burke Gilman trail. She felt so full of energy it was hard to stay at her training speed. Her feet wanted to push her faster. Thoughts spooled out, flowing like her movement.

At Log Boom Park, she stopped for water and a restroom break. Paddle boarders and swimmers and kayaks brightened the dark blue lake. Maybe half as many as just a few weeks ago, and all bundled up in their bright pink-and-yellow dry suits.

Fall.

She shifted into an even more flowing state, her thoughts like air, her breath easy. She raced through the Woodinville wineries. Bicycles swarmed around her and she missed her bike, swore she'd ride on her rest day after the race.

She couldn't be everything. Not a runner and a biker every day. Not Outside with Lou and Inside helping her.

She had to choose, and her choices had to matter.

She pulled her gear on and requested a playlist tied to her pace. The constant beat and her footsteps matched almost automatically, and she pounded along the slough.

A runner she had competed against went by, going the other way, and when Coryn waved at her she waved back and smiled, and, while Coryn didn't turn, she sent a message suggesting they should train together some day.

The small act felt almost as good as going out with Imke.

In the end, as she ran over the 520 bridge back to Seattle. Finally tired, she found her night with Imke and her message to the other runner filled her as full as the answers she finally had to the questions everyone had been throwing at her.

She finished strong, legs flying, a few strands of damp hair clinging to her sweaty cheeks, her feet sore but unhurt.

CHAPTER TWENTY-FIVE

At the office, Coryn checked in with Lou, who was out darting deer with tiny transmitters so she could follow them over the winter, and, not incidentally, also looking for mushrooms. The farm was quiet, the ecobots well behaved, a late harvest underway to beat a forecast thunderstorm, and basically all was well enough.

A note from Jake suggested he'd show up later this afternoon.

She flipped though her transcribed audio notes from the run and made them into sense. Then she sent Julianna her answers.

> *The three things that threaten Seacouver:*
>
> 1. *Whoever fought us a few months ago. Hackers and Returners?*
> 2. *The complexity of our systems. Maybe even the systems themselves?*
> 3. *Our own sense of safety.*

She felt proud of that last one. It had come to her near the end of the run—the idea that the city was so sure it would always exist that it didn't consider itself vulnerable. She was guilty as well. When she ran here, she felt safe. Outside, even with a robotic companion, she'd had to worry about dangers from all sides. People who wanted her robot, people who wanted her, people who wanted whatever she had. Outside, one had to be part of a group or a tribe to be safe.

But nukes? What would nukes do inside of a dome? Did they all trust the city's security too much?

Admitting that maybe she had been acting a little too entitled about her own safety made her feel more honest, and a little older.

The three things that threaten Lou:

1. *Whoever wants to attack Seacouver. (She's helping us look for them. If she gets caught, they might kill her.)*
2. *Weather (storms and fire).*
3. *Her own stubbornness?*

Number three didn't look right after she wrote it down, so she crossed it out and wrote *disease*.

Then she skipped down a line or two and wrote, *I want to work on diplomacy. After Lou is safe, after this summer.* After they got through whatever this coming attack was and the city was safe again. Or not.

The message didn't feel ready to send yet.

Thank you for giving me these opportunities. Aspen went with Pablo. My run was great this morning. I'm not seeing as much of Jake as I'd like. I hope you are okay.

She left it unsaid that she hadn't seen Julianna for a few days, either. When she hit send, she felt a lot lighter. Who knew that unanswered questions weighed so much?

She settled down to look up as much as she could about Imke.

At the end of her shift, Jake hadn't come. Neither had Julianna. Nor had Julianna answered her questions, or even acknowledged she got them. Imke hadn't messaged her. The silence left Coryn irritated as she turned out the lights and opened the door. Namina waited just outside, as always, lifting her head and smiling. "I have a message for you."

Well. "Okay."

"Julianna would like to invite you to dine with her this evening."

"Tell her I'd be happy to join her." She felt a sudden worry about her answers. Had Julianna liked them?

"Of course." Namina paused a moment, undoubtedly messaging Julianna's house systems. "It's a formal occasion."

Really? Coryn glanced down at her clothes. Simple black pants and a casual T-shirt. When would she learn to dress better? "All right. Should I go home and change?"

Namina cocked her head for a moment, maybe in conversation. "Julianna will lay out some clothes for you."

"Who will we be meeting?"

"I cannot say. But you'll start by having a quiet moment with Julianna and Jake."

Ten minutes later, one of Julianna's housemaids handed her three shirts to try on. She chose a sage-green tunic to top her own pants with, and russet boots that made her think of Imke and smile.

Julianna and Jake waited for her in a small parlor they often used before dinner. Tall ceilings gave the room an airy feel. Natural light spilled in from high windows and skylights.

Both looked ready for a fancy event. Jake wore a loose-fitting gray suit coat with black lapels, offsetting the funereal look with a pale mauve shirt. Julianna wore a black and silver pantsuit.

They looked at least a year older than when she'd last seen them. "Are you okay?" The words were out before she realized how vacuous they sounded. Jake was dying, Julianna loved him, and the city they built together was apparently under attack.

Jake smiled thinly and gave a soft nod that seemed designed to avoid pain. He looked both pale and frail.

"Sorry we abandoned you," Julianna said. "I keep meaning to fill you in."

She did look sorry. And tired. Coryn gave her a hug before she took water from the maid. "I'm okay."

Adam came in; his hair was braided so the streak of gold wove in and out of only one strand. The bottom of the braid was caught in a gold band studded with glittering white stones of some kind, probably zirconia. He had even applied pale gold eye makeup.

As usual, even after she dressed up, he outdid her.

She smiled at Adam. "I like the view."

He smiled immediately and then clearly understood that she meant the view through the window in his old apartment. His cheeks reddened. "I'm glad. You're right, there's no room for the chairs. But maybe we'll trade back some day."

With a start, she realized she liked where she lived now better. Who'd have thought? She turned her attention to Julianna. "What's up?"

"Sit down. We have twenty minutes."

Coryn sat on an ottoman. "Twenty minutes before?"

"There's a dinner that was already planned, a regular diplomatic affair, and after the dinner there will be an emergency meeting. It could affect the work you do for Lou."

She felt her throat and stomach tighten. Another challenge.

"There's a good consensus now about who is behind this. We've been working with Chicago, Calgary, and Portland. After we lost so many Listeners, we needed to rebuild a network. Lou, of course, is part of that."

Did Lou know she was a node in a bigger network? Coryn made a mental note to fill her in.

Jake picked up the thread of conversation, his voice more gravelly than usual, his cadence so slow that Coryn winced. "We need you to hear what we hear."

"Why?"

"Lou may be able to confirm some information, and your morning conversations are more secure than anything but Blessing and Day's travels."

"Oh!" she exclaimed. "That's why they killed so many Listeners. They were far more secure than technology. And that's why you sent Pablo." She felt certain she was right, and proud of herself for figuring it out. Except it meant Pablo and Aspen were in danger.

Julianna's slight nod confirmed it. "We needed more people in more places." She paused. Her voice softened. "It was generous of you to let him take Aspen. Thank you."

So they had read the note with her answers, and shared it between them. "Of course I'll come." Maybe Imke would be there.

Jake spoke. "We've identified some of the people behind this. One is a family who fought us tooth and nail when we did the taking. Smith."

When we did the taking. Sometimes she forgot the power they had once wielded. Still did, in some ways. "I think there are Smiths in Chelan."

Jake continued, still slow in spite of the power of his words. "Most of them appear to be there, or nearby. Henrietta is rumored to be in Chelan. She used to be one of the four most powerful Returners."

Julianna twirled her water glass in her hand. "I met Henrietta twice. She's a few years older than me. She could be dead."

That earned her sharp glances from Jake and Adam, and Julianna smiled. "She believed in her cause as hard as I believed in mine. They sent her in to negotiate—I think for better optics. Woman on woman and all that shit."

Coryn startled; Julianna did not curse often. Or lightly.

"She's ruthless. She's also a good marketer. Strong. And she has a huge family, all of whom do her bidding."

That sounded like Valeria. Huge family. But the two women weren't the same. "Lou mentioned Henrietta," Coryn said. "I don't think she's met her. But she mentioned her once."

Adam spoke up. "So she must be there."

"Is she leading this attack?" Coryn asked.

Jake spoke slowly. "Probably not. But we're willing to bet she's directing at least one wing of it."

"They're calling it the Last Fight." Julianna raised her water glass, and the others did the same. "We cannot lose."

Surely the city had more defenses than the Outsiders had offenses?

Still, she remembered the loss of the transportation grid, and how much damage that did. And how fast. The city had come to a hard stop.

"And there are nukes," Adam added.

Her hand stopped with her glass halfway to her mouth. "You know that?"

"There are so many small signs of it that we're eighty-five percent certain. That's yes, as far as I'm concerned. Small ones. Not missiles. Could be dirty bombs or something in a backpack. Maybe as much to create fear as anything."

The news made her throat dry. "And they're succeeding."

Julianna gave her an approving look.

She straightened in her chair, not wanting Julianna to see her fear. "But what do they really want to do? They can take down a few buildings, breach our dome—that's easy enough. Pablo's people just walked through it with a little help from hackers."

"We didn't design this city to withstand an army," Julianna snapped. "Who'd want to hurt us? We're the hope of mankind." Her voice was bitter. "All the cities are. We are the future, unless we want to kill nine out of ten people. Maybe more. Maybe ninety-nine out of a hundred. Knock humanity all the way back to hunter-gatherers with a few technologies they can keep up and a few good survival manuals. It's just stupid."

Jake remained silent, but he smiled and put a hand on Julianna's hip.

Adam started picking up glasses. "It's an attack on our leadership. The feds are behind it. That's the other thing we heard. They've been working here as well, convincing some people to be on their side. Not enough, we don't think. They're clumsy. But they want to get control of one city, and from there to influence the others."

A new and unpleasant twist. Coryn frowned. "We're under attack from our own government?" The same people she was getting permits from?

"They have plausible deniability." Julianna gave her a hard look. "Besides, you should know by now that governments are made up of people and organizations, often with competing desires."

Coryn smiled in spite of the sting in Julianna's words, or maybe because of it.

"Let's go," Jake said. "I'm not as fast as I'd like to be."

Sure enough, he leaned on Julianna as they left, and after no more than a few hundred steps, Adam moved up to his other side and took most of his weight, eventually shooing Julianna back to escort Coryn.

CHAPTER TWENTY-SIX

Their destination turned out to be a ballroom at the top of a new Ritz-Carlton near the harbor. Windows all the way up, so high Coryn felt like they pierced the dome. They were north of the busy waterfront where she'd met Imke last night, and the view south took in the bridges, the skyscrapers, the vast swirling length of the seawall, and even West Seattle. For a moment she just stopped and stared, remembering why she loved this place so much. It looked invincible.

But it wasn't. She knew that now.

Maybe she should see all the cities, and work to save them all. Every one. She had heard Chicago had a great wall around the downtown, that Salt Lake City had the best engineering anywhere, that almost every building had been redone without the weird sentimental history that kept Seacouver a contrast.

Adam's hand plucked at her sleeve, and she turned to be introduced to the junior ambassador from Salt Lake City, an older woman with gray hair, bright eyes, and a blue kimono that draped over a slightly plump body. Marie Severson. Coryn tried to impress the name, the face, into her memory. Politicians did that. Leaders did that.

The introductions continued, the effort quickly reminding her of the Ambassador's Ball, even though the only music was live piano from a single woman playing in the corner, and the dress was at least one notch down. Fancy, but with a serious edge the ball had lacked.

The security expert from Portland took Adam away from her for a private conversation, and Coryn looked for Imke. She couldn't remember meeting anyone from Chicago in the last hour, although she'd been listening for that.

She slid carefully around small knots of people deep in conversation, grateful that no one stopped her. After twenty minutes, she felt like she'd seen the whole vast floor, and passed all of the artfully arranged tables, which had flowers in the middle and food arranged all around in small colored-glass bowls.

She wasn't hungry, but wandering around introducing herself to strangers had become wearying. She found a chair with a view of the city and sat, grateful for a few minutes respite from the crowd. A hand grazed her shoulder. She looked up and behind to see that Adam had found her, and that he had Imke in tow. He looked a little quizzical. "Imke here seems to think you'll be sitting by them. They're calling us to dinner."

Coryn smiled and stood up, straightening her shirt. She caught a mischievous look in Imke's eyes and returned it with a smile that seemed to come from her belly. "Why yes, I think that could have been arranged."

Adam gave her a look that might be confusion, or might be hurt. She steeled herself against it. He could always sit on her other side if he wanted.

She followed Imke in, admiring the way they moved, and the easy, flowing black robe they had chosen. Imke's hair jewels were almost the same as yesterday, only all in white and gold.

It turned out there was not one table, but four. The current mayor of Seacouver was at one side of the long head table, Julianna and Jake seated about five people away from him. Adam, Coryn, Imke, and about twenty others surrounded the table farthest from the decision-makers and closest to the doors.

The tables were set for fall, with yellow and red-orange leaves and great bulbous blue hydrangeas lording it over gold tablecloths and freshly made plates with the name of the occasion on them: *Quarterly Dinner for Central and Northwest Cities*. She laughed at the stuffiness of it, then paused. Why had they asked her to come?

Adam sat at one side, she and Imke far down the farther side.

Coryn leaned toward Imke, keeping her voice casual. "I thought you were playing tonight."

"Doubtful." They shrugged. "If I get out of here on time. We have two leads in the band because this happens."

"Is your mayor here?"

"He flew in yesterday with news."

"What news?"

Imke narrowed their eyes briefly and shook their head. Rather quickly, they leaned across the table and started introductions. Coryn took careful mental notes. It helped that she had met most of her table-mates in the first whirlwind moments when Adam introduced her around.

Luckily Adam and Imke both drew far more attention than she did. Both knew how to work a table so well that Coryn decided they wanted to be actual politicians in their secret hearts of hearts. That left Coryn free to listen to the small talk of big cities, which varied from conversations about what to do with surplus power to how to attract immigrants from each other. Surprisingly little of the talk was petty or even inconsequential.

Sitting next to Imke and not being able to touch them was tanta-lizing and a little frustrating, although twice she caught quick, smoky glances from the singer's dark eyes. After the second one, she looked up to find Adam watching her. He raised an eyebrow, and she realized she couldn't interpret the expression on his face. He seemed . . . intrigued.

Shortly after Coryn finished the one-bite each trio of pumpkin crème brûlées that made up dessert, Imke rose from the table and took her hand. Adam had stood as well, along with a tall woman who had been sitting beside him watching his every gesture as if she was dreaming his hands would touch her instead of the air.

A band began to tune up. The lead singer began talking people toward the dance floor.

The four of them walked right through the dance floor and through a door she hadn't even seen, then through two more doors and up a flight of stairs onto a rooftop patio room fully enclosed in thick glass that silenced the city noise. The top third of every window was tinted a deep security gray. Guards stood watch, their backs pointedly toward the room. This still left a view almost as good as the one Coryn had admired on the way in.

Imke took her over to a tall black man with a wide smile that drew attention away from his wide shoulders. As soon as she saw him, Coryn recognized him as the mayor of Chicago. Imke stopped in front of him, and here it was harder to focus on his smile. He was one of the largest men Coryn had ever met. Tall, broad, and well-fed, although not fat. "Mayor Broadbridge," Imke said, "I'd like to introduce you to a key board member of Julianna and Jake's new foundation. This is Coryn Williams."

Coryn grimaced at the way Imke made her sound far more important than she felt.

The mayor's attention felt like a mountain looming over her, and she couldn't tell if his reputation as a strong mayor or his physical presence was more intimidating. "Pleased to meet you," he said, his deep, resonant voice pitched for her ears alone. "I'm always pleased to meet people whom my esteemed mentors know."

Just then Julianna came up on her far side, a surprised smile flitting ever so briefly across her face.

Good. Coryn gave her a quiet nod and returned her attention to Mayor Broadbridge, aware that he'd just asked her a question about the foundation; she'd almost missed it.

She smiled and launched into the logistics of getting the permit, thankful that she'd met with Julianna and Jake and heard how the cities were—again—fighting the feds.

Imke pulled her to the side as people started to take seats at the table, and she sat between Imke and Adam in a row of vaguely comfortable seats at the back of the patio. Most of her view was obscured once she sat down, although the tops of buildings glowed with colorful patio lighting and the top of the curve of the Bridge of Stars was visible, it's observation decks a comforting white light.

"We get to listen," Adam whispered to her. "Don't speak unless someone asks you a question. Take your notes mentally. If there's anyone I—we—haven't introduced you to, let me know."

She sat back, working to take in the whole room without looking like a curious child.

The head table included Justin Arroya, the current mayor of Seacouver, Julianna, Jake, Mayor Broadbridge from Chicago, Susannah Biker—the tiny woman who was the new mayor of Portland Metro—and a taller woman whose name escaped Coryn but who came from Calgary. The gallery of watchers like herself was about twice that big, and mostly gathered in small groups that probably represented the cities.

Not one robot.

Very few of the people from the dinner outside had been included. Were they having their own meetings? Or still dancing while the important people talked?

The whole political thing seemed like its own dance. Blessing had described it that way. Thinking of him got her to sit down and pay attention.

Imke touched her knee briefly and whispered, "I'll find you after the meeting." They rose and moved over to join the Chicago delegation.

Imke had said that she was important, or lucky, or something. That she was in a place and time that mattered. Not like the people in the middle of the room, of course, but who would have expected her to even get to see such a meeting? Drawing a deep breath, Coryn silently vowed to prove that she belonged here.

CHAPTER TWENTY-SEVEN

The high-powered meeting room appeared plain, but complex touches made it look classy. Every corner held vases full of flowers above small trays of appetizers. The scent of summer flowers felt at odds with the fall colors of the trees on nearby roofs.

Mayor Broadbridge towered over his colleagues even seated, and when he stood he looked like a giant. "Thank you all for coming. I'm sorry to meet like this, but there are dangers that must be communicated."

He paused, letting everyone settle, and then said, "As always in these meetings, information is not to be shared outside of this room unless the mayors collectively choose to do so." He glanced at the staff area, his gaze taking in Coryn, Adam, Imke, and everyone else as he paused to make his point. His attention turned to the collected presence of the mayors. "We are all under attack."

Whispered conversations stilled.

"We are under attack," he continued, "from Inside and Outside. Our systems are under attack. Our values are under attack. The planet remains under attack. This—" He paused, spreading his arms out, smiling. "This is not new. It is how we live. But this time, it is a *coordinated and widespread* attack. Seacouver and Portland Metro took the brunt of the first exploratory sorties. Some people died. Others were harmed. The cities continued, and they have stronger defenses.

"The next attacks will be fiercer. Some of our best analysts will tell you why they have concluded this. Please pay close attention."

People sipped at drinks, shifted uneasily. A chair leg scraped across the floor. "First," he said, "We will pledge our support to each other. This is our tradition, and this meeting may be the most important that I have ever called."

He took a single slow breath. When his deep voice broke the silence, he spoke clearly and loudly. "I, Rufus Broadbridge, pledge to maintain a strong city, a just city, and a free city. I pledge to assist the mayors of other cities in the great Federation of North American Mayors to remain strong and free. I pledge the uninhibited flow of information, trade, safety, and security."

Coryn had seen the words in a high school text. She'd even heard a recording of Julianna and Jake saying them. But she'd never heard them live, spoken by people in power.

They had force.

Justin Arroya stood next, dressed in a dark blue suit with his usually wild hair slicked down. Julianna and Jake stood beside him as he spoke, although they were silent. At first, it surprised her that they didn't each speak the pledge, but then it dawned on her that they demonstrated unity by standing in support of the man who had replaced them in power.

Susannah Biker's voice trembled as she spoke. Perhaps this was the first time she had said the words out loud. She hadn't been running Portland Metro for long, and the pledge was not a part of governing a single city but a binding between cities.

When the woman from Calgary pledged, Coryn recognized her name from stories about a difficult election she almost lost. Helena Hall. She was nearly as tall as Mayor Broadbridge, thin almost to bony, with dark hair and eyes, pale skin, high cheekbones and a tattoo of a sun on the far side of her forehead, the rays shading down to her eyes. Her voice was far stronger than Susannah's, and the last few words seemed to hang in the air as she completed the pact.

I pledge the free flow of information, trade, safety, and security.

Each time, Coryn felt the words shiver through her. She'd never thought about that before. The flow of these things. Information flowed, trade flowed, but safety and security? Perhaps. Systems connected inside of each city and between cities.

The cities had not made a mistake when they starved the land between them of any but the most basic connectivity. It strengthened them to have more capacity for information, computing, and communication.

Mayor Broadbridge drew her attention back to the table. "There are always dangers. But there is currently an unprecedented amount of coordination among our enemies." He paused, looking around the room again, apparently a habit of his, a way of demanding attention. "We will share four primary dangers. These are threats to our systems, erosion of values, collecting forces, and the building and preparation of small armies."

A few hands went up, but the Mayor held one of his large hands up, and the others fell.

"Please hear the speakers out. To begin, I'd like to call up one of my aides, Imke Boro, who will discuss the dangers to our systems. Imke has been working with staff here in Seacouver for the past few months, but they began their discovery at home in Chicago. They have much to tell us. Please listen carefully."

Imke didn't even glance at Coryn as they took the front of the room. They held themselves so upright they looked taller than they were, and they had the presence of mind to stand still a moment before starting. Wall screens lit up with a pale blue background and a timeline. The presentation data stream appeared on Adam's slate, and he held it at an angle so Coryn could see.

Imke began. "The first alarming event was the ruthless murder of many Listeners."

Which Coryn finally understood. Poor Liselle. Aspen had come to her from Liselle's murder, and now he was out there again. She shivered.

"Next, Portland Metro and Seacouver both suffered successful attacks on external and internal infrastructure. In Portland Metro, the hackers sent in compromised ecobots, starting with a fairly simple attack. The primary purpose appears to have been testing whether or not Wilders and other NGO staff could be turned against the city."

Coryn winced. Adam, who knew a little of her participation in that attack, put a hand on her knee. She kept her face still, staring at the slate.

Imke continued. "They followed this with a second attack, which included trained fighters and more severely compromised ecobots. This, again, took place mostly in Portland. At the same time—and this is significant when you think of the pledge that you all just spoke—at the same time they attacked Seacouver's primary transportation and utility systems. A few people died immediately, and some less fortunate or more fragile people died because they couldn't reach the medical care they needed. The water system in all of Seacouver was turned off by a delicate and effective hack, and restored only with Seacouver's best programmers and the help of a number of cyber-war fighters who don't even work for the city."

And a few warriors who worked for Julianna. LeeAnne, Day, Blessing, and Pablo. The memory made Coryn smile.

"There were other heroes as well. Two sisters and Jake, who talked Seacouver's people through the last hour or so. One of them is here, in this room."

Imke pointed and all eyes shifted to Coryn.

Coryn fought down an absurd desire to wave.

Imke winked and turned back to the crowd. "I believe a far larger attack is planned."

Those words drew everyone's attention back to the screens. Adam's hand finally slid away from her knee as he fiddled with his screen.

"All of our systems are connected. We have multiple safeguards and many ways to kill the connections from one city to another, one neighborhood to another, one street or even one household to another. But as we sever those connections, we lose information, we lose effectiveness, and we lose trust. If connections remain severed long enough, we lose the integrity of our systems. For example, if a sewer lift station is compromised and shut out of the system, it will revert to its most basic duties for some time. It will still pump sewage uphill and into the systems that take it to be treated. But if external conditions change, such as a comprise of any kind at the treatment plant, the lift station will not know that. It will continue to do the most basic part of its job until sewage begins to back up, and then it will stop taking more.

"You can imagine the domino. *All* of our systems are *that* connected. The sewage system talks to the water system, since sewage get recycled back into the water system after it's purified. It also talks to the parks maintenance systems, and from there to the robotic forces that do the harder work in the parks and to volunteers who earn their basic income weeding and planting.

"Misinformation can spread and do significant damage, and that misinformation can start with any connected system and go through all of the others."

This seemed basic. But perhaps Imke was just making sure that everyone in the room shared the same understanding.

Imke stepped closer to the head table. "We have evidence that all of our cities have been compromised. This shows in small ways. Very small ways."

Beside her, Adam smiled. It dawned on her that his surprise that Imke would choose to sit with her might have been jealousy of Coryn. What a tangle. If she could only see inside of people's hearts.

Imke used Seacouver and Chicago systems to demonstrate a slight, broad, uptick in small compromises, quickly fixed. "Whoever did this—" They spread their arms wide and paused. "Whoever is orchestrating this knows the alarm thresholds of all of our infrastructure systems, and how to disturb them without causing a single human to notice."

They stopped, the implications clear. Only programmers or artificial intelligences inside of the city could know that much.

Imke looked beautiful. Strong. Entirely at home on a stage. Coryn could barely tear her attention away from them.

Imke nodded. "This compromise is not limited to just the megacities, but includes smaller metro areas like Spokane. It includes Chicago as much as Seacouver and Portland Metro. I'm willing to bet that it includes Calgary."

Helena with the sun on her forehead nodded in agreement.

Imke had said nothing about who was doing this, only what was happening. Coryn was willing to trust the mayor, but curious. No one clapped as Imke went to sit down, but Coryn wanted to.

She expected the next speaker to be from another city, since there were four topics and four cities, but Mayor Broadbridge called another of his staff up, an older slender man with a goatee and a bald head named Clifford Smith. "This will not seem connected, but you will understand. Please pay close attention."

Clifford spoke of concepts she decided she should have grasped long ago, but hadn't really, not until he said them. His voice was so soft that they all leaned in to hear as he built a case that suggested that the people in the cities were no longer in touch with nature. "The taking severed city-dwellers from wilderness, and many see the Wilders as mere gardeners."

He delivered his news with a storyteller's cadence, and at the end he summed up his information by saying, "Many of the people who live inside domes cannot see out of them. They know that forests exist because they see pictures. But they do not know what a cedar tree smells like." His voice grew sarcastic. "They ask *If we can manage things as great and wondrous as the cities, why can't we also manage everything about the earth?*" He stopped and looked at his audience, as if accusing them of the same beliefs.

Susannah's cheeks looked pink. Jake and Julianna simply looked sad. Helena's back was to Coryn, stiff and a little affronted. Mayor Broadbridge let the moment stretch for a few minutes, and then said, "Thank you, Clifford."

Susannah startled as if she suddenly remembered she had a role. She stood. "I'd like to introduce Ty Loomis. He'll talk about gathering forces."

Ty was almost a visual twin of Adam's, tall and athletic except with darker hair and eyes, and skin that had been lightly brushed with sepia. Adam leaned in, paying more attention to the reaction of the middle table than to Ty or his slides, which were sparse. No wonder: it was all numbers and graphs, easy for Adam. He seemed to have seen the material before anyway.

Coryn took the slate and slid her AR rig out of her purse, watching closely as three-dimensional graph and graphic after three-dimensional graph and graphic slowly built a case for many enemies working together. Returners, who wanted their old land back and the rise of the cities stopped. Moneyed members of the old federal government, building power. These funded people in the cities who preached the things Clifford had talked about, and encouraged peaceful protests. They also paid for operatives planted in the cities to do far worse, seen more by the signs of their communication trails than anything else.

Russians, for one. Russia was still a strong centralized state, with the strongest cities in Russia beholden to national interests, and far less powerful than the Western megacities.

Helena nodded at this, and whispered, "I know," loud enough for Coryn to hear.

Mayor Broadbridge nodded at her.

Maybe that was why Helena was here. Calgary was smaller than the other cities, and she hadn't contributed an analyst to any of the four problems, at least so far.

As Ty kept talking, Coryn watched him carefully. He fascinated her. They all had. They spoke well, clearly, cleanly. Words were crisp. Cadences perfect. They had all worried her; Ty frightened her so she caught herself breathing fast and forced her body to calm.

All of the groups Ty mentioned were growing. They weren't large, not yet. Not as far as anyone could tell. But in a connected city, ideas could rage and flame overnight.

Again, Mayor Broadbridge allowed for a moment of quiet. Coryn kept hold of Adam's slate as he went to the front. He talked of what he had been telling her about weapons across the last few weeks. It had frightened her as he fed it to her in dribs and drabs, mostly because she had been able to see how he took it. Here, in this context and presented with the other information, it sounded worse.

As soon as Adam sat down, the table erupted with conversation and chatter as Mayor Broadbridge called for a break. She handed Adam back his slate and leaned toward him. "It really is scary, isn't it?"

He nodded.

She gazed through the glass at the tops of the city's most beautiful buildings and at the bridge she loved. "It will be all right. It has to be."

"It doesn't." He stood, looked down at her. "We've only got the winter to prepare."

CHAPTER TWENTY-EIGHT

Coryn still dreamed of attacks and weapons and Lou five days after the meeting. But at least she had slept as long as she wanted to. So long that it was early afternoon. A day off of running. A holiday.

Thanksgiving.

Not something she'd ever celebrated much. Not really. But there had been days of ads and decorations, of free food to taste in hopes you would buy some, of the city being orange and pale red and deep brown.

Except where the Christmas colors overran the Thanksgiving colors.

Still in her pajamas, she made her way to the god-awful green chair closest to the window and stared out. A Northwest-gray sky hung low over a dark gray sea, but in spite of that the city looked warm and she felt good.

Namina brought her a cup of coffee.

"Thanks. Happy Thanksgiving."

"To you as well."

"Thanks." She went outside on the balcony. The wind was cool, but not cold. The green wall just across from her was straggled by fall, but a few yellow marigolds thrived here and there, and bright purple cabbage grew from one corner.

Namina came outside and stood beside her. "What are you looking at?"

"The city. Thinking about how it all works together. Tell me what you can talk to."

Namina smiled, a vacuous robotic smile with little nuance. Paula had showed far more range in the emotions she mimicked for Coryn. But then, Coryn and Paula had been together for all of Coryn's remembered life, and she and Namina had known each other maybe two weeks. She cocked her head and asked "Everything?"

Coryn nodded.

"All of your house systems. The refrigerator, the thermostat, the water filter, and the meters that go to the sewer and power systems. I can talk to the elevators and to the buildings safety systems and the weathervane on top of the building. I am prohibited from talking to the building systems other than through your interfaces to it, but if I were not prohibited, I would be able to talk to things like the HVAC and the building's energy monitoring systems."

"I expected nothing less. Can you talk to the front door?"

"Yes."

A seabird flew between buildings, startling Coryn for a moment. Namina didn't react at all. "Did you know that bird would fly by?"

"Only three seconds before it did. There are cameras that notify us of interesting events."

"Why did you need to know about a bird?"

"What if it was a security drone?"

Fair enough. Coryn took a deep breath and a sip of coffee. "What of mine can you talk with?"

"Nothing you have not enabled."

Stupid robot. "What have I enabled?"

"Your A/R rig, your alarm system, your wristlet, your tablet, your coffee machine."

"Please disable your access to everything except the coffee machine."

"Done."

Coryn raised an eyebrow. "So what city systems can you talk to?"

"Transportation, water, sewer."

"How do you see them? Are they data?"

Namina frowned and hesitated, her expression switching to puzzlement. "I don't know if I could explain. Everything is data. Vision. Hearing. All of our senses. You might say we live inside of a permanent augmented reality. We know what's real in the physical world, but we have other worlds layered inside of us as well."

Coryn stared at the shifting ocean. "Is there a network of robots?"

"Of course there is. But we can only touch the outer surface of each other—temperature, movement, etc. I would know if there is another robot in your bedroom, but not what she could do or who she worked for."

Coryn nodded. It was about what she had thought. She and Julianna had exchanged words about robots a few times right after Paula died. She really should go put on clothes, but it felt good to be out here on the balcony, even if she was alone except for a robot she couldn't let herself trust.

Thanksgiving dinner started at noon on the farm. Coffee and pumpkin pastries made with real bread flour that Coryn had sent out from Wenatchee for them as a surprise. The table was decorated with leftover dried allium globes from the front yard, cut short and poked into glasses. Alondra had gathered fall leaves all the previous day, and scattered them artfully in the middle of the big table.

It was sunny and cold, and they all went outside and played silly games like three-legged races. Lou brought the ecobots up for the children to climb on, and left only two people on guard at a time, on shortened two-hour shifts.

For dinner, she let them all come up. She kept her wristlet on. Coryn watched from Seacouver, using the satellite shots and her voice for security so that everyone could eat together.

There was no turkey, but Felipe had sacrificed six chickens and Matchiko, Cheryl, and Astrid had baked them into root vegetable pies with the other half of the same fabulous, fine-ground flour.

Lou, Matchiko, and Shuska took the first shift after dinner, leaving all of the men to join in with the after-dinner music. They took care of the horses and then stood watch together, watching the sun set over the lake. "It's going okay," Lou said.

"Yes," Matchiko agreed, taking her hand and squeezing.

"It's entirely too quiet," Shuska said.

Lou laughed, and far away and behind them, a pack of coyotes howled as the moon came out and made a streak of white on the nearly black lake.

CHAPTER TWENTY-NINE

The Saturday after Thanksgiving, Lou woke early. Matchiko had slept beside her the night before, and still lay stretched out on the bed with her dark hair tousled from sleep and her back rising and falling in a sweet rhythm. Her damaged ankle stuck out from under the covers, still slightly swollen and deeply scarred.

Lou found Shuska in the living room, drinking coffee and staring out of the window. Morning light bathed her face, illuminating thin wrinkles around her eyes and mouth. She was rarely beautiful, but in this light and in this moment, a stateliness settled on her, a beauty born of strength and loyalty and steadfastness.

Lou stepped near Shuska and slipped her coffee cup from her wide hand, stealing a sip while looking down on the garden. Already, Sofia, Astrid, and Diego moved between the beds, using dented water cans to get water only where it was needed. The soft sounds of their morning conversation were barely audible, sounding more like bees than words. They sounded happy.

Shuska took the cup back and curled an arm around Lou's waist in greeting. "They never stop, do they?"

"No. And I've never beaten them awake. I'm going to their bar tonight. Would you like to come?"

Shuska shook her head. "I think you should go without us. Valeria talks more openly with you than with us."

That was true, although it galled Lou a little. "We should try to fix that."

"I'm getting along with the -o boys."

They had started calling them that. Diego, Ignacio, and Santino. Middle children. Felipe and Astrid were ahead of them, Angel and Sofia behind. They moved in a group, doing the family's business but not the foundation's work. She seldom saw one without the other. "What are they like? I haven't talked with any of them."

Shuska fell silent a moment. "They are quiet, but they have anger in them. I see it in the way they carry themselves, in the way they glance at me sometimes. All of the others here seem to have become used to us, or to accept that they need us or at least that they cannot escape us. But these three? I think they wish they had never seen us."

"They work hard. I never see them stop, in fact. They're always moving." Lou watched a red-tailed hawk circle high up above the fields, looking for breakfast. "One of them is married. Ignacio?"

"To Ana. He is the quietest of them all. I have no idea how he managed to ask anyone to marry him."

Lou smiled at that. "So how are you getting along with them? Where do you see them?"

"They're often in the main barn. Staring at the horses, helping with the horses, whispering to them. I think they'd like horses of their own. It might be a way to tie them to us."

"Do we need more horses?"

Shuska turned toward her. "Is that a question?"

"All right. Sure we do." Lou took the cup from Shuska's hand and stole another sip of the coffee. It was getting cold but still more tempting than making her own cup. "I'm going to Wenatchee in a few weeks if the weather holds."

Matchiko stirred, and Lou called out, "Coffee for you, too! We need to finish and file the plan for the month."

Five minutes later, the three of them sat around the large kitchen table, which had a hidden erasable surface under the wooden top. She'd been surprised to find it here, but pleased. Maybe it had been used to plan parties during the farm's incarnation as a bed and breakfast inn.

Shuska projected a map from her tablet, the lake a long fat line of blue bisecting the center. The eastern edge had an irregular figure drawn around it to indicate the area they'd decided to consider as occupied, a near-oval that included the building they sat in. Shuska pointed to a spot north of them, on their side of the lake. "We'll survey here this morning. I've already marked some places we can begin to take down. If we block them, normal vehicles won't be able to pass, and we'll have an easier time reclaiming these wineries." She circled two complexes of farms with large houses, the buildings wrecked by wind and rain and neglect. "No water. We sent some drones out yesterday to take a look. Neither appears to be occupied."

Lou nodded. "I'm still pondering how wise it is to destroy them."

"The ecobots are demanding it. Apparently, Julianna didn't think it would be a big deal if we helped them reach their goals. Something about trading human oversight of the destruction of Chelan for robotic protection of the destroyers."

How could Julianna be so utterly naive? "Damn all rigid programming and clueless leaders to hell," Lou muttered, completely unsurprised when no one bothered to respond.

"What about the survey?" Matchiko asked. "I'd like to take one of the bots today. We want to go west." She pointed to a spot closer to the mountains than the one Shuska had claimed. "I want to ride to here"—she tapped a finger on the map—"and do a walking survey along that stream." She zoomed in. "It's dry now, but there are a lot of living trees beside it. I'm pretty sure it runs with water most of the year."

Lou remembered her last conversation with Coryn. "Storm in a few days."

"Bad?"

Matchiko pondered the map. "Might be the first real cold one of the year."

Lou nodded. "Let's finish. If we file the plan today, we can take tomorrow off."

In spite of the dark circles under her eyes, Matchiko nodded. Shuska zoomed in on a different part of the map and started talking.

How lucky was she to be with these women?

✝ ✝ ✝

As had become her habit, Lou made a sandwich from fresh bread and eggs and took it and a second cup of coffee outside to one of the tables on the front lawn, sitting by herself to call Coryn.

Coryn answered right away, her face a small round oval on Lou's wrist. She was in the same office she always took the calls from, a sterile place that made Lou shudder inside. After a few light greetings, Coryn began as she always did, launching straight into business. "There's no significant new activity in Chelan this morning. A small caravan may get to town tonight. We think it's twelve horses and ten people. A storm is coming in day after tomorrow and may linger a few days. That's Monday. Pablo is two days out of Wenatchee, four out of Chelan."

Lou stuffed her own words into the stream of data. "How are you?"

The Coryn-figure on her wrist watched her in silence for a few heartbeats before she said, "I'm fine."

"You sound different. Are they working you too hard?"

A slight smile crossed Coryn's lips, and as usual Lou wished for a bigger view of her little sister's face.

Coryn said, "I don't think I can work too hard right now. None of us can. It's no different from you anyway."

Coryn had never seemed like the workaholic type. Lou nodded, exaggerating the movement to be sure Coryn would catch it. "True enough. But you need your sleep to run."

"I've a race Monday. Wish me luck!" She smiled again, looking more upbeat.

"Sure. Good luck. I'm going to find a wolf next week."

"You always were sure of yourself."

That made Lou smile. Nothing Coryn had said so far had stopped her worrying. "Tell me what's happening in your life."

"You never care about the city."

"I care about you."

Coryn's face lost its smile. She leaned in and said, "I know. I love you too."

"You've been like this for four days. Tired-looking and not talking about anything you don't have to." A small flash of insight touched Lou. "Are you keeping secrets?"

Coryn went quiet for a moment and then spoke softly. "I'm worried. The nukes. The planned attacks. I can't even tell you everything I know."

Lou sighed again. "Is there anything I should know about the caravan that's coming?"

"We'd like to know anything you learn. They'll be coming from the north."

"Okay. I've got to go. I have a barn to finish before a storm comes in."

"It looks like you don't have much time. I love you."

"I love you, too." She hung up and then whispered to herself, "But I wish I knew what you're going through."

Lou finished her sandwich on the way to the barn. Something had changed in Coryn's personal life. She had both more confidence and a harder edge.

Angel looked up and greeted her as she approached the work party, before returning to pulling out rotted wood and salvaging nails. Blessing and Day joined them shortly, and Lou reveled in the sweaty teamwork of discarding old, rotted boards. With luck, they'd have fifteen or twenty horses soon instead of six. With luck.

CHAPTER THIRTY

Lou walked down the center of the street to the bar, Blessing and Day beside her. She hadn't asked them to come, but they had been waiting at the end of the drive, watching the stars and joking, and had simply gotten up and flanked her.

Now, in the dark street, she felt grateful for their presence. She had never expected them to stay so long. Surely Julianna would call them back sometime. They were her creatures, even though Lou had once thought Blessing was hers.

She pointed out the door to the bar. "Here." A pale yellow bulb spilled a soft circle of light onto the handle. She took a deep breath before opening it. Other than Valeria and her family, there was a good chance that everyone in here thought they were an enemy.

Live music and conversation enveloped her as she slid inside quickly, followed by the other two.

A crowd filled the space. Most of the women wore dresses and the men button-up shirts, probably the best clothes these people had.

Valeria looked up from across the bar and offered a welcoming smile. She wore white, as always, bright in the dusky room. Lou shouldered through the crowd until she was close enough to speak without shouting. "It is as busy as you promised."

"Drink?"

"Wine."

"I've only got two choices at the moment. Chardonnay or Merlot?"

"Merlot."

Valeria poured the glass herself, a careful pour measured to about five ounces.

Lou sipped the wine and nodded, turning so she could look over the room.

Almost a hundred people crowded around tables or stood in small groups talking animatedly. Most were men. Most were white. A noticeable whiteness. Every one of Valeria's family members stood out for their brown skin, except of course Felipe's wife, Cheryl, who was as white as Lou, and Mathew, who either wasn't there or was in the back.

A complete contrast to the city, where skin color made a vast palette. This was a distinct whiteness, even for out here, where those in power were often white.

It made Lou twitch. These were the people who had killed Paulette's young, frightened husband, Rick, and made her watch. For disobedience and love.

She couldn't let herself forget that about them, not for a moment. They looked normal, but clearly they were not.

In one corner, a tall white man wearing a black beret played instrumental music on a guitar, the music nearly inaudible over the sounds of the crowd. A drummer sat beside him, simply watching him and stroking the top of his drum.

Valeria's adult family all appeared to be here. That puzzled her until she heard the high slip of Alondra's laughter from the kitchen and decided they might *all* be here. Even the children. Family business.

She recognized the woman she'd passed in the group that Valeria had shepherded them through on the way to town. She turned to ask for her name, but Valeria had slid down the bar, talking to a young couple.

The woman glanced up from her table, seeing Lou and nodding in recognition. Her square face, wide lips, and earnest hazel eyes suggested strength and power. A scar marred her nose, and another one her left cheek. She pushed up from her table and came to Lou, extending a hand. "It's the woman with the balls to ride in here on the backs of wilding machines."

Even though the woman seemed genial, Lou took it as a test. She tried to sound casual even though adrenaline pounded through her system. "The ecobots? They come with my job." She took the woman's hand, a firm grip at least as calloused as her own. "I'm Lou. We're running the Outside-N Foundation, working on restoration ecology."

The woman spat the term back at her. "Restoration ecology? Stealing is more like it."

Lou answered with a more measured tone than she felt like using. "We're permitted. We're Wilders. I wish you no personal harm."

"Once you're established, you'll take down everything that makes this a human place." There was no question in her statement.

No point in mouthing the tenets of her work at this woman either. She surely knew them. Instead, Lou simply said, "We're not planning to work close to town. We'll be light on deconstruction and heavy on survey and protection."

The woman tilted her head to the side. "Your choices here could be very important. We are well armed."

Lou swallowed a surprised response. "I see." Most of the men wore visible weapons, some knives, some stunners, some projectile guns, and she felt certain the invisible weapons were far more numerous.

"You don't appear to be afraid of us," the woman said.

"Are you afraid to give me your name?"

For a moment, Lou thought the woman might actually smile. She didn't. She did say, "I'm Agnes."

"Nice to meet you."

The look on the woman's face suggested that was the wrong response, and Lou was suddenly certain this was Henrietta's older daughter, the woman Valeria had told her ran the town. She took a risk. "It's good to meet a strong woman."

Agnes nodded. She kept an even voice as she said, "Do not underestimate the ability of this community to survive." She went back to her table, sitting down and raising a beer in a toast with her tablemates. The noise in the room prevented Lou from hearing it.

Her own glass was still full. She sipped at it. She had considered not coming in tonight because she could be seen as a threat, could be killed easily enough. But that was true if she hid or if she didn't, and there was her secondary purpose. Finding nukes. She had fled the city to be rid of it, all those years ago.

But here was Julianna, pulling her with strings made of money and goods. The damned city she couldn't escape. If she severed the strings she'd allowed to be put on her, she'd have trouble finding work. She might have to go feral. Ferals died.

She watched the room quietly, marking who spoke to whom, noticing when people tried to glance at her furtively and failed.

Blessing worked his way over to her, smiling. "I saw the queen of terror talking to you."

"Do you know her?"

"Just of her. It's something a woman I was talking to said. She's afraid of her. Rumor has it she orders people killed."

"You're always talking to the ladies."

He grinned and tipped his hat at her.

"She was straightforward. Basically told me not to mess with her."

That wiped the smile off his face. She wondered if Agnes had ordered Rick's death.

The man with the guitar got up from the stage.

Lou glanced around the room, locating her crew, and when she looked back, Sofia stood at the front of the stage, wearing a black sheath dress that probably came from some rich woman's closet. It was demure and revealing at once, and it made her look older and absolutely stunning. She spoke to the crowd, her voice amplified by a microphone Lou couldn't spot. Maybe a cheek mike. "And in five minutes, my mother, Valeria of the Hills, will sing for you. Please refill your drinks, order more food, and relax."

Valeria of the Hills?

People began shifting chairs and checking their glasses. On impulse, Lou grabbed pitchers of cold water and moved through the tables, refilling water. She made sure she stopped at Agnes's table, and that she smiled sincerely at her as she filled her glass. Agnes gave a short nod, but her eyes were hooded and filled with a cold silence.

The overhead lights flashed. People rushed to find their seats and stilled, and the room suddenly felt like a theater.

Lou stayed at the bar, and Day and Blessing stood against the wall on the opposite side of the room. A good choice. She didn't want to look like she needed bodyguards.

Sofia returned to the front of the stage, a sweeping look taking in everyone, as if making sure they were still and quiet. She said, "Please welcome Valeria of the Hills, who can sing the world awake in the morning and send it to soft dreams at night."

Lou blinked at the ritualistic description, but noticed that people grinned and settled more fully into their seats.

Valeria hugged Sofia and just as Felipe helped Sofia off the back of the stage, Valeria reached the front. "Tonight I will tell you of peaceful living on the land."

Lou stiffened.

"Amen," one man said.

"Yes," a few other voices murmured.

"I will tell you of the time of families farming, of the sun bringing the rooster to wake the hens to scratch in the dirt and shining upon us for hours before the chickens seek the safety of night and sleep."

She found Felipe near her, as rapt as the others.

As Valeria began to sing, her voice sounded like it came from her toes and then worked its way up and out, and only then filled the entire room. It was a husky alto, a sensuous and serious sound.

Lou had heard her sing before, had sung with her walking down the hill to town just last week. But she had not sounded this good, this full. That had been a playful moment.

This was her soul talking with them.

The song *was* about the sunrise. It felt like a morning at RiversEnd

Ranch. She knew how the light would creep over the horizon as a softening of black to gray before a sudden infusion of yellow rays spilled momentarily through the sky and then faded in their turn as the ball of the sun rose and the soft light of true dawn touched the land awake.

As Valeria finished, her voice rose higher and stronger, and Lou thrummed so with energy that she stood up from her barstool.

A few others had done the same.

She swallowed and forced herself to sit down.

Valeria began to speak, her words measured, rhythmic.

> *Horses stamp their feet and lift their noses,*
> *smell the timothy hay and oats*
> *dangling from my fingers. They snuffle*
> *from my open palm, fragrant with grass,*
> *full of pasture dreams of running free.*
>
> *The brown bristles on the brush flick dry dirt*
> *from their sides, sweep small yellow specks*
> *of fly eggs from their delicate hocks.*
> *The saddle smells of leather and soap,*
> *sweat and afternoons in dusty light.*

A simple poem that lulled Lou after the rousing song. There were eight stanzas, a steady rhythm that drew on her memories of getting ready for patrols in the morning.

Sofia refilled her water glass.

Valeria sang again, a song of watching over the animals, of caring for chickens and vegetables and goats.

Lou almost expected her to talk of impossible things like cattle, which had been banned for a hundred years at the great taking, except for small survival herds.

The things she sang of would be legal in Yakima. Not here. But they were imaginable, and positive, and full of messages about family and neatness and the importance of caring for animals. They were also enough out of place to worry Lou.

When Valeria stopped for a brief break, Lou turned to Felipe. "Did she choose this subject for me?" she asked him. "Why is she singing to these people about ranching and small farms, and not about . . . I don't know . . . not about things they might . . ." Her voice trailed off. Valeria couldn't sing of revolution. Not to these people, and not with Lou. She couldn't sing of equality. There was no protection for her. So she had chosen something that would appeal to them even if it wasn't their goal.

Felipe smiled, looking for all the world as if he saw her work it out and approved. "She is singing what she can. She chooses a theme for every night. Last week it was raising children, and she ruffled some feathers with that. This week, it's something safer."

"Why do they love her so?"

He shook his head, his expression a war between pride and worry. "Sometimes she sings of things that make me expect to find her in a ditch."

"Like?"

"Like equality for women. Hispanic heritage." He grinned, looking as if his mom were a child who had done well in school. "She's the bravest person I know."

"She is brave."

Valeria started again, and this time she took them slowly down into the evening. Dinner was a poem, and after that she took the audience to the bar—right to where they sat now—and together they all sang a song. Two. Then three. These songs were almost like sea shanties, although they spoke of rolling hills and rivers and stars.

Then she took the solo stage again and crooned of people speaking warm things to each other. As far as Lou could tell, she was making it up on the spot, a spontaneous half-talking, half-singing song that captured the exact moment it spoke of, and to some extent shaped the moment.

Despite her fascination, Lou found herself yawning.

Beside her, Felipe laughed softly. He leaned close to her and spoke in a hushed voice. "That's how she wants you to feel. Next she will sing or tell you a lullaby to send you home peacefully. Don't let her make you too sleepy."

He was laughing at her, although in a good-natured way.

Felipe's wife, Cheryl, came by and whispered in her ear, "Don't mind him. He likes to tease his friends."

The comments sounded good-natured. "I won't."

Cheryl went on to the next table, and Valeria started a lullaby. She chose a deep and melodious song that elicited a few more yawns from Lou, and a little more ribbing from Felipe.

As the song finished, the lights came up. Valeria's family was already picking up glasses and plates quietly, with only a little clatter. People began to file out of the bar.

Lou got up to help clear as well, finding herself a little stunned. She would never have expected poetry to be so powerful. Maybe song, but never poetry. Right now, her sharpest memories of the evening were the poetry.

There had been something vulnerable and tender between Valeria and her audience. And tense. The complexities of the bond between Valeria and these people were as amazing as the poetry.

The topic Valeria had chosen rubbed at her. It described her life as a Wilder, although she usually had fewer domestic animals than Valeria had referenced. It had enchanted her, yet it was vaguely seditious.

She stopped at a table near Felipe and pointed at the mural. "Alondra told me you painted that."

"I did."

"Tell me about Akita?"

His lips thinned. "He is an alpha wolf. Strong. But I haven't seen him for weeks."

"But you have seen the pack?"

"A few times."

He was lying. He worked for her, and she couldn't afford to have him think he could lie to her. But she didn't want to rat Alondra out either. "Could you have found the wolves last week?" she asked him.

"I looked for them with you."

She stopped right in front of him. He held dirty glasses in each hand and looked like he wanted to walk right around her.

"Do you trust me?" she asked him.

"With what?"

"With this place?"

"It is my home."

He was so frustrating! "I am supposed to work to save the wolves. I am paying you to help me find them."

"And I took you to try and find them."

His language was so careful. She didn't want an argument. It had been a long and interesting night, and an argument with Felipe wasn't her preferred way to end it. But she felt even more sure that he had led her *away* from wherever the wolves were. "I will find them." She stepped out of his way and let him pass her and then followed him to the kitchen, where she stood in the middle of a drying line with a clean cloth. The repetitive, simple work calmed her.

Felipe scrubbed the floor in the main room. Blessing and Day helped him by moving tables and chairs. As they were nearly finished, Valeria came in dressed down in simpler clothes than she had worn on stage, her hair braided back loosely from her face, small wisps escaping from it. She looked as exhausted as Lou felt. "That was beautiful," Lou told her.

Valeria nodded. "Thank you for helping. It was a busy night."

"You're welcome."

No one sang as they left the bar, but stars shone above them, and there was soft laugher and tenderness hovering in the air among them. Felipe carried his son, and Day utterly surprised Lou by taking Alondra onto his shoulders, her legs dangling almost to his knees.

A shout came from the end of the street. A greeting?

More voices. Horses.

The caravan her sister had mentioned? She jogged a few steps to catch up with Day. "We should stay in town."

"Yes," he said, lifting a hand up for Alondra to take. "Let's get you down," he told her. "Go to your mother."

Valeria noticed the conversation and must have read something in it, since she was too far away to hear. "Is everything okay?"

"I believe this is the caravan Coryn told me to watch for. Go ahead and get the children home. We want to learn more."

Valeria stared at her, all the considerable force of her personality going into her words. "Come home with me."

Lou recognized the command but shook her head. "I can't. We'll be along soon."

"These people are dangerous."

"So are we," Lou snapped.

Valeria glanced between them and her family. Nodded stiffly. She turned and took up Alondra on her shoulders, walking fast as if the child weighed nothing. She and all of her family continued the way they had been, walking with purpose while also looking like there was nothing at all in the world to be worried about.

CHAPTER THIRTY-ONE

Day signaled them all to stop in a shadowed part of the street under an overhang. They waited in silence for Valeria and her family to reach the end of the road and turn. Before Lou could give an order, Day held up his hand. "This is the work I trained for. Blessing too. This is why we are still here."

She slapped his shoulder, which felt like a rock. "I'd been wondering about that."

He put a finger to his lips, withdrew it, and whispered, "You can go back if you like."

She shook her head. "My work, too."

Day nodded and gave her the hand signals for *We can't be seen*, *Stay quiet*, and *Follow me*.

He led her and Blessing behind dark buildings. She tried to match their silence, but the toe of her shoe slipped across gravel in one place and two strides later she stepped on something plastic that emitted a large crack.

Neither man mentioned her transgressions.

As far as she could tell, they didn't breathe. Her own breath rasped loudly in her throat.

A waxing gibbous moon offered just enough silvery light to see streets and buildings and make out the difference between sidewalk and street. At the end of the road, Day stopped. He pointed left.

They walked down a wider road now. She felt watched, though she saw no one in the shadows of the buildings or peering from windows. With the bar closed down she couldn't imagine any excuse to explain their presence in town.

She focused on her steps, on the wind, on places where people could hide.

An animal rustled in a dry bush, and she startled, scraping her foot along the road.

Blessing glanced back at her but said nothing.

She drew her jacket closer against a cool wind.

They turned a corner and they were behind buildings again, tall concrete towers with broken windows. The lake flowed to their right—here in the end of the lake it was more like a river, the water gradually picking up speed as it made for the spillway that would send it down a fall and toward the Columbia.

Day stopped and cupped his ear. She heard the sounds of hushed conversation, too far away to make out distinct words.

Day turned them abruptly toward the water and laid down on the face of a small hill, gesturing to them to do the same. Grass tickled her nose but she held every worried muscle as still as she could.

Two men cut across the grass toward town, maybe twenty feet away from them. A tall one with light hair and a shorter one with dark hair, the exact color of their skin or eyes impossible to determine.

The men didn't even slow as they passed. Perhaps it was the line of the dark shadows Day had chosen to conceal them in, or maybe it was that they were talking to each other. The tall one was saying "—we missed the bar."

"Can we break in?"

"Agnes won't allow it."

"Bitch."

"Don't let any of hers hear you say that."

Soft laughter, and then they were gone. Day motioned for Lou and Blessing to scramble up and follow him closer to the water. Lou had an easier time walking quietly on grass, and the rustle and swirl of the water created a white-noise sort of background anyway, making the night a bit more forgiving.

Day motioned them down again, only this time it was to sit. He cupped his ear as a signal to listen.

She did, hearing only water at first, and her own breath. Then, another conversation. She did her best to follow it, barely making out a few words. Nothing she could make sense of.

She glanced at Blessing, who shrugged and smiled his inimitable smile. Even though she could barely hear over the sound of the water and the night birds, the conversation clearly ensorcelled Day. She heard the word Seacouver once, a few curse words, and about ten minutes in she also realized that one of the voices belonged to a woman. Agnes? There were three voices. What she couldn't hear specifically as words, she felt as intensity. They were excited.

Her joints began to stiffen with cold and fatigue.

The two that had passed them going the other way returned, talking more loudly than the other three. "We finished. It's stashed."

What was *it*?

Agnes's voice, louder to match these men. "When will the next shipment arrive?"

"When it does."

"We would be better able to help you if you delivered more regularly."

"Just store this stuff. And drill. The best thing you can give us is men who are ready to fight."

Agnes laughed. "I might also give you some women."

"If they can fight."

"Better if they're past childbearing," another said.

Lou stiffened.

"Hail to freedom," Agnes said. "I'm going to bed."

"We're leaving early," the other one said. She thought the shorter one.

"I'll have someone bring you enough salvage to fill your packs at first light."

"Good."

Their voices shifted a little in place and then softened as they wandered off, and Lou didn't catch any more. It was enough.

Coryn had been right. Weapons were being stored here.

They sat for a long time before getting up. The cold had crept so deeply into Lou that Blessing needed to give her a hand up. He held her close for a moment and then stepped back and chafed her arms with his work-roughened hands, whispering, "Warm up."

She nodded, not yet trusting her voice to speak quietly after being still so long. They slipped quietly away from town and started up the hill.

The night deepened as the moon fell over the mountains, and she had to focus sharply on her footing. Halfway up, she turned and looked back at Chelan. Not a single light showed. Discipline.

"Lou," a voice hissed.

"Valeria?"

"Are you all okay?"

"Yes."

"What did you learn?"

She turned toward Day, but he shook his head. "Not much," Lou replied, feeling duplicitous, and tired enough to be irritated at the necessity for the lie. "We did see the caravan, but we didn't learn what they have."

"Too bad." Valeria walked beside them. "What did you think of the bar?"

"I loved your performance. I'd forgotten—maybe I never knew—the power of poetry spoken out loud. I think I might have known it once. In second grade."

Valeria laughed so loud that Day glared at her.

Even though they didn't sing or talk it seemed easier to make it up the hill with Valeria along. Walking warmed her up, and her pace quickened as they got closer to the house.

Funny. It was starting to feel like home.

Lou wished Valeria good night at the top of the wide, center stairs in the silent house. After her door closed behind her, Lou glanced meaningfully at Day. He gestured for her to follow him again, and they went into the suite that he and Blessing shared and sat in overstuffed chairs while Blessing served them all water.

The water tasted like heaven. She drained half her glass and took a breath. "So what did you learn? I could barely hear a thing."

"I made out much of it," Day said. "These are people John Smith and Agnes knew."

"Who was the other person with them? Weren't there three? A man, right?"

Day nodded. "I don't know. Younger than Agnes. Someone from the caravan. I'll recognize the voice if I hear it again. They've got weapons. They're leaving some here and some in Wenatchee. Others are going to Cle Elum and Yakima. They've apparently been doing this for a few years. They're planning a coordinated assault. They get the communities to give them goods in trade for weapons." His voice had gone quiet and contemplative. "It's a good deal for them. For the community? Not so much. They get guns instead of butter and actually give some of their butter away."

"Butter?"

"Sorry. A term for things people need, like food."

"Oh."

"This is bad. I heard rockets once. I didn't hear nuclear, but that doesn't mean there aren't any. Conventional shoulder-fired rockets could still do a lot of damage to city buildings or bridges. But of course they all knew what was there, so they didn't describe it. They just crowed about the power of whatever it is. I heard the phrase city-killer."

"Coryn told me they think something will happen in spring."

"That seems right. The winter is supposed to be hard." Blessing stood up and stretched, glancing toward the window where the sky was already lightening a bit with dawn. "We should go down and see their faces in daylight."

"You haven't slept," Lou remarked.

"We're trained for this."

She threw a dirty shoe at him.

He caught it and laughed.

"I'm too tired to go." She was, too. Every muscle felt heavy. If she went she'd probably do something stupid. She wanted to go, but clearly their training gave them power she lacked.

"That's okay," Day told her. "We have a job for you. Ask Valeria how many locals are in on this. How many recruits they made, in other words."

She nodded. "After I wake up."

Blessing held his hand out and she took it. He pulled her up and led her to her door.

She gave him a brief hug. "Stay safe. Find me when you get back."

He hugged her back. "It might be a little while."

"I know."

CHAPTER THIRTY-TWO

Late in the afternoon of the day after Blessing and Day left, a cold wind blew down from the mountains, wicked and full of the knives of winter. Lou stood inside of the newly rebuilt barn, listening as the fresh wood bore the brunt of the storm. Wind whistled between boards just above her head, behind her, and to her right. She reached into a bucket she'd hung on a peg and took out moss that Astrid had harvested for her, wedged it into knotholes and cracks where boards didn't quite meet. Then she listened again. After about an hour, she thought she had shut most of the wind out.

Matchiko appeared, a slender silhouette in the doorway. "Are you ready for the horses?"

"Yes. Best hurry."

Lou followed Matchiko and found that Daryl and Shuska held fractious horses on lead lines just outside. Buster stamped his big feet and shifted his weight, but his ears stayed forward. The others danced and tossed their heads, rolling their eyes, even Mouse.

She led Mouse in first. Matchiko followed with Buster and Daryl with Pal. They led them into freshly reinforced stalls. Mouse settled slowly, but Lou kept whispering and her ears eventually swiveled forward and her breathing slowed.

Only a few spears of light came into the barn through the high windows, even though it was a full hour before sunset. They threw armloads of hay into the metal feeders on the walls, and the food calmed the animals some.

"I'll stay out here," Daryl said.

"Me too." Shuska grabbed a water bucket. "You shouldn't be alone."

They probably both preferred the company of horses to people most of the time, but nevertheless Lou suggested, "Why don't you come up for supper first?"

Daryl eyed the roof. "This storm's got my back up. I'd rather have tested our barn-building with a mild storm, and this one's not that. Besides, I think the horses will want company. Maybe Felipe or someone can bring us something down after you all are done."

It was a long speech for Daryl. Lou nodded. "Thanks."

"It'll be raining soon," Matchiko said. "I'll see what we can find now."

"Or snowing." Lou and Matchiko walked side by side to the big house, leaning into the wind. Matchiko put an arm briefly Lou's waist, pulling her close. She whispered, "The barn looks great."

"It does." Lou stopped briefly, letting herself marvel for a cold moment, enjoying a hug so tight the wind couldn't get through the spaces between them. She felt lucky to be here, lucky to have gotten the barn done, lucky even to have found Valeria and her family, since it had, in truth, taken all of them to get the house ready for the storm.

She felt even better when Felipe and Angel took food out to the barn, including a few late apples for the horses.

Before they returned, hail pelted the roof and windows with a startling rattle. Angel and Felipe came in soaked. "We're going back," Angel proclaimed. "There's a leak in the roof."

Lou set down the plates and straightened in alarm. "Where?"

"Above one of the stalls. It's not bad, but better to stop it now."

Most of the adults began sliding on the parkas, coats, and boots that Alondra had set by the door earlier. Lou started toward the melee, but Valeria but a hand on her arm. "Stay with me. It won't take ten people."

"I should help."

"I'd like to share a glass of wine with you. Welcome the storm in."

Valeria looked so solemn that Lou swallowed her objections and went to the kitchen for wine.

They settled into Valeria's suite, the dark red wine looking almost black in the low light of a few fat candles. Even though neither wall faced directly into the wind, the windows rattled anyway and something outside banged repeatedly. Valeria spoke more loudly than usual, and still Lou had to strain to hear her. "What did you find, that night? When you stayed in town?"

The question startled Lou a bit. She sipped her wine, her thoughts as rattled as the windows for a moment. She took a deep breath. "You know we work for the city, or at least for people in the city? I don't mean directly. Wilding itself is for the land. For the grass and the rabbits and the wolves. But it's also for the city."

"I know you believe that."

"I care whether or not the city survives." A great sound-drowning gust of wind blew something hard against the house, probably a tree branch that had snapped free. Lou stood, but sat again. It didn't make sense to stand by the window. "There are people and things in the city that I care about greatly. My sister, for one. And many of the resources that you now freely enjoy come from there as well. The lumber to fix up the big barn, the new nails, those all came from the cities."

Even in the dim light it was easy to see the slightly mocking smile on Valeria's face. "The nails came from Wenatchee."

Lou returned the smile. "The money for them came from the foundation."

"I did not need the barn. You did."

Lou bit back an exasperated sigh. "But you did ride in to intercept us, including our horses and our robots. You wanted muscle up here. I'm pretty sure that was to strengthen your hand against the likes of John Smith and his family, in spite of your truce with them."

Valeria raised her glass, her face gone slightly more serious. Her hair fell loose around her face, cascading over her shoulders in a soft wave of dark threaded with silver. She spoke softly. "I did seek you out. The new people in town have mostly been bad influences. They've made our people, my people, make bad choices. Ever since the taking, the town has stunk of patriarchy."

Lou wondered if Valeria was referring to her neighbors or her children. Was this the moment to ask her how many people in town had gone bad? Before Lou could decide how to frame her question, Valeria continued, "I knew you led the ecobots—we'd been told that. A woman. I wanted to see. What are strong women to do but stick together?"

Was that an offer of friendship? Or a challenge? Lou raised her glass, and Valeria did the same and then leaned toward Lou. "But I cannot afford for you to turn the town against me. You must be careful. Let me advise you. There are many things you cannot know."

Lou knew it mattered to find the right relationship with this exasperating, fascinating woman. But one that wasn't subordinate to her. Never that.

Coryn had urged her to keep secrets from Valeria, but instinct suggested that she trust her. Maybe not to support everything Lou believed in, but surely she could trust Valeria to be kind and quiet? "I don't trust the people I've met in town, not any of them. Except you. I don't want a fight. What I want most is to get settled, find the wolves and an elk herd or two, and to work on the science I'm supposed to be doing. I came out here to restore a scarred world, not to spend my energy on a difficult town."

"Leaders don't get to choose what they work on." Valeria smiled. "Not often, anyway. You have all of the choices, and yet you really don't." Valeria took a long slow sip of her wine, looking lost in thought. "If you get caught spying on these people, we could all die."

"We needed to know what that caravan carried. We have reason to believe there are a lot of weapons stored here." Lou stood and paced the room. The conversation and the storm—now gone from hail to hard rain—made her nervous. "I can't ignore threats to Seacouver."

"You can't fight these people. There are more of them than of you, and more of them than all of us."

Now she could ask. "Do you know how many? How many people came in from Outside and are influencing the people who were here before?"

Valeria pursed her lips. "Half?"

"How many is that?"

"Fifty?"

That was a lot. Still. "I'm sure there are more than a hundred people in town."

Another burst of wind rattled the windows harder, and Valeria stared at them. "I should have boarded those up, too. I'm counting the people in John Smith's group. Some were here before, but there were only a little trouble then. I could tell a few stories, though . . ."

Lou laughed.

"But you should not spy too hard. It could put us all in danger."

"I'm being careful."

Valeria grunted. "I have protected my family for a very long time. I admire what you are doing here, the wilding part. I admire looking after wolves and counting deer and restoring streams. At first I wasn't sure you were really going to do that at all. I thought it might be a story you told us just to spy. But I know better now that I've watched you. In fact, I'm sure you'd rather just do that."

Lou smiled. "I would."

"But now your two spies have left."

"Blessing worked with me on a farm in the Palouse. For a long time. He knows the Outside."

"That doesn't mean he isn't a spy. And the small one with him is only that. He has no love for the wild or for the horses."

Day had done the work that needed to be done. Still, Valeria was right. She raised her glass, tipped it toward the other woman in salute. "Day does love action. Wilding is as much watching and learning as doing."

"Is that why you ride off for whole days at a time?"

"Yes." Another gust of wind rattled the windows, and Lou sat and listened to the storm, wondering if the barn roof had been fixed, and happy that Valeria could be quiet.

Eventually, Valeria said, "I'm grateful for the removal of fences that are no longer used and houses that have fallen into ruins. I'm grateful you helped me rip out the dead grape vines. I need you to be careful."

Lou's jaw tightened. "I'm far more interested in wolves than threats, but I cannot ignore either."

Valeria looked equally determined. "I will stop you if you endanger my family. I'm glad the other two are gone."

"I'm not. They were good fighters, and we might need fighters."

"You can hire more of my boys."

"I can't. You need some of them to farm."

Valeria watched her, silent and looking thoughtful in the way a cougar looked thoughtful sitting on a tree branch.

"I can't pay you to farm, and I cannot take orders from you. But I will try to keep your family safe."

Valeria's nodded stiffly. "Thank you."

It must gall Valeria to need someone as young as Lou, but Lou couldn't let it worry her. She had to maintain her leadership in spite of the doubts anyone else had, or that she had for that matter. It would be easy to fall into letting Valeria give orders. She stood. "I want to see if the roof got fixed."

"I haven't heard them come in."

"The sound has changed," Lou said. "It's not rain anymore."

Valeria cocked her head. "Sleet. Maybe going to snow."

"That's not good." Lou paused, eyed the other woman. In many ways, Valeria was still a mystery to her. A brilliant, helpful mystery, but her goals remained unclear.

"What if you have to choose?" Lou asked. "What will you do if you have to choose between us and the town? It could happen."

A door banged, and Felipe yelled up the stairs for Valeria.

Lou had never heard him yell.

She followed Valeria out her room and down the steps at a near run.

The foot of the stairs emptied into the wide hallway that led to the front door, and a chill stung Lou's cheeks. Someone lay on the ground.

A man, based on the boots and the size of the feet. Not Daryl. Matchiko stood beside whoever it was, blood running down her right arm.

Valeria cried out, "Angel!"

Matchiko moved aside, and Lou noticed that his arm bent in the wrong direction, before Valeria knelt beside him and blocked her view.

There were enough people right around Angel that Lou took a place near the wall behind Matchiko, assessing. There was no obvious blood on Angel, so Lou's eyes darted to Matchiko. A bleeding gash marred her forehead. In spite of the blood running down her cheek and dripping onto her shirt, all of her attention was on Angel.

Lou felt someone behind her. She turned. Alondra, her eyes wide with worry.

"Can you get me a clean kitchen towel?" Lou asked her.

The girl turned away toward the kitchen, but Astrid was already there with a fistful of towels and two long wooden spoons in one hand and duct tape in the other. She handed Alondra a towel and knelt beside Valeria.

Valeria carefully examined Angel's arm, which appeared to have broken neatly just above the wrist. Astrid handed her a spoon, which she placed in Angel's mouth. He bit down on it and Valeria tugged and twisted his arm.

Matchiko grunted.

Astrid turned her face away.

Valeria set the arm down, it looked *right* again.

There were two bones in the forearm. Doing that correctly wasn't easy.

Astrid calmly took the spoon from Angel's mouth, and he whispered, "Better."

Valeria said, "You'll need a doctor when we can get you one."

When she had pulled on his arm, he had made no sound, but there were deep teeth-marks in the fat wooden handle of the spoon. In just a few moments, Valeria and Astrid transformed the towels, spoons, and sticky tape into a decent splint. Felipe reached down to help Angel stand, his face white.

By now the whole family had gathered. The hallway was chock-full of people, most of them still in coats.

Lou handed Matchiko a clean towel, which Matchiko held up to her head. Blood quickly stained it near her fingers.

Valeria asked, "What happened?"

Felipe spoke. "It's gone to ice out there. Freezing rain. Angel slipped, Matchiko tried to catch him and fell herself. Two or three of us fell trying to help them up, and then we had to almost skate back, slow and easy."

Valeria nodded.

"Are the others still in the barn?" Lou asked.

Felipe smiled, a brief twitch of the lip. "Just your two. I don't know if we fixed the leak. Maybe. But everything is frozen now, so ice will plug the hole until the storm passes."

"Are they okay?" She glanced at Angel. "Do they know to stay put?"

"Wrapped in horse blankets." Felipe smiled reassurance. "They have a bottle of wine between them. I think they were glad to see us go."

He was probably right. She smiled in return, then turned to Matchiko. "Let's go to our room and clean up."

Alondra put her hand on Lou's arm. "Can I help?"

"Of course. Maybe you can bring Matchiko a cup of tea, and bring me a fresh clean towel? You can bring tea for yourself, too."

Alondra's nod looked quite solemn, and she turned quickly to her task.

Lou went to the window and looked out. "Is it snowing?"

Felipe spoke from behind her. "Yes. It will make the ice even harder to see. Hard to feed the animals in the morning."

"Or the people." Shuska and Daryl had survived a worse storm the year before, so she trusted they would be okay.

As soon as she closed the door to their room behind them, Matchiko turned to her and said, "We have tea."

"I know. I wanted time for a kiss." She leaned in and gave Matchiko a kiss on the forehead, then one on the lips. "And Alondra likes to have jobs to do."

"I bet she does."

Lou ran hot water to wet the towel Matchiko had already been using and started scrubbing at her face. "I hope the house batteries out here will hold through this storm."

"Probably. I looked at the system. It's a decent one. Old. But everything seems to work. Ouch!"

"Sorry."

A soft knock announced Alondra's presence, and Matchiko called, "Come in."

"She probably has her hands full." Lou opened the door. Alondra had three cups of tea on a tray, and two bowls with warm water. "Thank you. We appreciate the help."

Alondra smiled. "Thanks for letting me come. I wanted to be with someone, but Mom is working in the kitchen and Dad's gone."

"Your dad is gone a lot, isn't he?" She had seen him recently, but not since the storm started.

Alondra nodded.

"Can you can help wash off Matchiko's arm?"

Alondra took one of the towels off of her own arm and started in. She was efficient, and willing to scrub hard where the blood had dried. "Dad is in town," she said. "He's in town a lot. Sometimes he travels."

"But I've seen him here, too."

"He was home for two days last week."

She didn't sound bitter, just resigned. Lou had only seen Alondra and Mathew together a few times. Mostly, Alondra shadowed her mother. This family was like that. Strong women. And Felipe. He had the strength of a favored first-born. Everyone else? Less. But what did Mathew do in town? Was that part of why Valeria wouldn't allow fights? Or was it really all about economics?

Mostly clean now, Matchiko took her cup of tea. "I'm going to sit on the couch. Want to join me?"

Alondra regarded the couch. "It's pretty close to the window. Can we sit at the table?"

That was as close as the girl was likely to come to saying she was afraid. "That will be better for drinking tea anyway," Lou agreed. She sat and curled her fingers around the cup. It smelled of cinnamon and cloves, and when she touched her tongue to the liquid, it tasted spicy. "This is great. Where did you get it?"

"It's my favorite. Dad brings me some from time to time He brought this on my birthday."

"When was your birthday?" Matchiko asked.

"Two months ago. I'm eleven."

Lou smiled. "I would have guessed at least twelve."

The three of them listened to the storm, which was quieter now, turned to snow and the occasional soft rattle of wind. "I want to help you," Alondra said.

Lou reached a hand across the table to her. "You just did."

"I want to work for you. I want you to hire me."

Lou laughed. "I can't hire a child."

"I want to ride your horses."

"I can let you do that," Lou said, tipping her cup to finish the last of the tea. "You don't even have to help for it."

"Yes." Alondra paused, twisting her held-empty cup so the liquid swirled near the edges. "Yes, I do. Mom said we can't be beholden to you, that we have to work for anything you give us."

"Good advice," Matchiko said, pushing up from the table. "I'll let you two talk trades. I think I'd like to go wrap up in some blankets."

"I can help you find the wolves," Alondra said, all in a rush. "I know where they are."

CHAPTER THIRTY-THREE

Namina drove Coryn through morning wind sprints, sending her back and forth endlessly across a small park with some other runners and their robotic coaches. Coryn merely wanted to be finished so she could get to work. The storm had hit Chelan overnight, and she wanted to see the satellite pictures on the big screen even if they showed nothing but the tops of clouds. She felt closer to her sister when she had the feeds up, even though they were also sent to her wristlet. A five-foot tall image was so much better than a one-inch picture.

She also, finally, had questions for Jake.

As soon as Namina let her stop, she rushed to the office, where she asked Namina to wait outside. Inside, Jake looked up from a note he was making on paper.

"I suppose it's too late to tell you a slate works a little better." She smiled, teasing him.

"For you." But he returned the smile.

She glanced at the sat shot. Just as she expected, a beautiful picture of clouds, with the glory of the sun turning the tops of them a blinding white and only the barest glimpses of dark gray. The clouds moved quickly, which might or might not mean serious wind at ground level, but it did make the storm look bigger and more threatening. No lightning. "Where do you keep all that paper anyway?"

"I shred it. Some days I burn it. Paper is much more secure than any computer system. Besides, I only write things down to remember them. After I write them down, I don't forget." He pushed the paper away from him. "Even now."

She reached across the table and took his hand. It felt almost like ice in hers, the fingers stiff and knobby. The words he'd been putting on the paper were so spidery she couldn't read them, but she didn't mention that. Maybe his trick worked whether or not anyone else could read his writing. "Are you well?"

"No. My head hurts now. All the time. I wanted to make it to the spring, to see us keep the city safe again." He pulled his hand back and rubbed at the back of his head.

Her eyes felt hot. "Can I ask you a few questions?"

"Sure." He reached for the paper again and pushed it toward her. "Sometimes it helps to write down the answers."

She dug through the pile on the table to find a purple pen. "I'm curious about relations between the cities. I really liked being in that meeting the other day. I mean, it scared me. What was said. But I liked the oath and the way people were working together."

"Good to have you there. What was the most interesting?"

"The meeting was almost like a dance. The mayor—Mayor Broadbridge—he knew what he wanted to tell us, and it was a lot, and he figured out how to make it happen. And everybody agreed. I really liked that."

He leaned back and smiled. "I think you'd be a good diplomat."

"I don't know if I'd have wanted to do the talking."

"Not now. You hardly know a thing. But you work hard and people like you. Do you have any questions about what you heard?"

"I probably have a hundred." She stood up and leaned against the wall. "But one thing is really puzzling me. How are the people attacking us paying for it?"

Jake's smile widened. "Very astute. A lot of money went missing during the troubled years. We never knew if it lost itself forever in the failed markets or if it was simply hidden. We always suspected some of both."

"And you can't track it? Not even Adam?"

Jake shook his head, slowly. He looked a little faraway, like he was lost in memory. He tapped his fingers on the table for a while, and she sat back down and started doodling, letting him work out what he wanted to say.

"Money from then went into a million holes. Some people had been saving it up since the very beginning, when climate change was big enough to see but not yet big enough to get attention. People ignored it. Inconvenient, hard . . . a lot of reasons. But some people started saving up and stashing away then. This might be that coming back to haunt us, or it could be from the underground economy."

"I thought that was a story they made up to torture econ students with."

He laughed. She hadn't heard him laugh for a while. Then it turned to hacking and she brought him water and tissues and waited him out, worried, rubbing his shoulder.

After he got his breath back under control he heaved once and finally spoke. "Sit down. I'll live another hour. We don't know. If anybody knew where the money came from, they would have said so in the meeting. I suspect everyone is looking."

She nodded.

"Do you know how a meeting like that gets pulled off?"

"I'd like to." She started doodling on the corner of the paper, sketching his face badly. "A lot of planning."

"Days, maybe weeks, of work. Meetings about the meeting, and I'd bet everyone practiced the presentations together. Did you see how they didn't repeat a thing, and how the presentations just built on each other?"

She had. That kind of puzzle would be worth the work. "It was like being in a class, only it was so real it made every class I've ever been in seem fake. That meeting was worth a few days of work."

"Probably a few days of work each for about twenty people."

That shocked her. "So much?"

"Yes. Diplomacy requires a competent staff."

"Like Imke."

"And Adam."

She nodded. Whatever else Adam was, he was certainly competent.

"Julianna shared the note you sent her with me."

She had almost—but not quite—forgotten about that. "Did she like the answers?"

He smiled, and for a moment he looked far away, like a memory scooped him away from the conference room. "She did. I did, too."

Coryn blinked, relief spreading through her and unknotting muscles in her shoulders. "Were they the right answers?"

"Can you pull them up?"

"Sure." She glanced at the screen again, the white clouds, the certain fury of the storm right over Lou. She probably wouldn't be able to see anything useful until morning anyway. Maybe there'd be a small break in the clouds she could use to check on the new barn. She'd spent so much time finding materials she wanted it whole. She pulled up her note.

> *The three things that threaten Seacouver:*
>
> 1. *Whoever fought us a few months ago. Hackers and Returners?*
> 2. *The complexity of our systems. Maybe even the systems themselves?*
> 3. *Our own sense of safety.*
>
> *The three things that threaten Lou:*
>
> 1. *Whoever wants to attack Seacouver. (She's helping us look for them. If she gets caught, they might kill her.)*
> 2. *Weather (storms and fire).*
> 3. *Disease.*
>
> *I want to work on diplomacy. After Lou is safe, after this summer.*

Jake stared at the screen for a moment, squinting a little, so she made the font bigger. He nodded at the list. "Do you see what you did there?"

"Saw a lot of bad things?"

"Even though Adam says you'll never be a data analyst—"

"Hey!" she interrupted.

"You can't be everything. There are precision thinkers like Adam and intuitive ones like you."

She leaned back in her chair, a smile threatening to sneak up on her. "Julianna is the precision thinker. And I'm like you."

"Yes, although don't be fooled into thinking you or anyone else is just one way."

She nodded, the flash of insight dulling a little.

"Your intuition *is* good. You listed three of the four things that we presented in that meeting. And you did that *before* the meeting."

She stared at it. Had she?

"See?"

"I suppose." She'd screwed her face up, perplexed, and consciously relaxed it. "I learned a lot in that meeting."

"Of course you did. Anyone would have. One of the most important senses for a politician is instinct. Knowledge that just comes, and is right. Your answers show instinct." He sat back, pain tightening his face.

"Are you okay?"

"Please stop asking that question. It's a silly one. I'm as okay as anyone who's about to die."

She winced and hurried on. "I didn't get it that the cities have to work together at all, even though we read about that in school. I didn't understand. But they're all islands of information, aren't they? And we need rivers of good will in between. We need to share, and we're far more likely to win together."

He smiled. "Maybe."

She narrowed her eyes. She was right.

He held a hand up. "Maybe. Maybe we'll win. As humans. That's what you'll need to remember to be a diplomat. That to win as humans is to win for everyone. Not just for the people in the city who have it good."

"All the people in the city," she mused.

"All the people everywhere. Everyone. Even your worst enemy. Even the people who might kill your sister." His voice was stronger than she'd heard it in weeks. "The fight is for us and every other plant and animal and tree we've accidentally managed to leave alive. If we fight among ourselves, we will kill everything and then we will also die."

There was such conviction in his voice. Even sick, even almost dead. He had so much—bigness. Sometimes she felt his presence this way, in the things that he talked about easily that were impossible things. Mayor Broadbridge had sounded like that. Bigger than a human. Larger than life.

She fell silent, glancing again at the image on the wall. "I hear we never used to have storms like that."

"We've always had storms. But not as often, and almost always smaller. The storms won't get better for a long time, not for generations. If ever. But we *are* making progress. We're slowing the carbon trends, flattening the curves. Taking out fewer species at a time, putting a few back. Helping others. Keeping animals safe from us. The wilding is helping the most."

"There are people out there." She pointed at the screen, but she meant further out. "There are people out there who would stop that. Selfish people."

"Only because they don't know better. What did your textbooks say was the reason we got all the way here?"

"We fought."

"That's only a little bit of it. We didn't listen. It's not that two sides fought, it's that they spent all their energy fighting each other without listening, and none of their energy forging a future. It's a human risk. I see signs of it every day."

She reached for another piece of paper and started another picture of him, getting his thinning features all down before she said, "Lou and Valeria aren't exactly alike and they're working together."

"That's good. But the people in town and Lou are on opposite sides, and are they listening to each other?"

She shook her head. "No."

"You have to fight that in yourself. There are times when you talk instead of listening."

She stared at the paper and let the sting of his words roll over her. Were all leaders so blunt?

"Julianna and I forged the great taking by bulling our way into it and through it. But that was listening to our time." He gestured toward the smaller screen with her notes on it. "You're listening to your own time. Change happens fast." He stopped for a moment, steepling his long fingers and resting his head on his hands while he winced through whatever internal hell his cancer was creating in that moment. "You and Lou. Everyone in your generation. Imke. Adam. It's not your job to finish what we started. That's not even possible. The world almost always moves on before you get all the way to a goal. It's your job to do what needs to be done now."

She blinked back unexpected tears. "How do we know what to do?"

"No one does. You do your best." His whole body shook a bit, his cheeks sunken; in the artificial lighting, his eyes seemed to recede into his skull. "We'll help you. Julianna and I have talked about what to do for all of you, what your special gifts and roles might be. But you have to want the things we want to give you."

"What is that?"

"For you? Schooling. After spring, after Lou is safe. If you survive." That made her flinch.

"We'll send you to school. A good one. We'll have a job for you back here, even if we're gone, something like Imke's or like what you're doing for Lou, only for Blessing and Day and LeeAnne and more people we'll introduce you to. You won't be the only one. Part of a team. But that's only if you do well in school and *if you want that* after school. But we wanted you to know. In case we're not here to tell you."

He wouldn't be. She felt like he could fall over now, just put his head on the table and not wake up. "Surely Julianna—"

"Is my age. We don't know what will happen to her, or when. The rest of this year might be dangerous. Her guards could fail. So many things . . ."

She swallowed. "I'll help keep her safe."

He smiled indulgently, as if at a child. "Thank you." He stood up. "I have to go lie down."

She stood as well, walking him to the doorway.

He stopped and looked down at her. His hand on the doorframe started shaking. "I'm sorry we can't let all of this play out over years. That we're asking so much, so fast."

"I'll walk you back."

"I have a companion."

"I'd like to."

He smiled, and then grimaced. "Okay. Let him take my weight."

To her surprise, his robotic companion, Evan, picked him up and carried him down the hall. She had the sense it went more slowly than it might have if she weren't there. They were quiet, but it felt like having company, and like Jake got as much from her simply being there as she got from his being there.

Namina trailed behind.

As they parted at the doors to Jake's suite, Evan turned toward her, and she could see that Jake had fallen asleep in his arms.

CHAPTER THIRTY-FOUR

Alondra scampered up a hill in front of Lou, heading toward a stand of ponderosa pine and Douglas fir trees. Even though she was shorter than Lou, her legs were at least as long. She bounced from rock to root to rock, avoiding the mud left over from the storm. It seemed as if the wild places loved her, and poured power and grace into her.

Lou glanced back down the hill to check on Mouse, who stood in a small corral with no tack other than a halter. She and Alondra had ridden double to the corral, which was by itself next to a burned-out foundation with a scarred stone chimney. They had watered the horse in a lake on the way up, and Mouse looked perfectly happy munching on grass. They were already far enough above her that she looked like a toy horse.

Alondra reached the trees. Lou redoubled her efforts, panting by the time she caught the slender preteen. "You look like a forest nymph or something," Lou told her. "And you move like one, too."

Alondra didn't slow down.

"Stop for a second so I can catch my breath?"

Alondra laughed, a high friendly laugh. "Keep going. It's flat for a bit and where I'm taking you isn't far. Really."

Lou gave an exaggerated sigh, and Alondra giggled. Twenty minutes later, the girl stopped under a copse of trees surrounded with vine maples that still clutched a last few brilliant scarlet leaves, even after the last storm. The sky was clear and blue and the air cold enough to demand a coat and warm gloves.

Alondra led her to two rocks that made good seats. As soon as they settled, she pointed at a steep hillside full of tumbled rocks opposite them. "There's a den there."

Lou squinted at the hill, searching the tumbles of rocks and dead wood, the small bushes and trees that clung to the slope. "I don't see it." She reached into her pack and brought out a set of silver binoculars about the size of her fist. She scanned the area where she thought Alondra was pointing, but the hillside looked utterly unremarkable. No wolves, no cave mouth, nothing that looked like a den.

Lou handed her the glasses.

Alondra peered through them. "These are great."

"Find me three wolves and I'll buy you a pair."

Alondra smiled broadly. She directed Lou's attention toward a twisted tree and a rock shaped like a rabbit before passing the binoculars back. Eventually, Lou figured out where the girl wanted her to look. It wasn't exactly a cave mouth, just a dark spot between rocks with a ledge around it and some low flat bushes. A few thin game trails led to it, but then the entire hill seemed full of game trails.

"I don't see any of the pack there now," Alondra said.

"It's fall. Do they den here in winter?"

"No. But they shouldn't have left yet, unless the storm drove them away. But it's warm again."

Lou stared at the vapor trails of her own breath. "This is warm?"

"You'll see." Alondra handed the glasses back to Lou and started unpacking lunch. Astrid had sent fresh carrots and flatbread and late-season blueberries and flasks of water.

"How do you know so much?" Lou asked her.

"I've come up to help Felipe a few times. He found them years ago, and he watches over them."

"Has he ever come up here and not been able to find them?"

"Of course."

Lou bit down on a sweet carrot. "Does he always come here to look for them?"

Alondra drew her brows together and thought before she said, "Every time he's brought me, we came here."

Lou held her questions. Alondra adored Felipe. She fought back the dismay that wanted to settle onto her features. Had Valeria known they wouldn't find wolves on their ride either? Were they testing her? Or did they just not trust her?

Either way, it bothered her. She turned to Alondra. "So we just wait?"

"That's all there is to do."

"We can wait two hours," Lou declared, conscious that she was responsible for the girl.

"Three?" Alondra asked. "I haven't seen the new pups."

Lou smiled in spite of herself, just the sound of the word drawing up happiness. "Pups?"

"Felipe told me there are three of them. There were, anyway. Pups don't always make it."

"So how old were you the first time you came up here?"

"Eight."

She was eleven now. Did she have any idea how lucky she was to be raised out here instead of in the city? When Lou was eleven she'd never even seen a wolf. She'd printed pictures and taped them up on her bedroom wall and stared at them until she fell asleep. She'd dreamed of seeing trees and vistas and feeling the bite of real wind and rain. She'd studied everything she could about Wilders and the NGOs that funded them, and written about them in her school papers.

Here she was, shivering in biting cold the dome never let into Seacouver. She and her companion were the only humans for miles. This life had been a dream, and now she lived it.

How long had it been since she thought of her younger self? "Hey, Alondra?"

The girl looked at her, brushing a strand of dark hair away from her face. "Yes?"

"What do you want to be when you grow up?"

The girl stared across at the den, which still showed no activity. "I don't think about it much. I guess I want to be like Felipe or like you and care about things out here."

"Good girl," Lou said.

"I don't want to be in a war, or even a fight though." She made a face, and shivered.

Lou felt a sudden fear for Alondra, a visceral feeling with no reason about it. "I don't either. And I hope you never are." She took a deep breath. "But I have been." She thought of all the weapons in town. Blessing and Day had learned little more when they'd gotten back to town, although they had been able to get good pictures of the people in the caravan and sent them to Coryn.

Alondra tucked her legs up close to her, her eyes focused of the far hillside and the den.

They sat together in silence for some time. The girl was uncannily good at being quiet and stayed still against the cold while Lou rubbed at her arms from time to time.

A doe and her nearly grown fawn wandered slowly in front of them, coming so close Lou held her breath to keep from spooking them.

After they left, Lou whispered, "How many wolves live here?"

"I think there are eight now. The alpha pair, Akita and Ghost. The three pups. Three solo wolves. Maybe it's different now, though. Felipe has been saying that one of the males might run off this year. That's Cazador. He'll be three now, and not strong enough to tackle the alpha. Akita is only six, and so Akita might not get old fast enough for Cazador to be alpha, and he wants to be."

"Felipe told me Akita is old."

She smiled. "Not too old to fight."

"You know a lot," Lou said, settling back and getting as comfortable as she could in the cold.

Two hours passed. Soon it would be time to give up and leave, however little Lou wanted to. She stood, shaking her arms to get the blood to run tingling back to her frozen fingers.

Alondra tugged on her pants leg. "Stop moving."

Lou stopped with one arm in front of her, then lowered it slowly. She glanced toward the den.

Nothing.

Alondra wasn't looking that way. She was looking behind Lou, totally still, her eyes wide.

Lou turned her head, slowly.

Right behind them, a pair of yellow eyes stared at them both. They were so compelling they were truly the first thing Lou noticed, and the ruff of white and gray fur and the pointed ears and long nose that surrounded the eyes, then the large paws and the casual stance, the wolf's weight on only three feet.

The wolf stood no more than fifteen feet from them, watching them almost straight on. It could have easily stayed deeper in the vine maples.

She had seen dead wolves this close, had touched them. She had seen live wolves, but not so close. She'd seen them running, even seen a hunt once when two wolves drove a deer into three more wolves and took it down quickly. A thing of efficient beauty, that hunt.

This, though. It was different to merely be regarded by such a wild thing. The power of the animal seemed to combine with an unexpected gentleness. The fur around its muzzle was more gray than white. It had one brown sock. A scar marred one cheek, a wide swatch of hairless skin that must be cold in winter.

"Rumpus," Alondra breathed.

It turned its great head toward the girl.

When Alondra addressed it, she spoke in a soft, calm tone. "Hello, Rumpus. It will be fine."

As if it had been waiting for her words, the wolf turned and trotted away.

"Did it know you?" Lou asked softly.

"I know them all. So they all know me." Alondra looked past Lou, almost through her. "There. Now."

Lou turned. There indeed. Another wolf, large, with darker fur along its back and on the tip of its ears stood on top of the rise. It watched them with an unblinking and unreadable stare.

Akita. She didn't even have to ask. He looked like Felipe's picture. Besides, *this* wolf had to be the alpha. She has seen two other alpha wolves, and there was something unmistakable about them, an aura of power. A white wolf stepped out from behind him. She had a beautiful pelt, and her body spoke of speed and power. Ghost.

Below them, two other wolves. One was darker, sienna and brick colors blending with black, and the other was as tall as the one they had just seen, but redder in color and with a slight limp.

Behind that, a smaller wolf. A pup. She watched carefully but only saw the one.

All of wolves except Akita disappeared, one by one. Akita lay down on top of the hill and put his head on his paws.

They sat, listening to the wind ruffle the leaves on the trees above and around them, and to the patter of rodents in the leaf detritus under the bushes. Smaller birds sang while two crows argued with each other, unseen but nearby.

Lou had the distinct impression that the wolves and the humans were sharing the peace of this moment together.

She let the moment go on a long time before breaking it with a soft whisper. "Do you recognize all of the wolves?"

"Akita, Ghost, Rumpus, Rosie the Red, Brown-Back, and a pup. The pup doesn't have a name."

"Do you think we missed a pup?"

"No. I think we lost two. Ghost—that's the mom—Ghost would never leave two behind."

Lou whispered, "Why did Felipe name her Ghost?"

"I named her. I was only eight, and she was the whitest pup that year. That's also what some people called '06."

Lou knew that story, about an early Yellowstone wolf, but she was surprised Alondra did. "That was a good idea. You gave her a lot to live up to, though."

"I did." Alondra smiled. "She's that good."

"Why did that wolf get so close?"

"Rumpus? He wanted to smell us. The wind is blowing away from the den and toward us."

Lou nodded again. "You really have done this a lot."

"Yes. I thought *you* protected wolves. Shuska told me that one night, by the fire. She told me you were pissed off about a wolf being killed the day you met her."

"So was she. But I never had an assignment about wolves in my old job. We were protecting buffalo and eagles. There were wolves around, and we helped other people track them sometimes. We wanted to keep them alive to keep the buffalo healthy. Bison, really." She realized she was letting her thoughts and words wander. "Mostly I protected wolves by stopping hunters." She glanced appreciatively at Akita. "I've killed people who wanted to kill wolves. I've killed people who did kill wolves. I've seen many wolves, mostly alive and some dead. But I've not had time to just sit and study them like this. Although I know some packs, there is no pack that knows me."

"This one does. Rumpus knows what you smell like and Akita knows what you look like."

"Good. I want to come back. I want to protect this pack. I hear there's another one near Stehekin. I want to protect those wolves as well."

The crows screeched extra loud above them and then flew off. "What are you protecting them from?" Alondra asked.

"What killed the pups?"

Alondra shrugged, for a moment looking as young as she was.

"Could it have been humans?" Lou persisted.

"I don't know."

"Where did Rumpus go? I didn't see him go into the den."

"He's around."

Lou stood up.

Akita stood as well, not making a sound.

"Do we have to?" Alondra asked.

"Mouse will need us. And we have to get home before dark."

Alondra nodded, although she didn't take her eyes off of Akita. The slender brown girl with dark hair and eyes and the rangy light-colored wolf seemed to be telling each other something, although Lou couldn't tell what, and Alondra said nothing.

They'd been traveling back for almost ten minutes when the first wolf howled.

A tumble of words swung toward Lou's tongue, but they competed and she couldn't decide which one to say. *Magic. Haunting. Beautiful. Frightening. Lovely. Natural.*

Still, she startled when a howl came from right behind them. It thrilled up her spine, making her stop in place as if she had turned to a statue.

Rumpus, following them?

Howl on howl created a song that blanketed the mountainside, echoing for fifteen or twenty minutes before the wild call faded, as one voice after another dropped off and away.

When she could move again, Lou hurried them along, worried about the cold, the loss of light, and about Mouse. She'd promised Astrid they'd be back tonight, and if they didn't hurry they wouldn't be. She topped the rise above the old ruin and looked down, hoping Mouse had remembered the howl of wolves and known not to panic.

The corral was empty.

CHAPTER THIRTY-FIVE

Lou wanted to rush down the hill toward the empty corral, to call out for Mouse. Instead, she shrugged her light pack off, took the stunner from it, and dropped the pack behind a rock. She whispered to Alondra, "Wait here. Stay safe. If anything happens to me, get home." Her fingers and nose already felt the freezing cold, and it was bound to get worse as dark fell. "Don't stop though. Keep moving."

Alondra nodded, and the voice she spoke to Lou with sounded just like the one she used with the wolf. "Don't worry. I'm used to being out here. I can go with you. I'll stay with you."

In spite of her worry, Lou almost burst out laughing at her tone. "I need you to be safe. Your family needs you."

"I can help you."

"Stay."

There wasn't any way down to the corral that didn't feel exposed, but Lou flitted as quietly as she could from rock to rock, tree to tree, scuttling quickly down the open places in the switchbacked trail.

The ping of a bullet against rock startled her. Someone had shot at her!

She stopped, flattened herself against a rock, took a breath, checked her weapon.

Stupid. She knew better than to relax.

At least whoever had shot at her had missed by a long way. The bullet hadn't been close.

She found the next cover and stopped again, breathing hard. Someone wanted her attention, had taken her horse. And now she knew they were still nearby.

Why?

She peered carefully around the rock she had settled behind.

Nothing.

A voice. Male. "Come down. Now."

"Who are you?" she called.

"Stop it, Daddy!" Alondra's voice. "Don't scare her."

Mathew? Lou stood up and looked around. She couldn't see him. She called out, "What are you doing here? Where's my horse?"

"I have her."

"Why?"

"I needed to see what you would do if I took her."

"What do you mean?" If he was trying to find out whether or not she'd stun him, he might not like the answer, not now that he'd filled her with adrenaline by pulling a stupid stunt.

"I wanted to see if you would keep my daughter safe."

That made her angrier. She didn't trust herself to answer.

Alondra scrambled down next to Lou, dropping her pack. "It's going to be all right. He's just mad."

Just mad? He'd shot at her!

"You should put your gun away," Alondra whispered.

Lou hesitated. Chances were Alondra knew more about her father than Lou did. She compromised by sliding the weapon into her coat pocket and shouldering her pack again.

Alondra kept her control of the small scene. "We're coming, Daddy. Did you ride up here?"

"Diego has the horses."

There were two of them? Horses? Had they stolen the horses? How had they come up here? But Lou held her tongue as they climbed the rest of the way down to stand on the flat ground beside the metal-post corral. Mathew leaned on the rails, looking like a far angrier version of Daryl. He looked down at them, his expression unreadable except for the look in his eyes, which was cold and mean. He held an old-fashioned long-rifle in his hands.

Alondra walked right up to him and gave him a hug, which he

returned with one arm while barely softening. Then the girl stepped back near Lou.

"Why are you here?" Lou demanded. He might not work for her, but much of his family did, and she wasn't willing to be pushed around.

"Shuska sent me to find you."

A brief knife of cold made her shiver. "Why? We were on our way anyway."

"The farm is under attack. They needed to stay to wield the robots."

Wield the ecobots? Did he know anything about them at all?

"Me and Diego took two horses and came up here. When we saw that you'd left your horse, we decided to teach you a lesson."

Bastard! "Attack from who? Tell me."

The look he gave her was condescending at best, and when he told her, "The town didn't like your ecobots tearing things up. They came to tell you," he sounded almost proud of the attackers.

Which side was he on? She wanted to let the anger sparking through her nerves out and confront him for the horse, for the tone in his voice, for his utter arrogance. But that didn't matter. The farm did. "Where are the horses?"

He led them to a sheltered spot behind a stand of trees. She gritted her teeth and bit back foul words over and over as she checked Mouse's girth, tightening it a little, letting the thousand thoughts in her head settle. Deciding which questions mattered.

"Is anyone hurt?" she asked finally.

"No," Diego said with amused affection. "Except Angel. He got stupid and tried to get out of bed, and then he tripped."

She mounted and leaned down to offer Alondra a hand.

"She goes with me," Mathew said. "I'm keeping her safe. You go with Diego." He pulled her up behind him so roughly that Alondra winced before she settled onto Pal's broad back.

Even though she didn't like it, there was nothing to argue about. Alondra wasn't hers. And it wouldn't hurt to see one horse and Alondra safe, although she had the brief uncharitable thought that it was also keeping Mathew safe and out of choosing a side.

Lou tugged her pack around and pulled out the binoculars. She held them out across the gulf of air between horses, and Alondra's skinny hand reached for them, snagging the strap. Her smile was nearly as wide as her face as she slung them over her back, but it faded as she slid her arms around her father's waist.

‡ ‡ ‡

Lou and Mouse were ahead of Diego by the time she reached the first overlook that showed the farm. Smoke rose from the old barn they'd stayed in the first night on the farm. An ecobot circled it, although from here she couldn't tell what it was doing.

A few people seemed to be helping it. It wasn't quite dark enough to see flames, but it would be soon.

A crowd of about thirty people surrounded the house. For just a moment, she wished she still had her binoculars.

The cold wind that almost bruised her cheeks also kept her from hearing anything from up here. Diego said, "Some people didn't like the ecobots tearing up the old farms."

She startled at his tone. Did *he* agree with the people attacking his own farm? Mathew wasn't family, but the -o boys were Valeria's. Not the moment to ask. "They were all dead anyway," Lou said. "We didn't destroy anything worth saving."

"Maybe not. But you made a lot of people angry."

"How?" She'd kept her word to Agnes and funneled the ecobots' demands to work into places that wouldn't hurt the town, and even asked them to leave any completely reusable building materials in a stack that people could choose from. She'd skirted all the edges she could if she wanted to keep their permit. Probably more.

Diego came up beside her and looked down. "Hatred."

He just said the one word and nothing else, and she nodded.

It took twenty minutes to reach the back side of the property. The flames were visible now, snaking along the barn roof. It would have gone up fast. Wood and hay and leather. At least the horses were out. She dismounted and thrust Mouse's reins toward Diego. "Take them both somewhere safe."

"But—"

"I know you don't work for me. But I'm needed in there, and I need my horses safe."

He stared at her, not speaking, a look somewhere between defiance and disbelief in his eyes. "I can help."

"Take the horses. That's help."

"Yes, ma'am." He turned away, and she hoped she hadn't made an enemy of him.

CHAPTER THIRTY-SIX

As Lou started to circle the outside of the farm, two rabbits and a deer raced across her path in a panic. Ash caught in her nose and stuck to her hair. Anger and fear both pulled at her as she neared the burning barn. She could not lose her headquarters now, their home! She could not!

She rushed toward the fire. The entire structure was engulfed now, the bigger timbers burning with extra brightness, falling one after another like a shattering skeleton.

Had they lost the goats?

As she circled, a huge figure loomed up, covered in ash and soot. An ecobot. She half-expected to see one of her crew on its broad metal back, but it had no a rider. It used its massive front claws to scrape the earth, moving fast, dirt flying up into the air. She blinked at it. It looked like it had gone crazy. Lou shook her head, realizing it was building a firebreak. Its drone swarm buzzed around it, some riding high enough to have a good view of the whole farm.

Hopefully Shuska could access a feed.

An ember separated from the flaming roof and twisted on the cold wind. Smaller sparks trailed behind it. One of the drones followed the bright ember, and behind that, the ecobot.

The ember landed on the ground.

The bot stomped on it, a quick, decisive move, and turned on tank-like treads to resume building the firebreak.

What magic words had Shuska whispered into its ear to get it to defend the farm as violently as it would defend a wetland full of endangered species?

She giggled, a nervous reaction. The barn was certainly extinct now. At least it wasn't their new one.

What was she thinking? *Someone had destroyed one of their barns!* She turned toward the house.

"Pshtt."

She recognized the hiss. "Daryl?"

"Good to see you, boss."

He had come from nowhere. Light played on his face, brightening the whites of his eyes. He looked determined and calm. Her man for emergencies. The noise of the bot and the fire almost demanded she yell. "What are you doing out here?"

"Making sure no one is stupid enough to take on the ecobot."

"Ahhh."

"If you stay around the perimeter, I think you can work your way toward the house."

"Very good." He looked happy. As long as she'd known him, he'd come alive around danger. A surge of love for him swelled in her. "Stay safe!"

He lifted a finger to his forehead, hand and face both sweaty and stained with ash and smoke. "You too."

She skirted the outside of the fire, close enough for its searing heat to draw sweat from her forehead.

She heard screaming over the roar of the flames. It came from the lawn, most of it directed at the house. She jogged toward the crowd.

Torches spread flickering light on faces, letting her see they were mostly men.

Not all.

She didn't see Agnes.

The second ecobot was parked between the crowd and the house, completely still, its drones all resting in the small hangars on its roof. The great round red bowl of its head waved to and fro above the body, slowly, as if making sure that none of the farm's antagonists got too close.

She walked quickly around the back of the crowd, trying to make out the words. *Traitor. Destroyer. Damager. Unclean. Evil.* A lot more she couldn't hear. All of them angry, building on each other, then dying down, then building up again like a wave.

Thief!

Evil!

Unclean.

Once, *Witch!*

Witch? The word startled her.

Someone drowned that speaker immediately with more calls of *Traitor!* How could these people understand so little? What right did they have to burn things?

She looked for a leader, for someone running the crowd. There was no evident single person in charge, although two young men and a young woman circled the outside of the group, exhorting people to keep chanting and screaming.

She slipped around to the back of the ecobot. Shuska leaned against the machine, holding her tablet, one big hand flicking over its screen and changing the color of reflected light on her face over and over. Red, green, red, blue, red, maroon. Lou came up beside her. "What's so fascinating?"

Shuska's big arm rolled over Lou and pulled her in tight. "I'm trying to talk this dumb robot into shooing the rabble away."

"Is everyone okay?"

"We're down one barn. Two kids ran off with the goats, as if they'll be able to hide them. But at least that means they didn't burn. The other animals are probably safe. The horses are gone."

Lou breathed out a sigh of relief. "Diego has two of the horses. Mathew took Pal and Alondra. Who has Buster?"

"Ignacio. I told you he was in love with the horses. He has both of the ones that were left."

"Are there any injuries? To people?"

"Safe. So far." Shuska smiled. "Angel twisted his ankle."

"I heard." Lou pointed toward the crowd on the far side of the bot. "When did this start?"

Shuska spoke quietly, still staring at her screen. "They've been here three hours. Valeria needs to give them a talking to, but she said she's waiting for Henrietta. Whoever the hell Henrietta is."

"Rumor has it she runs the town."

"Apparently Valeria thinks she's going to save us. Do you know her?"

"No."

"Do you know what she looks like?"

"No."

Shuska frowned, hesitated a second as the device took her attention. "Glad you're here."

"You're okay?"

Shuska nodded, obviously more intent on her tablet than on Lou. "I couldn't call you. Our data seems to have been cut off. I have an open voice line to Matchiko."

"How?"

Shuska held up a two-way radio. "Felipe gave them to us. There are six people with radios. Me, Matchiko, Daryl, Felipe, Valeria, and Angel."

"Angel?"

"It makes him feel useful to monitor communications. Matchiko and Felipe are in the kitchen running ops. Go!"

Lou sprinted around the house to the back door. Her way was clear. There were enough townspeople to surround the house, but they hadn't done that. They had gathered in a bunch and treated the ecobot like a fence when they could have swarmed around it.

Someone opened the door for her, and she ducked in.

Valeria, Felipe, Matchiko, and Astrid stood over the kitchen table, scratching notes. Matchiko waved. Astrid glanced up and asked, "Where's Alondra?"

"With Mathew."

Astrid's lips thinned. "Dammit."

Lou glanced at the window. "She wouldn't be safe here."

"No one is safe with him. Pray for her."

Had she made a mistake? Alondra had gone with him willingly enough. "He shot at me, but won't he protect his own daughter?"

"He shot at you?" Astrid stared at Lou, and then the look on her face softened. "He's a bastard."

Lou frowned. "Where are the others?"

"Sofia went to town. Tembi took the youngest kids out to the back field, away from all of this. Maybe even into the hills. Everyone else is in the kitchen. Diego went to find you."

Lou answered the question in Astrid's voice. "He has the horses with him. To keep them safe."

Valeria looked up, her eyes narrowed. "Was he with Mathew?"

"Yes."

"But they're not together now?"

Lou hesitated. "I don't think so. Diego is nearby and Mathew rode away from near where we saw the wolves."

Astrid frowned. "Did it look like Mathew was trying to keep Alondra safe?"

Lou hesitated. "I think he would have ridden away anyway."

Valeria visibly bit back words and went back to whatever she was writing down.

The room felt full of tension and anger, but less activity and action than Lou had expected. She jerked her head toward the front door. "Are they going to attack the house?"

"Maybe," Valeria said. "Not right away."

"Do you know why they're here?" Lou asked.

Felipe looked up and across the table. "To destroy the ecobots."

"They can't do that."

Matchiko put a hand on her shoulder. "They don't understand."

Lou glanced at Valeria. Her hair was uncharacteristically messy, and she wore no makeup. She looked puzzled at Matchiko's comments, so Lou spoke loudly enough for everyone in the room to hear. "Ecobots can protect themselves. And they will. You don't need to worry about them."

"Can they defend us?" Felipe asked.

Lou glanced at Matchiko, sure it wasn't the first time the question had been asked. "I explained," Matchiko said.

Lou sighed. "Probably not. We're damned lucky the one is defending the rest of the property from the fire. I have no idea how Shuska made that much progress."

Matchiko smiled. "She convinced them they need us, and that we need this headquarters."

"Good."

Felipe's face was drawn with worry. "If they need us, why won't they defend us?"

Lou answered him. "They're programmed to do a job. That job isn't defending humans, except when we can convince them it is. Most importantly, they can't harm humans. Bad PR. That's what the algorithm that runs them says. Shuska is outside arguing with the algorithm."

Felipe drew his brows together, looking confused.

Low spread her arms. "They're neither self-aware nor mere machines."

Valeria still looked perplexed and Astrid lost. Well, they were hardly alone; many people failed to grasp the subtleties of the ecobots' mission. There was nothing to do about that now.

Shuska's voice spilled through the radio Valeria held. "I think I got the bot to agree that it can shoot at the ground if I ask it to. It won't shoot people but it *will* scare them."

"Perfect." Astrid raised an eyebrow. "Would now be a good time?"

Lou hated the idea. "We're trying to prove that the ecobots aren't a threat to them."

Felipe stared at her. "Something needs to threaten them."

"Someone." Valeria sighed audibly. "I'll go outside."

"They're armed," Felipe warned. "Are you going to sing to their guns?"

"Maybe I will. Give me a minute. Lou?" She handed Lou her radio.

"Sure. I got it." Was Valeria giving her command, or just a radio? She would take it as command. "At least no one is hurt."

Felipe laughed, breaking a little of the tension. "Just Angel."

She smiled. "I already heard that story."

"How many weapons did you see out there?" Felipe asked.

"A few rifles. But I wouldn't see pistols or knives. There could be a lot." Pots rattled from inside the kitchen. Lou glanced that way. "Is someone cooking dinner?"

"Cheryl is heating up chicken stew. People need to eat."

Lou nodded.

"We're making enough for them." Astrid gestured toward the crowd outside. "Maybe after Henrietta arrives, they'll settle down for dinner."

Lou wanted to ask them if they'd lost their minds, but instead she said, "I heard Valeria is waiting for Henrietta. What do you know about that?"

"Valeria thinks she'll hate this as much as we do, and she'll stop it. It's wasteful. Coffee?"

But wasn't Henrietta the one who ordered people killed? Or was that only Agnes? She noted that everyone seemed calm. But then they had been attacked three times in the past. "Coffee would be great. We'll help."

"That's why we invited you," Felipe snapped. "Only now the robots won't help."

Shuska must still be listening, since she popped in with an answer. "It's very hard to make robots kill people."

"Especially ecobots," Lou added, since they kept missing the point.

Felipe frowned, and she wondered if he wished Valeria hadn't invited them. Well, he'd gotten a new barn, assuming it survived the night. Astrid handed her the coffee and she took a sip, the scent and taste both bracing. This was another thing Felipe had gotten. Coffee.

Coryn sent it to them, and the first time Astrid had seen a bag in the supply run she'd hugged it.

Lou sipped her coffee while staring out the window, angry. She needed something more active to do than just be pissed off. But what?

The shouting outside intensified for a moment and then slowed down. Coryn keyed her radio. "What happened?" she asked Shuska.

"Someone started a fight." She almost sounded bored. "There's a small minority of three who want to attack the house, but the others seem to have come up here to yell and burn a barn."

"Thanks." Bless Shuska for her huge pool of exterior calm.

A scraping sound from behind her caught her attention. She turned to see Valeria coming down the steps. She wore black pants, black boots, and a voluminous white shirt. A black cape swirled over the whole outfit. Her hair had been twisted into a bun, and she had applied enough makeup to belong on stage at the bar. She wore dangly earrings that caught even a small amount of light.

She looked as beautiful as she had on stage, as ethereal and strong. She pulled the hood up over her head, wrapped the cape close enough that it hid the white shirt, and took Astrid's radio. "Shuska," she said. "I'm coming out the back, and I want to get on the ecobot."

"On?"

Valeria hurried out, the door barely making a sound as she closed it behind her.

"Now you did it, Felipe," Astrid said.

"She was going to go anyway."

Lou headed closer to the window, looking for a way to peer out.

"You'd be better off out there," Matchiko said. "I can manage in here."

Lou glanced at the door, back at Matchiko, and then at the door.

"Someone needs to keep her safe," Astrid whispered.

"Go," Felipe said. "She won't care if you do. Maybe she even wants you to."

He was probably right. Lou slid out the door.

✝ ✝ ✝

Valeria kept her head and blouse covered with her black cloak, making it hard to follow her in the dark. At least Lou knew her general direction. Even though she lost sight of her twice, she was close again when Valeria came up on Shuska and asked, "How do I get up there? On the ecobot?"

The faint light from Shuska's screen illuminated a cold look on her face.

"It's okay," Lou said. "Let her up."

Shuska waited for Lou to come up beside Valeria. She stared down at them both. "Neither of you should be out here."

Lou looked up at Shuska. "I'm not going to let anyone destroy our house or our new barn."

Shuska nodded. "Me either. But don't be stupid."

"I need to quiet them." Valeria spoke with fierce determination. "I'd expected Agnes or even Henrietta to come bring the miscreants home, but they're not here. So I will do their job."

Shuska glared at her. "The ecobot won't obey you."

Lou spoke up. "But it will obey me. And it will obey you. I'll go up with her."

Neither Valeria nor Shuska looked pleased at that.

"You can start," Lou whispered. "I don't sing as well as you do anyway."

Valeria laughed as she scanned the shadows and the dark side of the ecobot. The torches and lights of the protestors were all on the other side.

Shuska shone a thin, dim light at a ladder. "The robot can pick you up, or you can climb up a leg, but it's less obvious if you use the maintenance ladder."

Valeria climbed quickly, her black skirt swishing loudly enough that Lou heard it over the raised voices on the far side.

Shuska held Lou back in a brief, tight embrace. "Stay safe. Don't underestimate an angry mob of white people."

Lou started up, the rungs hard and cold under her hands, flat and almost as thin as paper. Before she reached the halfway point, Valeria disappeared over the top. Lou found her standing on the crowd-ward edge of the flattest part of the ecobot's back, right in the middle, shedding her coat.

Apparently no one was looking up. Valeria stood there for some time, waiting to be noticed. When that didn't happen, she began belting out a song, something about family and food. Lou didn't recognize it, but apparently the angry crowd below did. Lou slid across the bot's back and lay down on her stomach, peering over the edge.

The crowd quieted slowly, the way a group of fractious horses in a small pen quiets. One by one.

Valeria finished the song; all of the faces below her were upturned, anger and curiosity and even amazement warring for dominance. She stepped even closer to the edge. "I welcome you to our farm. You are always welcome. But you are not welcome to burn our barns or our home or our animals. This is the place where your food is grown before we bring it down to you, and it is a place that you need."

A screech came from the back, from a woman. "Traitor!"

"To what?"

"Yourself!"

"Bot Lover."

Valeria smiled. "I am standing on the back of the robot, using it for a stage." She lifted her arms, an exaggerated gesture. She turned her fingers down to point at the machine. "This beast." She stamped her foot on the metal. "This beast is strong enough to kill me, to kill you, to kill you all. But it does not. But if we begin to hurt each other, we will draw its attention."

The crowd shifted restlessly. A few young men in the back elbowed each other.

Lou's stunner was still in her pocket. She drew it out, primed it, and waited, clutching the radio in her other hand. She sat, breathing carefully, watching.

A tall young man with blonde hair and a black baseball cap stepped forward. "There are enough of us to take the ecobot."

Lou depressed the bottom for the mike. "Maybe now would be a good time for the ecobot to shoot the ground."

"Not while you're on it," Shuska said.

"Why not?"

"They'll think you are making it shoot."

Lou frowned. She usually trusted Shuska, but the people below them looked angrier. How angry would they have to get to shoot at Valeria? Or at her?

Valeria took her skirt bottom in her hand and pulled it up a little, curtseying and bowing. She looked both ridiculous and confident. Brave as hell.

One of the men in the back held up something long and thin. A rifle? "This is not a good night for you to die!" Valeria shouted. "Calm down. Talk with me."

"No talk!" someone yelled. A woman.

Lou, still seated, shot past the crowd, and for a moment, silence fell.

The radio crackled in her ear. "Someone's coming."

A vehicle rocked its way up the rutted road. Lou stared at the low headlights as they cut through the darkness. She hadn't seen any working cars in Chelan.

"Henrietta," someone said.

The car turned out to be a jeep, with tall rugged wheels and seating for four that was occupied by two. Sofia jumped down from the driver's seat and walked around, holding her hand out to help a very old woman out of the car.

Lou glanced up at Valeria and whispered, "What's Sofia doing there?"

Valeria shook her head. "She has always loved the wrong people."

There was no time to ask for clarification. Everyone turned toward the two women, watching the older woman emerge. She was short, maybe even under five feet tall, wearing a simple black dress, with a white hat over silver hair. She moved with stiff determination.

People whispered at her.

She walked over quite close to the ecobot, staring up at Valeria. Fearless. "Performing a stunt, as usual, I see."

"I am trying to stop your people from doing something they will be very sorry for soon."

"I see that." The old woman lifted one of her hands, and it took a breath for Lou to recognize that for a signal.

A shot rang out.

Valeria grabbed her arm, blood running through her fingers. She kept her footing, swaying slightly, eyes wide with shock.

"Now," Lou told Shuska.

The ecobot slammed its largest foot down into the ground, shaking their perch.

Valeria moaned and sank to a sitting position, shock giving way to a look of surprised betrayal.

Another shot ricocheted off the top of the ecobot.

The drones started to rise, an eerily small army. Two of them tilted up and spat bullets into the ground, sending puffs of dust into the air.

Someone shot at one of the drones, missed.

The drones hummed and buzzed like angry bees.

Lou stood, making sure that she was mostly shielded from the crowd below by one of the robot's great arms. "I wouldn't do that." She thought she'd identified the man who shot Valeria. A squat man, middle aged. Older than most of the crowd. Not the young hothead she would have expected. He still held his gun pointed at the top of the bot.

Henrietta's arm started up again.

Lou used the ready button and pointed her stunner at the matriarch. It *might* reach her from here. She squinted, aiming hard.

"No!" Valeria screamed.

CHAPTER THIRTY-SEVEN

Lou hesitated; had Valeria screamed at her, or at someone else? Lou dropped her hand, but only a little, keeping the stunner ready.

It had fallen quiet, as if Valeria's screamed single word had stopped everyone. All she could hear was low conversation and the barely audible whine of the ecobot's drones in flight.

Lou glanced toward Valeria. She had crumpled to sit on the top of the ecobot, clutching her arm. She scooted toward the edge.

"Stay down," Lou hissed at her.

"I have to see Henrietta."

"No." Lou belly crawled across the far said of the bot toward Valeria. "If you can see them they can see you. With bullets."

No one was shooting right now. Probably *because* they couldn't see either of them. They were lucky the bots were huge.

The chanting and name-calling started again.

"Is your arm okay?"

"I won't die today."

Lou smiled. "Good. Me either."

"Deal."

Lou keyed her radio. "Shuska?"

"Are you okay?"

"Valeria is hurt. Her arm. Shot. We're staying down. Keep the drones high."

"You think I can tell this damned thing what to do?"

"Yes." Thoughts raced through her head. "Keep the crowd out here. I don't want them near the house."

As if they heard her, the voices grew louder, preparatory. Maybe it was her imagination. Preparatory for what?

"What are they doing?" Lou asked.

Felipe answered her from the house. "I think they plan to come here."

"Can you make this thing keep them back?" Lou asked Shuska.

"I'm trying."

People below them screamed louder. Pent up adrenaline. Young men trained to fight but denied the chance. Henrietta's arrival had charged them up.

The drones buzzed lower, swooping just above the crowd.

Lou crawled to where she could see, scraping her right elbow as she clutched the radio. A few people bent away from the drones or walked backward from them. Henrietta stood her ground, staring up at a drone. Half the crowd stayed near her, protective, staring up at what she watched, defiant but quiet.

The looks on their faces were—curious? Hopeful?

One of the drones fired into the ground right between the ragged front line of the crowd and the ecobot.

Everyone took a step back except Henrietta.

"Atta girl," Lou whispered to the ecobot. Not that it would hear her.

Someone near Henrietta shot at a drone, missed, shot again, and clipped the wing of one of the smaller drones in the swarm above it. It fell, tumbling to the ground.

The other drones massed and buzzed like gigantic, angry insects.

A voice came from behind her. Valeria. "I need to talk to Henrietta."

Lou hesitated. After the old woman had demanded she be shot? "Are you sure?"

"Yes."

She didn't have a better plan. She didn't have a plan at all. Just a set of objectives. Save her people. Save the house. Save the new barn. Save all the people, no matter what side they were on. She keyed her radio and asked Shuska, "Can you ask the ecobot to capture Henrietta?"

Shuska cursed, then said, "I'll try."

Bless Shuska. A group of men raced off toward the fire. "Daryl!" she snapped over the radio.

"Here."

"Company. Be ready. Five, I think."

The ecobot extended a leg down, setting a multitooled "hand" flat on the ground. Lou spoke, loudly enough to make herself heard below. "That's so you can come talk to us, Henrietta. Come up here and talk."

One of the young men with her screamed up, "No."

A drone buzzed him. It didn't shoot, but it made him step back. Pretty soon Henrietta would be standing alone.

"Henrietta?" Lou called. "What do you say?"

"If Sam comes with me."

Who the heck was Sam? "He comes unarmed."

The man who had just taken a step back screamed. "You're armed. I saw it."

"A stunner."

"Throw it down and maybe we'll come up." He bent to confer with the old woman.

Maybe this was Sam?

Lou glanced back at Valeria. The only light she had was starlight, and it was too little to make out much more than the black pools of Valeria's eyes and the dark slash of her mouth. A slight glint from her earrings. "Do it."

Lou turned back. A drone hovered just above her. Protection, she assumed. "Do you promise to bring no weapons? No knife, no stunner, no gun, nothing."

"I have my hands."

Bastard! Well, so did she.

She heard a scream far off, near the barn.

Time to stop this. She took her stunner and threw it over the side of the machine, so it landed just in front of Henrietta.

Sam helped Henrietta onto the flat foot of the bot, his big arm curled protectively around the older woman.

She moved slowly, not nearly as youthful-looking as Julianna. More like a brick, whereas Julianna was a feather, light and agile.

Henrietta braced herself on the bot's leg just above the hand, and Sam hung on just as tightly, above her. He looked grim.

To their credit, neither looked frightened.

The bot moved its leg slowly, taking its passengers in a wide circle that avoided tilting its giant and currently flattened hand.

Behind them, a gust of fresh flames licked the night sky.

The new barn.

She called into the radio. "New fire. Barn, I think. The new barn. Dammit."

The reply was a stream of invective.

At least they all knew how to cuss. "Daryl?" she called via the radio.

Nothing. Hopefully he was busy and not hurt.

Someone else would have to deal with it. She had to focus on Henrietta and Sam.

The ecobot demonstrated its gracefulness, stopping so that the old woman and her protector could step easily from their perch to its wide back.

Lou met them, taking them to sit on a five-inch-wide ledge of the drone parking space, which was the closest thing to a decent chair on top of an ecobot.

A perimeter light built into the side of the ecobot snapped on, allowing Lou to see the old woman. Her dark eyes receded deep into a wrinkled face but still managed to convey a great sense of purpose and power.

They reminded her of Akita.

Sam was broad but not fat, simply big. His eyes were small and suspicious, with chunky cheeks above a wide mouth that probably looked great when it smiled. Not that she could tell right now. He sat almost behind Henrietta, his posture protective.

She turned to Valeria. Blood soaked the left arm of her white shirt, the whole effect one of a bit-player in a horror movie until Lou looked into her eyes and saw the deep determination there. If Henrietta was alpha, so was Valeria.

She helped Valeria to a seat and took up a position much like Sam, a place where Valeria could lean into her if she needed to. She could also see both the house, which was quiet and well lit, and the burning barn. Barns.

The arm had to be painful, but Valeria merely kept it near her, cradled. She leaned a bit toward the old woman, a cold smile on her face. "You would be welcome here if you did not bring me violence. We kept our word."

Henrietta said, "We cannot allow these things." She tapped on the back of the ecobot. "They cannot be here."

"I and my family did not bring them," Valeria said. "But we took them in, took in the people who brought them, because we feared the size of the rabble in town. You keep your own in check, but there are many new people, and I will not have my family harmed."

As if in answer, the flames burst even brighter behind them, and a gust of wind blew the sounds of angry voices toward her. Three drones flew low over the back of the ecobot and away, toward the fire.

The ecobots appeared to be working together.

Henrietta said, "Most people in town came here at my request. We believe we no longer need you."

"Winter will be upon us. We have always helped feed the town."

Sam said, "Perhaps they'd like horse meat."

Lou managed not to hit him.

Henrietta tapped his knee. A signal of some kind. She did not look at him.

Valeria laughed. "You know you need us. We can help you, protect you if necessary."

Henrietta stiffened. "I need no protection."

"You gave the order to shoot me."

"I did. You were my staff once, loyal to me. But you have grown proud." She tapped the ecobot with her knuckles. "We cannot afford to have people stained with the city so close to us." She glared at Lou, her eyes hard. Then she turned her attention back to Valeria. "You could join us."

"I have never. I will not. I wish you no harm. But I will not stop you from throwing the lives of your young men away."

"Some of your young come to see me," Henrietta said.

Valeria spat her daughter's name out. "Sofia."

"And some of your boys." Henrietta didn't wait to see if her words stuck Valeria hard before she continued, "Some of your boys need ways to express anger. You give them songs."

Valeria's chin was up, and her eyes glittered with anger and maybe even hatred. "I do!"

Henrietta tapped the ecobots. "Will your Wilders stay neutral?"

Lou interrupted. "Valeria does not speak for us. Nor we for her. We have a job to do. I met with Agnes in town. I promised her we would not destroy the occupied parts of town this year. We did not. That is a compromise I may be in trouble for, and it is all I *can* promise. Some of my orders come from *my* bosses."

Henrietta spit on the top of the ecobot and ignored Lou, keeping her eyes on Valeria. "Join us and we will keep you safe."

"I will not join a war," Valeria said. "The way to life and happiness is peace. I will protest peacefully. I will convince, and you know I can do that well. But I will not fight."

"Some of your boys will fight."

Valeria stiffened.

The old woman spoke as if she had all the power in the world, but Lou wondered what she actually had. These people had come up here without her, and if it had been on her orders, why was she here?

The radio crackled, and Shuska's voice said, "The other ecobot has chosen to stop the people who fired the barn." Shuska's voice was deadpan, utterly devoid of emotion. "It is asking if you would like them back or if it should keep them contained."

Lou almost broke out into a cheer, but managed to control herself.

Valeria also kept a poker face. "If you want your looters back, you will need to promise to take them all and to leave."

Henrietta sat very still. "You can let them go *and* come with us. Then none of us will be back until after we win our freedom. We might even help you rebuild."

Valeria shook her head.

The old woman was still for a very long time.

Valeria clutched her arm tighter, her face white with pain.

Sam looked furious.

Lou tried to tell if the flames were growing larger or smaller. The smudge of smoke had thickened enough to obscure the stars in one direction and above it. Probably larger. Anger burned in her belly and she looked away. For now.

An airplane flew over them all, quiet and bright with blue and white lights, a reminder that the cities and their prodigious technologies existed.

Sam lifted his arm up and spoke into his wrister. "Report." He held it to his ear.

She had wondered if they had any good communications.

His jaw tightened as he listened. "Give us a minute to talk," he said.

Lou walked to the other side of the bot. She crouched near the edge, looking toward the fires. She couldn't make out anything near the flames, just smoke and less noise than before.

Below them, people sat talking in small groups. No yelling.

A rustle made her look behind her. Valeria had stood up in all of her bloodstained white glory. Somehow, she had gotten her hair loose with one hand, and it spilled about her shoulders. She looked glorious and dangerous now, a key actor rather than an extra in a bad movie. She stared over the edge of the bot until all of the eyes directly below them looked up.

Drones flew circles of protection over her head, a damning halo of city technology.

"We've given them long enough," Lou said.

"They can come to me." Valeria leaned over the edge, almost far enough to lose her balance, and then stood straight again. She started speaking:

> *"The cost of hatred is death, the cost*
> *Of death is death, and the cost of death*
> *Is hatred. Peace flows from the brave."*

A poem. Lou had no idea if anyone other than she herself could hear. But after Valeria spoke, she turned and went back to Henrietta, standing over her with a soft smile.

Henrietta stared at Valeria, her expression completely unreadable to Lou. After what seemed like a long time, she said, "We will leave now."

"All of you?"

"Yes."

"And you will not come back."

"We will not return this winter."

Valeria seemed to be considering this. When she opened her mouth, it was to repeat the poem:

> *"The cost of hatred is death, the cost*
> *Of death is death, and the cost of death*
> *Is hatred. Peace flows from the brave."*

It was powerful, and yet it left Lou wondering how sane it was to say such a thing. It was not an answer.

The words didn't seem to take Henrietta by surprise, though. She nodded in accord, and Lou sensed the thickness of the history between these two women.

"Perhaps I will see you next Saturday," Valeria said.

Henrietta snorted. "I don't get out much."

"Come." Sam helped Henrietta to the edge of the ecobot. It picked the two of them up as before, and set them down on the ground.

CHAPTER THIRTY-EIGHT

The next morning dawned cold and bright. Lou paced the perimeter of the still-smoking barn with Shuska beside her. The new barn. Dammit. The twisted metal and ash remains were shades of blacks and whites, with no brighter color anywhere. It mocked her. She had finally felt like they were done with the big things, that they had an adequate base. "I was so proud of this barn."

Shuska wore her calm face this morning, a deep sadness showing only in the drift of her shoulders down and the lack of a smile. Always steady. "I already sent one of the ecobots to the debris pile to see what we can use to rebuild."

Lou toed the edge of the wide, jagged firebreak the bot had dug. If the ecobots hadn't helped, the fire would have taken more, maybe even taken everything. They were lucky it hadn't sparked the other outbuildings or the farm house. A little more wind . . .

"Did you hear me?" Shuska asked.

"Sorry. I'm distracted. I spoke to Coryn this morning and she said she stopped Pablo in Wenatchee. He's going to obtain materials for us."

Shuska looked over at her. "So our communication came back. Do you know why we lost it?"

"Coryn can't tell either. She's working on it. At least it's back."

"I bet our enemies include some hackers." An eddy of wind picked ash up and coated their pant legs, and Shuska waved a hand as if to fan the air clean. "Do you need an ecobot to deliver the materials?"

"I'm hoping for a horse and wagon."

Shuska grunted.

The only thing left of either barn was twisted metal. The tines of a pitchfork, one edge bent open by something—an ecobot's foot or even the heat. Hard to say. She pointed. "We might save that hay feeder."

"Yes."

"I haven't seen Alondra."

"No."

"You are a woman of one-word answers."

"Yes."

Lou smacked her playfully on the arm and Shuska picked her up and hugged her close. "I'm glad you didn't die."

"Me too. Put me down."

Shuska did.

Lou nodded, amused. "Thank God you're my friend."

Shuska smiled down at her. "Only that?"

"Never." Shuska's smile warmed her enough that she smiled in spite of the destroyed barns. "I'm going up by the wolves. I'd really like to find Alondra. I plan to take some cameras."

"I can go."

"Felipe is coming with me. He will be enough. We probably need you here to work with Daryl on the barn."

Shuska only looked mildly annoyed. "Good for you and him to get along."

"I'm leaving for Wenatchee tomorrow morning. Weather says I can probably do it, but that five days from now there will be snow."

"It'll be close."

"One of you needs to go with me."

Shuska pursed her lips. "Take Matchiko. Daryl and I will clean up this mess."

"Okay." She'd have been all right with either, but Matchiko blended into crowds better. "Take care of Valeria."

"That woman needs no help."

"Don't overestimate her."

"Don't underestimate her."

"Deal."

"Deal."

They both laughed.

Lou turned her back to the barns. They would rebuild. Henrietta and her mob would not stop them, and neither would weather or the incessant demands from the city.

Lou and Felipe reached the den just after midday. The sun lit the ridge and birds called and fluttered in the forest behind them. Akita came out of the mouth of the den as soon as they reached the spot where she and Alondra had watched, almost as if he had been waiting for them. He lifted his head and howled softly. It sounded like a greeting.

Ghost emerged, standing beside her mate. She was so beautiful Lou nearly forgot to breathe.

To her surprise, Felipe howled back. He sounded like a wolf, his voice echoing and reflecting from the rocky ridge opposite them, and then fading into the forest at their backs.

"What are you saying?" Lou asked.

Felipe turned his always-serious face toward her and held a finger up to his lips.

She frowned, but rather than showing him that the gesture irritated her she got up and started looking for a good place to mount cameras.

"Wait," he said. "I have to ask first."

"Ask who?"

"Akita."

These people were crazy. But she was also a bit at their mercy, and this trip was partly designed to show Felipe she wouldn't disrespect or hurt the wolves. Hardly the position she'd expected to be in, but if he wanted to consult the alpha wolf, so be it.

She could be patient and watch.

Felipe and Akita stared at each other. Felipe brought out a flute that she hadn't even known he carried, small and slender. As he touched it to his lips, she realized it was more like a Native American flute than a concert flute. He blew softly, then arranged his fingers and started playing.

He reminded her of Valeria playing to the deer by the mountain stream. The music captured her attention and seemed to take her floating with it on the wind.

She stayed quiet, breathing slowly, trying to figure out what he was doing.

The pup peered out.

Rumpus was nowhere to be seen.

The music sounded ethereal.

The three wolves—mother, father, and child—all sat and listened to him. From time to time an ear twitched. Otherwise, they were quiet.

Felipe played for half an hour. When he stopped, Ghost and the pup retired to the den, leaving Akita to watch them.

Felipe stood, put the flute away, and nodded to her.

It turned out that he was excellent at putting up cameras.

Mathew hadn't come home or sent word by the time Lou left just before dawn the next morning. Presumably Alondra was still with him. The clear sky promised warmth that hadn't yet materialized; Lou wore a thick coat, wool socks, and a scarf, and still she shivered. The only warm spot was her back, where Matchiko rode behind her on Buster.

Diego led them down the road. She had chosen Diego when Matchiko reminded her of the injured Angel. Diego had offered to take no pay, presumably so Angel could be paid, but Lou had made them settle on half each, which seemed to please everyone. Such a practical family.

While she hated to separate the -o boys for anything, Diego had done a good job keeping Mouse safe, and he had followed her orders when he clearly didn't want to. Both things recommended him.

After a few hours, the sun warmed them enough make them strip off their coats as they rode just above the Columbia, the day so flawless it seemed like everything just had to turn out all right.

They were still outside the edges of Wenatchee when it grew dusky enough that Lou suggested they stop for the night. Diego selected a lone tree for them to sleep under, and Lou helped set up camp and feed the horses. Stars began to prick the cold sky, and silence slowly fell over the night except for the occasional stamp of a horse's foot as it fought the deep cold.

She took the first watch. Early in, a few coyotes howled in the hills, and after they fell silent a rabbit's death scream startled her. Two owls talked back and forth between two trees, and from time to time she hooted at them. The constant white noise lulled her, and toward the end of her shift, she paced to keep both warm and awake. No traffic went by on the road. By the time she shook Matchiko awake, she was cold and shivery, and it took a while to warm up enough to sleep.

She woke to a dead fire and a soft whistle. Diego had the third watch, and he pointed at a brown man on a brown horse, who looked a lot like an older and grayer version of Diego himself. The man was whistling a low tune, watching the river but clearly aware they were there. "I think he wants your attention," Diego murmured.

She smiled and pulled herself up and out of her sleeping bag, certain she knew who he was. "Pablo!" she called.

She had never seen him, but Coryn had sent her pictures, and his smile matched one of the photos almost exactly. Warm, almost soft, and full of knowledge. A preacher's smile if she'd ever seen one.

Come to think of it, not that different from Valeria's smile.

He bent low over his horse and made a sweeping gesture. "May I offer you access to a house with a working kitchen."

She laughed. "That sounds wonderful."

"I'll feed you breakfast there. It's not far."

The suggestion of breakfast made her belly growl. By now, Matchiko was up as well, and just as curious as Lou. Diego looked a little doubtful, so Lou said, "Coryn trusts him."

"Very well." He started settling Buster's tack on his broad back as the two women broke camp. Diego was ready by the time they were. About ten minutes after she first heard Pablo's soft whistle, they were on the way to town.

Pablo remained silent for the few moments it took to reach the house. A chain-link fenced yard surrounded it, perfect for the horses. As soon as he opened the door, a ball of white fur leapt up into his arms.

"Is that Aspen?" Lou asked. "Or Aspen's evil twin?"

"Yes." He put the dog down, and it came over to snuffle at her feet, whining for a pat.

She knelt and obliged, feeling like Aspen's presence made Coryn feel a little closer. "You must have seen Coryn. How is she?"

"She's working too hard and worried about too much. She spends a lot of time thinking about you and what you need. Come on in. There's coffee."

The kitchen did have running water. A potbellied stove with a stovetop sat against a wall in the living room. It looked so normal that she almost expected a working toilet, and she had to sigh when there was no shower. "The water comes in but there's no sewer," Pablo explained. "Someone jury-rigged the kitchen pipes to run to a ditch outside the house. They can treat gray water, so maybe a shower could be rigged up, but there's no sewer treatment."

"Still, not bad. Did you know this was here?"

He didn't look up from the open door of the stove, where he was shoving a lit paper under dry wood in a fire he'd clearly prepared before they arrived. "It was offered."

She frowned. "Because you're a preacher?"

"I brought a few trade goods. The address cost me a bottle of whiskey."

A mock-serious look crossed Matchiko's face. "Do you have any left?"

"Now?" he asked, his face equally full of mischief. "No."

"Well then. We'll have to wait and see what's left by the time we're done trading." The fire caught, and he closed the door and stepped back.

There was a small bowl of butter, another one of eggs, and a fresh loaf of bread on the counter. "Did you trade for breakfast, too?" Lou asked.

"No. That was a gift as well. But I traded for a wagon and nails. No wood yet. That's dear right about now."

"Horses?"

"Coryn told me you'd want to pick them out."

"True enough. Can we go right after breakfast?"

"Yes, if I'm done telling you things."

"What things?"

"Over breakfast."

Diego shook his head and went out to take care of the horses.

"What's wrong with him?" Pablo asked.

"I think he misses his brothers," she quipped.

Matchiko watched him walk down the path. "No. I think he thinks you are a goddess and that Pablo should not be teasing you."

"Let's hope not," Lou whispered.

"Should he hear all of the things that Julianna sent me to tell you?" Pablo asked.

"How would I know? I don't know what you plan to say yet."

He hesitated, glanced at Matchiko.

Lou placed a hand on her partner's shoulder. "Matchiko is like me. She and I and Shuska can hear all of the same things. Always."

To his credit, Pablo didn't even raise an eyebrow. "Good to know. The water is nearly hot. If you sit by the window, I'll bring you coffee."

"There could be no better food for a goddess."

"Don't blaspheme." His voice contained laughter and warmth. Who knew preachers had a sense of humor?

Pablo's coffee was bitter and black and made her purse her lips. After a sip, she held it down in her lap and waited for him to begin.

"I'll be quick," he said. "And then you can ask me questions in the cracks of the day when we have time. I want to get this out, get you breakfast, and get us up to get horses. There's five minutes before the stove is hot enough for eggs."

She nodded.

Matchiko sipped at the coffee, clearly braver than Lou.

Pablo spoke without his usual smile. "There are two things. Your permit is under threat. It could get pulled. Probably not until the spring. But be ready."

She blinked, stunned by this unwelcome news. She had never heard of a permit being pulled except for a gross violation.

Pablo wasn't done. "If you lose it, the ecobots will leave, and you will also lose the rights to where you live. The feds can evict everyone. Everyone. Julianna is trying to stop it. She wants you to winter in Chelan, to get close to people."

"What does she think I'm doing?"

"That. But here's the second thing. The city's security analysts have become convinced there are nukes in Chelan. Julianna wants you to help find them."

Lou took a long, slow sip of the coffee, suddenly happy with the bitterness. "I had heard a whisper of that from Coryn. The nukes. She didn't think it was true."

"Julianna is fairly certain they are there."

She pushed the word *nukes* back in her head to think about, and focused on the first threat. "How can they pull our permit? We've met every requirement."

Matchiko came up behind her and put a hand on her shoulder, gripping hard. "The feds do not need to be fair," she said.

Lou kept her focus on Pablo. "Can Julianna protect us?"

"Coryn is trying. Julianna's helping when she has time. Her hands are full. Jake is ill, and he is the love of her life."

Matchiko frowned. "I thought that was a rumor."

Pablo smiled softly. "I worked for her once, a long time ago. That is no rumor. She and Jake are like one person. How else could they have made a single city?"

Lou raised an eyebrow at him and shook her head.

"The griddle is hot. We'll talk more on the way to the farm."

"Can I take a cup of coffee to Diego?"

"Yes."

She found Diego leaning over the low fence, watching the horses. When she handed him the cup he nodded at her and took it. He felt distant, maybe even a little lost.

"Be careful. It's stronger than I like. We'll have breakfast soon. That is, if you want to come in for it."

"Thank you." He spoke down at the black liquid. "Sorry I walked out. I don't like politics. I want to fight, not talk about fighting."

She studied his strong face. He was a handsome man, wide cheekbones and dark hair and eyes, a rare but tender smile. Out here, away from the shadow his mother and older brother cast over him, he seemed more willing to express his feelings. "What do you want to fight?"

"Anybody that says we can't make our own choices. I want my own land."

She grimaced. "None of us can have that. Not anymore." The great taking had wiped the concept of ownership away and replaced it with permission. "Who do you see as the enemy? Who is saying you can't have what you want?"

He stared at her, and for a moment she thought he was going to name her. But instead he said, "The city. All the cities. Mathew has been to a few, and he says they're so crowded he can't breathe."

Mathew had Alondra. "Do you know where Mathew is now?"

He shook his head and sipped at his coffee. She had the sense he felt like he'd said too much, so she changed the subject away from Mathew. "My sister is in the city. She loves it."

He kept his eyes focused on the horses. "Do you know why?"

"I don't think the cities are ever boring," Lou mused. "There's a lot to learn, to do. A constant stimulation." She shivered a little. "I've been, but I don't like it. I'm here because I want a sky with no weather dome. I want to see forever."

He smiled at her like he approved. "I don't think I'd like the city."

"I don't think you would either. Let's go eat."

CHAPTER THIRTY-NINE

Lou pushed away from the breakfast table, still contemplating the news Pablo had delivered. Their permit was a shield, but she had played a little loose with rules, allowed Valeria to farm, shared the house. But dammit—those were the *right* things to do! Nothing was as black and white as the rules and laws about it, and out here there were no police. She'd had to make do. And what if Jake died? What if Julianna died? Would she even have a foundation to run if that happened?

What would happen to Coryn if she lost her benefactors?

Diego raised a hand to get her attention, and then surprised her by saying, "I don't want to go to town. I want to be sure nobody steals from us."

"I'll stay, too." Matchiko looked like a cat protecting a secret. "While you were outside, I saw what's already here, and I think you'd want to have two of us for guards."

Pablo opened the doorway to the garage, and she counted four boxes of precious nails, a spool of rope, and a pile of tools that included shovels and trowels. There were a few unopened bags bulging with who-knew-what, but she didn't take time for them. She and Matchiko shared a glance. "Yes," Lou agreed. "Do stay. And be careful."

She and Pablo walked side by side down a short hill and up another. Pablo carried a pack full of trade goods, and she wore one full of rope leads for the horses. In spite of the news Pablo carried, the preacher was clearly a gift to them. If nothing else, he was a fabulous trader. Maybe she should hire him.

She had found the open-air market the last time they were in Wenatchee. It operated all day and offered everything from old clothes to bicycles and carts. It was noisy and chaotic, at least ten times the size of the one in the warehouse in Chelan. As she walked past a few of the less fortunate merchants, she remembered poor Paulette. She turned to Pablo. "Can you spare something small to trade with?"

"For what?"

"A gift."

In answer, he pulled a bag full of buttons and needles and thread and spread the contents of the top of the bag across his open palm. He hadn't gotten those from the city, so he must trade and trade again. Her estimation of him kept rising. She plucked three matching blue plastic buttons from him and went in search of something Paulette might like.

When she found it, she had to return to Pablo to get two more buttons. After she traded them to an older woman in a broken-legged rocking chair, she returned to Pablo, holding up a medium-sized plastic horse in her hands: a young bay mare with a white stripe on her face and one white foreleg. He laughed. "I thought you wanted real horses."

"It's for a teenager."

He looked pleased.

"Lou!"

Someone from two aisles over calling her name. Familiar. Who? She turned, searched.

"Lou!"

There were the Silversteins, side by side, smiling and coming toward her. They looked like they'd lost a little weight since she'd first met them in the cabin in the hole in the hills. "We thought we'd never find you."

Lou gave them a warm hug, a sudden burst of happiness at the small size of the world making her grin widely. "You were looking for me?"

"Yes!" Ray's smile was so broad it touched his hazel eyes. "Coryn hired us away from No Fences. She said you needed us." He laughed. "She pays well. And we were ready for an adventure."

Greta stepped near him, fitting herself into his arms and smiling as well.

Lou shuddered as a great wave of relief swept over her. "I do need you. I do." Experienced staff would matter. Valeria's family was great, but the only trained Wilders she had were herself, Matchiko, Shuska, and Daryl. "Do you have horses?"

Ray was still smiling, delighted at her delight. "We brought six horses—four for you."

"That's great news." But then she remembered. "You know our barn burned down?"

He shrugged. "We know how to build barns."

Greta added, "It's more fun than tearing things down. We even brought enough food for us for the winter, and bags of grain for the horses."

Lou stared. "Where did you get bags of grain?"

"We grew grain at No Fences. They needed credit to buy other things and parted with the grain they'd saved for the six horses. Win all around. Coryn's awesome."

And to think she hadn't even known Coryn was working on getting her help. She'd wanted to pick up six horses. Here were four, free. The good fortune was almost too much to bear, too big a counterpoint to the awful night of burning barns. Maybe she could get two extra horses for the -o boys.

Oh, to be home, right now, sharing this news. She smiled at Pablo. "Horses next?"

Choosing four horses took a good hour, and bargaining added more time. Pablo and Greta were clearly good at this, and she knew it wasn't the best-honed skill in her own bag of tricks. She watched for as long as she could stand, but as soon as they'd acquired the first two horses, she offered to lead them back to the little house and get them ready.

"Sure." Pablo seemed happy enough to be rid of her and the horses.

These two came with tack, so she left her pack and just took them by the reins, bridled and saddled, and walked out through the rows of tables and toward the house they were staying in. One was a light gray, almost white, and answered to the name Sugar, and the other was reportedly her sister, a bay named Spice. Lou wasn't sure she bought the sister story, but both horses appeared sound and well-trained, and she was amazed Pablo had gotten them at all. Much less for a pile of credit, a case of whiskey, and four pairs of good city-printed winter boots.

Well, no one had to feed the boots.

She was whispering to the horses, working to gain their trust and recognition, when Pal crossed her, and Mathew pulled him to a stop and looked down at her. "Finally."

"What?" He looked harried and unkempt, a little wild. And alone. "Where's Alondra?"

"I'm sending her with you."

"Where is she?"

"I'll bring her."

A deep knot of worry unraveled inside her chest. She took a deep breath of relief. "Where is she?"

"I'll bring her. Stay put." He wheeled away. She whispered to Sugar and Spice, the cold soaking into her in spite of the sunlight. Her toes felt numb. Maybe boots did make sense after all.

Was he going to give her Pal back?

It took ten minutes for Mathew to bring Alondra to her. He no longer rode. He just brought the girl, tugging her behind him, and shoved her toward Lou.

Relief took her at the sight of the child, and unexpectedly, joy.

She looked up at Lou, her eyes wide. She shivered in spite of new red coat she wore over the same clothes Mathew had taken her in a few days before.

He growled, "Keep her safe. You'll have your horse back someday."

Anger made Lou's cheeks hot, but he vanished before she could say anything to him. She glanced down at Alondra. "Are you okay?"

She hesitated, as if assessing. "Sure. I'm okay. Now. But he's really mad."

"So am I," Lou whispered. She still had Paulette's horse. She leaned down and looked in Alondra's eyes. "This is for Paulette. Would you like to carry it back for her?"

Alondra took it and held it close to her. She smiled, and said, 'Thank you."

"Anything, my friend." She meant it, too.

The snow started to fall the next day, about halfway home. No more than a spit at first, small flakes that melted as soon as they touched anything. They made a long line—thirteen horses, six people, and one child with one wagon. To make matters worse, one of the new horses refused to be led, and danced and fretted so much under saddle that Greta had to ride alone without leading another horse. Even at that, Lou wasn't sure she was going to make it. She leaned over to Ray and asked, "She knows how to jump off if that damned mare takes her over a cliff, right?"

He laughed. "Don't worry. She'll get her there."

"Good." She rode up behind Pablo, leading Sugar and Spice.

They were short three saddles, so three of the horses could only be led. All of the horses packed at least some goods, and it was a struggle for her to keep Sugar away from the grain in the back of the wagon. Spice was less demanding, but it was still tough to manage so many horses. Mouse helped by being her usual steady self.

Snow started to fall. Ten minutes later, the flakes fattened and began to cloak the hills. In another twenty, she could no longer see the whole train of people. Matchiko rode in front, setting the pace on Buster, wedged between sacks of cloth and bags of coffee, tea, and flour. Pablo's horse pulled the wagon, with Pablo and Alondra perched on the seat, and then Lou, the Silversteins, and in the end, Diego.

By the time they reached the outskirts of Chelan, the snow rose up over the horses' fetlocks, white and wet.

In the hour it took to slog the rest of the way home, so much snow fell that Lou lost visual track of everyone else except the back of the wagon and Pablo's bobbing head. She started a roll call of numbers, front to back and back to front; she could hear Matchiko's shouted "One!" and through the two Silversteins, but the only way she knew Diego was still okay was when Greta called out "Five!" in between cursing her fractious mount.

Near the top of the drive, Shuska materialized like a snow-covered ghost and led them to a lean-to made of a combination of parked ecobots and materials they'd scavenged from destroyed houses in the four days of the trip. The other -o boys met them there and helped unload the wagon before they started fawning over the new horses. Lou didn't tell them two were theirs, not until she could talk to Julianna and get Pal back. Surely there'd be a good moment for a special surprise.

They were going to have to raise a barn in the dead of winter. But for now, they needed to get warm. She reached for Alondra's hand and headed toward the kitchen. She couldn't wait to see the look on Astrid's face when she saw her daughter.

CHAPTER FORTY

Seacouver was bright blue and white and downright loud this close to the holiday. Every religion seemed to have a holy day in or near December, and for those of no particular religion, there was always the solstice on the twenty-first and New Year's Eve. As usual, prodigious displays of seasonal fashion brightened all levels of the city.

The city's weather systems had allowed it to rain for three of the last five days, but tonight Coryn managed with no umbrella as she hurried through the streets at ground level, her new silver coat tight about her. She'd grown up here, but after she started working with Julianna she'd taken to the richer heights of the city, traversing it mostly on bridges except for her longer runs. Imke had reminded her that this city, the one that touched the ground, was the one she needed to understand if she wanted to lead anything.

She passed small short-stay rooms designed for travelers or students on basic-basic, a few for slightly richer tourists, and the street-level entrances to fancier hotels and apartments. At this level, the disaffected walked the streets, those the city had lost other than to provide a minimum level of sustenance for. She passed quiet autistics minded by drones, old people with bent bodies, and others who had simply chosen to accept the most basic deal and be happy enough. Some reminded her of her itinerant parents, moving year by year in search of something they never found, and now dead by suicide.

Imke was right, though. It was important to remember *all* of the people in the cities. She had been spending her time with those in power, with those who thrived on the technology-driven soul of the city. She had always loved the city, fit inside of it, but no one else in her family had done the same. These were her roots, these people down here.

Imke had been good for her in a thousand ways, and now Coryn would see them again soon. Soon, the delegations and work of governing the northwest would shut down for the holidays, and Imke had invited Coryn to loop to Chicago.

She had been counting down for ten days and still had another two left. So she kept on her way to help Julianna. Jake no longer left home. Whenever Julianna needed to attend a meeting, go to a social event, or even get her own runs in, Coryn came over. That meant she lived in Jake's suite half the time and did most of her job running Outside-N from there as well.

She caught the elevator from the bottom floor, holding the door for Namina to catch up. They rocketed through ninety-six floors to get to the top.

Julianna waited by Jake's bed, already dressed up in a pale pink dress with a dark blue coat and a string of pearls. She nodded sadly at Coryn, and then at Evan, who stood at the ready right by the head of Jake's bed should his master need anything at all.

Jake himself was nearly invisible—one bony, twisted hand resting on a blanket.

"I'll probably be late." Julianna stood up, looking momentarily lost.

"That's all right. I can sleep over," Coryn assured her. There was a couch near the bed that she'd used rather often in the last week, and she even had some extra clothes stashed in a drawer in the coat closet.

She stopped by the side of the bed and sat briefly where Julianna had been, reaching a hand out to rest on Jake's shoulder. "I'm here. Let me know if you need anything."

Jake didn't open his eyes, but he gave a soft smile of acknowledgment and moaned a little. The designer drugs the medical machines gave him were meant to keep him a little floaty. He was lucid for a few hours every day and asleep or nearly asleep the rest of the time.

Julianna reached out and touched Coryn's cheek. "Thank you for coming."

"Always." Her own parents had abandoned her. These two, Lou, Blessing and Day, and now Imke were all of her world.

Julianna swallowed and looked down at her dress. "I missed my run today."

Coryn took her hand. "I'd offer to run with you tomorrow, but I've a rest day. The Jingle Bell Run is the day after tomorrow."

Julianna glanced at Jake. "It's all right." She left, although not fast enough to hide the damp shine in her eyes.

Coryn blinked back a tear of her own before she crossed to a small desk in the corner to work. This long death vigil was one bad moment after another, and the few good ones were just as emotional. Maybe there was something cheerful in Chelan. She scrolled through the recent sat shots until she found one with a big enough break in the clouds to show her the farm.

Snow blanketed everything. The horses were still in the lean-to, with one of the ecobots still making up one wall. The new barn had a roof and a wooden wall, and if she zoomed in she could see figures clambering around the outside in the snow.

She texted Adam and Imke. Imke told her she was beautiful, and Adam promised to meet her for breakfast.

Coryn scooted her chair near Jake and sat and watched his face, waiting for him to stir. She sang softly, and then gave up and played music through the speakers. After a while, she turned the music off and read him some poems. Her sister had developed a new love of poetry, and she was trying to figure out why. So far, she didn't get it.

Jake opened his eyes. "How about some Whitman?"

"Huh?"

"You're researching poetry. Find *Leaves of Grass*. I think the line I want starts, 'There was never any more inception . . .'"

His voice trailed off, but Evan had already produced what he asked for, and displayed it on the wall-screen closest to her. The companion robot said, "He's always liked these lines. He likes the whole thing, but he told me once that these lines helped him stay present more than once."

She nodded and began to read:

"There was never any more inception than there is now,
Nor any more youth or age than there is now;
And will never be any more perfection than there is now,
Nor any more heaven or hell than there is now."

"It's kind of old-fashioned," she said.

Evan laughed. "Well, it was first written in 1855."

"Do things get second written?"

"Whitman re-wrote this one a few times."

Jake spoke up. "The first version is the best. Maybe you should read the whole book for homework."

"Is it recorded, so I can hear it while I run?"

"Help me sit up," Jake asked. "Please. And yes. It's been recorded a thousand ways. But can you read to me a little more now?"

She did, occasionally stumbling over the diction. It did make the night go by quickly, and she giggled at her own mistakes more than once. Sometimes Jake asked Evan to read for a while, and she and Jake sat side by side, listening and drinking water. That was all Jake took in any more, water and food pastes, and of course his medicines. He took those mixed into the pastes. "I refuse to be tube-fed," he told anyone who'd listen, most often Evan. "I'll die in my own bed without any needles stuck into me."

When he said such things, Evan nodded sagely, often reminding Coryn of her dead Paula.

‡ ‡ ‡

Whitman's poetry infected her dreams, even though she wasn't really sure she liked it. She woke remembering a line that had stuck with her. Something like, "Has anyone supposed it lucky to be born? I . . ." Something she didn't remember. ". . . just as lucky to die, and I know it." Jake had read that one out loud, and he'd been looking at her when he did it, clearly wanting her to know he felt like that.

He had been alive when she left him and Julianna curled in the bed together this morning, with Evan watching dutifully over them. She didn't think he had much longer to go.

Adam brought breakfast to her headquarters conference room, since it was one of the most secure places that they knew. "What's up?" she asked. "Learn anything more about the nukes?"

"I have two theories."

She started to peel her hard-boiled egg. "Show me?"

"If you peel my egg, too." He pulled up a screen that showed pictures of two backpacks. One was rounded, as if it held a small oil drum. It was covered in camouflage and screamed military. The other looked like a typical hiker's backpack, with nothing about it to suggest it was dangerous. "These are heavy. They are both theoretical, as well, but likely to have existed. Or worse, to exist."

She finished peeling her egg and started in on his. "But can you trace them to the feds?"

"The first one. Almost for sure. The second one was a rumor. But I found three references to it. It doesn't look like a bomb at all."

"Is it?"

He gave her a mock look of horror at being questioned and reached for his egg. "Thanks. I don't think it will make a mushroom cloud. The first one might. It's not like there are videos of tests or anything. But I think it's a newer and smaller version of a nuke that used to be called the Davy Crockett. The thing it's in—the round thing—converts to a launcher of some kind. Maybe not a literal city killer, but it could kill a lot of people."

Nuclear weapons had been used twice. Well, depending on how you counted. Once in World War Two, and one early in the Gasoline Wars that led to the big cities and the wilding. But never in America. Nukes made her shiver. History come back to haunt the present. "What about the normal-looking one? The camping pack?"

"It's supposed to be heavier than a camping pack. Almost eighty pounds. So it's likely to be on a big man or a horse. Or a cart. It's rumored to spread radiation around, maybe a lot of it. Other rumors suggest North Korea built them for war with us, but, of course, they never used them. One old report suggests just one could make whole areas uninhabitable."

"But you can't really tell?" she mused.

"They were born in an age of misinformation."

She laughed. He was so serious sometimes. But then, nukes. Wow. "So how theoretical is it that the feds have these?"

"Not very for the first one. They probably do have them. Maybe even a few of them. We think they hid weapons in Canada during the early power fights and the denuclearization orders. I found three heavy rumors anyway. The second one—I don't know. Careful analysis of everything I've been able to find so far suggests there's a little less than a 50 percent probability of even one ever existing—much less being here. But we'll look for it anyway."

She sat back, the enormity of it making her feel heavy and confused. "Why would people do this? Want to blow up people? For power?"

Adam pursed his lips. "For an old idea. A lot of money went missing during the last wars. I told you that. Old money mostly—thus the name. Gasoline Wars."

"But almost no one burns oil anymore."

He shrugged. "Most execs were big enough to change. Exxon Mobile used to be a fossil fuel company."

"I know that."

"Most people think of them as dome builders. Wall builders. They didn't even stay in the same business, other than being sure to make something we cannot live without."

She started eating her egg. "You sound cynical."

"About businesses? Aren't you?"

"Don't we need them?"

"Of course we do. But maybe they shouldn't be run by people.

Some old oil execs hid their money instead of transforming their business. A kind of insanity, I think. Algorithms wouldn't do that."

"But why blow us up *now*?"

"So they never have to admit they were totally wrong."

She frowned. "Stupid people keep trying to destroy our world."

"Why do you think I drink?"

"That's not the answer." She hadn't meant to snap; she turned to him to apologize, and saw he wasn't even hurt. He might as well have not even heard her. She settled for changing the subject. "I can share this with Imke? The nukes?"

He looked mildly troubled.

Surely he was big enough not to let his unhappiness that she was going to Imke for the holidays affect his work. She waited him out.

"Of course."

"Why are you hesitating?"

"I want more certainty. I'm a numbers guy. Chances less than half make me think they are even lower."

"The stakes are so high," she whispered.

"I know. I don't like this."

She swallowed. "I don't like the uncertainty, and I don't like the idea of either of these weapons being near Lou. And I can't tell Lou. Not over the cellular."

"No. And you can't travel there. Maybe you can suggest she look out for backpacks though."

"Yes." She finished her egg and started on her banana. "At least I get to carb-load tonight."

"Are you worried about the race?"

"No. Are you?"

"No." He grinned. "We're both going to win."

She threw her banana peel toward him, making sure it fell short. "Don't jinx us."

✝ ✝ ✝

When she woke up on race day, she was thinking of Whitman's poetry again. Not the lines about death that had stuck with her the night before, but a simple line. *I am larger, better than I thought.*

She could win a race with that line, and with the general questing joy of *Leaves of Grass* inside of her. It might even be better than the fake lions she used to use when she had nothing but augmented reality running games to train to.

Outside of the dome, it was below freezing, and the weather report suggested it would be dry through the race but might actually snow in the evening. A bit of holiday cheer for Seattle.

People lined the course, stamping their feet against the cold while looking beautiful in festive coats and hats.

Coryn jogged in place, keeping her muscles warm and her blood flowing.

Just before the start, Julianna messaged her. *Good luck!*

So Jake had to be okay. If he wasn't, Julianna wouldn't be watching a stupid thing like a race.

The elite runners started first, by speed group. Behind them, there would be twenty thousand casual runners dressed up in holiday hats and bells. Two years ago, she'd run in *that* crowd. She'd been near the front, but nowhere near the elites.

Adam was in the one group ahead of hers, and probably at mile five by now. Behind her, the elites would get older and slower and then give way to the casual runners dressed in holiday clothes, out for a lark.

There were twenty runners in her class, and since they started in time-seed order, she was third. She let the start go slow, staying in third place, falling back to fifth, holding it there.

She sang in her head and heard lines of poetry and said little prayers for Jake. By mile seven she'd fallen to seventh, and Namina sent her messages goading her.

I am larger! Better than I thought!

By mile ten she was in third again.

At mile twenty her back hurt and her feet screamed, but her breath was strong and even, powerful. She overtook the woman in front of her, Elisa, and started in on the long-legged Nigerian in front of Elisa. The leader. Tambara. Tambara had won two of the last three races, Elisa the other one. Coryn had been second twice and third once.

She put her head down and dug in, needing speed.

Tambara's stride was long, her legs beautiful.

Coryn began to catch her. The cold was more help than hindrance. Her fingers felt the cold, but they still moved easily, and the winter tights Julianna had ordered for her the previous morning worked great. In some ways, the cold seemed to make her faster.

By mile twenty-five, she and Tambara ran side-by-side. Neither woman looked at the other, but Coryn knew every movement of Tambara's, and felt Tambara knew hers. For nearly a mile they kept the same pace even at different strides. Their breathing didn't match. Tambara breathed more slowly, quieter.

Coryn almost fell back because of Tambara's perfection. She was so beautiful, so like a metronome.

I am Larger! Better than I Thought!

The words had capitals now, in her head. Exclamation points.

If she was ever going to win a race, it would be this one.

For Jake.

She reached deep, found scraps of energy, pounding over the line a step ahead of her beautiful competition.

Adam met her, running her down, slowing her down with him, and then he picked her up and whirled her around, and she screamed in triumph.

Snow began to fall, small controlled flakes that didn't stick to anything but made Seacouver beautiful.

CHAPTER FORTY-ONE

The after-party for the race picked away at her good mood with its noise and demands for attention. Drones buzzed nearby, barely keeping the legal three-foot distance. People kept trying to hand her champagne, which she refused with a wave of her hand. In the far corner of room, she noticed Adam taking two drinks, and she resolved to get out before he did, and without him.

When she had imagined what it would be like to be a winner, she had thought the attention would be wonderful. Maybe, if she weren't more interested in spending time with Jake, it would have been.

She did her best to smile and to say nice things. Just as there was a bevy of celebrities, of which she was now a small one in a small subclass, the city also had many celebrity interviewers. One, a fat woman named Ruby Seattle with way too much makeup plastered onto a kind, round face, asked, "What about your sister who's wilding? We got snow, but I hear there is a lot more in Promise."

Coryn nodded. "Yes." The question felt a little disturbing.

"That's all? Yes? What's it like for her?"

"It's very, very cold. And wet. And she has to stay inside a lot." Coryn forced herself to smile. "She also says it's really pretty."

Ruby Seattle cocked her head. "How do you have it all? Winning a prestigious race, working for the most powerful people in our city's history, and having a Wilder sister? What's it like to balance all of these things?"

Coryn gaped for a moment before answering. A bad idea. With so many cameras, any awkward facial expression could end up on the city feeds. "I don't have time for much of a social life." She started to turn away, then thought better of it and turned back. "I believe in all of those things. Exercise. Hard work. Family. They all matter." She hadn't known she was going to say that, but it was true. Julianna had taught her. And Jake.

Ruby Seattle nodded and looked like she was about to pop out another question.

Coryn smiled. "Thank you."

She turned away, looking for a few moments of peace before the next interviewer. Adam had warned her people would start researching her. At least no one had mentioned her parents' suicide yet, or figured out that Jake was dying.

It took an hour before Coryn managed to get away from the media show, and even then two drones followed her until she turned around and ordered them to go away.

She traveled along her new trails through the city streets, the afternoon sun all but completely blocked by the height around her. She was shivering by the time she hit Julianna's building. Some of the other people in the streets looked even colder, and everyone seemed to be in a hurry. The elevator was air-conditioned, and she cursed under her breath and fidgeted. Yet she bounded out of it at the top, holding her bright gold winner's medal on its blue ribbon and her glass trophy, and stopped in her tracks.

Jake lay in bed, eyes bright. He held Julianna's hand. Both of them were carefully watching Blessing, who sat in Coryn's work chair, and Day, who leaned on the wall right behind him.

She squealed with happy surprise, bouncing toward him like a puppy. "How are you? How's Lou? When did you get back?"

Blessing rose to meet her, laughing at her with his good-natured wide smile, arms wide. Day merely looked amused.

She stepped easily into Blessing's arms, holding him tight for a heartbeat before pushing away. She kissed Julianna on the cheek before leaning down by Jake. "Did you see me win?"

"I did. We all did," he murmured, his voice soft and focused, as if speaking required all of his energy. The way he said it made her wonder if any of them were watching. But she didn't really care. They were home safe. She turned back to Blessing. "When did you get back?"

"Just a few hours ago." He was still grinning. "I might have come back early to watch you win your race if I'd known. You should communicate better."

She laughed. He knew she was forbidden from talking with him outside of the boundary. He had a new scar on his cheek. The thin undissolved edges of the medi-tape that held the wound closed were still visible. She reached up and touched it. "How did you do this?"

He smiled. "I'll tell you after. We're still meeting."

"Oh!"

"You can stay," Julianna said. "What we've done so far is learn more about how the Returners get weapons around. It's all on horseback, and these two learned of five routes. We assume there are more." She paused, her expression grave. "There may be a bigger arsenal out there than we thought."

She remembered the meeting. "Isn't hacking supposed to be the main attack vector?"

Julianna smiled. "Good girl. That's what we were told. Always question assumptions, even if they've been put into a presentation and delivered. We think that's still true. If so, if nukes are a distraction, can you imagine what kind of cyberattacks might be leveled at us?"

Coryn shivered. "Is it just us?"

"And Portland, at least." Julianna let go of Jake's hand and started pacing. "Adam thinks Calgary, too. I don't know about anything else for sure."

Blessing said, "We heard about a route that goes further south. So there might be attacks on cities that are farther away. This could be bigger than we thought, although I can't imagine there's enough army or arms out there to bother more than a few cities."

Coryn thought of Imke. "Chicago?"

"We don't know," Day said. "That's so far away we couldn't verify anything. There are many rumors. Misinformation may be part of the attack, or part of how they are shielding the attack."

Coryn leaned forward. "So there's no way to know what we're facing?"

Jake held a hand up, and when the room quieted, he whispered, "Misinformation was common in the old days. It's coming back. Getting around the old controls we created." He collapsed back down into his covers, his eyes closing, and for a moment she thought he'd simply fallen asleep. But then he said, "Write down all the rumors. Coryn and I will look at them tomorrow."

"Did you see Pablo?" she asked Blessing, but Day answered.

"Yes." As usual, Day sounded calm, shading toward unconnected. "He gave us messages from you. Did he get to Lou's?"

"Yes."

"Good. Is Aspen okay?"

Blessing offered a slow, slightly teasing smile. "He's good. He's losing some of his city fat."

"Hey!" Coryn swatted at Blessing, who dodged, and then glanced at Julianna. "Did you tell them everything we learned? At the meeting?"

Julianna smiled. "It wasn't the only meeting in the world. You can fill them in after we're done. I'm sure you need a celebratory drink, and that they need one as well. I'll buy you all a bottle of wine to share."

Wow. That wasn't on her training diet. "Thanks!"

The door swung open and Adam came in, weaving a little. "Did you see we both won?"

Julianna stood up and went to him, her face suddenly sad. "Yes, and we have guests. Can you sit down?"

For the first time, Coryn felt sure Julianna knew Adam drank too much. She resolved to ask her why she allowed it, but for now she just wanted him gone. She didn't want him out for her wine with Blessing, and she could tell Julianna didn't consider him welcome either.

She crossed to Adam. "I'll walk you to your room. We're about done here. Jake should rest."

He looked at Jake, lying still and white but wide-eyed in the bed, and then took in Blessing and Day. He waved. "Hi, guys. Hi. Glad you're safe."

Julianna gave Coryn a grateful look, and then looked over at Adam. "Yes, we saw you win. You won by a lot, at least a hundred yards. That might have been your best win yet. Congratulations."

Adam looked a tiny bit mollified.

Jake waved a finger.

Adam nodded. "I see how it is. After you win enough nobody cares." He turned to Coryn. "Let's go."

Coryn glanced back at Blessing, trying to pin him into staying there with her look. "I'll be back."

He grinned. But then Blessing grinned at almost everything. It might mean he was glad she was handling Adam, or that he was looking forward to the wine, or it might mean he remembered their kiss. Or it might mean nothing at all.

Coryn led Adam back to the room she used to sleep in. He managed to keep his feet without weaving too much, and mostly stayed silent. When they got there, he stood in the doorway. "Come in."

"I need to get back." She frowned, and then said, "I left my trophy there." She felt a little disingenuous, but she needed to get away.

"Just for a moment."

She hesitated without meaning to, and she saw him see her hesitate, and then she nodded. "Just for a minute. To make sure you drink a glass of water."

"I'll be fine," he said. "I'll be just fine. I think you like Blessing more than me. And I want to tell you I like you more than Blessing."

What did that even mean? Maybe he had been drinking more than she thought. "I like you fine," she said. "But I don't like drinking."

"Then I'll stop."

Not likely. "I have to go."

"Hey." He put a hand on her arm. "I can use a friend. Someone who knows me. Someone else who knows what it's like to be one of Julianna's pets. You're one, too."

"No. I thought that once, but I don't think so now."

"What do you think? Come sit by me and tell me?"

"No." She turned around and separated herself from him by an arm. "I like you. I like running with you. But I am not you, or like you. I am not owned. I am not beholden to you."

"Wow," he said, his words only a little slurred. "I didn't think you had guts."

"There was a time when I didn't think so either. Goodnight, Adam."

"Goodnight, Coryn."

He was saying it again as she closed the door. "Goodnight Coryn. Goodnight Coryn." Like a chant.

Maybe she should go have water while Blessing had wine.

✝ ✝ ✝

"I'm heading home to sleep." Day lifted his small glass of champagne. "To being home, to good friends, and to safety." He took a sip and left the rest of the glass on the bar. Even though he'd hardly drunk a thing, he seemed more loquacious than usual. "Have a good night," he said. "Dance a little. It looks like we'll have some hard times ahead."

He left abruptly, sliding easily through the crowd on the rooftop bar with no looseness in his gait. "Is he worried?" Coryn asked. "I've never seen him worried."

Blessing leaned down and whispered in her ear. "We're all worried. But dancing helps."

He led her to the far corner of the bar and took her in his arms. Out here at the edge of the roof, the space heaters couldn't keep up, and one side of her grew cold, so she snuggled a little tighter into Blessing's rangy form.

This felt very different than dancing with Imke, warmer and more sensual without being as hot or driving. She pushed back a little from him. "I've been seeing someone."

He looked down at her, his grin still in place, and not an ounce of concern or even surprise of his face. "Of course you have. You are breathtakingly beautiful."

Breathtakingly beautiful? Her? She almost stumbled.

"Anyone I know?" Blessing asked, with no more than friendly curiosity.

"I doubt it. A person from Chicago."

He immediately slid into the right pronoun. "Are they kind?"

She laughed. "And smart." She hesitated. "But it still feels good to dance with you."

"Did you and they make any agreements?"

"Oh no. No. Not . . ." She didn't even know what she wanted. Just to not hide things from him. Blessing had saved her life, had ridden beside her, had taught her to act like she might die every day. Blessing had given her the courage to see Imke in the first place.

"Then you can kiss me?"

Startled, she looked up at him, hesitated.

"I will not ask for more until you return." He smiled down at her, nothing but warmth and happiness on his face. Not one little grain of jealousy. "Love can build on love, and love can multiply love. The human heart is huge unless you make it small." He ran his finger along her chin, and his touch created a line of heat.

"You know I'm going to Chicago?"

"I do. And I expect to be here when you get back. We'll winter here and go east again as soon as the thaw begins. There's mountains to go over, or a long trip if we go to Portland first and follow the gorge. Nothing will happen out there for a few months except cold and down time, and things your sister will have to handle."

Coryn smiled. "She can handle a lot."

"I know," he said. "Especially with such good support. We'll take over while you're gone. Julianna told us to take your morning calls."

She felt a rush of relief. She'd planned to take her job with her to Chicago, but days off might be heaven.

The song switched, and Blessing took her in his arms again, and danced with her in silence. He smelled of Outside still, of horse and fresh air and wind. The snow had stopped falling, but the cold had grown slightly sharper, and this warm moment with her friend and the music made her feel safe and soft.

When Blessing walked her to her door half an hour later, she offered herself for a kiss, and he took her up on it, the kiss as wonderful as the first time he kissed her.

"You remind me of Walt Whitman," she said.

He cocked his head. "How?"

"You love life that much. Whitman loved life."

He gave her a mock-accusatory glance. "You've been hanging around with Jake."

She laughed. "Guilty as charged. He made me read all of *Leaves of Grass*."

"You're lucky."

"Do you ever write poetry?"

"I might go write some tonight," he teased. "And dream of safe places in tall cities full of beautiful runners."

Her cheeks grew hot. She didn't invite him in, and he didn't ask, but she felt a small pang of regret as he walked away.

CHAPTER FORTY-TWO

Coryn bundled up before she headed for the loop. Chicago hadn't chosen to control the weather as finely as Seacouver, or couldn't. They used walls for most of their physical protection and had small weather domes here and there, but no city-wide dome. And while they didn't have as many bridges as Seacouver, they had three buildings that were taller than anything here. She could hardly wait to see it.

To her surprise, Imke stood outside of the Seacouver station, dressed in a dark blue pantsuit with big lapels and a light blue coat, and wearing silver chains and silver boots. A sly, slightly hungry grin crept across their face when they spotted Coryn.

Coryn's reaction matched the grin with a sudden heat. "I thought you'd meet me at the Chicago side!"

Imke leaned down and kissed her, and Coryn kissed them back, and remembered her conversation with Blessing and his kiss, and kissed them even harder. Heat flared in her center.

Imke raised a glittering eyebrow.

Coryn shrugged, her cheeks hot. "Show me how this works?"

"You've never been on a loop?"

"I've been on a plane."

Imke looked surprised. "Okay."

They climbed into a hyperloop pod with just room for the two of them, and Imke sat behind Coryn, running their hands along her shoulders and scalp. It felt . . . fabulous.

The ride was over so fast she expected that the door to the little pod would open onto an intermediate stop somewhere. But when the pod door sprang open, Imke gently pushed Coryn out and bounded out of the small car carrying Coryn's bag. They gave her an enigmatic smile. "There's so much to show you. I have a dinner planned with two of my best friends. You'll love it."

Even though it hadn't quite turned to dusk at home, it was full dark in Chicago, the sudden shift jarring. Six inches of snow blanketed the ground, blown into taller piles in the southern corners of buildings. The loop station was a mile from downtown, and the buildings near the station were as tall as the higher buildings in Seattle. With fewer bridges, the streets were more crowded. The green walls had mostly been put away for the winter and lay bare or covered with decorative lattices, although a few well-lit greenhouses illuminated indoor gardens like Seacouver's. The buildings got taller as they moved toward the lake, towering above them, lit like beacons. Gaudy. "You don't care much about light pollution, do you?"

Imke laughed. "We do. This light goes up, and that's admittedly bad for birds and the like, but it doesn't go *out* much, so we don't throw light for miles like we used to."

She and Imke spilled out of the city onto a lakeshore park, the dark water still in the windless night, the seam of the horizon where night sky met night water nearly invisible. In spite of the snow and the cold, the lake hadn't frozen. Small boats with dull orange and blue lights ran along the edge, taking people for tourist rides. A few people went by on strange contraptions. "Are they riding bicycles on the water?"

Imke laughed. "Sort of. There's a track. Can you see how big the tires are?"

They *were* big. As tall as Coryn and at least a foot or two wide. "Can we try it?"

"Tomorrow. Dinner's in twenty minutes, and the walk is almost that long."

"Can I touch the water?"

Imke cocked their head, looking bemused. "Of course."

"We're bordered by water like this, but it's hard to touch. There's the seawall, which is always between me and the water. There's a place where Julianna and I run where I could touch the Sound, but we never stop there." Coryn handed Imke her small pack full of toiletries and technology and walked to the edge of the water. She knelt there, took her glove off, and trailed her fingers in the top of the lake. It felt cold and sweet and silky, as if the water were thick with the night.

When she stood, she found Imke right behind her. They leaned down and kissed her. "You are a delight."

"It feels so lovely to be here. It's an adventure."

"Are you ready to eat?"

"It's only five my time."

"Can you manage?"

"Of course I can."

On the way, Imke told her they'd watched the race, and how they'd screamed so loudly when Coryn won that Mayor Broadbridge jumped, startled. Coryn giggled and told them about Pablo and Aspen, but left off her worries about Jake. She had no idea if they knew or should know.

Imke took her up the tallest building in Chicago, to a rooftop bar exposed to the cold night but warmed by space heaters in the floor and walls. It reminded her of dancing with Blessing. "Imke?" she asked.

"Yes?"

"You know I love to dance with you?"

"Yes." Imke grinned and bumped out a hip.

"And you can dance with others, too."

"Of course I can." Imke leaned over and kissed her in the nose, a glancing wet kiss full of play. "Yes. You can dance with whoever you want. If I want a different deal, I'll ask."

Coryn nodded, hoping she hadn't taken any magic away for Imke. Or for herself.

Imke took her hand and led her to a table. Another couple sat there, both of them about Imke's age, both as gender-indeterminate and as beautiful, and as well-dressed. "This is Rudolf and Russy, part of my Chicago band."

"Pleased to meet you." Coryn felt like a token female for about a minute, but then all three of them had her in stitches talking about the city and telling jokes, and she ate chicken skewers and spring rolls and drank sake and got as giggly as they were.

The four of them walked back to Imke's together, and Rudolf and Russy left them in the vestibule, still giggling.

Imke lived in a small room on a high floor. As soon as they got inside Imke led her to the window, pulling the drapes to expose a panoramic view of the big sparkling bright downtown clothed in white snow and light. Even though it had been noisy on the walk here, she couldn't hear the city now. Just her breath and Imke's. "It's beautiful," she whispered.

"As are you." Imke touched her on the cheek, and ran their finger along her lips and along the soft edges of her chin. They started at her temples and massaged her scalp and her shoulders, much like on the loop. Then they slid Coryn's shirt off and moved a warm hand to her belly, tracing a large circle and bringing it in, making a spiral of heat on her skin.

Coryn quivered.

Imke pressed themselves against her and touched her nipples, and Coryn's breath caught in her throat, and her center thrummed with heat, her pulse loud and knocking against her throat.

Imke spoke softly in her ear. "Do you want me?"

"Oh, yes."

"You're certain?"

As if she weren't standing there half naked and exposed, on fire, spreading her legs apart as if on command and leaning into Imke. "I'm certain."

Coryn lay curled up in a small ball, surrounded by Imke, savoring the smell of Imke's arm where it draped over her waist. She had never slept a whole night with anybody else, and waking up so close to someone was both magical and slightly jarring.

Imke slept naked except for their wristlet, an artsy device that ran from wrist to halfway up their forearm, the flexible material an amazing color that wasn't black or gray or dark blue, but all three at once, blending into Imke's dark skin. Tiny lights flashed bright yellow three times, and then began to emit a series of low beeps.

Imke turned their wrist so Coryn couldn't see the screen, and groaned. They sat straight up. They pushed a few buttons and then flopped back down on the bed. "Sorry. Into the shower. There's a meeting in half an hour. Emergency."

"What?" Coryn asked.

"I don't know." Imke slid of the bed, holding a hand out. "Now. Shower."

Coryn followed, the hot water bracing. As Imke ran shampoo and warm water through Coryn's hair with strong fingers, Coryn asked, "What shall I do?"

"The mayor said I'm to bring you."

"Oh." She didn't ask more, just soaped Imke's back. All too soon the shower's triple heads shut off and Coryn's skin prickled with sudden damp cold. A soft lavender towel fixed that. She barely had time to dress and comb her hair out before Imke's hand tugged her toward the door. "Bring your things."

"Oh." Coryn grabbed her pack, zipping it as they climbed into the elevator. She contemplated how to keep her wet hair from freezing.

The elevator started hitting negative numbers. It stopped at negative ten. "This way." Imke stepped out of the elevator into a white corridor with red metal railings and a brightly lit floor.

"Oh," Coryn repeated.

"There's a Seattle underground," Imke said. "I've been there."

"Not ten stories of it, except a few old parking garages and a few tunnels." Julianna and Jake had built tunnels into the city during its heady growth days after it declared itself free of federal rule. "I don't think we could go this far down, not even with nano walls. Seattle's built on fill."

Both of them wore soft flats, and they made little noise in spite of their speed. They rounded two corners and traversed the length of two long hallways, one at least half a mile, passing multicolored doors and elevators and a few people.

All of the people looked grim.

Coryn felt an urgent need to check her wristlet for news, but Imke showed no signs of even pausing, much less stopping.

An elevator with white doors opened as they approached. Imke gave it no instructions. It went down rather than up, and they got off again at negative seventeen.

Three minutes later they were in a huge and quite plush conference room filled with camera walls, which were currently off. Mayor Broadbridge stood at the head of a table of people who sat, watching him. He looked angry. They looked serious, and most wore uniforms. Coryn had the sudden wish that they'd arrived five minutes earlier. It would be nice to know what had made everyone so angry.

The mayor looked at them, nodding curtly. "Good. Welcome to one of our Emergency Operations Centers."

"What do you know?" Imke took an empty seat at the largely full table and gestured for Coryn to sit beside them.

"Let us fill you in." The mayor waved a hand, and one wall of images came alive. "That's Flagstaff. Arizona. One of the largest cities in the Southwest, now. A lot of Phoenix Metro went there in the tough years."

Phoenix was a ghost town now, hot and dry as hell. It was often held up as the greatest of the failed greed-time cities. "I read about that in school."

"Have you ever been there?"

"This is the only city I've been to, except home, of course. And Portland Metro."

He grinned. "Do you like it here?"

"Of course."

He narrowed his eyes. "All of the cities matter."

She sat up straight under his gaze. "I agree."

He looked so hard at her that it kept her attention from analyzing the moving pictures of Flagstaff to the side of her. "Why?" he demanded.

"They have all the people. If they fail, the people have to go to other cities. This could be hard, especially if more than one fail at once. We grow all the time, but there are limits to the speed we can grow at. If refugees don't go to other cities, the land has to sustain them, and wilded land is not meant for that."

"There's not much wilding in the seared desert," Imke mused.

The mayor stared at Coryn. He was really quite imposing. "Why else should we care what happens to Flagstaff?"

Coryn would really like to have some coffee before being interrogated like this. And maybe something to eat. "Because we're good people."

The mayor smiled.

A man in a simple blue uniform and black boots, with his hair back in a ponytail brought Coryn and Imke coffee, water, and a plate of mixed breads and fruits.

Had he read her mind?

"We are good." The mayor nodding. "Weren't you in our meeting in Seacouver?"

"What's happened to Flagstaff?" Imke asked.

"The mayor and deputy mayor were both murdered. Three of five councilors have disappeared. The other two have called for the right to appoint. They are known to disagree with many of the principles we just mentioned."

"It's a coup," Imke breathed.

"Now?" Coryn stood, worry driving her to move; she paced behind her seat and Imke's, up the length of the table, unable to settle.

The mayor's lips thinned. "So what do we do? Send protection down there? Risk getting thin so it's easier for them to target us in the spring?"

Coryn moved around the table and stopped close to him, looked up into his broad face. "What are you *supposed* to do?"

He sighed. "Help."

She let that sink in and thought about the magnitude of the problem. "What are you asking me?"

"I'm not—not exactly. I needed to see if you grasped the implications. I'm sending you two back to Seacouver to see what Julianna and Jake think. Jake is one of the best tacticians I know." He was speaking more to Imke now. "It would be suspicious for me to travel. But you two can do it."

"When?" Imke asked.

"Now."

"I'll get my things."

"No. Now." Mayor Broadbridge glanced at Coryn. "Before any more people die."

"Oh." Imke glanced at Coryn. "Are you ready?"

She wasn't really. She'd only had a few sips of her coffee and nothing to eat. She wrapped a few biscuits in a cloth napkin and said, "Sure."

✝ ✝ ✝

Coryn spent the short loop trip back messaging Julianna. Adam met them at the station and escorted them to the conference room she used for an office. As soon as they were seated, he said, "What's up?"

"I need more coffee," Coryn said.

"Your robot's outside. Ask her."

Coryn hadn't seen her on the way in. But when she looked out, sure enough, Namina stood against the wall outside. "Can I have coffee please?"

"Anything else?"

She hesitated. They might be here awhile. "Fruit?"

"I'll bring breakfast."

"Thanks."

Namina gave her a genuine smile.

Well, that interaction had been easier than most. Maybe she and Namina were finally getting used to each other. She ducked back into the room and immediately started calling up her usual methods for watching over Lou. Sun spilled on snow around Chelan, and here and there, bare patches glistened wet. She glanced at the temperature. Almost forty degrees.

The barn wasn't quite done, but if the weather stayed like this, maybe they'd finish it before Christmas. For Imke's sake, she stood up and pointed out the farm and the barn and even the chicken coop, narrating a little story about the farm.

Surprisingly, Adam didn't stop her. Were they going to keep hiding Jake's illness from Chicago? Or did Mayor Broadbridge know?

Julianna came in looking both exhausted and stern. "This had better be as important as you think it is."

"It will be," Coryn said.

CHAPTER FORTY-THREE

While the first two-thirds of December had been all snow and ice, the week running up to Christmas itself was sunny, and warm enough that the crowd on the lawn outside of the big house wore only boots and light sweaters the morning of the holiday. Glittering hair pins and jewelry sparkled in the sun. All of the women, even Alondra, wore dresses.

Lou, on the other hand, wore her cleanest jeans, a red flannel shirt, and a knitted black beanie to keep her ears warm. She stood just outside of the circle, more a guard than a participant in the impromptu holiday services. Pablo presided over the festivities while standing on a decent-sized tree stump.

She fidgeted as he talked, making lists in her head. Animals she should expect to see in winter. Elk and deer might have drifted lower, but there would be coyotes and rabbits and other hardy species to count and maybe sample. Birds.

Already, the service had lasted almost an hour. There had been song, talk of being brave, and prayer. Now, Pablo started them on "Silent Night," which was incongruous at this time of the morning but beautiful with Valeria's sultry alto. It felt hopeful, everyone standing together and singing, the couples and families almost all holding hands. She was almost sorry when the preacher said, "Thank you," and hopped down to the yard.

Alondra came up to her and took her hand. "I have presents for the horses. Will you come with me?"

"Of course" She carried Alondra to the barn on her shoulders, both of them laughing. The girl's legs hung down past her waist, her heels digging into the top of Lou's thighs. "It's a good thing you don't weigh much," Lou said.

Alondra merely laughed harder.

The week of good weather had allowed them to finish rebuilding, although the new barn wasn't a work of art. They'd paint it in summer, but until then it would hold and keep the animals warm and dry.

Alondra gave each of the horses half an apple. Both Mouse and Buster let the girl kiss them on the nose.

As they walked back up toward the group breakfast in the big house, Alondra said, "I have more tea. Dad came to town yesterday, and he brought me a tin of it for Christmas. I can make you a cup for your Christmas present this afternoon."

"I'd like that. Did your dad say why he was in town?"

"No. But he told me he might not see me again." Her voice had a quiver in it. "He made me promise not to forget him."

Coryn took the last bite of a piece of warm cinnamon bread, savoring the flavor. They were halfway through a quiet party in Jake's rooms, a Christmas breakfast with the best buffet Coryn had seen in some time. Julianna had declared Jake too weak to go out, so a dozen or so people lounged around the room.

She felt a strange combination of somber and excited as she prepared to read out loud. Julianna had asked them all to bring stories or poems, and it was her turn.

Eloise had started it all with a simple haiku. Day had read a poem from a famous Puerto Rican poet who had died recently. Blessing had sung a song about the moon. A man she barely knew had told a story about the great taking. And so on.

She had chosen to read a few lines from Whitman's *Song of Myself*.

Jake's cheeks had sunk into his face. Even lying down he looked smaller than just a few days before, as if he were falling into himself. She hesitated, but when she looked at Julianna, who sat by his side holding his hand, Julianna nodded.

Coryn set her coffee cup down and started in:

"I exist as I am, that is enough,
If no other in the world be aware I sit content,
And if each and all be aware I sit content.

One world is aware and by far the largest to me, and that is
my-self,
And whether I come to my own to-day or in ten thousand or ten
million years,
I can cheerfully take it now, or with equal cheerfulness I can wait.

My foothold is tenon'd and mortis'd in granite,
I laugh at what you call dissolution,
And I know the amplitude of time."

Jake's smile was nearly luminescent with the life that seemed to fight the clear wasting of his flesh. He hardly ever spoke any more, but he croaked out, "Thank you."

She wondered how much effort it had cost him to thank her. She swallowed back a sudden urge to cry and beamed at him as she sat back down, hardly listening to Adam's story about a sheep and a sheepdog.

Most of the people in the room smiled along with Jake when the sheepdog drove the sheep home just in time for the holiday.

Someone knocked.

Evan opened the door to admit Imke. Cory had expected them for dinner, but not for this small ceremony, which was really meant to be private. They looked troubled, and came over to Coryn and bent down. "I have news."

Coryn glanced around the room. The only person left to go was Julianna. She shook her head. "Give us ten minutes."

"Should I leave?" Imke whispered.

Coryn curled her arm around their waist. "Of course not."

Julianna smiled at Jake, and then held her arms up, dropped them, and Evan started the background music for Seacouver's anthem.

Julianna sang the first verse by herself. By the second chorus, others in the room had joined, and by the last chorus, even Imke sang along.

It was perfect. A tribute to Jake, to the city, and even to the season. Without him, the song would never have been written.

Silence fell. Jake nodded his thanks to Julianna, reached up for her hand, and the look between them was so sweet and deep it brought a sting to Coryn's eyes. She hugged Imke a little closer and smiled across the room at Blessing.

Jake lay back and closed his eyes.

Julianna gave Imke a long, questioning look.

Jake tugged at her hand. "I'll hear it."

"Very well," Julianna said. "Merry Christmas, Imke."

They smiled, calm and collected, in complete control now that they had the floor. "Merry Christmas. I've just come from Chicago, where I had breakfast with Mayor Broadbridge. First, he wanted me to wish you all well, and ask you to have a lovely holiday morning no matter what you celebrate."

Julianna inclined her head and spoke equally solemnly. "Tell him thank you. While we are not religious, we recognize the deep roots of ceremony and greetings, of gifts and song that is often shared at this time, and we wish all of our friends in other cities the best."

Imke stepped a few feet away from Coryn. "I have less happy messages." They glanced around, as if asking Julianna if it was truly okay to share with everyone here.

Julianna chose to answer the unspoken question out loud. "Everyone here is briefed. Evan's communication capabilities are hand-coded and monitored by my staff and as safe as a technology can be."

"All right. Our enemies in Flagstaff were confirmed in their positions in spite of the number of troops our collective cities have committed there. We've detected helicopters approaching many of the places we believe that fighters and arms are collected. We've also identified two robotic ocean tankers that came into Seacouver last night and that appear to be at least partly full of contraband cargo. The president of the United States of America has called on Seacouver, Portland Metro, Chicago, and Silicon Frisco to open their doors and borders."

"I thought this was happening in the spring!" Coryn blurted out.

Julianna frowned at her. "We knew that false messaging was part of the campaign." She steepled her hands and turned back to Imke. "Did you inform Mayor Arroya?"

"A message has been sent to him."

"Did Seacouver find any of this?"

Imke shook their head. "Just us. And yes, we find that strange."

Adam was already standing. "We'll need to go the Emergency Operations Center."

Julianna shook her head. "You should go, but to ours unless you are called to the main EOC. All of you. Namina can run messages. But I will stay here, with Jake and Evan."

For a moment, Coryn thought Jake might object. But he merely nodded and kept his hold on Julianna's hand.

Julianna stood, gave his hand a final squeeze before releasing it and crossing to Coryn. She reached up to lay a hand on Coryn's shoulder. "Go to the EOC in this building. Namina can lead you. It's set up to monitor our holdings. I'll see that it does that, but I will also offer it to Mayor Arroya if he needs a secondary command post. Send Namina to get food. Contact Lou."

Coryn tried to commit every one of the stream of commands to memory. "Okay."

Julianna kept talking. "I need Eloise for a few minutes and then I'll send her along to help. Just start turning the room up and do what you can in the meantime."

Oh. Of course. They needed to keep up the fiction that Jake was well, or at least that Jake wasn't dying.

Eloise could help. The woman was strange, but she was also always calm and always effective.

Who would start a war on Christmas Day?

CHAPTER FORTY-FOUR

Lou and Valeria finished giving the horses holiday treats, their hands flat as wide, warm lips nuzzled carrots and dried apples from their palms.

When they arrived back in the kitchen, the scent of butter and bread and coffee and candles rolled over them, warm and sweet. Sofia and Tembi and Alondra had spent the previous night carefully decorating the tables with homemade wreaths and candles, and this morning they had set them with good woven mats and silverware. Matchiko was in the kitchen helping Ana and Tembi make pumpkin pancakes and heat up chicken-apple sausages the -o boys had made from some of this year's culling and late harvest.

Astrid poured coffee, Cheryl poured water, Sofia ordered the children around, and Valeria hovered. The men had been sent to bring in firewood and perform other chores that got them out from underfoot. Lou leaned down to Alondra. "Go help Matchiko."

Alondra bounded off, and Lou grabbed a cup of coffee and pulled Valeria outside. "Have you heard anything strange?"

"No." She narrowed her eyes. "Should I have?"

"Alondra saw her father. He told her he might not come back. She thinks that means she might never see him again."

Valeria worried at her bottom lip. "Mathew is an idiot. He could have just been trying to scare the girl. Maybe Astrid will get lucky and he'll commit suicide tomorrow."

"I didn't know you liked him that much."

Valeria sighed. "I loved him once. But he's fallen in with the Smiths and the idiots that are driving them. He cares more about them than his family. That's selfish." She spat on the ground.

"Who is driving them?"

Valeria stared at the sky. "Angry people."

"The day the barns burned, Diego said one word. He said *hatred*."

"That's right."

"Could anything be happening already? Other than drills?" Lou glanced up at the bright blue sky. "It's not spring yet."

"No. But it *will* be Saturday tomorrow. I'll keep my ears open at the bar and see if there is anything to learn."

Lou nodded. "Maybe I'll go with you."

"Is that a good idea?" Valeria cast a doubtful look at her.

"I'll bring Shuska."

Valeria laughed. She had kept up the bar routine. There had been two Saturdays since the attack and the fire, and the only change they'd made was sending Shuska down and back with the family, and posting her near the door as a visible enforcer. There had been no incidents. "Leave it for now. There's nothing to learn during Christmas breakfast." Valeria took her arm. "Everyone has been working hard, and the preacher and his little dog are here."

Another mystery. What was Coryn up to that meant she didn't have time for Aspen? She kept meaning to capture Pablo and ask, but he was wildly popular with this family. You'd think they'd been starved for religion.

Everyone had been working extra hard to repair the barn and shore up the planting beds and the fences during this last unusually glorious week. It had felt like a late Indian Summer, a strange gift after the freezing rain.

Lou went upstairs to find Shuska.

The big woman was looking out over the fields. "I hate holidays," she said as Lou came up behind her. "Particularly Christian ones."

"Would you like a job that will take you away from the table?"

Her broad face brightened.

"Alondra mentioned something creepy her dad said about maybe never seeing her again. It's probably nothing, except my sixth sense is itching. Will you go wake up the ecobots and make sure they keep watch? Can you keep watch, too?"

Shuska pulled Lou close to her. "Good day to be outside."

"Grab a plate from Matchiko on the way out. Tell her you'll be on guard duty."

Shuska changed her indoor shoes for boots. "I understand what Pablo did out there more than I'll understand the prayers they'll say in here."

"Me too."

Lou followed Shuska down the steps and resolved to stay cheerful, and even to enjoy Pablo's indoor prayers. She did find them oddly comforting, even if she had no deep sense of their meaning. Out here, it was easy to understand the pull of religion. Life was hard.

Pablo had the good sense to offer a very short prayer so nothing grew cold. "Dear God, keep us and our families safe on this day."

Even Shuska wouldn't have minded that.

The sausages tasted fabulous and the pancakes had emerged warm and fluffy, and smelled of cinnamon. There wasn't any syrup, but Sofia had revealed a bag of powdered sugar she had been saving for a special occasion in a tin on the top shelf of the pantry. The Silversteins and the other new staff had all been found places, so the table was crowded in a happy way. At one point, Lou noticed Diego looking sad, but he was across the table from her and there was no easy way to ask him about it.

At the end of the meal, all of the new people properly mentioned that this was the best feast they'd had in a year. Astrid and Tembi almost glowed, and all of the household women looked pleased. Most of the women went to the big sitting room, and most of the men spilled outside to exercise the horses.

Since Lou hadn't helped cook, she stayed in to clean alongside Valeria and Felipe and his small son, Hila, who brought him dishes with a solemn look on his face. Felipe took them one by one, thanking Hila for every plate. Alondra was with them as well, cleaning up the floors and giving Hila directions from time to time like a rather annoying big sister.

Lou hummed as she washed, happy to have a simple thing to do.

The kitchen was clean, and they'd started boiling water for Alondra's holiday tea, when Shuska came in and pulled both Valeria and Lou outside. She walked them a few feet away from the house. "Hear that?"

At first it sounded like a strange wind, except that it was too steady. "Drones?"

Shuska shrugged. "Maybe big ones. Helicopter drones carrying people? I can't see them, but the ecobots compared the sounds to their databases of machine sounds, and they think they are troop carriers."

Valeria frowned. "We can't see them?"

"From the ridge," Lou said. "But we can't get there in time."

They listened until the sound faded away. She needed to know more, and she needed to know now. She stared at her wristlet. If only—

To her utter astonishment, it buzzed her, signaling a call.

"Coryn?"

"Merry Christmas."

She shook her head, the greeting a little jarring. As far as she was concerned, the holiday was over. "You too. Look, we just heard something—"

"What?"

"We don't know. The ecobots think they are troop carriers."

"The ecobots told you what they think?"

"Shuska has a way with them."

"They're probably right. We have a sat shot from a few minutes ago that shows six pretty big vehicles against the lake. There are signs that the attacks are going to happen now."

"Now?" It wasn't spring yet. It was Christmas Day. Lou stared at the tiny image of Coryn on her wrist and tried to tell what she was feeling. It was as impossible as trying to read Julianna. "We'll see what we can find out."

"We don't think you should go to town. Not today. Not after the barn burning. Let me know if anything happens. I have to go."

Lou stared at her wrist for a long while. The advice not to go to town today was probably good. Tomorrow she would go in with Valeria and she would be well-armed.

She ignored the hoofbeats on the road at first. After all, the -o boys were exercising the horses. Then Alondra raced past her, and she looked up to see Paulette on Buster's broad back, her baby slung in a pouch on her back. She had Sugar and Spice on lead, trailing obediently behind her.

Lou felt a chill run though her. She broke into a jog, stopping when she reached the horses.

Buster held his nose out and whickered at her.

"Good boy," she murmured, looking up at Paulette. She wore a red-and-green Christmas dress and a gold cross, her eyes wide above cheeks streaked with tears.

"What happened?" Alondra asked.

"Diego told me to bring the horses back to you. He and Ignacio and Santino left with the other fighters."

Diego's sadness at breakfast made sense. She remembered talking with him in Wenatchee. *I want to fight.*

Could she have done anything to stop this?

Lou knelt down in front of Alondra. "Can you tell your mom? And Valeria? I'll help Paulette put the horses back."

Alondra ran as if she could outrun the information she carried.

Lou and Paulette led the horses into the new barn. She hadn't told the -o boys the horses were for them. She was going to do it today, as a holiday present. Damn.

Paulette moved easily around the horses, taking off tack and whispering in their ears. The child stayed quiet against her back, occasionally making tiny sounds as they brought the animals fresh water and buckets of grain. Lou kept expecting it to cry or be frightened by the smells of damp horse and the sound of stomping feet, but it didn't object to any of it, not even when Buster put his head down and sniffed the baby's head.

After the horses were all settled, she asked, "Can I see your baby?"

"Of course." Paulette twisted the carrier around so the babe rested in front of her and pulled back a corner of its warm blanket. Dark eyes and a tiny wisp of dark hair above round cheeks and a small mouth.

"This is Jude. He's named after my oldest brother." She chewed on her bottom lip and looked down. "He went, too. Jude. To war."

"Do you know that? Do you know where they went?"

A brief bitter pain tightened Paulette's features. "They don't tell me anything since I ran away."

And she'd still named her child after one of them? Jude opened his small, circular mouth and let out a significant screech for such a tiny thing. "How old is he?"

"Four weeks." Paulette rocked him against her and he snuffled and twisted in her arms. "He came two weeks early, but he weighed seven pounds, so the midwife said he would be fine." Her voice was soft and still a little full of the wonderment new mothers often had. His soft cries seemed to fade into Paulette's heart while they crawled up Lou's spine, making her want to move, to do something. But Paulette simply gazed at him, her eyes soft. "Isn't he beautiful?"

The baby let out a wail.

"He is. And loud."

"Can I feed him?"

"Of course. Sit right here. I'll be right back."

Lou jogged toward the house. As she neared the front porch she heard angry words and then a woman screamed in anger, frustration, or pain. Lou couldn't tell if it was Valeria or Sofia. One of them. Alondra must have relayed her news.

Lou wanted to get back to Paulette, so she snuck in and up the stairs without stopping, retrieving the small plastic horse from her rooms.

She ran into Alondra at the bottom of the steps on her way down, and waved the horse at her. "Let's give this to Paulette."

Alondra ignored her. She looked quite small and alone at the bottom of the stairs. The other women were probably thinking of everything else. But of course, Mathew must have been in one of those troop carriers as well. He had even told Alondra he was leaving, only she hadn't known quite what he had meant. Lou should have done something, gone to town instead of having holiday breakfast.

But there was nothing to do now. The carriers were gone, the fight started.

She bent down and whispered in Alondra's ear. "Do you want to come with me to give this to Paulette?"

"Yes." He voice sounded small. "Yes, I would."

Poor baby. "Here, you can carry it."

"Is she hungry?"

"Of course she is. I should have thought of it myself. Can you bring her a bowl of soup?"

"Can you carry the soup so I can carry the horse?"

So they ended up walking back together through the unseasonably warm night. Owls hooted and a slight wind barely cooled them. In the barn, the baby still nursed hungrily, and Lou held onto the warm bowl until it finished, and after that she gingerly bounced the warm baby until Paulette finished eating.

Only then did Alondra hold out the small horse. "This is a gift from Lou."

Paulette looked up at her. "Really? For me?"

"Yes." Lou didn't really know what to say, so she stayed quiet.

"Thank you."

"Lou likes to help people," Alondra said. "She helped me get home, and she let me carry the horse."

If she said anything she might cry. Lou took three deep breaths, and then asked, "Can I give you a ride home?"

Paulette nodded.

Alondra took the bowl and gave the baby a small, sweet kiss, before heading back toward the house, her head bowed.

Lou and Paulette talked of small things all the way back to town, Paulette behind her on Buster, the baby between them. Buster didn't seem to mind the triple burden.

CHAPTER FORTY-FIVE

Their impromptu Emergency Operations Center was a hive of confusion. Coryn and Imke both started to turn on the same devices. Adam pushed Imke away and muttered something about being better at searching. Imke said, "Fine, but think about what we're searching *for* first."

Coryn had the fleeting thought that all of them, even Adam, were used to taking orders.

Eventually, Adam stared at news screens and data feeds, flipping content so fast it made her dizzy when she glanced at it. Imke used a secure line between them and Chicago to talk to the Chicago EOC, and to two people from Chicago who were in the formal Seacouver EOC.

Coryn called Lou, and together they started writing down everything they thought might be a fact, and when Lou begged off, she sat beside Adam and wrote down the facts he pulled out of news articles, using paper and a purple pen. Half of the "facts" she wrote down seemed contradictory. The paper quickly became a mess, but when she tried to move to the computer it was hard to type, since Adam was using all of the screens.

Namina brought coffee. After she handed it around, she stood staring at the table full of notes, looking perplexed. After a minute, she started taking photos of the notes and ordering them into lists that she sent to the printer and taped onto the wall.

Relief flooded over Coryn when Eloise opened the door.

Eloise had never been talkative. She didn't bother to offer a greeting, but simply came and leaned over Coryn's shoulder, looking at her list. She pointed at a statement that troops had been identified on a boat outside of Tacoma. "Cross that one off."

"Why?"

"It's a rumor. I don't have time to explain everything. Add that the

Camas Gate has been fortified and the road remains clear, but Portland also has two suspicious tankers."

"What about city systems?" Coryn asked. "Adam saw a transportation knot up in Lynwood."

Eloise shook her head. "Those happen without hackers. Remember that nothing is true until it's verified and even then it probably isn't. And that's worse in this case. We know there's bad information being injected into our systems."

Coryn swallowed. "How do I tell?"

"Use multiple sources when you can't find a human to verify." Eloise offered her a rare smile. "You're doing well. Keep it up." Then she went to interrogate Imke, and Coryn gave up on listening as Adam already had a list of three other news sources for her to review.

After Eloise had visited all three stations, she clapped her hands for their attention. "Short briefing," she announced. "We're going to keep this center running as a backup center. More people will join us, some from the city, some from our teams. Most of you will end up with assistant jobs. Coryn, when you get relived, I want you to work with Imke and handle communications with Lou."

"Where are Blessing and Day?" Coryn asked.

"We sent them to bed. They'll be second shift."

At least they weren't out trying to save the world like last time. But then this was far more serious. The last attack had felt bad, but the question had always been how quickly the city would win, not *if* it would. Before she had time for more questions, three new people came in and reported to Eloise.

Coryn returned to the news reports. It was the only way she could think of to manage both the chaos in the room and the fear and adrenaline that kept spiking through her.

A few people trickled in, but the work didn't slow. Shift change finally came. Coryn had never been so happy to see Blessing in her life. Given that he always made her happy, this seemed significant. It felt like she had been checking and rechecking facts for no more than an hour and no less than a week. Her shoulders were tense and her neck hurt and her forearms ached from so much typing. She felt wrung out of energy, sugarless and pale.

At the end of the briefing, Eloise came by and touched Imke on the shoulder. "We have a cot for you in the room next door."

Coryn almost protested, but Imke had seen the look on her face and shook their head slightly, smiling a secretive and sweet, if tired, smile. Coryn understood. They were both, after all, envoys of a sort. And Imke held a more formal position than she did, and worked for a mayor, not an ex-mayor.

So Coryn walked home with Namina, and let the robot give her an upper-body massage before she went to bed. Namina's fingers knew exactly where to poke and prod, which muscles to run long on and which to treat with strength. Best of all, Namina demanded nothing in return, not even polite conversation. This was good since Coryn's throat was sore from talking for so many hours.

Coryn kept her sleep to seven hours, ran for two, and showered and ate in one. She arrived in the outside corridor fifteen minutes before she was supposed to report back for her next shift.

First, she called Julianna. "Are you okay?" she asked. "Do you need anything? I could send Namina."

"I'm okay." The words were flat, and they both knew Julianna wasn't okay. The etiquette of disaster. Multiple disasters, really.

"Do you need anything?"

Julianna sighed. "You're helping the city. That's the best any of us can do. Is your sister okay?"

"As far as I know. She sent a text an hour ago and said the night had been quiet."

"Good. Give me an update when you can."

Coryn had learned to recognize a polite dismissal. "I'll call if I get news."

She stared at her wrist for a few moments, but she'd have all the news she needed soon, and there was no one else to call.

When she opened the door, she barely recognized the EOC. There were four times as many people, the big table had been pulled apart into four smaller tables that each had four to eight people huddled around them, a coffee service filled one corner, and the room smelled like tired people and fresh bread.

She went to check in with Eloise, but couldn't find her. She found Blessing and asked him what she should do. He grinned her, of course, but it was an exhausted smile. "Are you okay?" she asked him.

He pulled himself up to his full lanky height and took a deep breath, then gave her a little bow, as if she were a queen. "Of course I'm okay."

She smiled. "It looks good in here. A lot must have happened."

"The real cavalry rode in to the rescue." He pointed across the room at a tall gray-haired woman with an apple-cheeked smile and a red hat. "That's Lucille Moore. She acted as our Incident Commander, like Eloise did for you. She knows her stuff. She called in all these people and all this food."

"Did anything important happen?"

"The operation team worked on reporting viruses and hacks. They found a lot. A whole neighborhood water system went down, and another neighborhood's sprinklers went on full speed and stayed on. The transportation grid stuttered a few times during the morning, and they think some of it is still in trouble." He shrugged. "But who knows? Since it's Saturday, there's no school or anything, so the grid isn't stretched."

"No threats?"

"The cities have an ultimatum to answer the president. It's tomorrow at noon. But they won't give in and he knows it, so it doesn't really mean anything. No one thinks the feds have political teeth, whether or not their weapons are real." He stopped, and a rare frown crossed his face. "Except maybe those few who know where the nukes are, or if they're real." He lowered his voice. "I did get to go see the city's formal EOC. If you get a chance, go. It's—wow. I can't even describe it. Screens everywhere, and robotic everything, and the situation status is really neat."

"Hey! My sit-stat boards were neat!"

He laughed. "I didn't mean it that way. It's . . . organized and searchable and the AI's and the robotics are pretty fabulous. There's real-time reporting hanging in the air. Literally."

"So why are we even here?"

He arched an eyebrow and spoke in a low and overly serious tone of voice. "What if those systems are hacked?"

She curtseyed at him. "How do you know ours aren't?"

"I don't. But they're not government systems, and maybe no one knows about them."

He pulled her briefly to him, and then turned and went to answer a question from someone he'd been working with.

Eloise came in and clapped three times loudly, and then climbed onto a table with Lucille Moore. Lucille was old and burly, almost but not quite fat. She wore plain dark gray clothes and comfortable shoes, with only her red hat and a red belt to add color. In contrast, Eloise looked ready for a board meeting, in navy and white with low-heeled black boots and her hair pulled into a neat ponytail.

Lucille spoke first. She sounded precise and calm. "There are three primary fronts that we are monitoring. These are the port, city systems, and the physical land perimeters.

"First. As of last night, we identified two tankers we were worried about. One has been cleared. The other has . . . defenses. The city's teams have been assembling around it, and there is an assault by city forces planned for 11:00 a.m., which is in exactly one hour and fifteen minutes from now. Other teams are sweeping the waterfront looking for anything we might have missed. We are backup communications and logistics for this assault, and our operations team will need to pay close attention.

"Many cybersecurity challenges have been identified. There is a list on the right side of the situation status board. All response is being coordinated through the Seacouver Cybersecurity Unit, with three backup teams that work is being spread to. None of them is us. We are monitoring only. If we are assigned a role, it will be to mitigate damages but not to clean systems.

"We have a team assigned to Julianna's and Jake's holdings. They will come to the Incident Commander for this room if they need anything."

Lucille paused and caught her breath, made sure everyone paid attention. "We have identified at least ten possible strike teams approaching or already near Seacouver. Estimates suggest there are more. We are one of three locations working on identifying enemies approaching. The other two are listed by the board. One is in Vancouver and one is in Tacoma. Any questions?"

There were, of course, and after about ten minutes the collected staff from two shifts fell silent. As long as they were meeting, less work was getting done. Lucille nodded. "I'd like to thank my crew. Go home and sleep. Eloise will brief you all on the next shift."

Eloise stayed on the table, watching the room like a predatory bird, while the shift Coryn and Imke were replacing all filed back to their desks to wait for the briefing to end so they could go home. Blessing and Day joked and laughed. Coryn frowned at them, wishing they would act serious. Being part of an EOC seemed so solemn, so important.

She sighed and kept herself from trying to change him. If Blessing had taught her anything, it was to use humor in the face of great odds.

Eloise drew her attention. "The operational plan for this shift is to work on all of the tasks as outlined by Lucille. Your assignments are on the check-in table. If you haven't yet checked in, do so." She called out a few specific jobs. At the end, she said, "Coryn, Imke, please see me," and jumped lightly off the table.

Coryn hadn't even seen Imke so far this morning. She searched the room and found them wading toward Eloise from the far side by the coffee.

Eloise pulled them both quite close to her and spoke quickly, voice low. "I need to talk with you, but none of us is free right now. I've assigned you to be the liaison for the city's main EOC."

"How many EOCs are there?"

"There's one central hub. It's here—just two building's over. Easy to get to and from. You'll carry messages today. Some messages don't belong on electronics, especially in a cyber fight."

"Okay."

"Namina will take you. Go."

Imke looked puzzled. "Are there any messages for us to take now?"

"No. You're to be on a schedule—fifteen minutes in each place, and fifteen to get back and forth. Both places will see you about every forty-five minutes. Don't get sucked in over there. Do your jobs."

This must be the job Blessing had done. "We'll do our best."

A small line had queued up close to Eloise, keeping a barely respectable distance from them. She whirled away from Coryn and started answering other people's questions.

CHAPTER FORTY-SIX

Valeria had just opened the bar half an hour ago. Only a third of the chairs were full, and most of the people there were women—or the old. So far, neither Henrietta nor Agnes had appeared. Lou served; it gave her a chance to talk to more people than sitting still would.

There was an air of sadness and resignation, with none of the sense of guilty escape she'd felt here the last time she came. Patrons either drank extra or a little less than she would have expected. Some hushed conversations ended when she came close.

Another hour passed, and the bar remained quiet. Lou led Valeria into the back room under the pretense of asking where a certain type of wine was stored. "They're all shocked and surprised." She thought of Paulette's complaint about being kept in the dark. "Maybe no one told their women. Paulette was shocked." She paused. "Maybe we should get them drunk. I want to buy a round for everyone, but you can say it's from you. A holiday wish for the town. And then if you could sing something sappy about safety and war, I'll serve and listen. We can engage Felipe in the same thing, and Cheryl. Even Alondra. So if you can pass that along, maybe we can shake some information free."

She expected Valeria to be excited about the idea, but she looked stiff and angry.

"What?" Lou asked.

"These are my people. Most of the ones that are left. They are the ones who've been here a long time, or the children or the wives of the newcomers. I don't want to betray them, or to spy on them."

What was a bar for if not to gain useful information? "Do you mind if I buy them a drink?"

"No."

Lou pushed a little further. "What about singing to them? Songs that might comfort them?"

Valeria started straightening bottles of ketchup and mustard and canned pickles on the shelf in front of her. "I don't care about the cities. You know that."

"My sister is there. And so are your sons!"

Tears welled in the corners of Valeria's eyes and her hands shook. "I know."

"*And* the funding for what I do comes from the city. *And* neither of us wants everyone from the cities to spill out here." All of that felt inadequate. "We don't want innocent people killed, right?"

Valeria stepped back, still looking at the shelf and not at Lou.

Did she know something she hadn't told Lou? "Talk to me!" Lou demanded.

Valeria turned to her, her face a mask of frustration. "I have lived here and sweated here forever. I've protected my family here. You've been here what? Months? If I betray these people, *I will have to leave.* I have a few rules that have helped to keep us safe. One is that I *do not spy.* My family *does not spy. I will not put my boys—who are with these people's own children—in jeopardy.* We *cannot* help you."

Lou sighed, and spoke softly, aware her words were going to hurt. "Isn't one of your rules to keep some distance? But Diego and Santino and Ignacio broke those. War breaks rules."

Valeria blinked at her, pursed her lips, and turned back to the neat shelf, counting salt and pepper containers.

Lou leaned close to her and whispered, "What if you sing, and I buy drinks, and I listen. No one else. Most of the people who may be left are not your people. I need to know what is going on. I'll be careful."

Valeria rolled her eyes.

"What will happen to these people if all of the young men they sent off die? What will happen to you?"

Valeria flinched and took in a deep breath, blowing it out sharply. "If I sing, then you may listen." Anger edged her words. "But only you. No one else."

✝ ✝ ✝

An hour later, Valeria climbed up onto the stage. She had pulled her hair up and tied glittering strings of faux-diamond flowers into it and made up her eyes with sparkly dark blue shadow and dramatic paint. She should have looked beautiful, but as she moved toward the stage, she looked more reluctant than showy. She paused for a long time with her toes on the edge of the stage, watching the crowd, letting them finish sentences and sip drinks and slowly slide their attention to her.

Valeria usually shone when she was performing for a crowd. Any crowd. Right now, she looked vulnerable and a little shaky. Lou almost wanted to go rescue her.

Valeria shivered and then spoke quietly. "We have empty beds in most of our homes tonight. There are three in my household. We are here in this bar sharing drink and stories because a community must come together in hard times." She licked her lips, her movement and voice completely devoid of the subtle sexuality that usually imbued her. The lack of it made her look almost her age, more grandmother than goddess.

She continued. "Do I have your permission to sing healing songs and share some poetry? It would help me, but I only want to offer it if it will also help you."

Lou shook her head slightly, amused despite the gravity of the moment. Valeria was, in fact, playing this perfectly.

A woman near the front spoke. "I'd like that."

Others nodded and offered encouragement, and Valeria began with a low, sweet song of love between families, between father and son and mother and daughter.

Lou took water, wine, and cider out to the main room on a tray, offering it freely. About half the people in the room took it, most of them murmuring thank yous. A few refused, some with looks that suggested they wouldn't take a perfect rose or a gold coin if it came from her. Still, when she finished, all of the wine was gone and most of the water. A few glasses of cider remained.

She ignored the slights as best she could, and sat in the back, listening. Valeria sang three more songs and recited a poem. The room began to feel warmer, and at least one woman shifted her hands to her eyes to hold back tears. An older man and woman held hands near the back.

How did Valeria do this?

Alondra came into the room with more water, and Lou added a few fresh glasses to the tray of leftover cider and followed her out. Twice she perched briefly on the edge of chairs or just paused and made small talk, trying to get people to relax some. She refrained from asking any direct questions.

No one spoke to her of anything important. The men were gone. They apparently hadn't felt like telling people where, although the city could probably tell via satellite shots. But did they have bombs? What were their plans?

Valeria started a poem about men coming home from war, and then she stopped, her voice choking. She turned it into a lullaby, and then she stepped away from the small stage, almost stumbling. Astrid went to her, holding her, and Sofia passed them both, taking the stage. She looked hesitant.

People gave her the benefit of the doubt, waiting quietly.

She said, "Three of my brothers went wherever the men who are not here also went. I will sing three happy songs for them. Think happy thoughts and think of your loved ones while I sing, and perhaps we can send them a smile on this cold night."

Sofia's songs succeeded in making Lou smile, although they didn't shake any information loose from anyone. Lou raised her half-empty cider glass with the rest of the room when Sofia finished the first song.

She realized she hadn't been able to take her eyes off of Sofia for the last few lines. She might, some day, grow into Valeria's place. If she didn't let Henrietta woo her into danger.

Even though it was still early when Sofia smiled and gave a flouncy bow and stepped down, the women and old men began to leave. They talked in low tones, a few of them glancing back at her, or over at

Shuska, who stood quietly by the door even though it was clear her services as a bouncer wouldn't be needed tonight.

Henrietta hadn't come. Neither had Agnes.

By ten o'clock, the bar was fully empty. Lou brushed up against Valeria as she carried a set of dirty plates to the kitchen. "Thank you," she said.

"Did it help?"

"It didn't help me. But maybe it helped the people in the room."

Valeria nodded, looking weary.

This time, Lou did feel sorry for her. The bar felt hollowed out with so many people missing. Two generations had been plucked out of the community and sent away.

Felipe stroked the floor with a mop, the water running clear from it as he finished the last rinse. Sofia and Alondra stood by the door, laughing and pulling on gloves. Lou helped Astrid wipe up the cabinets with rags so hot they turned both women's knuckles red.

The door opened and Paulette stepped through, her baby in a cloth carrier that held the infant at her chest. "Lou?" she called.

Lou dropped the rag and went to her. "Are you okay?"

Paulette nodded, although her hands shook. She looked like someone had stolen all the color from her face. Lou led her to a table in the part of the bar that had already been cleaned up, ignoring Felipe's frown.

Paulette stayed standing, rocking, one hand on the back of Jude's head and one hand on the back of the chair. She whispered, "I know something."

"What?"

"Jude."

"Yes?"

"Jude kept a diary."

It took Lou a moment to understand that she meant her brother and not her baby. "He did?"

"Electronic. On his wrister. But he backed it up at home. No one is there now, and I wanted to know where they went. I downloaded his diary to my wristlet and I listened to some of it."

Lou sat, and gestured for Paulette to join her. "What did you learn?"

"If I sit the baby will cry. I can't sit."

"Okay."

Paulette licked her lips. "Mathew."

Lou waited.

"Mathew. Do you know Mathew?"

"Alondra's dad. Yes. I do. He shot at me once."

Paulette's eyes widened. "He had an ID. A real city ID. I mean, one that the city didn't even question, with his own real biometrics coded into it. He worked for an institute. The Modern Training Institute." She paused, staring at the wall above Lou's head. "I'm sorry. I need to tell you the right thing."

Lou smiled, her throat tight. "Take your time."

"Mathew was supposed to be helping people like us get into the city. Not us, we don't want to go. But helping people do well there." She leaned down and kissed baby Jude on the head. "Mathew used the classes and his job to take bombs into the cities. Nukes. He went from the loop in Spokane to the cities."

Lou felt stuck to the floor, frightened. She whispered, "To which cities?"

"Seacouver. Portland Metro. Chicago. Calgary. Salt Lake City. That's all I found. But I think some other cities might have them too. I didn't listen to it all. I thought I should tell you."

Lou felt cold, and slow. It was hard to even get the words out to ask, "How many?"

"I don't know. Jude called them payloads, and he rambled about nuclear war and all that. He talked about Korea and Fukushima and Hiroshima, all the accidents and the bombs mixed up. He liked them. I had no idea my brother liked bombs."

Lou took in a deep breath. Another. Her heart was racing. "What does he plan to do?"

"Bomb the cities. Kill as many as he can. Scare the rest."

Lou took another deep breath. She looked around. No one was close enough to hear. She didn't know if she wanted an audience or if this should be secret. Shuska would be good, but she wasn't in the room right now. Valeria had said something about taking her to move boxes in the back of the store. There was Felipe, still concentrating on his mop. Alondra and Sofia, but *they* shouldn't hear this.

"Do you know when?"

"He took them over the summer. One at a time. I don't know why." She fell quiet. Jude wriggled and stretched his arms out. Paulette looked down. "Oh—you mean when they want the bombs to go off, don't you? No. Maybe New Years. Maybe sooner. I can give you the files. I have them. They're on my wristlet. Someone else needs to read it."

Yes. Julianna. The city needed to know this now. "Yes. Soon."

"Will you take them? I can't leave and take care of Jude. I don't want to be caught with this, either. Maybe people will listen to you."

"Did you tell anyone else?"

Paulette's eyes widened. "Of course not. I don't want anybody to know I can do this."

Lou winced. "I'm glad you're capable. You did right. I'll take them." She held her hand out, and Paulette sat down and leaned back, maybe to keep the baby in the position she wanted him. She took both hands off the child and used one to unbuckle the strap of her wristlet and hold it out. "I'll say I lost this. If anyone asks."

Lou took it, sliding it deep into her pocket. "I'll get this to someone. Is there anything else you remember that I should know? Did you learn where Jude or Mathew went?"

"No. To the city. Seacouver I think. North. They have weapons."

"More nukes?"

"No. But big things they can brace over their shoulders and fire. And rifles that fire fast. And more. I never got to see it all. But they've been saving ammunition and testing a little from time to time. Jude wants to blow up a court. Why would he want to do that?"

Lou hurt at the loss and sadness in the girl's voice. She would hug her, except then she'd crush the baby. "I'm sorry. I'm sorry the world's not that good."

"You've always treated me well. You're the only one who ever has."

"I hope that's not true." The girl's wristlet burned in her pocket. Maybe Shuska could pry its secrets free.

She had to call Coryn.

Julianna needed to know.

Everyone needed to know.

Lou shook with the need to do something, anything, to move the information to others who could do more with it. She took Paulette's hand in hers. "Unless something happens to me, don't tell anyone else about this. Then tell my people. Shuska or Matchiko, or even the priest—Pablo. Not your people. They might know, or they might not care, or they might hurt you for knowing."

Paulette nodded. "I understand." The baby squirmed, and she comforted him by patting his back.

"So go home. I'll take care of this."

"Okay. Thank you. Thank you for listening. Can I come talk to you some day?"

Lou smiled "At the farm? How will you get there?"

"I'll walk."

"Will you be safe?"

"I think so."

"Be sure."

"Okay. I gotta go now."

"I know. Take care. You're always welcome." She paused. "Thank you."

Paulette offered a small, tremulous smile. Tears shone in her eyes.

Lou watched as she and Jude pushed through the door and out into the night. She clenched her fists, drew in a deep breath, closed her eyes, and tried not to imagine what could happen if nukes went off in the cities.

CHAPTER FORTY-SEVEN

oryn and Imke followed Namina to the main city EOC. Every screen they passed on their way showed breathless news. They had to thread through so many people and robots they almost lost each other, and once Coryn's foot got stomped on.

Outside of the main city EOC they joined a large group standing in line, waiting to be vetted into the room. Security staff used wands and small pricks of blood that flowed into tiny white tubular containers that turned black when they were full. After that, there was a five-minute wait in a pressing crowd while a small square machine on a shelf examined the blood. Namina merely watched.

Apparently robots were easier to identify than humans.

Coryn asked Namina, "What is the machine looking for?"

"Nanobots you don't have a prescription for. Pathogens."

"Not just DNA?"

"It's not allowed to."

"Oh."

Imke looked irritated. "I already have a diplomatic security clearance."

"That's not enough for this EOC."

Imke tapped their foot and crossed their arms, and then blew out a deep breath and adopted a more relaxed stance that looked entirely forced.

A young woman with five long black braids came up and requested their AR glasses. She set them on a belt that ran through a machine and then handed them back with an insipid smile. Coryn half-expected to be asked to strip next. But the woman waved them toward the door. "Go on in."

When Namina opened the door, Coryn gasped. The room was huge—ten times the size of the ballroom they were using for Julianna's

EOC. Colorful displays hung on all of the walls and in the air, a richness of information that dazzled her. People in multicolored vests hurried throughout the room. Nonhumanoid robots scooted along the floor carrying everything from food and coffee to paper maps and what looked like special communications gear.

Coryn stepped in. Just above her head, a display shimmered, drawing her attention. There were seven lines of data on it, all of them accompanied by arrows:

Ports
Cybersecurity
Utilities
Medical
Data
Partners
Media

Imke's eyes followed the "Partners" line, which led to a map of the United States, Canada, and Mexico. They led Coryn toward the board, their eyes fixed on the bright colors and their grip tight on her wrist.

A location blob for Seacouver glowed in a variety of colors, mostly sick yellows with a few greens and a few reds. Chicago was mostly green, with one dark red spot to the south. Flagstaff was a swirl of crimson, burgundy, and rust. Coryn began to look down the coast, but a tug on her arm made her turn to Namina, who looked quite stern. "You are not cleared for the whole room. If you don't arrive in the liaison area in the next five minutes you might set off an alarm."

Coryn tugged on Imke, managing to register that Portland Metro was yellow and green and Spokane a swirl of blue and green before she turned and had to quickly sidestep a waist-high robot.

There were two other people already in the liaison area, both of them wearing their AR rigs and sitting quietly, looking through them.

A tall, square-shouldered robot with a design that merely nodded at humanoid features watched over them. Namina introduced it as the liaison check-in-bot. He wore a red uniform and didn't appear to have been programmed with any sense of humor whatsoever. He led them to the far two seats and went back to his place.

Namina stood behind them, one hand on the back of each of their chairs. It felt as if she were guarding them.

Coryn stared at the swirling bits of data, some of it in three dimensions and so crystal clear it looked like she could walk right into it. Namina nudged her and made a gesture for her to drop into augmented reality.

She pulled her glasses up from around her neck, and her fingers reflexively clutched the seat of her chair.

Looking ahead of her, the same places that had been utterly confusing made her mouth drop open. The entire EOC appeared to be suspended over the city, as if it floated on a platform above the dome. She felt unmoored. The imagery was so good that she pushed down with her feet, searching for the floor. When she found it, her stomach stopped spinning. She knew augmented reality, had spent years making it her friend, and this was so far beyond anything she'd experienced that she *needed* the literal toehold in the real world to center.

She'd never seen graphics rendered so realistically on such a vast field. The outlines of the real tables and chairs and doors and even people all moved through her field of vision, but they had been dulled to see-through shadows. She let go of her chair and leaned forward, fascinated. Her glasses responded the way they always had, but the places they showed her filled her with awe. Eye blinks moved her fast, the vision so real she felt as if her body moved with it. She could move between EOCs and between locations in Seacouver with the whispered beginning of words.

These were the things she knew or was being prompted for in this place, like the shelter EOC or West Seattle. What would render for words she didn't know?

A whisper in her ear. Namina. "Turn around."

She did, drawing in a breath and fighting sudden vertigo at the unexpected. The wall behind them had been transformed, as if she were looking through a clear window with fine lines of metal threading through it at three-inch intervals. Just enough disturbance to keep her from trying to walk through the now nearly-invisible wall and right into what must be another room in a different building. North of them? The map under it flowed seamlessly into the one she had just been watching, and she recognized two of the Canadian Vancouver's iconic buildings. The Spear of Hope rose straight up next to blocky Pearson Tower. She figured out how to zoom in and look over the squat top of the Pearson building and see that hothouses still produced bright red tomatoes.

She pulled her glasses up and leaned down to Imke. "Go into AR."

Imke pointed. "We're about to get some work to do."

Bitter disappointment washed through Coryn. There was so much she hadn't yet really seen in here! But sure enough, the liaison-bot was leading a tall woman over to them. She wore a red vest with the words Corporate Liaison in capital letters on it. She handed Coryn a small envelope. "Please take this to Eloise."

"What is it?"

Her voice was just barely to the good side of condescending. "It's sealed."

Coryn stiffened. "Very well."

Namina led them out. They were checked for security again, their glasses scanned again. At least there was no line, and no real wait this time. As the door-minder-bot handed them back their glasses, it said, "All records of your time here have been permanently erased."

A brief and bitter disappointment shocked Coryn. The magic she had just experienced had been ripped from her. No wonder Blessing had warned her. Thinking of him helped her center. If any day was a good day to die . . .

Coryn held her tongue until they left the building, and then she couldn't help herself. "Oh my gosh," she said. "Oh my gosh. So good. I've never seen AR like that. You should look, Imke. Maybe the cities can be knit together like that. Oh—sorry. The EOCs are together. Not ours. But all through Seacouver." She realized she probably didn't make much sense to someone who hadn't *felt* the AR, so she tried to be a little more understandable. "They have a view from above, way above. The whole city on a fly through. It looks live. Where did they get that view? Are they using drones?"

Namina looked over at her, almost scolding. Her large dark eyes had narrowed and her jaw tightened just like some of Coryn's teachers might have done once. "If I were a human, I'd be amused. Settle down for a moment. Think about all that data being knit together. How safe can that be?"

Imke answered immediately. "Not very."

A soft shushing alarm warned them to step to the side of the hallway and let a string of three robot cars through, trailing the aromas of coffee and fruit. "Your glasses should be safe enough as they don't broadcast anything," said Namina, ignoring the interruption with the imperturbability of someone who didn't need to eat. "But I wouldn't take any serious electronics in there with you."

"What about our wristlets?" asked Coryn.

"I should have warned you to turn them off. As liaisons you'll be targets of anything trying to get out of there."

Coryn wandered how much of a target Namina might be. She'd seen ecobots hacked, and city systems, but thankfully never companions. Namina was theoretically hand-coded by Julianna's staff.

But did that really mean anything? For the fiftieth time in the last month, she swore to try and follow the cybersecurity news better. Security always felt like it mattered greatly, but she couldn't grasp the details beyond normal precautions. The invisible threats posed by hackers felt like dangerous gnats she could neither see nor understand.

As if to underscore Namina's caution, Eloise took the small envelope and handed it right over to the technology security team and asked for a scan before she even tried to read the messages on the small data seed the envelope carried. "What did you think?" Eloise asked.

"Amazing."

Eloise smiled. "Best I've ever seen. But I asked Namina to fill you in on the dangers. I presume she did."

"Yes."

"Okay—eat, and I'll read this. If I have something to send back I'll have it ready in ten minutes." With that, she turned back to the security people.

Imke pulled Coryn over to the coffee and poured two cups. They took a sip before they led her into a quiet corner. This EOC had far fewer gimmicks, but it had at least as many people swirling among and between each other as they pursued their different, connected missions. Imke stood so close that their shoulder touched Coryn's, creating a small point of tantalizing heat. "We have something like that in Chicago. Eloise has a point. It's got cybersecurity, everything the city does has that. But I heard a presentation once about the dangers in EOCs. They aren't as hardened as public safety dispatch or utilities, and the last attack here got to the utilities."

"You'd think they'd be extra safe." Coryn leaned closer to Imke, savoring the touch, doing her best to turn it into comfort she could use now rather than fire. "I mean, they're the center of any responses."

"They're toys that people run drills in. The one here and the one in Portland were activated during the last attack. How long do you think it was before that? Other than for drills?"

"How do I know? I was a lost orphan girl, then I was Outside."

Imke laughed. "Fourteen years. The last activation was for a dome weather system upgrade, and not a disaster at all. Just something that might have become one. And before that?"

"How would I know?" Coryn said again, trying not to sound irritated. "Ten years?"

"Seven," Imke corrected her. "For a law passed in Russia that glitched the transportation system and closed all airports internationally for two weeks. All the EOCs were activated. In Seacouver, the primary emergency was a bunch of protests. Three people were trampled to death. In Chicago, we had a brief spate of shooting and lost one police officer and two robots."

"That was the year before I was born."

"Which is my point. And before that it was the fire that took out Leavenworth. That was a year-long activation, but the city was really running backup and support, not handling the direct incident management."

"You know a lot about emergency management."

Imke laughed. "That's because I work for the mayor. Did you know you're three hundred times more likely to die of suicide than an accident or an act of war in the city?"

Coryn winced. Did Imke know her parents had killed themselves? She searched for a change of subject and raised her empty coffee cup. "Want more?"

Imke smiled. "No time."

Sure enough, Eloise was halfway across the crowded floor and clearly coming toward them.

Each loop between EOCs took at least an hour, regardless of the posted expectation of half that. Security slowed them down. The crowded corridors took longer than usual to get through. Now it was mostly delivery-bots, as if everyone in the city had decided they needed a month's supply of food when they usually had, at best, a day or two. Worse, Imke had been sent to Chicago's Seacouver embassy with a message last round. So Coryn breathed a sigh of relief as Imke crossed the crowded, multicolored floor and sat beside her. "How was the embassy?" she asked.

Imke smiled. "Fine."

So they weren't going to give up what their messages had been, at least not here. That was okay. Coryn still hadn't told them that Jake was so close to death. Maybe politics always included secrets.

She had become more used to the big EOC and its huge glitter map of all of the hot spots in the city. This was her sixth time, and she began to focus on details. What if she could help Lou find the -o boys? She examined routes and identified threats from and around Chelan.

At first, she thought she was misreading the data. The numbers were too low, the travel directions wrong.

She grabbed Imke's hand, leaned close, and whispered, "Something's wrong."

Imke squeezed back, hard, and let go. Coryn interpreted it as a sign to wait, and returned to looking over the statistics. She turned her attention to Wenatchee, and then Spokane, her stomach souring slightly.

She spoke the numbers she saw softly, recording them to playback later.

It seemed to take longer than usual before they were let out of the room. The liaison-bot finally approached them with another package of data to take back.

Coryn slid her glasses down and took the package.

As they were walking out, Namina tripped on something and bumped into her from behind, and her glasses fell to the floor. The robot picked them up and handed them to her, fumbling for a second. It took five minutes to make it to the door. They stopped to sign out, and as they did the minder-bot held its hand out for her AV glasses.

She wanted to resist. But the bot was big and quite metallic, and it looked at her with a sincere patience that demanded compliance. She handed over the glasses, and the bot sent them back through the machine with the belt. When it handed them back, it said, "Your settings have been restored to where they were on entry. There is a number to contact if anything is wrong."

She nodded, both angry and more certain that something was,

indeed, quite wrong. But she smiled and slid the glasses back around her neck, walking out after Namina and before Imke. She said nothing until they were back inside the security perimeter of Julianna's building. She was still debating whether to try and talk to Eloise alone, which might be impossible, or to tell Namina and Imke what she thought. First, though, she had a suspicion. She turned to the robot. "What made you bump into me?"

"I chose to save your data."

"You copied it?"

A slight smile was the only answer Namina seemed willing to provide.

Coryn let out a long sign. "Why would they erase it?"

"What do you think is wrong?"

"How do you know I think something's wrong?"

"I have very good hearing."

The flatness in Namina's voice made her laugh. She was so different from Paula. Slyer. More subtle. And never like a mother. More like a slightly obnoxious spinster aunt, in spite of her exotic younger-woman's body and tendency to wear prodigious amount of makeup for a robot. Coryn took a deep breath and gathered her thoughts. "The data they're displaying about Chelan is off. They claim less occupancy, and they only identify a group of about five people as possible enemy combatants heading toward the city. But I know it's three transports full. Over thirty. They list our permit—I guess they'd have to. But they say there are five people working, and there are more, and we've filed our updates every month. They should know we have more than five staff. Even before you include the Silversteins. Shouldn't the EOC have perfect data? Or at least as good as ours? They should be able to see even the sat shots that I've been blocked from."

"Perhaps you are not as naive as you seem to be," Namina replied.

Imke gave the robot a strange look.

When they arrived back in their home EOC, it was so crowded Coryn had to look hard to locate Eloise in a corner talking with a pair of uniformed men. She led Imke and Namina into a short line that had queued up to get Eloise's attention.

Eloise's entire job in here was handling the next emergency and the next. While Coryn waited, Eloise convinced the head of security in the building that operations below the EOC could and should remain normal, told the head of communications where the spare radios had been taken last shift, and then ordered three of Julianna's restaurants to deliver food for the main cybersecurity EOC.

When it was their turn, Coryn opened her mouth to speak, but Namina pulled Eloise away, gesturing for Coryn and Imke to follow. They went all the way into a small room with a metal door. After the door clanged shut, Namina said, "The main EOC appears to have been compromised. We need to stress test our systems."

Eloise didn't look as startled as Coryn felt.

"Tell her what you found," Namina prompted.

Coryn did. Eloise nodded, and said, "Thank you."

Coming from Eloise, it was almost praise. But before Coryn could bask in the glow of accomplishment, Eloise added, "You can skip the rest of shift change. Julianna wants you. Meet me there in an hour. Tell her this."

"May I go?" Imke asked.

Eloise hesitated, frowning. Then she said, "We'll call you. Do you have a secure enough line with Chicago to tell them this?"

"I can get to one."

"Will you do that and then call us?"

"Of course."

"Wait," Eloise said. "Maybe if you learn anything important, you should come directly to us."

CHAPTER FORTY-EIGHT

Coryn crept into Julianna's room. Evan stood at attention, nodding his permission for her to enter. The dim light showed Jake sleeping half-under the covers. Julianna lay curled around him, uncovered except for a coat, her fingertips touching his shoulder. She didn't stir.

Jake looked like a skeleton barely cloaked in skin; she couldn't imagine how he still lived. The fingers of his right hand splayed across the sheets, no more than skin-covered sticks defined by knobby knuckles. His cheekbones looked ready to emerge from his skin.

She shivered and turned away. Perhaps she shouldn't wake them just now. She tiptoed to a recliner and sank into it with a tired sigh. The sadness and waiting that permeated the room, the chaos of the scene in the EOC, and her worry about the city all collided at once, weighing her eyelids down. A strange not-sleep drifted over her, a waking doze, where her limbs wouldn't move but her brain kept going, playing conversations from the day over and over.

She lost track of time, and maybe even slept some, although she couldn't be sure.

The sound of the door opening startled her. Eloise, with Adam trailing behind her. She looked as wrecked as Coryn felt. Coryn blinked and stretched her toes out, rotated her ankles, and managed to coax enough movement from her body to sit up.

Eloise crossed the room and shook Julianna's shoulder. "Wake up."

Julianna leaned down to Jake's back, listening for breath. A tender, sad smile escaped her lips. She scooted carefully away from him before sitting up and moving from the bed to a square work table they'd been using for a kitchen table.

At a signal from Julianna, Evan nodded. Coryn knew from multiple nights here that coffee, fruit, and nuts would appear soon. In the meantime, the robot drew a pitcher of water for them.

Eloise glanced at Julianna. "Report?"

Julianna whispered, "The doctors say hours. Maybe a day. He's mostly out of it."

Eloise took one of her hands, and Coryn rose and took the other.

Adam tried to comb his hair with his fingers, although the effort largely failed.

Eloise spoke quietly. "We're losing the cybersecurity wars so far. Water has been compromised again, and Portland lost its core transportation system. The hyperloop has been cut between here and Chicago, and again between Chicago and Flagstaff."

She took a deep breath, let it out slowly, clearly working for energy and control. "Our borders are more permeable than usual. The only good news is that our attack on the container ship worked. We pulled a number of robots and some weapons off of it."

She'd forgotten about the ship. "Were any of the weapons nukes?"

Adam answered. "No sign, not so far. But the dome has been penetrated so many times I can't track all the possible entry points. We should have built a wall instead of a weather dome with holes everywhere." He paused and looked over at Julianna. "Sorry."

"It's okay. You might be right."

The table fell silent until Coryn realized it was her turn. "Some of the data in the main EOC looks wrong to me. I'd like to call Lou as soon as we can."

Julianna twisted her hand around in Coryn's so she was doing the comforting for a moment. Coryn smiled, a sudden wash of warmth for the old woman almost making her cry. Her hand started to shake in Julianna's. She glanced toward the door, willing it to open and admit a tray full of coffee. Adam's words sank in. "Do you think there's an attempt to cut Chicago off? With two hyperloop systems down?"

Adam answered her. "Hard to tell. The loops are manned by security-bots and drones. There have been four hundred attacks in the last year, with almost a hundred of those in the last three days. The fact that both successful sabotage attempts go to Chicago could be accident; almost everything goes to Chicago. There are still three ways to loop there, including via Spokane and up through Calgary and down, or Spokane to Flagstaff to Portland to Chicago."

"So couldn't you go Seacouver to Portland to Chicago?" Coryn asked.

Eloise shook her head. "The Seacouver / Portland Loop has been commandeered for military purposes. No civilian use until this is over. Besides, it's a main target." She cleared her throat and focused on Julianna. "I have worse news than that. Namina brought back a lot of data. We put her through a series of stress tests and her code appears clean. We ran our EOC through some. We removed two sleepers, but of course . . ."

She didn't really need to say that nothing was ever really secure. The whole city had been reminded of that in the attacks a few months ago, and there had been frantic news about security every day, a few small protests, and many programmers swearing they were doing their best.

The door opened, and Evan came in with a tray of food and coffee. He was followed by an older male doctor, who sat down beside Jake and took his hand.

While the doctor examined Jake, everyone else reached for coffee and calories. By the time the doctor came over to their table, Coryn's hands had stopped shaking, and she felt like she might be able to stay awake a few more hours.

The doctor leaned over Julianna. "He's the same."

She nodded. "I know. Thank you. Come back in an hour?"

"I can stay until . . ."

Julianna spoke firmly. "No need."

The doctor nodded curtly and then left, although Coryn had the impression he'd be hovering close by.

"Can I call Lou?" Coryn asked.

Eloise said, "Do it from here. This is the only place in town that is less than fifty percent likely to be compromised."

Julianna lifted her weary face. "That bad." It wasn't even a question, merely an indictment.

"Yes. Go on back," Eloise said. "Rest."

Julianna nodded tiredly and sat beside Jake again, running her hands lightly over his shoulders and back.

Eloise handed Coryn a wristlet. "Put this on. Keep it for a few days. Not as a replacement—in fact, use yours. We don't want to create anomalies that pop out of the watcher algorithms. You are probably a high priority for them. But keep this, too. It's more secure."

The device was as spare and beautiful as Eloise herself, with a simple band that snapped shut around her right wrist, and a flat face that was about two inches across. "What if she doesn't answer? How will she know it's me?"

"It will spoof you—pretend to be you—whenever it calls anyone on your list of contacts. So don't lose it."

"I won't." She glanced at the clock. Eleven at night. She told the device to call Lou, and was surprised at how quickly Lou answered. Clearly she was awake.

"I was about to call you." Lou's hair looked unkempt and she looked tired, although it was hard to tell on the tiny screen.

"Perfect."

Words tumbled out of Lou. "We . . . learned some things you need to know. Bad things, things I can't help you with from here. We have data to get to you." She paused.

Coryn spoke quickly. "We think this line is secure. I'm in a room with other people. Julianna, too."

Eloise said, "Can you describe what you learned in just a minute or two?"

"Yes. The nuclear weapons are already in the city. They've been there awhile."

The entire room stopped, silenced. Julianna's hands slowed as they roamed across Jake's shoulder and side. Eloise froze, staring at Coryn. Adam set his cup down and leaned in close.

Lou continued, "I have an electronic diary from someone who may have known some of the details. There is some data in there, but I don't know the cities well enough to parse it. It's just clues to me."

Eloise leaned in. "You can't send it here. Not directly. We can't tell what communications are secure any more, if any. Can we meet you somewhere?"

"Wenatchee? That's a place I'd be likely to go."

Adam was parsing through maps. "What about Spokane?"

"On horseback?" Coryn asked. "That would take days."

"On an ecobot," Eloise said. "We can program one to get you there. Spokane is better. It's got a loop, at least so far."

Lou hesitated, some kind of hushed conversation going on in the room with her. "Yes."

"Leave as soon as you can," Eloise said. "In an hour or less. We'll track you. I'll send an override code to make sure the ecobot obeys you. It will be good for a week."

There's was a moment of silence, and when Lou came back onto the line, she sounded . . . controlled. "Thank you. I'll see that Shuska gets the code."

"Someone will be in Spokane by end of the day tomorrow."

"It will take me longer."

Eloise's smile was as tight and controlled as Lou's voice. "Leave now. We'll beat you there if the loop system holds up."

Coryn leaned over her wrist. "I love you."

"I love you, too," Lou said. "Stay safe. See you in Spokane." With that, the connection closed.

They all stared at each other. There wasn't anything else to do, not after hearing about nukes in the city.

Adam's fingers drummed on the table.

"No," Eloise told him. "Don't change your search parameters or double down. We don't want to tell anybody what we just learned."

Coryn stood up. "I'm going to Spokane."

Eloise simply looked at her, her face utterly devoid of any emotion other than simple exhaustion. She glanced at Adam. "Do you have the strength to track the ecobot's progress for a while if I give you the next shift off?"

He nodded.

"Can you make eight hours?"

He nodded again.

"Okay—go to your room and sleep. I'll wake you when they start off. You come back here and work from this desk."

He nodded a final time and left.

Eloise turned to Coryn. "Okay. You're coming with me. So you need to sleep now. I'm going to arrange for someone else to take my shift tomorrow, and then I'm going to sleep."

Coryn opened her mouth to say she was too wired to possibly sleep, but the look on Eloise's face stopped her. Evan handed her a blanket, and she went back to the same recliner and snuggled under it, her eyes pasted open with worry and her brain full of little nuclear backpacks hiding in parks and on bridges. At least she was going. At least she would see Lou.

Soft sobs woke Coryn. She had been deep in the kind of dream that often haunted her after a long training run, and it took a moment to realize she was sprawled awkwardly on the recliner in Julianna's suite.

The sobs came from Julianna, quiet but raw.

Coryn stretched and climbed out of the uncomfortable chair, twisting her head to relieve a muscle in her neck that felt like a tree trunk. There was no one in the room except her and Julianna and Jake. If he was alive.

She suspected not.

Evan wasn't in his place.

The room was quiet except for Julianna's cries, a deep gray darkness that felt like a chasm of grief. Coryn went to the bed and sat down quietly next to Julianna, entirely unsure what to say.

Julianna kept her head down.

Coryn handed her tissues, which she took without comment, clutching them.

After a time, Julianna's sobs rose in pitch, becoming keening wails punctuated with uneven breaths.

Coryn sat still, breathing deep and slow, just being there.

After about twenty minutes, Julianna quieted.

Coryn brought her water, which she drank.

When Coryn took the empty glass and turned toward the sink, the sobbing started over.

This time, it slowed in half the time.

Coryn brought more water and reached her hand toward Julianna, offering it. She had seen death, but she had never been with someone she loved when they died, or with someone whose lifelong partner had just passed. Always, death had been sharp but offstage, like her parents' suicides, or the murder of her companion, Paula. She had just missed the bloody deaths of the Listeners who had been slaughtered before the last attack on the city.

This felt far more visceral, but also numbing; a little foggy and dreamlike.

Julianna's eyes were wide but didn't really appear to be looking outward at all. All of her being seemed to be focused inward in a sort of eerie control.

Coryn realized she was crying and blew her own nose, then got up and washed her hands and sat down again, close to Julianna. A line of Walt Whitman's went through her head, over and over, driving an odd feeling of peace through her pain. *Nothing can happen more beautiful than death.*

Julianna finally looked directly at her and appeared to see her.

Coryn held her hand out again, and Julianna took it. "I'm so sorry," Coryn whispered.

Julianna sniffled and nodded. "He woke up. He looked good, really good. He was smiling. He asked me how we were doing."

"And?"

"He wanted to know if we were winning. That's what he was really asking. Were we winning? Did this city he built and fought for make it?"

"What did you tell him?"

"I told him yes. What else could I have said?"

Julianna leaned forward and let Coryn put her arms around her. It reminded Coryn of the day her parents had died. Lou had seen their bodies, and Coryn had held her and Lou had taken from her, or perhaps *accepted* was the right word. Coryn had been able to give her big sister comfort for the first time in her life.

Julianna accepted from her now, and the moment was filled with grief and pain and comfort all at once. Coryn whispered, "We are winning. We will. We have to."

CHAPTER FORTY-NINE

Even though it was still a few hours shy of dawn, the lights in the kitchen threw a warm glow on Astrid's face. The scent of baking bread filled the entire room, along with brewing coffee. Matchiko, Shuska, and Lou were so bundled up they nearly filled the open spaces in the room.

Astrid pulled a tray of buns out of the oven and handed around coffee for all, the cups smelling of nearly unbearable bitterness. "There's no milk."

"That's all right."

The four women sat at the table. "I'm not happy all three of you are going."

This was the third time that Astrid had said the same thing. "Daryl and Felipe will do fine," Lou assured her. "And you're still working for us. You work hard."

Astrid hadn't touched her coffee. "You don't know anything do you? About our men?"

So that was it. She winced at the small elusive lie she would have to tell. "About Mathew? No."

Astrid sighed. "Mathew is an idiot. I should never have married him. But my brothers? I can't live without them. I can't. Please?"

Lou looked away. She couldn't lie to Astrid. "I don't know what I can do. If there's anything, I'll do it. But Mathew may . . . Mathew may . . ."

"Have killed my brothers," Astrid said. "He's been telling them to go to town when he goes, probably taking them to meetings. But you know people in the city. You know Julianna Lake."

"I do. But she doesn't run the city anymore."

"What if you don't go?"

"We have to."

A small narrowing of Astrid's features suggested Lou had just lost some of the trust she'd built up here. Guilt washed through her. The diary she carried did implicate Mathew. She hadn't seen anything about the others, but it was hard to know. The people in the city would get far more secrets from it than she and Shuska had been able to. *Damn the city to hell, and all of its endless needs with it.* She leaned forward and looked into Astrid's eyes. "I hope everyone is safe. *Know* that."

Astrid got up, remaining silent as she bundled up the buns and handed a heavy basket of food to Matchiko.

Lou put a hand on Astrid's shoulder and said, "Thank you."

Astrid brushed her hand off and stood still, looking away. It bothered Lou all the way out to the ecobot.

They used flashlights to climb up on the bot's cold metal back, which glittered with a light, slippery frost. Lou grabbed the basket from Matchiko, turning to settle it in a niche they'd also piled full of blankets. Whoever had designed these machines had left room for riders but clearly hadn't really expected them. Everything was an inconvenient distance away from everything else.

Shuska turned on the low running lights, illuminating the uneven surfaces.

Matchiko finished climbing up and settled, looking wide awake and perhaps even excited. Shuska sat, leaning against a metallic arm and poking at her tablet. The tablet and the machine had accepted the code word Eloise supplied, and Shuska and her tablet had been in a small and periodic fight ever since. Even now, with all her focus on the controls, Shuska swore under her breath every few seconds.

So here they were bundled up on a nearly frozen machine with the smell of warm food surrounding them, and no way to tell if the machine was actually going to move or not. It was almost six in the morning, but the nights were long this time of year, and it would be at least an hour before the sky began to soften toward dawn.

Shuska looked up suddenly and barked, "Hold on!"

There was actually no need. The machine twisted one of its arms around Lou and soon it was holding her, much like the ecobot she had ridden into Portland on. She could no more fall than she could stand or otherwise move.

The same thing had happened to the other two. Shuska had been gently pinned in front of Lou, facing her and looking at the back of the ecobot. Lou barely had time to brace before the bot took off, moving faster than she had ever seen it. The startled look on Shuska's face implied that she hadn't expected such a quick burst of speed either. It was managing this speed on six sturdy legs, which created a rocking gait that made Lou grab for the arm that held her, in spite of the fact that she probably couldn't fall.

At the end of the long drive, the bot went up and out, taking a route that she would never have thought it could manage. They passed far from town, scrabbling down steep hillsides and nearing the level of the river just as dawn spilled reds and oranges across the sky, and in a few places, an improbable pink.

A few hawks circled them for a bit as if curious about the dull silver-and-red machine lurching across open ground.

What other features hadn't the ecobot bothered to show them? They crossed the Columbia north and east of Chelan at Brewster, and then recrossed over a new bridge worthy of Coryn's attention. It took them off of established roads in the small, abandoned town of Keller Ferry. By then it was nearly lunch, and so Matchiko asked for a stop. Shuska found a small hill where they wouldn't be seen easily.

The bot's arms released them, and Lou stumbled as she stood up, stiff from the long, cold ride. They all walked around a bit to shake off stiffness and then gathered on a great flat rock to eat.

"I think we'll be in Spokane tonight," Matchiko said. "Maybe even before dark."

Shuska picked up her tablet, glancing at it quickly. "We've been going nineteen and a half miles an hour, average. Which means over twenty-five sometimes."

"And how fast does it usually move?" Matchiko asked.

"Five to seven miles an hour."

"I thought so." Lou found it hard to imagine them going so fast. The bot looked so ponderous. "If you'd asked me, I'd have said the best it can do is ten. Can it go even faster?"

Shuska shrugged. "I don't know. I don't know what else that code changed, what other governors it might have released."

Matchiko gave Shuska a startled look. "Do you think it will kill people now?"

Shuska stared at the machine for a long time. "Maybe."

"I bet it would," Lou muttered around a mouthful of breakfast roll. She looked at them, suddenly painfully aware of how lucky she was that they had each other. The three amigas, on an adventure. Lou smiled. "Let's do this."

Shuska smiled. "I want to see what this thing can do, or more accurately, what it will do absent some restrictions."

Matchiko said, "I guess they've always been able to do this. If that's so, why didn't they show us this before?"

Shuska stood up and started gathering their trash. "They're run by an AI network. Maybe it's afraid."

Lou frowned. Shuska often gave more emotions to AIs than Lou thought they had. "Don't go yet. I wanted to ask something."

Both women turned to her. Standing side by side they always looked so mismatched, with Matchiko weighing maybe a third of what Shuska did, but looking more like she weighed a tenth. It made Lou smile for a moment before she grew serious again. "The information we're taking. We know it might be used against the -o boys."

"By people who would destroy all of this." Shuska shook her head. "Don't worry about what you can't control. We need to do this."

Matchiko stood stiffly, arms wrapped around herself and lips thin. "We need to do what we came out here to do. Visit wolf dens. Destroy abandoned falling-down houses full of toxins that stupid people left behind. So let's do this and hope we can find a way to help the -o boys." She paused for a second, smiled softly, and continued in a lower tone. "You used to tell me people die out here. They do. That's how it is. If we spill all the people from the city out here, everything we're doing is for less than nothing."

That was quite a long speech for Matchiko. She was right, but that didn't make Lou feel any less guilty. She sighed and said, "Let's go."

CHAPTER FIFTY

Coryn fidgeted nervously between Imke and Eloise in the crowded loop pod. They'd been unable to get a private car. They sat in front of three people in military uniforms, and an older woman and her companion sat beside Namina in the last row. No one directly mentioned the attacks on loops during the thirty-minute transit, but Coryn noticed that everyone except the robots looked nervous. The old woman held her robot's hand so hard her knuckles were white.

Like Imke and Eloise, Coryn wore simple khaki pants and T-shirts. Eloise had convinced Imke to go with little makeup, so they all looked plain and unassuming. Just travelers out for a ride in the middle of a war.

Everyone in the pod seemed to breathe a collective sigh of relief when the car slowed and docked. Shoulders relaxed, people whispered to each other.

The Spokane station was far smaller than Chicago, with four stationary ticket robots and three wandering security-bots. By the time they climbed out, the three soldiers were already nowhere to be seen, and the old woman was making her way slowly ahead of them, her robot holding her arm to keep her steady.

They made it through the station exit with none of the security robots taking any obvious notice, and rode an escalator to a tram.

The sunset was a dull red wisp of light, and the air felt crisp and tasted of a coming freeze. Coryn sat back against the hard seat, scanning for the lights of Spokane. They looked small and far away. "It's going to take us longer to get to town than it took us to get here from Seacouver."

"Not quite," Eloise said. "Besides, we have time. We're about an hour ahead of them. They'll have to walk in."

"I guess they can't just ride an ecobot into town."

"Not exactly." Eloise tightened her lips and shot a repressive look at Coryn. To stop her from talking? The entire tram car they were in was empty.

How did Eloise know where the others were right now? Coryn glanced down at the newer wristlet that she wore. The screen was annoyingly blank.

The tram dropped into a busy building, where instructions about bikes, cars, and other transportation options flashed info at them.

Coryn perked up. "Can we ride?"

"That's the plan," Eloise said. "But no AR. Spokane doesn't require it, and I want to be less trackable." Her face remained carefully blank, but Coryn thought she saw a happy sparkle in Eloise's eyes. Maybe she liked being out of the city.

Namina found a bank of bicycles outside of the station. Eloise passed her wrist over the machine to release three of them, and one at a time Imke, Coryn, and then Eloise pulled out bikes and tweaked the seats and handlebars to size them. As soon as they sat on them, lights bloomed on under the frames, encircling them in pools of brightness.

Namina ran.

At first, Imke was a bit wobbly, but in a few minutes they steadied, looked back and grinned, and promptly fell with a clatter. Coryn helped them back up, laughing, and Eloise looked grumpy. Soon, they were all back in line, the lights of Imke's bicycle occasionally wavering from side to side.

After about two miles, Eloise stopped at another bike rack. They parked the bikes and walked into a park, the park lights coming on as they entered, and staying on just until they passed, telling the world exactly where they were. Coryn wished they'd stop it, and suspected Eloise wished for the same.

They found a bench and sat, and after a few minutes the lights went off. Eloise whispered, "They're only about fifteen minutes away."

"Why are you whispering?" Imke whispered.

"So the lights won't hear us."

Coryn laughed, and the lights flickered on in response, which earned her a glare from Eloise. They went off again in a minute, and this time Coryn sat as quietly as she could. She had to work not to rock or get up.

A runner went through the park, the lights flicking on and off in a string.

When Coryn set the light above them off a second time by kicking her foot, Eloise silently stood and took her hand as if she were a child and led her out into the grass, a hundred feet or so from any of the lights. They sat on the grass. The lights went out again. Cold settled over them. From time to time, Eloise's wristlet lit up with dull white texts.

A light came on at the far side of the park. Another. The three figures silhouetted in the light were obviously Lou, Matchiko, and Shuska; a jitter of excitement warmed Coryn, banishing the evening's deepening chill. They looked like the three bears from the old children's story—hulking Shuska, willowy Matchiko, and average-sized Lou.

Cory got up and started toward the light, feeling almost like her much-younger self, finally going to see her sister. Imke, Eloise, and Namina followed, a little behind.

They met in a dim spot between lights that threw shadows both in front of them and behind. Coryn fell into Lou's arms and breathed her in. She smelled of night and wood smoke and even a tiny bit of horse. She smelled like everything but the city.

Coryn untangled herself and looked into her sister's face. She'd seen her almost every day in a talking-pictures fashion, or as a tiny figure in satellite shots, but feeling her hand and being close was so much better. Lou had developed tiny lines around her eyes, little wrinkles surely born more of exhaustion and worry than age. Her hair was a mess, and she looked tired and a little angry, but her smile was pure happiness, and her eyes shone with joy as they met Coryn's.

Maybe no one but Coryn would be able to see so much in that face.

But she knew her sister, and knew how hard she'd worked and how heartbreaking the last few months had been.

Eloise pushed them apart. "We have an hour before the loop back to Seacouver. Let's sit down, and you can tell me everything you know."

Lou raised an eyebrow.

They all sat on the grass in a circle, seven women if you counted the robot, or six if you did not. Coryn held Lou's hand as she told her story. From time to time Matchiko added a detail, but Shuska stayed silent. There was a time when she had mistrusted Coryn completely, and, given the guarded look on her face, Coryn decided she still didn't trust her. That was fine. Coryn didn't need to talk to her; she didn't need to say anything. For the moment, it was enough to sit holding Lou's hand and listening to her story.

Eloise asked a number of questions, mostly about Paulette, clearly verifying her as the source of the information. After a while she seemed satisfied that the data was good and not a plant.

When the story was mostly finished, Eloise held her hand out for the wristlet.

Lou held it out, but hesitated. "The men who left town? The ones from Chelan? Can you do anything to protect them?"

"The men who planted nuclear devices in the city?"

Lou winced. "Only a few of them. Valeria's children. They didn't plant the nukes. Saving them might go a long way toward helping us in the future."

"Helping you with what?"

"With this." She waved a hand around the park, but Coryn realized she meant the Outside. "After this, after the city is safe, we'll still be out here. Those are good men. They are the children of my friend." She dropped the wristlet into Eloise's hand. "Please?"

Eloise closed her fist over the prize they'd come for. "I can promise nothing." She glanced down at her own wristlet. "There's twenty minutes before we need to head back to the bikes. Why don't you two take a walk?"

"Thanks," Coryn said.

"And try not to set off any lights."

Coryn took Lou's hand again, and they walked off toward a dark spot on the lawn, far from paths or lights. "I wonder how much fun Eloise will have with Shuska?" Coryn mused.

"My two can take care of themselves," Lou replied. "I meant it about Valeria's boys. I'd like to see them make it home."

Coryn swallowed. "Of course."

"Who's that with you? The boy?"

"Imke's not a boy or a girl. They're my . . . friend, though."

"Is that what's keeping you so busy?"

Coryn laughed. "I wish. We've been working the EOC, and before that we were traveling back and forth between Chicago and Seacouver."

"We?"

Coryn's cheeks grew hot. "We both have the same job."

"They're not taking care of me."

"That's not what I meant. We are both working for diplomats. Imke works for the Chicago mayor. And they play in two bands."

"Ah. Struck in love by the band," Lou teased. "You're such a city girl. Surely there's more to tell me?"

Coryn couldn't. Not yet. What she had with Imke was too fragile to share it all. "I wish you could see my apartment. I love it. I can see the ocean."

"Is that robot yours?"

"I don't know. Julianna at least loaned her to me." She talked about Julianna and Jake for a bit, and choked up when she told Lou about Jake's death. "You can't tell anyone, though," she said.

Lou hugged her close, and Coryn almost let herself dissolve into tears. She was so tired. But she couldn't bear the idea of spending this unexpected gift of time with Lou crying.

Lou cleared her throat. "Can I talk to you about something?"

"Of course."

"It's Valeria and her family. Not the runaway boys, although I care about them, too. But about an idea. Valeria calls it *keeping*."

"Keeping?"

"Right now, outside of the towns, there's only Wilders. Supposedly. We're all that's legal, anyway. Except Listeners, who mostly all got killed."

"Right."

"Well, what about small farming? Allowing some. Vegetables and chickens. Not cattle or pigs or anything big. Nothing that needs ranges, nothing that would undo the work we're doing. People who couldn't get a job wilding but who can't bear the cities would have a way to go on, to be out here."

Coryn frowned. "Isn't that the opposite of everything that established the wilding?"

"I don't think it would be right to offer land ownership. Just leasing."

It still seemed like going backward to Coryn. "You mean sharecropping?"

Lou sighed. "We just might need some other way. What we're doing might be too extreme, and might be part of why there's nuclear bombs in the city. Everyone has to live there now. But I think some people could live lightly on the land these days. Valeria calls it *keeping* because she sees it as complimentary to wilding."

"You listen to Valeria a lot. Is she like Julianna to you?"

"No." Lou seemed to be struggling for words. "I can't let her make all the choices. I can't give her too much power. I'm responsible for Outside-N, and I'm more beholden to Julianna for that than to Valeria." Lou paused and listened. An owl hooted from somewhere across the park, and Lou smiled in response. Then she continued. "She's survived out there for a long time. I learned a lot from her. And she's helped me. But I have to be her equal even though she's older than me."

"I think I understand," Coryn whispered.

"Just take the idea back."

"Okay. Julianna told me *we* need to decide on the world now anyway."

"We?"

"The young. But we have to get through this crisis first."

Lou sighed. "I know."

The raw tone in Lou's voice made Coryn wish she could help her. "I can't promise anything. About keeping. About Valeria's boys. I'm not that important."

"Of course you can't. Not by yourself. But you could come stay with us for a little this summer, after this is all over."

"You're pretty optimistic," Coryn observed.

"Aren't you?"

"I'm not sure how it will be without Jake. What I'll do. What resources we'll have. Any of us."

Lou hugged her again. "Of course you aren't. It will be okay. There's no other choice. We aren't our parents, you know? We'll find a way forward."

"Always."

They both laughed.

Coryn's wristlet flashed a command. *Time.*

As they walked back, Coryn found herself dragging her feet. She forced herself to pick up. She needed to get back. They had to find out if the data Lou had brought them was true. And if it was, they had to find the bombs. If they didn't find the bombs, she might never see Lou again. Coryn slipped her hand into her sister's hand and squeezed.

Lou leaned over and kissed her on the forehead.

CHAPTER FIFTY-ONE

At the doorway to the loop station, Imke paused and drew Coryn's attention with a touch on her shoulder. "I'm going from here to Chicago. The route is still open, and I have to tell the mayor."

Startled, Coryn bit back a protest. She should have known. She took in a deep breath, adjusted. "Of course you are. Will you be able to tell if your EOCs are compromised?"

"I know people who will." Imke glanced down at their clothes. "But first, I'll have to change. No one will recognize me looking so plain."

Coryn smiled.

Imke took her hand and squeezed it. Their voice was husky as they said, "Stay safe. I'll see you soon."

"You, too," Coryn replied, a little lump in her throat.

Eloise, Namina, and Coryn were the only three people in their pod. They took the front row. Namina sat beside Coryn, and Eloise across the aisle.

As soon as they left, Eloise said, "You really need to be more careful. Inside, you can be as crazy as you want. You're young. But Outside? Never, never draw attention."

Was Eloise still mad about the park lights? "Isn't Spokane Metro a city?"

"Not a megacity. It's far more dangerous than Seacouver."

She didn't like Eloise's tone of voice, but she had to ask. "Why not?"

"The city itself isn't as sophisticated."

"What does that even mean?" Coryn asked. "Is 'the city' even an entity? Do you mean the systems aren't as sophisticated?"

Eloise turned toward Coryn, looking just condescending enough to get Coryn's back up.

Coryn continued. "Seacouver looks far more hacked than Spokane at the moment. All of the systems here work. The damned park lights worked." She almost giggled. "Too well."

Eloise did not look amused. "You should not underestimate the dangers Outside."

"You think I don't know that?" Coryn snapped. When she heard her own tone of voice, she managed to get out a "sorry."

Eloise nodded but said nothing at all.

"It doesn't matter," Coryn said into her silence. "We're leaving anyway."

Eloise remained stoic, which made Coryn feel like Eloise thought she was stupid. But maybe she was just tired. And frightened. *Nukes in the cities.*

She didn't want to sleep, but she started to drift down anyway, half-dreaming of Lou standing on an ecobot's back.

Klaxons screamed at her, startling her awake. The brakes slammed on.

Her body kept going forward. Her seatbelt dug into her shoulder and waist.

Namina's arm shot out and cushioned her head, protecting it from hitting the metal handrail in front of her.

Eloise's head smacked into the metal of the railing. She flopped back in the seat, bounced again, and moaned.

The brakes kept screeching in Coryn's ears.

Oxygen masks flipped down from holes in the roof. Namina reached for one, but Coryn said, "Eloise," and pulled the mask in front of her toward her mouth.

Namina crossed to Eloise, her balance perfect even in the wildly slowing car.

Coryn tightened the elastic band that held her oxygen mask on and gasped for breath, trying to control her hammering heart.

She couldn't tell if the mask was working, except that it must be since she was okay. She reached for her seatbelt buckle, but Namina looked up from Eloise's side and said, "Not yet. Wait until we stop."

The whine of the brakes rose so high Coryn slapped her hands over her ears. After a final squeal, the car lurched to a halt, silent except for a hiss of escaping air.

Namina walked backward, toward a panel marked as an emergency door. She threw it open and looked both ways. "Here!" she called.

Coryn unbuckled, but the oxygen mask didn't give her enough play to do more than just turn. She leaned down and shook Eloise, who huffed in a deep breath through the mask but didn't open her eyes. Coryn's voice shook. "She's not okay."

"I know. I'll carry her. Come here."

"Really?" She plucked at the elastic holding her mask on.

"Take a breath," Namina instructed patiently, "drop it, come back here, pick up this one. Besides, it's not oxygen-free in here. Just low from depressurizing."

Of course.

Namina's instructions worked, and Coryn soon peered through the doorway that the robot had opened.

"See that number on the wall?" Namina asked.

"Fifteen? Followed by L?"

"That means it's fifteen yards left from here to the next doorway to the service access path. As long as the tube stays depressurized, the door to the service path will open."

"What if it doesn't?"

"It will. You can hold your breath for fifteen yards. If you have to let air out and take some in, do it. There's still fourteen percent oxygen in the air, but it could drop fast. As you get closer to the door, there will be more, since the air in the service path is from outside. You'll be able to breathe there."

"Do you want me to open the door?"

"No. I will go first. You follow. After you're through, I'm going back for Eloise."

Coryn nodded. "Go. I'll stay here."

Namina practically flowed through the thin space between the pod and the wall. She barely fit, and Coryn had the fleeting thought that they were lucky it was them. Shuska wouldn't fit, and Lou would find it close.

Namina pressed on the wall.

Nothing.

She kicked.

Nothing.

She stopped and stared, and kicked again, and her leg passed through the wall. Something clunked on the far side. She stepped through the doorway and moved whatever she had kicked through. Her head poked back into the corridor and she gestured to Coryn.

Coryn took a deep breath and slid out sideways, nervous about leaving Eloise alone. She had to twist to get into the narrow passage. The claustrophobia made her want to gasp for breath. She used the palms of her hands to push away from the wall and stay upright, shuffling her feet, lurching. How had Namina moved through here gracefully?

The opening seemed to be far more than fifteen yards away.

She made it, blowing out a breath only as she felt Namina's hands pull her through. She breathed in. Again.

She met Namina's eyes. "It's fine."

"It's only eighteen percent right here, which might make you less coordinated, but I think it will be normal after we leave this door."

Handy to have a walking sensor with you when you needed one.

Something clattered from inside the pod.

Namina turned and slid back through the doorway. She returned with Eloise over her shoulder in a fireman's carry, her arms swinging back and forth. "She stood up and ripped her mask off and then fell."

"Is she okay?"

"She's probably dizzy. But she's breathing. The inside of the car is no worse than the top of a mountain."

Blood stained Eloise's hair, dripping onto the floor slowly. "Can you tell how badly she's hurt?"

Namina shook her head. "I had to move her anyway. Hopefully her spine is okay. If so, if we get back to the city safely, she should be fine."

"Then let's go. I need to get this data back."

"Follow me."

"What if we run into whoever did this?"

Some of Namina's makeup had smeared, which made her a look a little more human and a little less like a robot. "The value in the attack is holding up loop traffic. There's probably no one nearby who had anything to do with it."

Their mission mattered. "Shouldn't I have the wristlet? Eloise can't defend it, and you need to be free to defend Eloise."

Namina paused, cocking her head for a moment as if she were a curious dog. But then she laid Eloise down carefully. She tugged the wristlet out of Eloise's front pocket, handing it to Coryn.

It felt warm from Eloise's body heat. Coryn closed her fingers around it and slid it into her own pocket. "What about other people? Was there anyone else on the train?"

"If there was, by now they're safely sipping oxygen or they're dead. You said it yourself, we have to get the data to the city."

Coryn took a deep breath. "I don't want to leave people to die."

"I'd have to breach the pods. That might make them worse off, or mean we have to move at the slowest speed of whoever is in them."

And right now, they could move at Coryn's speed. "Okay. You're right. Let's go." She turned and started off, fighting a wave of guilt. But the data on Paulette's wristlet might save many more lives than they could save here.

The service walkway was wider than the thin place they'd just had to sneak through. Coryn could jog, so she did.

The tunnel had absolutely no natural or artificial light, but Namina handed her a handlight, which she used to illuminate the floor in front of them.

From time to time they passed doors to the left just like the one Namina had kicked though, but there were no windows or doors that led out.

The path felt endless.

Their footsteps slid along the metal, their voices loud in the confined space even when they whispered. At least the seal was good and they didn't have to contend with spiders or rats.

Coryn wished for water, or an energy gel, but she had nothing. She just kept thinking about nukes and about Julianna and home and the need to keep moving as quickly as possible.

The path began to slope down.

Coryn managed to gasp out a question. "Why isn't there a door?"

"We're underground here."

"Do you know where we are?"

"The loop route goes through North Bend. I'm pretty sure that's the exit. That might also be where the damage is, so if you see light, be careful."

Eloise coughed.

"Wait!" Namina set Eloise down carefully and stood over her.

Eloise coughed again and then put her hand to the top of her head. "My head hurts."

"We got in a wreck," Coryn said.

"On the loop?"

"Tell me what our plans were," Namina told her.

"Were?" Eloise looked confused, but then she brightened and said, "We have to get the data to the city."

"Yes," Coryn said. "I have it now. I'm not hurt, and as soon as we get out of here, I'll run with it. Namina will stay with you."

Eloise looked uncertain.

Coryn turned to Namina. "Is there water anywhere? She needs water."

"I know. My calculations suggest we are near the opening, and there will be water outside. We should keep going."

"What?" Eloise mumbled.

"We don't know what happened. The pods stopped. Sabotage, probably."

Eloise narrowed her eyes and managed a complete sentence. "Are you okay? You sound a little . . . I don't know."

"I'm thirsty," Coryn said. "I'm okay except for that. We've got to get out of here, and then I can run back to the city."

Eloise pushed herself up, but swayed and sat back down. "I can't—" She held her hand out, and Coryn took it. Eloise rose, swayed, but this time kept her feet. Dried blood stuck in her tangled hair and a steak of it ran down her cheek. Her eyes looked like she was staring into bright light. She looked at Namina. "Aren't there any emergency supplies?"

"They were in the pods. We didn't take one—I was in a hurry to get you out. It might have blown up. The train. We're probably far past the train now." Namina banged on the outside of the cylinder. "That's empty."

Eloise nodded. "We'd best keep going."

Coryn started off, moving more slowly. Dehydration tugged at her, wanting her to stop and rest.

A tall glass of water would be heaven.

"Faster," Namina said.

Coryn glanced behind her; Namina had picked up Eloise again. The other woman's face was the color of bone.

The slope increased, taking them farther downhill. It began to feel warmer.

Her head throbbed from dehydration and hunger. It hadn't been that long since the accident or the sabotage or whatever. Maybe an hour. She hadn't stopped to drink before they got on, and maybe not since they'd left Seacouver. Her focus had been on Lou. She'd been moving ever since.

She kept going.

After twenty more minutes, she spotted dull light ahead, more a softer shade of dark rather than a real light. She slowed.

Namina mouthed, "Go on. There's nobody there. Not unless it's all robots."

Unlikely. Coryn crept forward.

The dim, diffuse light brightened as she went. Some. It was the light of night, but still far brighter than the tunnel had been. They were taking a long and very slow curve and when they got far enough along, it was possible to see that they were about to run into a jagged hole in the loop infrastructure. Too bad they hadn't been two minutes further ahead. They'd have been through the hole then, and already back in Seacouver now.

"Turn your light off," Namina said. "You wait. I'll go." She put Eloise back down and slid carefully and silently past Coryn, moving very slowly to the jagged edge.

It held her weight without a jitter.

She crawled the last few feet, leaning over the edge and looking down before she started back. When she reached Coryn and Eloise, she said, "There's no one there. Not that I see."

And her senses would be good. Paula had been able to see heat as well as the things humans saw. She'd had better hearing, too. Namina was newer, and probably far more sensitive. "How high up are we?"

"That's the problem. Thirty feet or so. I'll go down, and then you have to drop Eloise to me, carefully, and then you have to drop down to me."

"Okay. Let's do it."

Eloise woke as Namina picked her back up, and they explained the plan as they walked carefully toward the opening.

When Coryn peered over the edge, the drop looked impossible. The tops of trees bristled below her. Coryn contemplated the jump. There were ragged edges to avoid. The pipe was essentially double walled. They had been walking through the space between the walls. The circle where the pod usually traveled looked bigger than she expected, the top of it far above them now that they had moonlight to see by. The outer circle that they were in was even bigger than that. A monstrosity of engineering.

The break had dropped the once-continuous loop track into a

jumble of sharp materials that had shattered trees. A few pieces of the tube had rolled partway down a slope before being stopped by cedars big enough to stop them.

"That was a big explosion," Eloise said.

It seemed like some kind of rescue should be on the way. Drones or military or bots or something. But the scene was eerily quiet. An owl hooted, somewhere below them in the dark tree canopy. Another owl answered.

Namina leaned over the edge, her balance looking precarious. She stared at the ground, probably seeing things Coryn couldn't. "There's some open ground. No rocks. Just a few saplings. To the right and ten feet out." She glanced back at Coryn, and before Coryn could object, she continued. "I'm going. I'll signal you with an extra loud hoot when I'm ready for you to help Eloise slide off."

Eloise nodded, looking completely unworried. She remained professional and inscrutable in spite of her bloodstained clothes and the bruise becoming evident on her right cheek even in the dark. Or maybe she was too out of it to be worried. It was hard to tell.

Namina slid off of the ragged edge.

Branches broke.

An owl hoot floated up, loud but very, very natural.

Was that real or Namina?

The sound came again.

Eloise nodded, scooting toward the side. "Push me," she whispered.

Coryn pushed, gently, with a whispered, "Sorry." She cringed.

This time there was only a small crackle of branches and a light thud, followed by silence.

The owl hooted again.

Coryn took a deep breath and dropped.

Strong hands caught her before she expected. Namina had jumped up to slow her fall. They landed together, hard, the impact jarring. Pain shuddered up from her heels and through her legs, but when she tried to move them, they worked. Nothing had broken.

Coryn looked back up. They'd dropped about two stories. She glanced at Namina, "Thanks."

Eloise leaned on a tree, holding her head.

"Water," Coryn said. "You promised water."

Eloise wiped her bloody hand clean on her shirt and slipped it into her coat pocket. She pulled out a small container of white pills and an empty plastic sack. "Take this. It will purify water. I hear a stream."

"Wow. What else do you carry around?"

Eloise smiled in spite of her obvious pain. "That's for me to know."

Namina took the sack. "I'll get it." She slipped between two trees and was gone.

Coryn checked her wristlet for news. The *unconnected* icon blinked on and off in the upper right face. There had been connectivity in the loop, but out here?

Eloise whispered. "I can't run. I can barely walk."

"I'll leave you Namina."

"Maybe she should go with you." Eloise slid down the tree trunk and groaned. "She's harder to destroy."

Coryn glanced around. "You need her. I can't send her on her own."

Eloise glared at her.

Coryn was too tired to let Eloise's attitude go, no matter how hurt she was. "Don't go silent on me. You're important to Julianna. So I'm not going to leave you out here by yourself."

Eloise's face was only dimly lit, but a pale smile seemed to appear momentarily on her face. "Don't fuck up."

"I won't."

Namina came back with sack full of water. She started to hand it to Eloise, but Eloise waved it toward Coryn. "Coryn's running. Water her first."

Coryn smiled. She wasn't a dog. But she took the sack and tugged on the fat straw that stuck out of it. It did taste as much like heaven as she expected. She left some, but Eloise said, "Take it. Carry it with you. I have another sack. We'll be okay."

"Are you sure?"

"Go!"

Namina pointed. "I-90's a little over a mile south. You can take that. Do you know the way once you hit the interstate?"

Coryn smiled. "I took that route once. This time, it will be downhill."

Eloise whispered, "Good luck."

Coryn assessed. Trees and blackberries and rocks. Mostly evergreens, with an occasional winter-bare tree pointing black branches at the dark sky. No path. Not even an obvious game trail. Trees and debris blocked her way in all directions.

The wristlet burned in her mind, in her pocket.

"Expect it to be slow going," Namina said. "It looks to me that you can go east a ways and then turn south. You'll have to cross a few streams, but it looks like it will be passable."

Eloise whispered, "Don't use your light unless you have to."

Because there could be enemies around? She didn't even ask. That meant don't use her own wristlet as well—it gave off an amazing amount of light in this much darkness. Its ability to give her directions would be slim here anyway. She just took a deep breath and started off. The forest was too dense to run through. It had not been burned or rewilded here. Big trees towered over her, and vining things pulled at her legs.

A few minutes into her trek, she put a foot down and it kept going, as if there was nothing under it. She grabbed blackened winter blackberry bushes to keep from falling into a hole she hadn't seen at all. Maybe an animal den?

The woods smelled of mulch and rot and water.

Some of the places she slid through would clearly be impassable in spring. Now they were slippery with rotten leaves.

Lights flashed briefly some distance away. She stilled for a few moments, then kept going, moving even slower.

A large animal of some kind rustled away from her.

A swirling, gurgling sound and a thick, bright darkness identified a stream. She made it halfway across before her foot slid on an underwater rock and she went down on one knee, one hand in the cold water, one knuckle jammed when she caught herself. She forced herself to stop right there and make more drinkable water, and to have some.

The water cleared her head. She thought about following the stream, but a tree blocked her way so she kept bulling through underbrush, finally settling on a strategy of moving from big tree to big tree. Cedars kept the ground under them a little clear and the footing was better there. She could push into the branches, smell the crushed needles under her feet, and catch a short breath.

A bit of pale light showed in the sky. The beginning of dawn. That would be east, and she was heading too directly toward it, so she adjusted to leave it at her left shoulder. The light drove her. A reminder of how much time had passed.

She stumbled out of the woods and into a ditch beside I-90. The road was empty in both directions.

She drank the last bit of water from her bag, shoved it in her waistband, and started off at a slow jog. The even, reliable footing was heaven, the lights of the city ahead of her a beacon, the rising light of day a flail.

She ran, thinking about how she was going to get back into the city and about bombs and about Lou and about Imke.

The loop train had broken about midnight, and she had been jogging, or jumping, or running ever since. She had run for longer, but not much, and not with scrapes and bruises and a hurt knuckle, not with no food.

She couldn't go as fast as she wanted to.

She started singing silly little songs and remembering the lions that used to chase her through AR worlds. Then she remembered Whitman.

I am Larger! Better than I Thought!

It gave her speed and balance. She remembered running with Tambara, the fast pace and cadence, the smooth beauty of Tambara's legs. The way she had raced to win, had won.

I am Larger! Better than I Thought!

A convoy of silent electric trucks headed toward her, and she stopped beside the road, jogging in place to keep her muscles warm while they passed.

When she started again the small break had given her some speed back, or maybe she was just way past caring, in some weird place where the exhausted could run forever.

Her shadow was a long gangly runner in front of her, thin as a stick. She laughed.

I am Larger! Better than I Thought!

The lights of a car came up toward her. She slowed and ducked under a tree. The car stopped, and Blessing climbed out.

She nearly swooned at the sight of him, found she could barely move.

He called out, "Coryn! I know you're here."

She found the strength to take steps to him, falling into his arms. His hug hurt her scraped and bruised skin, but she didn't care.

"We have to get to Julianna."

"I know." He stroked her hair.

CHAPTER FIFTY-TWO

When Blessing and Coryn arrived at Julianna's, they found her in the recliner, covered in a blue-and-gray blanket Jake had loved. His body had been removed and the sheets stripped, but Julianna clutched the blanket as if she were a child with a toy. A cup of hot tea sat untouched on the table beside her.

Coryn knelt in front of her and took her hands. She looked into her eyes, searching, trying to be sure Julianna was really there and even capable of listening. It was hard to tell. Blessing had assured her that he'd seen Julianna rally in bad situations. But the old woman sat so still it was hard to tell if she even knew they were there.

Coryn took a deep breath and pushed her panic away, hiding it from her voice. "Eloise is hurt, but Namina is with her. Blessing told your security staff where. I've brought the data from the farm. Eloise, Imke, Namina, and I believe it is very possible there are nuclear devices in the city. In many cities. I understand they are supposed to go off on New Year's Day. That's two days from now. But it could be sooner. We need to find out."

Julianna managed to nod, and her eyes began to focus. "Say that all again?"

Coryn did.

At the end, Julianna leaned forward and licked her lips. Coryn brought her water, which she drank.

Since Julianna was looking directly at her now, Coryn kept going. "The city's main EOC—not ours, but the one the mayor is in—was compromised. Blessing said that's still true." She glanced at Blessing, hoping for guidance. Julianna wasn't going to find the nukes. Blessing steadied her with a hand on her shoulder, and she swallowed and dug in. "We have to tell more people than us."

Julianna sat up and pushed the blanket back, blinking at Coryn. "Can you say that all again?"

She did, using almost exactly the same words.

"I understand." Julianna's tone had become crisp again. She picked up her tea. "Go on."

"Blessing and I talked on the way in. We think it's best to create a mini-EOC in here while we verify the data. Or at least read it before we send it on. Imke is taking the information—but not a copy of the data—to Chicago. So it will be out soon, or maybe it already is at some level. We'll send her a copy after we pass it to our EOC, but we need to know what we have."

"No sense in starting a panic," Julianna said.

"That's right." That had been a coherent thought. "Can I call Adam?"

"Okay." Julianna glanced at her. "Will you sit with me?"

"After I reach Adam." Coryn messaged Adam to come immediately, pulled up a chair, and sat down. Evan brought her tea, his handsome, robotic face settled into a quietly pleased expression as he handed it to her. Blessing sat in a chair on the other side of the room, staring at his wristlet. Probably contacting Day.

Julianna smiled up at Evan, and asked, "Can you call the mayor for me, please? Tell him I'd like him to come in person, and to bring a single human security guard."

Evan stepped through the door to place the call, and Coryn leaned over to Julianna. "We haven't even read the data yet."

"We know what it is, or what your sister says it is. That's too big to keep quiet."

She took Julianna's free hand in hers. "I agree. Thank you." She felt lighter to think others would know. "But will he come?"

"Probably not. But now we have cover, in case this is real. You should remember that." She leaned forward, still clutching the blanket, and met Coryn's eyes squarely. "Whenever you have a secret that's too hot to share, develop a plausible story for how you tried to share it. If it starts to look true, we'll draw more attention to it by screaming louder."

Coryn dropped Julianna's hand and sat back, thinking. "We don't want to tell the whole city until we're certain because of the panic it might cause. But just in case the bombs go off, we need people to know we planned to tell them." She didn't like the words as she said them. They sounded cold.

"If I trusted the city's systems, I'd tell everyone now."

Why was the world so complex? It made her want to slam the wall with her fist. But that would just result in Evan standing between her and Julianna. She took a calming breath and a sip of tea. At least Julianna seemed happy to have political problems to deal with. So Coryn kept going. "Just so I understand, what I hear you saying is that we don't know if there are any nukes. If this is a ruse to frighten us and we panic people, then our enemies can do more damage. Is that what you mean?"

Julianna said, "Much of the campaign against us is misinformation. The faster they can send lies to us and have us believe them, the more off-balance we are. The source of this data is Chelan. It's a plausible source for true information. But it could still be a plant."

Coryn swallowed hard and tried to think. She was tired, but she had instincts. "I think it's true."

"Because your sister is the source? The best lies come from sources we trust." Julianna struggled to push the blanket off of her shoulders. "I'm too hot. We should get this place ready. There'll be ten people working in here in ten minutes." She glanced at Coryn's arms, which were bleeding lightly from encounters with berry bushes even though she'd cleaned them up once.

Coryn went and washed, then helped Julianna fold the blanket and set it on the chair. By the time they finished, Julianna appeared to have buried her grief. She stood fairly straight as she pulled a box of the tablets and paper and pencils Jake had loved to take notes with out of a cabinet.

Evan stepped back inside. "The call went through. I don't know if

Mayor Arroya will get it in the current chaos. But I recorded it. Eloise is on her way in, as well."

Already?

"Thank you." Julianna managed a smile. "Help me get the room ready for a crowd?"

Evan took the box from Julianna, who began rearranging chairs. Coryn went to the small kitchen and rummaged for a pitcher of water and clean glasses.

As she worked, Coryn watched Julianna out of the corner of her eye. She looked so . . . unbroken. Like she and Lou had been, she supposed, after their parents died. You just kept going. Imke, too, had simply left her and gone to do what they had to do. Coryn dialed up the lights in the room and set the air freshener to release a light, healthy citrus.

Evan made the empty bed, even though it didn't particularly need it. He unfolded the blue-and-gray blanket and refolded it into a neat rectangle, everything orderly. Jake had liked neatness.

Blessing looked up a few times, but otherwise he was fully engaged with his technology.

The air had already shifted from sickroom to office by the time a light bell announced the arrival of the elevator. Eloise, Adam, Day, and a woman she'd never met walked in. Eloise had cleaned up, although her hair was wet from a quick shower and dripped onto her clothes. She had a bandage on one arm, but no bandage on her head. She went to Julianna and held her, muttering, "I'm so sorry."

The stranger's skin was nearly as dark as Blessing's. Her black and gray hair lay in fine beaded corn rows, and she wore a bright yellow dress that set off everything dark and beautiful about her. She gave Julianna a hug. "I'm so sorry."

Julianna's smile wavered for only a moment, and then she turned to Coryn. "This is my personal assistant, Coryn Williams. Coryn, this is my chief data scientist, and Adam's boss, Serena Hingbe."

Personal Assistant? Maybe that was just the easiest way for Julianna to introduce her. Adam had never told her he had a boss other than Julianna! Questions for another day. Coryn extended a hand. "Nice to meet you, Serena."

"Likewise." Serena met her handshake, her hand a bit like a bird's, with long bones and strong, slender fingers. Serena turned immediately to work, assessing tools and chatting with Eloise and Adam. Day stayed with them, and Blessing went to Evan, asking him questions.

Coryn couldn't quite tell what was being done, but it looked like Serena was running programs against the diary, some kind of diagnostic that looked for keywords. Adam double-checked her and cut out pieces of text with dates and location words in it. Another program parsed that data through city cameras, and time after time, Eloise marked its output, the look on her face growing steadily grimmer.

A mere thirty minutes after they'd walked in, Serena looked over at Julianna. "I think this is authentic. We can pass it on."

Julianna nodded. "Do it."

Serena nodded. She picked up her tablet and sent a code. Coryn sat back to wait, feeling shell-shocked; she looked around the room and saw her own shock repeated on each face.

The mayor hadn't come.

Julianna took Coryn's hand, pulling her away from the table and back to the recliner. "I need to move."

"You want to run? Now? What about the mayor?"

"I'm just going to the roof. Just walking. I've got to clear my head. It's full of mush and grief. Fresh air will help." She glanced at Evan. "Please come get me if anything happens."

Evan nodded, and Coryn slipped a pair of running shoes on.

No public elevator led to the roof. Although there was a private elevator in the back of the hallway, Julianna insisted that they take the stairs.

Even though Julianna was far slower than usual, Coryn could barely keep up with her. Her limbs were stiff from the long walk, the run, and then riding back with no cool down. One ankle was slightly swollen. Midday sun beat down on the roof garden.

She had been awake over twenty-four hours.

Julianna set the pace. She started slow and accelerated to a fast enough walk that Coryn had to work to stay with her. Coryn stared down at the city, wondering what worked and what didn't. What parts had been hacked? Smoke rose from two places in the distance, curling inside the dome and running slowly out. The dome's field was designed for that. Otherwise, the city looked normal except for the largely empty streets.

Somewhere inside the dome, engineers and programmers waged war with other engineers and programmers. The good guys were trying to protect the city's systems, but they probably weren't winning everywhere. They hadn't been yesterday, when she was bouncing between EOCs.

Cyberwar was fast. Blessing had warned her that they could win or lose in an instant and have nothing but cleanup left.

A few sirens went by far below them, the police cars looking like toys.

Julianna must have noticed her attention as she led her to an overlook that showed two rooftop parks below them, and below that another park. "It looks peaceful."

"I feel like it's damaged."

Julianna leaned out over the guardrail, looking down. "The streets *are* too empty. But the city's systems have many layers. They all connect at the middle, but hackers would need to get deep and far to cripple us. They can hurt us at the edge, but they can't kill the city from the edge."

"But it *could* happen."

"Of course. Any system can be compromised, and we have many. But the city has an ethic. The systems here have ethics. We layered them in, everywhere. The same things we talk about—we put them into code. Equality. Health. Sustainability. It might be enough."

"How will we know?"

"We win." Julianna turned away from the view of the city. "Or we don't. Human history has always been about change. We've held onto power for over thirty years here. Study history. That's a lot of time for the same kind of leaders to run a city."

"Mayor Arroya isn't like you."

Julianna laughed. "Oh yes he is. He has different priorities. But he is like us in all the most important ways. He believes in cities, in humanity, and in wilding."

"Doesn't he want to go to space?"

Julianna started off at her fast walk again, and Coryn jogged a few steps to catch up. "So he's not as optimistic as we were. Space is a coward's way off the earth, and he is afraid." She swept a hand out at the city. "Maybe he should be? How would I begin to say, now? We had to keep everything positive, keep the messages all about hope. We were so close to so many horrible tipping points."

"We still are, aren't we?" Coryn asked.

"Of course. Some are different ones, though. We haven't saved the wild yet, but we're closer. We've figured out how to get power to everyone, everywhere, without fossil fuels. When I was little, power was hard and damaging. Now it's free and everywhere. We've created ways to recycle almost everything we use. We live in relative peace in the cities."

Coryn broke in. "Not right now."

Julianna smiled. "Relative. There have been peaceful periods as long as two decades in my life. At least in this corner of the world."

Coryn nodded.

"We haven't stopped the methane releases in the arctic. We should have expected the Returners to become dangerous, but we didn't. We thought they'd fade away." She waved her hand again, this time at the air. A gesture that seemed to say the list was longer but not worth talking about.

Coryn remembered what Lou had said about the concept of Keepers, but she didn't have time to bring it up. Blessing was coming toward them on the round track, moving fast.

He was nearly out of breath when he reached them. "Calgary," he gasped out. "A bomb. Inside the city. Five city blocks."

"A nuclear bomb?" Julianna asked, her voice hard and serious.

Blessing swallowed and nodded.

Julianna's eyes showed steel rather than the fear that coursed through Coryn. "Only one?"

"All I know of. I came right here."

The wristlet Eloise had given her jolted the inside of her forearm. Coryn twisted and held her arm up, shifting to keep the sunshine off of the screen. "Two bombs found in Chicago. Bring Julianna back."

Coryn would have stumbled if Blessing hadn't caught her and stabilized her. He looked down at her and smiled. "A good day."

She knew. A good day to die.

CHAPTER FIFTY-THREE

Julianna, Blessing, and Coryn rushed down the stairs from the rooftop and into Julianna's room. It had been transformed. Three new tables had been set up, and displays showed newscasters, an interview with Mayor Arroya, and a protest in the streets. Four more people now crowded into the room. Namina was there as well, working beside Evan, running a table with a sign-in sheet and vests, handing out water and snacks as people came in. Two young women Coryn had never seen sat in a corner, probably to run messages and errands.

As Coryn stared at it, one of the displays switched to Calgary. Drone footage from inside the city showed buildings with structural supports blown outward, debris shattering in the ground, nano-walls trying to self-heal. Companions walked the streets, carrying humans. Humans ran.

A *nuke*.

Were they all dead?

The display switched to a drone outside the city. Smoke rose from somewhere in the upper right part of the dome, curling inside of it. Namina jostled her.

"They're not letting the smoke out," Coryn whispered.

"Of course not. It's toxic."

Coryn stared.

Namina pushed a green vest labeled *Liaison* into Coryn's arms. She hesitated, wanting to stay here, but then Blessing took a vest as well. He looked down at her. "I'm no data scientist, but we can do this together."

She nodded. "All right." She fumbled for her AR glasses and ran a brush through her hair quickly. "Ready."

Namina had gone to stand by the open door, yielding her place at the table to Evan.

Coryn said, "We can find our way."

Namina smiled one of her more enigmatic smiles. "I will be taking you someplace different."

So not the main EOC? Ten minutes later, she and Blessing were following Namina through tunnels. Fifteen minutes after they started through the tunnels, they arrived at a nondescript doorway guarded by a single military robot. Beyond the door, a small vestibule was crowded by seven more military robots, two companion robots with fully humanoid features and dress—one eerily similar to Coryn's old companion, Paula, and the other a small companion that looked like she was impersonating a teenaged girl. The young-looking robot opened the door to let Blessing and Coryn in.

Namina remained behind.

Two human male guards passed wands over them. Inside, they found Mayor Arroya, three or four city officials Coryn recognized vaguely from videos and news clips, and the woman she'd met at Julianna's, Serena. She hadn't even noticed her absence in the hubbub of the expanding operation in Julianna's rooms. Serena nodded to her, and one of the human guards directed them to sit in chairs along the wall. A discussion was clearly just finishing.

A television screen showed continued images from Calgary, and on a separate screen she saw Mayor Broadbridge speaking. Without the sound up, she couldn't tell what he said, but he looked calm and professional like always.

Serena said something quietly to the mayor and then came right over to Blessing and Coryn, holding out envelopes. "Take these. One goes to the main EOC and one to Julianna."

Coryn and Blessing shared a glance. She wanted to see the city laid below her again, but Julianna had named her as her assistant. She should go to her. So she took the one for Julianna, and Blessing took the other.

Namina went with Coryn.

Back at Julianna's, Adam paced, twisting his beautiful hair in his fingers. Julianna waited in the recliner and smiled at her as she brought the missive from Mayor Arroya over.

To Coryn's surprise, it was a handwritten note. Julianna held it out to Coryn to read out loud.

Thank you for finding the information about the nukes. We will find them. Continue your own efforts. The core city systems are still standing, but it may be a matter of time. The main EOC did need help.

Coryn glanced at Julianna. "Does that mean it was hacked?"

"Yes. But he can't say that directly. Even on paper. Neither can you. Ever."

"I know that." Coryn returned to the paper. *I have ordered offensive actions. Open your code book to find a feed from the satellites we launched a few months ago. Thank you for your support.*

That didn't seem like much, but Julianna was happy with the message. "He's clearing us," she said. "Now if anything happens, we have this to say that we were on the city's side, on the mayor's side."

Adam whooped, and all eyes turned to him. "I think I found one." He looked ecstatic, maybe happier than he did when he won a race. She expected him to launch into telling them how he found the bomb, but he caught himself and asked, "Can I send someone after it?"

"Send the coordinates to the mayor."

Adam smiled and wrote them down on paper while Julianna composed a handwritten note in response.

Coryn found herself running again, this time racing behind Namina. They used the same elevator they had used before, and traveled down to the tunnels quickly. It failed to stop anywhere on the way down. "Is this locked for just us?" Coryn asked.

"Yes."

This time, there was no security except the wand swiping across the front of her body, but even that seemed to take a long time.

One of the officials took the note from her. "Shall I stay?" she asked.

"No."

So she was back at Julianna's in time to get another address, and she ran that to the mayor as well.

Twice, she passed Blessing briefly, and once he brought a message to the mayor's EOC at the same time that she did, and after that they were both sent back. She'd had no time to catch up on news, but in the main EOC Blessing would have been bashed about the head with status reports. "What's happening?" she asked him on the shared elevator ride.

"They've found four of the five weapons that we know were in Seacouver. They bombed out the attack forces from three places." He put a hand on her arm and looked into her eyes. "Including Chelan."

Her heart raced. "They bombed Chelan?"

"No. The people from Chelan. They don't think there are any survivors." He lowered his voice. "That includes the -o boys."

She stared at him for a second, relief that her sister was probably okay warring with the idea that the people Lou wanted protected had died. "You knew them, didn't you?" she asked Blessing.

He nodded. "I built a barn with them. They were good men." He sounded bitter for a man who regularly stated that he accepted death.

"I'm sorry."

He touched her face. "I know."

The elevator lurched to stop and they got out.

Coryn stood just outside the door long after it closed. Her feet felt so heavy she wondered if she could lift them enough times to get into Julianna's apartment. Blessing didn't move either. He faced her again. "There's much more. Chicago found all of their nukes. One detonated, but by then they had it in a pretty contained place. Three people died, but no significant radiation escaped. They're working on cleanup now."

So Imke was probably all right. Coryn closed her eyes briefly and sighed in relief.

Blessing wasn't finished. "Flagstaff is gone."

"Gone?" Her eyes popped open, and she stared up at him in shock. "I thought they were on the same side as our enemies."

"They were."

"Oh." It took a second for the implications to sink in. "We fought them?"

"The Alliance of Cities."

Oh, of course. It seemed like so much to take in. Each individual thing should be rocking her, but there were so many that she just kept absorbing, the only impact a deep sadness that the adrenaline in her body fought back. What did *gone* mean in terms of a city?

Without saying a word, they turned together and walked into Julianna's.

Serena nearly bumped into them as they came through the door. She paced beside Adam, both of them talking nonstop in mathematical language that Coryn couldn't follow.

Coryn waited until they passed and then sat beside Julianna. "Have you eaten?"

"Evan made me eat some nuts."

"Would you like to walk?"

"No. I want to see them find the last nuke. I want to know that this is over."

"What did they do with the ones they found?"

"The mayor had them taken to safe locations and defused. He promises to destroy them."

"Promises? Will he?"

"You're getting a better ear for the language of politics."

Coryn's smile felt bitter.

Adam and Serena returned to the table and leaned over it, arguing. Eloise stood behind them.

Coryn wondered if Lou would even be back yet. It had been a night and a day. She was probably back. Coryn pulled up a sat shot on her wrist, but it was too small for her to be sure that both ecobots were on the farm. She glanced at the table. She couldn't take over any of the big screens. She and Lou were small in all of this. Everyone in the room was small in all of this. Coryn took Julianna's hand in hers. "It's always about a lot of people doing their jobs, isn't it?"

"People and systems, working. The systems depend on the people who set them up."

Some of the city systems had been set up a long time ago. "How are the systems kept up to date?"

Julianna laughed. "Carefully. It's both more robust than it seems, and less, a network of systems like this. But the hacking seems to have been turned back, and I heard that the transportation system is about to be reported as clean."

Coryn gestured to Evan. As he made his way toward them, he had to step around Adam, who had taken up pacing again.

"Can we have some more tea?" she asked him. "And maybe some bread?"

Once more he looked as approving as he ever did. As he walked away, Coryn said, "Sometimes I get the idea that Evan likes me."

"He'll need a new job," Julianna said. She stood up and went to Eloise, conferring quietly with her. She came back just in time to be handed tea. After Evan left to return to his spot by the door, Julianna said, "They sent teams to four possible places. We'll know in fifteen minutes or so if the damned thing is in any of those. In the meantime, Adam and Serena are looking for more places it could be. We're off the data you brought and onto images of everyone we know who was associated with this."

"What about Flagstaff? Isn't that huge? A whole city?"

"Yes. Luckily, it had a dome, someone inside was smart enough to clamp it down. There's leakage, but a fresh dome will be built over that, and it will be contained."

"Everyone in Flagstaff will die?" Coryn asked.

"We don't know yet. There are medical teams and antiradiation meds and the like on the way. But yes, many will die from radiation or have died from the blast. You can't evacuate a whole city."

And this was *their* side. *Her* side. Julianna sounded resigned to this.

But it seemed so ruthless. Coryn could barely wrap her mind around the idea, the casual way she said it.

Something in her expression must have given away the sudden roiling of her nerves, as Julianna took her hand. "It's about the future for all of us. We cannot think only about individuals. Not anymore. We haven't been able to afford that since the climate wars began."

Coryn felt tears gathering in her eyes and forced herself to think about something else. She was too tired to deal with this right now. Maybe after a long sleep. "A bomb here. If a bomb went off here, it would do more damage, wouldn't it? It would kill more people."

"A lot more people live here."

Adam and Serena crossed directly in front of them, still chattering. "Don't they need to eat?" Coryn mused.

"They're hopped up on neural stimulators." Julianna's gaze followed the two with something like amusement. "They won't feel hungry until they come off of those."

"Oh." There had been signs warning about the dangers of neural stimulants all over Coryn's high school. "Will he be all right?"

Julianna sipped her tea, and for a moment Coryn thought she was going to answer, but when she spoke it was to say, "It takes many kinds of sacrifice for humanity to survive."

Maybe that was why he drank, and why he always seemed to be alone. He was a beautiful man, but she had never wanted to be close to him, far preferring Blessing and Imke, who were warmer and safer, in spite of being a little exotic.

It seemed strange to be thinking of relatively mundane things in the middle of a crisis, but her job right now seemed to be to spend time with Julianna. "You don't have an assistant like Evan. He was Jake's."

"I've never wanted one. I didn't grow up with one, except an old model that enforced all of the school rules." Julianna smiled. "I hated that robot. I learned to evade robots early on. I might just keep doing that. But you can keep Evan and Namina."

"Two? What would I do with two companions?"

Before Julianna could answer, Blessing came in and signaled for attention. "They found all of them except our last one," he announced. "All of them. The damage is only Flagstaff and Calgary, and Calgary will be fine. The damage is small. People are being treated now."

Blessing came and sat with Coryn and Julianna, reading good news to them out loud while they waited for word on the last nuclear device.

When it came, it was on the open news. Mayor Arroya announced, "All credible threats to our city have been neutralized. We will turn our attention to going back to business as usual, to helping other cities rebuild, and to rooting out all of the people inside of our great city who helped our enemies."

Adam and Serena hugged each other, Julianna smiled quietly, and Blessing smiled even more broadly.

Coryn stole some time on a bigger screen, counted two ecobots on the farm, and felt her own face relax into a smile. Lou was safe. Among all the huge issues, this tiny one mattered most to her. Next she messaged Imke, and got a hurried, "Busy. I'll see you soon!" which made her smile.

Evan shooed everyone but Blessing and Coryn out. He tucked Julianna into her bed, and Coryn into the recliner. Blessing curled his lanky body into a ball on a cushion in the corner, with his head on his coat, and began snoring softly. She stared at him for a long time, watching him breathe. He was always there at the moments when life and death rode close together, talking of what to do next.

Her last waking sight was of Evan standing in the doorway at parade rest, the silent sentinel who would keep them free of interruptions for at least as long as Julianna slept.

CHAPTER FIFTY-FOUR

Pablo stood on the tree stump again. This time, he was far more somber than he had been on Christmas Day. He wore black, with a thin navy-blue tie and deep blue boots that shone in the afternoon light. He held a black hat in his hand. Aspen sat on the ground near the bottom of the tree stump, staring up at him, a small dot of white in a sea of black and gray.

Valeria wore black lace and a black veil, both of which looked fabulous on her, and which somehow made her grief more ethereal. Lou stood near the back, Matchiko and Shuska on either side, and kept her head low while Pablo continued his tribute.

Paulette had brought a suitcase to the farm while they were in Spokane. She and baby Jude stood near the front, close to Alondra. Lou couldn't quite tell, but it was possible the two young women were holding hands. The baby cried softly from time to time, but no one seemed to mind.

When he finished, Pablo hopped down and held his hand up to catch Valeria's so that she could flow up onto the stump in a single, graceful move.

She stood there, catching each person's eye. After total silence had fallen, she spoke into it. "Bless you for being family. Bless us all for being family." Her gaze took in Lou and her staff, all of the adults, and ended on the children. She lingered the most over Alondra, who had lost a father. No one had told the girl that her father had brought the bombs into the cities, although some day she would figure it out.

Valeria began to sing softly in Spanish. The melody rose and fell, sweet and sad. Shuska leaned down and whispered in Lou's ear. "Las Golondrinas—The Swallow." As it ended, Shuska added, "It doesn't work in English."

Valeria took a deep breath, and said, "Please join me for this song."
Silence fell. Feet shuffled. Aspen whined.

Valeria started "Amazing Grace." At the beginning, it was just her voice, so deep and full of humanity and hope that dug into Lou's heart. Then the others came in on the second verse, even the children. Everyone knew the words.

> *Amazing Grace, How sweet the sound,*
> *That saved a wretch like me*
> *I once was lost, but now am found,*
> *Was blind, but now I see.*

When the song finished, Felipe pointed up at a bald eagle that circled high above.

After Felipe and Pablo helped Valeria down, people drifted into the kitchen and began to drink. Lou helped serve plates of fried chicken and mashed potatoes, and Shuska and Matchiko poured both water and wine.

After the meal and the alcohol, tributes began. With four people to talk about, and nearly everyone wanting to talk, the stories and occasional songs went well into the night.

When it was Lou's turn, she said, "Diego was lovely with the horses. He could even make Buster walk fast." She smiled, remembering. "The others loved the horses, too. Diego and Ignacio and Santino used to sit together and watch them when they took breaks. The horses seemed to make them happy." She didn't say she had bought them their own horses and never had a chance to tell them. She swallowed. "In honor of the -o boys' love of horses, I will give Alondra a horse."

Alondra came and sat beside her, looking up with the first smile Lou had seen on the girl's face since they had arrived back here. "Which horse?"

"Sugar or Spice?"

"Spice."

"You shall have her."

Alondra leaned into her, and Lou slid an arm over her slender shoulders.

After the festivities wore down, Valeria came over to Lou. "Come outside with me?"

Lou set her empty wine glass down and assessed her ability to get up. "Sure."

The two of them walked out into the night, Valeria still wearing black lace under a colorful blanket that Felipe had draped over her shoulders. Lou wore her black coat and black boots. Valeria did not turn on a light, and Lou felt no need to. The nearly full moon illuminated frost and bits of snow that paved the ground with white, and showed them where to walk well enough. "Will you stay?" Valeria asked.

"Of course we will. There are quite a few more conversations that I need to have with Akita."

"I'm grateful," Valeria said. She poked Lou in the ribs. "Do you think Shuska will help us guard the saloon doors for a few more Saturdays?"

Lou smiled faintly, trying for levity. "To ward off all of the old people left in town?"

"No. To guard against the Keepers who will come here. To help make sure the young men won't be causing any trouble."

Lou shook her head. Valeria was nothing if not insistent on her view of the world. "I don't know if that will happen or not. It's too early to tell. We might have an answer in the spring." She had said this before, but maybe Valeria had been so preoccupied with her grief she hadn't heard.

"It will happen," Valeria said. "It's the only way."

If the world was fair, it would. That, of course, was a big question. Maybe it was the wine talking, but Lou asked, "Do you think there's really any justice?"

"Justice for who?" Valeria mused. "Was it justice when the boys who went off to kill the city died?" A tear glistened in her eye but she ignored it. Eventually it streaked down her cheek. "Was it justice that poor Paulette saved your sister and gave you the information that killed her own brother, but also, maybe, saved her soul at the same time? Was it justice that my husband disappeared? That we've killed most of the wild things?"

Lou was sure Valeria didn't expect an answer to any of the questions. She, too, had been drinking wine. The questions hurt, each one of them. But they didn't have answers.

Moonlight made Valeria look like she could be any woman, any age. Maybe it even made her look like a goddess. At least, like a warrior. Her losses showed, but more than that, her strength. She fell quiet for a bit, but then she told Lou, "We can add some justice to the world. Maybe that's all anyone can do."

"You are a stubborn woman," Lou told her. "But I'm glad my sister directed us to your farm."

"Me too."

ACKNOWLEDGMENTS

There are always so many people to thank. I appreciate every reader. I want to extend particular thanks to all of you who have reviewed my work or sent me notes about it, or come to me at conventions to talk about it. The prequel to this book, *Wilders*, has generated more conversation than any of my other books, and I've loved every chance that's given me to interact with readers.

Thanks to my agent, Eleanor Wood, and to my editor, Rene Sears. More thanks to the ever-patient Sheila Stewart, who has copyedited many of my books. My father, David Cooper; Nancy Kress; Darragh Metzger; and John Pitts all read an early draft and provided fabulous feedback.

I wrote *Keepers* while I was a student in the Stonecoast MFA program through the University of Southern Maine. It was truly a peak experience for me, a place where I had fun and learned a lot. Special thanks to Justin Tussing, Robin Talbot, and Matt Jones. The first part of this book formed my thesis, and I want to thank Nancy Holder and James Patrick Kelly for helping to shape the work.

Some of the work in this book is inspired by Forterra, a nonprofit in the Seattle area that has protected great swaths of land and that is also working to provide affordable housing and increased livability in the city. The two are linked. Healthy cities can help protect and preserve wildness. It was also inspired by E. O. Wilson's brilliant book *Half Earth*. I read many books on wolves, and got to use very little of what I read. Still, I learned a lot and loved the research. In particular, I enjoyed *Of Wolves and Men*, by Barry Lopez, *The Hidden Life of Wolves*, by Jim Dutcher, and *American Wolf: A True Story of Survival and Obsession in the West*, by Nate Blakeslee. I probably need to write an entire book about wolves, although I'm not sure how to make that science fiction.

And last, but never ever less than the most of all, I thank my family. Toni Cramer has put up with many weekends away, many evenings when I stop to write on my way home, and other times when I am merely lost in my head. The dogs have also had to put up with nights they miss walks because I've stopped at a coffee shop to write.

ABOUT THE AUTHOR

Brenda Cooper is the author of *Wilders*, the Glittering Edge duology (*Edge of Dark* and *Spear of Light*), the Ruby's Song duology (*The Creative Fire* and *The Diamond Deep*), and the Silver Ship series. *The Silver Ship and the Sea* was selected by Booklist as one of the top ten 2007 adult books for youth to read and won an Endeavour award. The other books in that series are *Reading the Wind* and *Wings of Creation*. *Edge of Dark* was a finalist for the P. K. Dick Award and won the Endeavour Award. Brenda is also the author of *Mayan December* and *POST* and has collaborated with Larry Niven (*Building Harlequin's Moon*).

Photo by Toni Cramer

Brenda is a working futurist and a technology professional with a passionate interest in the environment.